THE PATH OF THE HERO KING

A harried fugitive, guilt-ridden, excommunicated, Robert the Bruce, King of Scots in name and nothing more, faced a future that all but he – and perhaps Elizabeth de Burgh his wife – accepted as devoid of hope; his kingdom occupied by a powerful and ruthless invader; his army defeated; a large proportion of his supporters dead or prisoners; much of his people against him; and the rest so cowed and war-sick as no longer to care. Only a man of transcendent courage would have continued the struggle, or seen it as worth continuing. But Bruce, whatever his many failings, was courageous above all. And with a driving love of freedom that gave him no rest. He was not a patriot as Wallace had been a patriot – that was a new conception in mediaeval Scotland – but he had a great love for his own oppressed people and a recognition of their rights, as well as his own.

Hounded from his land, he sought refuge in the Hebrides, then a semi-independent principality. Half-Celtic himself, he found his roots and renewal of strength, spiritual and military, amongst that strange, outlandish remnant of his people. From the Highlands and the Isles he launched himself back against the overwhelming might of his enemies, in as forlorn a hope as any history has to record.

In the process he lost everything but his life – wife, daughter, brothers, sisters, friends, health. But never his resolution and a kind of faith. For one day, he vowed to himself, he would compound for his sins and excommunication by leading a Crusade to drive the Infidel from the holy places. To do this he must first win his kingdom, whatever the odds.

In this the second of Nigel Tranter's powerful trilogy of novels, Robert the Bruce blazes the path of the hero king, in blood and violence and determination, in cunning and ruthlessness, yet, strangely, a preoccupation with mercy and chivalry, all the way from the ill-starred open-boat landing on the Ayrshire coast by night, from a spider-hung Galloway cave and near despair, to Bannockburn itself, where he faced the hundred-thousand-strong mightiest army in the world, and won.

Robert The Bruce

The Path of the Hero King

THE SECOND OF A TRILOGY OF NOVELS

Nigel Tranter

CORONET BOOKS
Hodder and Stoughton

Copyright © 1970 by Nigel Tranter
First published in Great Britain
by Hodder & Stoughton Ltd., 1970
Coronet edition 1972
Seventh impression 1977

Printed and bound in Great Britain for
Hodder and Stoughton Paperbacks, a
division of Hodder and Stoughton Ltd.,
Mill Road, Dunton Green, Sevenoaks, Kent
(Editorial Office: 47 Bedford Square, London, WC1 3DP)
by Cox & Wyman Ltd., London, Reading and Fakenham

ISBN 0 340 16222 8

PRINCIPAL CHARACTERS

In Order of Appearance

DAVID DE MORAY, BISHOP OF MORAY: Uncle of patriot Andrew Moray.

DEWAR OF THE COIGREACH: Hereditary Keeper of St. Fillan's staff.

DEWAR OF THE MAIN: Hereditary Keeper of St. Fillan's left arm-bone.

LADY ELIZABETH DE BURGH, the QUEEN: Wife of Robert the First and daughter of Earl of Ulster.

LADY MARJORY BRUCE: Eleven-year-old only child of the King.

ROBERT BRUCE, KING OF SCOTS: Fugitive, a few months after coronation.

SIR EDWARD BRUCE, EARL OF CARRICK: Eldest brother of above.

SIR NIGEL BRUCE: Next and favourite brother.

SIR CHRISTOPHER SETON: English knight and friend of Bruce. Second husband of Lady Christian, Countess of Mar, Bruce's sister.

LADY ISOBEL, COUNTESS OF BUCHAN: Sister to Earl of Fife. Wife of Buchan, who fought for English.

SIR JAMES DOUGLAS: "The Good Sir James" Lord of Douglas. Friend of Bruce.

SIR GILBERT HAY: Another old friend, Lord of Erroll.

SIR NEIL CAMPBELL: Chief of Clan Campbell and Lord of Lochawe.

JOHN DE STRATHBOGIE, EARL OF ATHOLL; Brother-in-law of Bruce's first wife.

SIR ALEXANDER LINDSAY: Lord of Crawford, a Bruce supporter.

SIR ROBERT FLEMING: Lord of Biggar, a Bruce supporter.

SIR ROBERT BOYD OF NODDSDALE: A Bruce supporter.

MALCOLM MACGREGOR OF GLENORCHY: Chief of Clan Alpine.

MALCOLM, EARL OF LENNOX: A great Celtic noble, friend of Bruce.

ANGUS OG MACDONALD: Self-styled Prince and Lord of the Isles. Second son of Angus Mor, Lord of Islay.

CHRISTINA MACRUARIE, LADY OF GARMORAN: Chieftainess of branch of Clan Donald; widow of brother of late Earl of Mar.

5

SIR ROBERT CLIFFORD, LORD OF BROUGHAM: English commander.

MASTER NICHOLAS BALMYLE: Official of St. Andrews: former Chancellor of Scotland.

SIR AYMER DE VALENCE, EARL OF PEMBROKE: English commander-in-chief in Scotland.

MASTER BERNARD DE LINTON: Vicar of Mordington. Secretary.

WILLIAM DE IRVINE: Armour-Bearer to the King.

JOHN COMYN, EARL OF BUCHAN: Lord High Constable of Scotland. Siding with the English.

SIR THOMAS RANDOLPH, LORD OF NITHSDALE: Son of a step-sister of Bruce.

SIR ALEXANDER COMYN: Brother of Buchan, Sheriff of Inverness and Keeper of Urquhart Castle.

SIR HUGH ROSS: Eldest son of the Earl of Ross.

SIR JAMES STEWART: 5th Hereditary High Steward of Scotland.

WALTER STEWART: Son of above.

WILLIAM, EARL OF ROSS: Great Celtic noble.

ALEXANDER MACDONALD OF ARGYLL: Chief of clan. Enemy of Bruce.

SIR ROBERT KEITH: Hereditary Knight Marischal of Scotland.

LADY MATILDA BRUCE: Youngest sister of the King.

LADY ISABELLA DE STRATHBOGIE: Sister of Earl of Atholl.

WILLIAM LAMBERTON, BISHOP OF ST. ANDREWS: Primate. Friend of Bruce.

MASTER THOMAS FENWICK: Prior of Hexham-on-Tyne.

SIR HENRY DE BOHUN: Nephew of Earl of Hereford.

GILBERT DE CLARE, EARL OF GLOUCESTER: Nephew of Edward the Second.

RALPH DE MONTHERMER: Step-father of above. Second husband of Edward the First's daughter.

SIR MARMADUKE TWENG: Veteran English knight. Former keeper of Stirling Castle.

SIR PHILIP MOUBRAY: Scots knight. Keeper of Stirling Castle for the English.

HENRY, EARL OF HEREFORD: Lord High Constable of England.

BANNOCKBURN

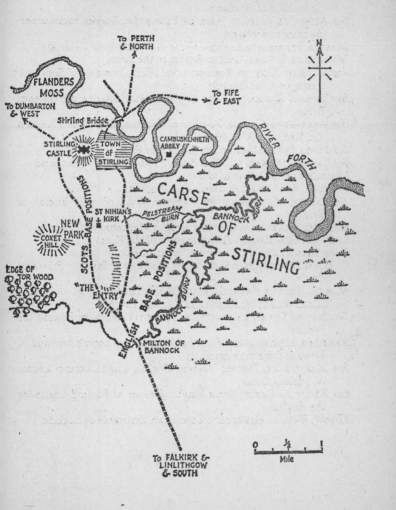

To PERTH & NORTH

To FIFE & EAST

FLANDERS MOSS

To DUMBARTON & WEST

Stirling Bridge

STIRLING CASTLE

TOWN OF STIRLING

CAMBUSKENNETH ABBEY

RIVER FORTH

CARSE

OF

STIRLING

St NINIAN'S KIRK

PELSTREAM BURN

BANNOCK BURN

NEW PARK

COXET HILL

SCOTS BASE POSITIONS

ENGLISH BASE POSITIONS

EDGE OF TOR WOOD

"THE ENTRY"

BANNOCK BURN

MILTON OF BANNOCK

To FALKIRK & LINLITHGOW & SOUTH

0   ½   1
Mile

THE HOUSE OF BRUCE

Robert de Brus or Brux, Lord of Cleveland 1st Lord of Annandale c. 1124

|

Robert 2nd Lord (fought at Battle of Standard 1138)

|

Robert 3rd Lord m. illeg. d. King William the Lion

|

Robert 4th Lord m. Isabel d. of David, Earl of Huntingdon, b. of William the Lion

|

Robert 5th Lord ("The Competitor") m. Isabel de Clare, d. Earl of Gloucester

|

Robert 6th Lord m. Marjory, Countess of Carrick

|

Robert (the King) — Edward — Nigel — Thomas — Alexander — Isobel (m. King Eric of Norway) — Christian (m. (1) Gartnait, Earl of Mar; (2) Sir Christopher Seton) — Mary (m. Sir Christopher Seton) — Matilda (m. Sir Hugh Ross)

Robert (the King)
m. (1) Isobel of Mar
   (2) Eliz. de Burgh

Marjory

THE SCOTS SUCCESSION

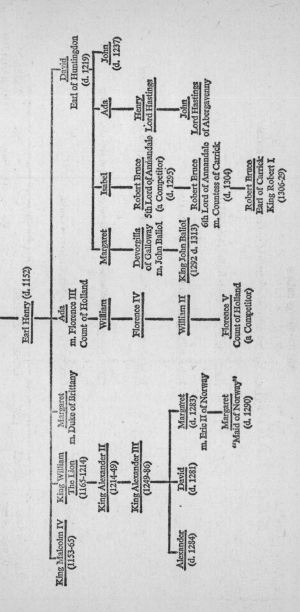

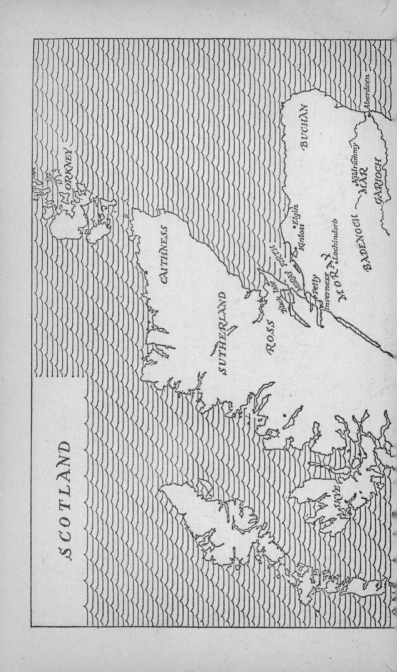

PART ONE

CHAPTER ONE

THE Abbey of Glendochart was a ruin, of course. Had been for centuries. But there was a little shrine there still, amongst the grassy mounds and moss-grown stones that nestled under the high heather hills. It could not be called a church or chapel, either from its appearance or its intrinsic character — indeed Holy Church itself would have been the first to deny it any such title, just as she would sternly condemn any suggestion that the mounds and heaps of masonry, of which this was the last remaining entity, had ever been a true monastic limb of the Body of Christ. Holy Church was, as ever, very strong about such matters, however much she might bend to the winds of expediency in others. And the ancient Celtic Church of the Culdees, long put down, God be praised, was still anathema.

That was why David de Moray, Bishop of Moray, though a cheerful and anything but pompously clerical exponent of the Church Militant, sat outside and a little way off, his back turned to the low, squat and entirely plain little building, more like a croft-house than a sanctuary, and contemplated instead the magnificent soaring skyline of Ben More and Stobinian, 3,000 feet above them, where the cloud-shadows sailed serenely across the quartz-shot stone and the purple July bell-heather, and the desperations of men seemed remote indeed. The Bishop, however, did not wholly idle away this rather deplorable interval; he honed the edge of his great two-handed sword with a most rhythmic and methodical stroke.

At a little distance, on the grassy haughlands of the River Fillan, the men lay at ease, some 500 of them, mainly Lowland men-at-arms but with some clansmen from the Southern Highlands, Campbells, MacGregors, MacLarens and the like, eyeing each other with no love lost, but glad enough to laze for a little in the smile of the July sun. They anticipated little lazing hereafter, for some time to come. Some of them took the opportunity to wash soiled and bloodstained bandaging in the clear sparkling water of the Fillan.

Inside the small low-browed building it was dark, by contrast, and not a little stuffy; indeed a blunt man might have called it smelly, despite the illustrious quality of the folk who crowded it — for unchanged clothing, untreated wounds and horse-sweat added to the human variety, can make a potent admixture, even without the smoke from the two guttering wicks that burned in beaten iron bowls at either end of the rough stone altar at the east end of the cabin. There were perhaps forty people crammed into that confined space, some kneeling or squatting but most standing, happy when they could lean against the walling, about ten of them women. Some bowed their heads reverently, some yawned, some frankly slept, with one or two emitting quite unknightly snores — though more than that, obviously, was required to halt the flow of liquid, musical-sounding Gaelic, quite unintelligible to almost all of them, that went on and on. Two men, up at the altar, produced this — and when one faltered for lack of breath, the other took over without pause.

If the Bishop outside did not look particularly priestly, in chain-mail and sword-belt, at least he had a cross and a mitre painted on his ragged surcoat. These two had not a single sacerdotal emblem or vestment between them. One was a young man, of stocky but good physique, red-haired, dressed in a short kilt of faded saffron stuff, with an open and sleeveless calfskin waistcoat, black and white, and nothing else. The other was an elderly stooping ruin of a man, of once mighty build, wrapped in a voluminous ragged tartan plaid, and grey-bearded right down to the massive gold belt of snake-links that winked in the flickering lamplight and kept his tatters approximately in place. They made strange ministrants for the singsong liturgical chanting which they gabbled endlessly. Yet none, north of the Highland Line at least, would have questioned their authority. They were two of the hereditary Dewars of Saint Fillan, custodians of the sacred relics of that royal saint of the ancient Celtic Church; the old man, the Dewar of the Coigreach, Fillan's bronze-headed pastoral staff of six centuries before, which now lay along the altar-slab; and the young, Dewar of the Main, the saint's left arm-bone encased in a silver reliquary, which lay beside the staff. The other three Dewars, custodians of less import-ant relics, were not present, being unfortunately under the thumb of Macnab, *Mac-an-abb*, chiefly descendant of the hereditary Abbots of Glendochart, a supporter of the unlamented and abdi-cated King John Baliol and of his Comyn kinsmen. But these two were the principal Dewars, and if anyone could convey the bless-ings of Saint Fillan and of the strange former Culdee Church, these could.

Crowded as the place was, a little space was left in, as it were, the first row before the altar, for three persons who knelt — a man,

14

a woman and a child. The man, in mail, auburn head bare, was in his thirty-second year, medium-tall of build, wide-shouldered, strong-featured with a rough-hewn sort of good looks, but strained-seeming, drawn, and bearing one shoulder slightly lower than the other as though in pain. The woman was tall, well-made, and of a proud and generous beauty, five years younger, her heavy corn-coloured hair bound with a golden fillet, richly dressed in travelling clothes somewhat crumpled and stained. The child, a girl of eleven, slight, dark and great-eyed, daughter of the man and step-child of the woman, stared about her in the half-dark and coughed with the lamp-smoke. She at least made no gesture at prayerful reverence.

Strangely enough it was her father, not normally a prayerful or very religious-minded man, who seemed most impressed by the proceedings, most anxious to take part, to be identified. Occasionally his lips moved. His wife eyed him sidelong almost as often as she looked at the altar and the two strange figures before it. She was attentive, concerned — but her concern was not really with what went on but with its effect on the man at her side. None knew so well as she did how important this curious interlude was for the King.

Almost, indeed, it represented a sort of salvation for a man sunk in guilt, the guilt of both murder and sacrilege, excommunicated by the Pope of Rome — whatever his own Scots bishops might say — beaten in battle within weeks of his coronation, a fugitive in his own country. This blessing and acceptance, by even this attenuated remnant of the former Church of the land, put down by the Romish order for over two centuries but persisting in these mountains in some degree still, was of vital moment. And not only to his bruised and harried spirit. The two extraordinary figures before him, lay Dewars though they were, nevertheless were accepted as holy men of major importance all over the Celtic Highlands and Islands. And since all the Lowlands, south, east and north, were barred to Robert Bruce, occupied by the English invaders, or his enemies the Comyns and their supporters, his future, in the meantime, must lie in these Highlands and Islands. This day's proceedings, therefore, represented hope.

Not all his followers, huddled in the ruins of Glendochart Abbey in Strathfillan, understood how vital all this was to the King, or looked on it as more than a passing madness on the part of a man tried to the limits. Catholics all, good, indifferent or only nominal, they looked askance at this outlandish performance by a couple of heathenish Highland caterans, in what was little better than a cattle-shed — and the only praying they did was that it would soon be over. Only those closest to Bruce — his brothers Edward and Nigel; his sisters Mary and Christian, with the latter's husband, Sir Christopher Seton; the Countess of Buchan who had placed the crown on his head those weeks before; and one or two of his surviving nearest friends, like Sir James Douglas and Sir Gilbert Hay, had any idea how much their cause might be affected by this weird ceremony.

How long it might have gone on had they not been rudely interrupted, there was no knowing. A messenger came hurrying in and pushed his way to the front, stumbling in the dark and cursing audibly. He reached and spoke to Edward Bruce, who rose, but gestured him on to the kneeling King.

"My lord King," the man whispered hoarsely. "Sir Robert Boyd sends me. From your rearward. The Earl of Buchan comes up Dochartside. In force. From the Loch of Tay. Two thousand horse, Sir Robert says. English with him, under Percy."

"A curse on it! They have found us, then . . ."

"Aye, we are betrayed again," Edward Bruce declared, from behind, not troubling to lower his voice.

"Buchan, you say? The Comyns?" The King glanced over his shoulder, shrinking with the pain of it, to where the Countess of Buchan knelt behind his sisters, his wife's principal lady-in-waiting and wife of the Constable of Scotland who was thus pursuing him even into these mountains. He sighed, and rose to his feet, lifting a hand to the Dewar of the Main, the young man, who was presently holding forth.

"My friend," he called, "I am sorry. Your pardon — but we must go. The enemy approaches. In strength. We must ride. I thank you . . ."

Had it been the old man, he probably would have paid no heed and continued haughtily with the ritual. But the other faltered into silence and became suddenly just a young and somewhat embarrassed Highlandman. His companion glared, tugging his long beard, and grabbed his staff off the altar in protest.

"I am sorry," the King repeated. "Your blessing I much value. Your faith and order I will seek to cherish. But now we must go. Remembering kindly Glendochart." He took the Queen's arm and nodded to the Princess Marjory. "Come."

Out in the sunshine the Bishop was waiting for him, leaning on his sword. "Trouble, Sire?" he asked. "Not the English? In these hills . . . !"

"The Comyns. Buchan leads them. With Percy." Bruce turned to the messenger. "How near are they?"

"They were past Luib when I rode, Sire. Sir Robert retiring before them. To the loch-foot . . ."

"Then we have but little time. Two thousand, you say? Too many for us, by far, as we are. We can but run for it."

"Where? Encumbered as we are with wounded. And women." Sir Edward Bruce, the eldest of the King's four brothers, was dark, thin, wiry and of tense-nerved disposition. "I say that we should fight. Seek a place to ambush them. Use this land against them . . ."

Sir Nigel, a little younger, handsomely dashing, laughter-loving and the King's favourite, agreed. "To be sure. Even though they are four to one. We have skulked and hidden enough, by God! Here, in this boggy valley, with the river and the hills, is no place for their chivalry. Hemmed in. We can bring them to battle on our terms . . ."

There were cries for and against amongst the circle of lords and knights that clustered round the King, fairly evenly divided.

Bruce shook his auburn head. "Use your wits," he requested his brothers. "Think you I would not stand and fight, if I might with any hope of success? But if the Comyns are riding up Glendochart, it is because they have been led here. No host would venture into these trackless mountains by chance. They must be guided to us. Which means that we have been betrayed. And the only folk who could betray us hereabouts are the Macnabs. When Patrick Macnab came not to greet us, in his own country, I deemed him no friend. Now, I see why he did not come! He has hastened to bring our enemies down upon us. And if they are so led, then think you we could ambush them? Take them by surprise? In daylight? This is *their* land. They will know every inch of it. And we have no time to wait for darkness. They would be on us in an hour. No — we have no choice, my friends. We must ride. And westwards. We must make for Sir Neil's country on Loch Awe. With all speed that we may. Forthwith. Sir Neil Campbell — you will lead . . ."

The Campbell chief, a dark, swarthy, youngish man of sombre looks but a notable fighter, was nothing loth. He had been anxious not to linger in this area of Breadalbane and Mamlorn, Saint Fillan's land or no, these last five days; it was too close and linked to the domains of his hereditary enemies, the MacDougalls of Argyll and Lorn. And the Lord of Lorn was wed to a sister of the late, murdered Sir John Comyn the Red, Lord of Badenoch.

Despite the complaint that they were encumbered with women, and wounded from the disastrous battle of Methven nearly three weeks previously, the King's small host was not slow about moving off. They had a sufficiency of practice. Campbell, with an advance party of four score, went first. Half an hour after the arrival of Boyd's courier, the haughland of the Fillan was empty save for the two Dewars and some of the local folk. With the enemy only about six miles behind, this was not too soon.

They rode up Strathfillan, the upper portion of Glendochart, making for Tyndrum, where the routes forked, one to go west by south, by Glen Lochy and Glen Orchy to the foot of Loch Awe; the other north over the mouth of Mamlorn and across the desert wastes of the vast Moor of Rannoch, to Lochaber and North Atholl. There was no other choice. The great mountain barriers hemmed them in.

The Queen and Marjory rode beside Bruce. It was nothing new for Elizabeth de Burgh, daughter of English King Edward's greatest friend, the Earl of Ulster, to be hunted, a fugitive. Since she threw in her lot with Bruce four years before, she had known little of peace and security in a savaged and war-torn land. But for young Marjory this was her first taste of campaigning. She had been reared in care and seclusion at her dead mother's old home, the remote, strong castle of Kildrummy in Mar, seat of that earldom, by her aunt and uncle twice over — for the late Earl of Mar had married Bruce's sister Christian, now Lady Seton, and Bruce's first wife had been the Lady Isabel of Mar. She had been brought south only to attend her father's hurried coronation. Marjory saw all as adventure and pleasurable excitement.

They had gone a bare two miles, and reached a stretch where the valley narrowed in and its floor was scored by quite a deep gorge through which the river rushed and spilled in foaming rapids, when an uproar in front halted them. The lie of the land and a thrusting shoulder of the braeside hid what went on — but there was most evidently a clash of arms.

Swiftly Bruce reacted. He pointed Sir James, the Lord of Douglas, forward. "Find me what's to do, Jamie," he commanded. "Campbell sounds to have run into trouble. Discover how much." He turned to Hay. "Gibbie — back, to halt and alert all the column."

Nigel spurred close. "If Campbell is beset, let us to his aid," he exclaimed, his sword already in hand.

"Wait, you," his brother said. He looked about him keenly. "An ill place for fighting."

It was. A steep bank of heather and scree rose directly on their right, to the north, curving back out of sight. Only a dozen yards or so to the other side what amounted to a cliff dropped to the river in its gorge. A place with less scope for manoeuvre would be hard to imagine.

Even as they looked, clamour and tumult broke out well to the rear, more violent than that in front.

"By the Rude — it is a trap!" the King cried. "An ambush! They have us." Quick as thought he jerked his horse's head round to face the steep slope, signing to his wife and daughter and the other women to do likewise.

All down the strung-out line there was confusion.

"Nigel — forward, and tell Douglas. And Campbell. We must up. Break out of this trap, this valley." He pointed higher. "Edward — back. To Hay. Get our people up out of this kennel. Then word back to Boyd and the rearward. Off with you." The rest, those near him, he waved onwards, upwards.

It was a steep climb for the horses, nearly 200 feet of rough going, demanding a zigzag ascent. They were perhaps half-way up this, in a long ragged line, perhaps 300 men, with the King and his immediate group, including the women, well in front, when the long ululant winding of a horn sounded from above, echoing amongst the enclosing hills. This was succeeded by a wild and savage shouting from hundreds, thousands of hoarse throats. And over the skyline appeared wave after wave of yelling, gesticulating men.

Bruce reined up in momentary indecision — although, in almost automatic reaction, he was tugging free the long two-handed sword sheathed at his back. He had suffered a grievous surprise at Methven, but never had he been so unready for battle as this.

The women, of course, were his first anxiety. Urgently he turned in the saddle. "Back!" he shouted to Elizabeth. "Down again. Get them back."

The Queen, daughter of a long line of warriors, neither panicked nor hesitated. Grabbing her step-daughter's bridle, she dragged both horses round, calling to the other ladies to follow her downhill. Bruce blessed her, even as he commanded his trumpeter to sound the rally.

There was no time for any positioning, any marshalling. The attackers had not much more than 200 yards to cover from their hidden waiting-place behind the rise. They were afoot, bare-shanked Highlanders to a man, but leaping, bounding in their charge almost as fast as cavalry, brandishing their Lochaber-axes and claymores, and yelling their slogans, a terrifying sight. Few wore more than the short kilt, to fight in, and many had cast away even these and were completely naked save for their rawhide brogans. On the face of it, mounted men in armour should have been vastly superior as fighting-men to these unprotected howling savages. But Bruce knew better than that. For one thing they had an enormous advantage in numbers; and they were on their own ground. Also they had the benefit of surprise, with the horsemen scattered. But most serious of all, the Highlanders were charging and the mounted men were not only stationary but were so on a steep and slippery downwards slope.

The Earl of Atholl, the Bishop, Sir Alexander Lindsay, Sir Robert Fleming and one or two others had spurred forward to the King's side, past the hurrying women. All along the hillside the knights and men-at-arms were seeking to draw together, to consolidate for mutual aid and protection.

There was insufficient time for this. Like an angry flood the Highlanders were upon them. Bruce, still in front, found half a dozen attackers leaping at him, each with a claymore in one hand and a dirk in the other.

His damaged shoulder, relic of the Methven fight, was a grievous handicap in wielding the great five-foot-long two-handed sword. Nevertheless, standing in his stirrups and aided by this elevation, he cut down three of his assailants with his first tremendous right-and-left slashes, before the residual wrench of his swing so tore his shoulder as to leave him gasping and it numb and useless. His efforts thereafter to lay about him with the one hand were less than successful. When only his chain-mail saved him from two crippling thrusts, he tossed his sword at one of the bounding men, and drew his battle-axe instead.

All around was chaos, complete and desperate. There was no line, no certainty — save that the mounted chivalry was getting the worst of it. Each horseman was an island in a sea of milling, smiting clansmen. And the island were steadily growing fewer. For the Highlanders were attacking in especial the horses, darting in and ducking beneath them, to slash open the bellies with their dirks. Everywhere the screaming, rearing brutes were falling, their armoured riders crashing.

Bruce, with a swift glance around, perceived that there was only one end to this, and that would not be long delayed unless something was done at once. Bending low over his mount's neck, he slashed furiously with his axe in a figure-of-eight motion, to drive back the two men who were at the moment assailing him, at the same time seeking to knee the horse round. It was the rearing beast's pawing hooves rather than the battle-axe which knocked over one of the men; but the other, a gigantic figure, claymore gone, hurled himself bodily upwards, hands clawing, in a crazy attempt to clutch the King and drag him from the saddle. Bruce managed to twist aside, kicking spurs into his horse's flanks. The giant failed to grasp the monarch's person, but one hand closed on the fine cloth-of-gold heraldic cloak that Bruce wore instead of the usual surcoat, embroidered with the red Lion Rampant of Scotland worked with the Queen's own hands. Tearing it away at the magnificent jewelled brooch that clasped it in place, the Highlander fell back clutching not the King but this trophy.

Bruce's trumpeter had disappeared, and his master had to shout, as he spurred downhill, lashing out at those who tried to stop him, with that wicked red-gleaming axe.

"A Bruce! A Bruce!" he yelled. "To me! To me A Bruce!"

That was a slogan for charge and victory, not for retreat and defeat. But something had to be done to break off this dire and fatal struggle, and to try to save the women.

Gathering blessed momentum the King plunged downhill, his brute sliding and almost sitting on its haunches. Momentum — that was what was required against these caterans, mounted momentum.

Sadly few of his company were in any position to perceive their sovereign's manoeuvre, or successfully to break away to join him. Close pressed and confined, most could by no means win free. By the time that Bruce was through the mêlée and could glance back and about him, no more than fifty or sixty out of the original three hundred appeared to be even mounted.

He did not slacken the speed of his descent, but plunged on down to the shelf above the gorge, where Elizabeth had the women clustered in an anxious, great-eyed knot, ten or eleven of them. Fortunately all were fairly young and good horsewomen — or they would not have been in this fugitive company in the first place.

The King had no pride in what he did. To be leading the flight from a stricken field was gall and wormwood for the Bruce. But it was necessary, if any were to survive — and no one else was doing it.

Down to them he came, his mount's slithering hooves scoring great red weals in the braeside. He pointed.

"Westwards!" he shouted. "On. Only way." Most of the women were in fact facing in the other direction.

"Robert! You are hurt?" the Queen cried. "Your shoulder . . .?"

"Nothing," the King threw back. "Wrenched, that is all." He looked back. Atholl and Lindsay were close behind, Bishop Moray and Fleming and a few others followed after, two horses bearing double burdens.

They dared not wait. Putting himself at the head of the little group of women, Bruce led on along the track above the river, westwards, at a canter. The foremost survivors caught up with

21

them, to form a sort of cordon, while others trailed along at varying distances. It made a sorry scene.

After only a few moments, rounding the bend in the glen-floor, they met Nigel Bruce, Douglas and Campbell with the residue of the advance guard, fleeing in the opposite direction. It was a pathetic remnant of not more than a score out of the eighty, with again some horses carrying two men.

Bruce only reined in, did not halt, and wasted no words on inessentials. "How many? In front?" he demanded, waving to the newcomers to turn round again.

"Two hundred. Three," Campbell panted. "Took us by surprise. Rocks rolled down. Arrows. Houghed the horses . . ."

The King cut him short with a chopping motion. "They follow? Pursue you?"

"Yes. If you continue thus you will run into them . . ."

"Better that than back. Thousands behind! More in rear. A trap. Come — form a wedge. Quickly. We must cut through . . ."

He did not have to explain. The wedge, or arrowhead cavalry attack, was a classic formation, given bold or desperate men and trained horses. Plus fierce momentum. Pressed close in a tight inverted V behind a purposeful and unflinching leader, each man keeping exactly his position, there was practically nothing, in flesh and blood at least, that could stop or withstand such a charge — even when, as often happened, the said leader, the tip of the arrowhead, and his immediate flanking men, who bore the brunt of the impact, were carried along dead or dying by the necessary momentum, borne up by the close press of the rest. All knew it. But not with a core of women and a bairn for the arrowhead!

They worked themselves into formation, nevertheless, a company of about forty now, hedging the women in, with stragglers adding themselves all the time. It was not so well-shaped and tight a wedge as many would have wished, but at least it made a solid and determined body, driving on at a fast canter once more.

Round a further bend of the trough, they suddenly were face to face with the enemy. Running along the shelf and some way up the bank to the north came a horde of Highlanders, in wild spirits and no sort of order or discipline, a bloodthirsty crowd elated with victory, chasing a defeated foe. Undoubtedly their shock was great at abruptly being confronted, instead, by a charge of cavalry however modest in numbers. The check in their racing advance was obvious and eloquent. But still they came on, though with less confidence.

The King, at the apex of his formation, did not hesitate. Instead he shouted, "Faster! Faster!" and raising his battle-axe on high, yelled, "A Bruce! A Bruce and Scotland!"

His companions took up the cry bravely, even some of the women skirling their shrill contribution.

Somewhere at the rear of the Highland party one of their war-horns began to wind, leadership tardily asserting itself. But it was too late, whatever the signal represented; indeed, probably it only increased the confusion, as some held back or faltered while the majority pressed on.

The horsemen crashed into the flood of wild-eyed, shouting men with enormous impact. No amount of valour or fighting skill could withstand it. Bowled over like ninepins, the Highlanders went down in swathes, more felled by the impetus and the lashing hooves than by the flailing weapons of the riders. As he was swept on through the throng of bodies, in fact, Bruce's own battle-axe never once made contact with a foe. His useless shoulder greatly hampered him, of course; but even so he was borne up and carried forward so closely by the press of his companions that there was little that he could do to affect the issue, other than to retain his position and shout his Bruce slogan.

It was not a matter of piercing a front, for the Highlanders were merely a mob streaming along a terrace of the hillside. It was like cleaving the current of a rushing torrent, rather, with loss of momentum the direst danger. So the riders spurred their foaming, frightened mounts even more than they wielded their swords; and spectacular as was the downfall of the foe, probably no great numbers failed to rise again thereafter. Not one of the horsemen was brought low, at any rate, and the women within the shield of steel and horseflesh scarcely saw their enemies.

At last they were through the main crowd. But the King spurred on as hard as ever, well aware that the clansmen would rally behind them and that all could yet be lost. On up the glen he led the hard-riding company, on to where Campbell's advance party had been ambushed, marked all too clearly by the litter of dead and dying men and horses. Here some dismounted and slightly-wounded survivors emerged from hiding-places to join them — but the King had to steel his heart against any waiting for these, mean-time. Some few got pulled up, pillion, behind riders, but to most Bruce gestured upwards, shouting that they should climb out of that fatal gut of the valley, north by west into the empty hills. He drove on.

He was making for a levelling of the trough which they could see some way to the west, where it looked as though horses would be able to get out without the dangers of steep, slow climbing. Beyond, half-right, there appeared to be a jumble of small, low hillocks with open woodland — the sort of cover they required.

They saw no more of the enemy and were able, presently, to set their beasts' heads to the lessened slope on the right and at last to win out of that grim valley. Half a mile more and they were amongst the knowes and scattered birches that spread over a wide area to the north of Tyndrum, the outskirts of the Forest of Mamlorn. Here, surely, they would be secure, for the moment. Thankfully Bruce drew rein, and turned to his wife and daughter.

"God be praised at least you are safe here!" he gasped.

Marjory, who had kept up throughout as well as any, now burst into tears of reaction. Elizabeth leaned over to put an arm around her.

"Hush you, hush you," she murmured. "It is by with, now. Remember — you are a king's daughter!"

"You have done well, lass," her father said. "Very well. All of you." He looked at the women. "Would that I could say as much for myself!" Sheathing his axe, he reached a hand out to his wife. "My dear — you ill chose a man to wed!" he said.

"*I* chose well enough. It is the others who chose ill!" The Queen shook her head. "There are over many traitors in your realm, my lord King!"

"Do not name them traitors. Not yet. I am too newly their king. I need time to win them . . ."

"An eternity will not win you MacDougall!" his brother Nigel broke in. "That was he. The Lord of Lorn and his clan. Come out of the west. Seeking you. He is wed to Comyn's sister . . ."

"MacDougall! So great a man! Then . . . Lorn is closed against us. Argyll. A whole province."

"I could have foretold it, Sire," Sir Neil Campbell declared sourly. "Not the ambush, but MacDougall's hatred. As Comyn's kin. He has been brought here by Macnab. They are close."

"Macnab, then, has cost me dear this day! Called both Buchan and MacDougall down on us, from east and west. To trap us in his Glen Dochart. What have I ever done against Macnab . . .?"

"While his creatures, those Dewars, kept you constrained, bethralled, with their heathenish mummery! Bait to his trap!" That was John de Strathbogie, Earl of Atholl, married to a sister of Bruce's first wife, and bleeding from two slight wounds.

"No! That I will not believe," the King cried, "The Dewars would not do that. Not so misuse what they hold most sacred on earth. The old man, I swear, was honest. His blessing true."

None might flatly contradict the monarch — but only one was prepared to agree with him; his wife.

24

"True, yes," she said. "These you may trust. The blessing was sure." Whether she believed it or no, Elizabeth de Burgh knew what that blessing meant to her husband.

"You were caught from the rear?" Nigel asked. "The main body? Where is Edward? Hay? The others . . .?"

"God knows! They came on us from above. In their thousands. We had to cut our way out. For the others, we can but wait. And pray . . .!"

* * *

Their waiting, at least, was not quite unproductive, whatever the result of their praying. In a couple of hours the King's party, hidden in the woodlands, had almost doubled itself, fugitives finding their way thither in ones and twos, exhausted, dazed, wounded or just dispirited, but none on horseback. Edward Bruce and Sir Gilbert Hay were amongst the last to arrive, the former still unsteady from being unhorsed and all but stunned by his own armour. The tail of the column had been as badly cut up as the rest, they reported, being overwhelmed before either of them could reach it. They had seen nothing of Boyd's rearguard, and feared the worst.

A long silence had now settled on the weary and dejected company. So far, the MacDougall host had not come seeking them here. But all knew that it was only a question of time. They would be reorganising, and possibly waiting for darkness. For if Bruce's own survivors could pick out this wooded hillocks area as an obvious refuge, then undoubtedly the Highlanders could do the same.

The King had been pacing, alone, a patch of green turf amongst the heather between two knolls, with the twisted gait of a man in physical pain, and the twisted expression of equal mental pain. Abruptly he halted, and it was his brother he looked at, not his wife and daughter.

"There is nothing for it," he said harshly. "We must part company. We cannot go on, thus. We are but playing our enemies' game. Here is no country for knights and chivalry. Or for women! Yet, out of these mountains, if I survive, I can raise thousands. Moreover, all else is closed to me. If I am to win back my strength, as your king, to challenge Edward of England, and the Comyns again, I must have time. As it were to lick my wounds, as might a lion. A sorry lion! And only in these Highland hills may I do it. But not as proud leader of a knightly host. As a cateran against caterans, rather. That way only lies survival."

It was a strange speech for the Bruce, for any monarch. They all gazed at him, unspeaking, waiting.

"So, Nigel — you will take the Queen and the ladies. With strong escort. Take them far north and east. To Kildrummy, in Mar. Out of this west country. To safety . . ."

"No, Robert — no! Not that . . .!" Elizabeth cried.

"Yes, my heart. It must be. I say yes. Indeed, it is my royal command. Here is no life for women. You would not tie our hands? Nigel will take you to Kildrummy. You will take all the horses that are left us — for you will need them, and they will serve us nothing who remain here. We shall do better afoot. We shall make for Sir Neil's country of Loch Awe in Argyll. And come to you again, when we may."

The Queen could not dispute openly, of course. But she looked unconvinced.

"And what if Edward Plantagenet comes for us at Kildrummy?" Nigel asked.

"Then you will go north. Even further. Ever north. Beyond the great firths. As far as you must, to gain these ladies' safety. Where Edward cannot follow. Even to the North Isles, if need be. They will receive you kindly, for our sister's sake who is their queen in Norway. These who I hold most dear, I trust into your hand. The married men, and the wounded, will go with you. My lord of Atholl. Sir Christopher Seton. Sir Alexander Lindsay. Sir Alan Durward. Sir John de Cambo. My lord Bishop of Moray. The rest will turn cateran, here. With Robert Bruce!"

The buzz of excited exclamation and comment that followed was interrupted by the arrival, mounted, of Sir Robert Boyd and about a dozen of his rearguard, weary and battle-scarred. Boyd was lifted down from his horse, sorely wounded in the leg. He gasped out his report. They had been caught between the two enemy forces, and had had no option but to fight their way out, towards their main body, with appalling losses. Boyd, who had been one of William Wallace's closest lieutenants, was a doughty veteran, though but thirty, and his survival of major importance; but the loss of almost nine out of ten of his rearguard was dire news. It meant that out of a total force of some five hundred, Bruce had now not one fifth remaining.

Boyd's leg-wound was also a blow. It meant that he would be unable to remain with the King's dismounted party — and he was the most experienced guerilla leader they had. But at least he was strongly in favour of the King's plan, and would be a source of strength to Nigel's party. He declared that the sooner they split forces the better. His own flight hither undoubtedly would have been observed, and it would be guessed that the royal survivors were assembling here. He urged that the Queen's company should make off immediately due northwards through the Mamlorn passes before these could be cut. The rest could then filter off through this open forestland in small groups, on foot, to come together again at a chosen rendezvous. In Glen Lochy perhaps. Campbell would know . . .

That was accepted. Bruce drew Elizabeth aside a little way.

"My dear," he said, "I am sorry. But . . . better this way."

"Better for whom? Not for me."

"For you, yes, also. In the end. Would you relish being a hunted fugitive?"

"So long as I was with you."

He shook his head. "I would not have my wife harried like a run deer. Nor can I have our men having ever to think of women's safety. You must see it, my love. But, by the Rude, I am going to miss you! The thought of it is like lead at my heart."

"Miss, yes. For me, life will be no more than an emptiness. And it may be long, long."

"Not a day, not an hour, longer than needs must. That I promise you."

"Must? Must? Robert — must indeed you do this? Must you go on with a hopeless struggle? You have tried and tried again. Why continue? Why not come north also? North indeed. Let us go to the North Isles. Together. To the Orcades. In your sister's husband's realm. Where none will assail us. Where we may live together in peace, you and I. Until a better day dawns. Edward of England is an old man, and sick. He will not live for very long. We are young, and can wait . . ." Her voice tailed away in a manner strange indeed for that strong-minded young woman.

The Bruce stared at her, closely. Never had he heard Elizabeth speak like this, the woman who had been his strength and stay. "Dear God," he whispered. "*You* ask that?"

Slowly she raised a troubled downcast gaze to meet his. And then her chin rose also, suddenly proud again. "No!" she said. "No. That was not I who spoke. Not Elizabeth de Burgh. Not your wife. Not the Queen. Forget that it was said. Said by a tired and foolish woman, in sorrow for herself. Heed it not, Robert — but go and do your duty."

He all but broke, then, more affected by her self-rebuke than by her pleas. "My love, my sweet, my very own," he said. "It may be that you have the rights of it. Who knows? But . . . I took the crown, for better or for worse. I swore to free and save this realm, if it is within my power to do so. As yet, I have proved but a sore king for Scotland. Two battles, and both shamefully lost . . ."

"Neither were battles. Both traps set by traitors, rather." That was more like Elizabeth.

"Perhaps. But in both I was taken by surprise. And should not have been. I thought that I had learned my lesson, at Methven. But no. Many have died for my error. I set up advance and rearguards, yes — but forgot that in these mountains that is not how war is fought. I must redeem myself, Elizabeth — not flee to safety."

"Yes, I know it. Forgive me. But I hoped that, though the other women, and Marjory, went . . . that I might stay with you. For I am strong of body, and care nothing for discomforts of camp and field. But . . . I see that it cannot be. I will go to Kildrummy, with your daughter. Or if need be, to the Isles. And await you there. There to assail the ears of all the saints in heaven continually, to watch over and preserve you, and bring you back to me!"

"Amen to that," he said. "Now — Marjory . . ."

So the leave-taking was got over, with haste and not a little foreboding — for none there required to have spelled out to them the chances against any swift or happy reunion. To Nigel the King spoke at greater length — for though he was his favourite brother, and trustworthy to the end, he was of a carefree and happy-go-lucky disposition, and Bruce was entrusting to him not only his wife but the heiress to his throne. He urged him, privily, to be guided by Boyd rather than by Atholl or Lindsay, more lofty in rank as these might be.

Elizabeth was the Queen again, calm in control of her women and herself. She bade her husband farewell with steadfast dignity and restraint, even though her lip quivered in the process. Mounting, they were gone, leaving about thirty men amongst the evening shadows of the trees.

They gazed after the departing riders, all young men, the King in fact the second oldest there, some ten knights and esquires, with a score of personal attendants and men-at-arms, all horseless for perhaps the first time in their lives. Whatever they said, whatever had been implied, they could not but feel themselves as lost, naked and abandoned — all perhaps save Sir Neil Campbell, the only Highlandman present. A month before, these had been amongst the very flower of Scotland's chivalry; today they were little better than broken men, hunted outlaws.

Bruce himself, after a few moments, deliberately set the pattern of it. Twisting round, and grimacing at the pain of his shoulder, he called, "To me, Jamie. Aid me out of this shirt of mail. Such wear is not for us, my friends. Hereafter. Off with your armour and helmets. Put away two-handed swords, battle-axes, maces and the like. Henceforth we use dirks and daggers. Tonight, after dark, we go down again to the field of battle. They will scarce look for us there. To rob the slain. The MacDougall slain. We want plaids and tartans and sheepskins. Brogans for our feet. Broadswords. Targes. From now onward we forget that we are knights and lords. Food we shall require, likewise — and must win it where we may."

The young Lord of Douglas, but newly of age, aiding his hero out of the chain-mail, tender for a damaged shoulder, protested. "Your Grace cannot turn cateran. Like any low-born bareshanked Erse bogtrotter . . .!"

"My Grace can, and will. Indeed must. Since only so will any of us survive. And I intend to survive, my friends. Do not doubt it. Come — we have work to do . . ."

CHAPTER TWO

SURVIVAL is a very compelling preoccupation, taking undoubted precedence over all others, in the last resort. Moreover, it carries its own built-in mental and emotional security system, excluding all other influences and anxieties which might endanger the individual's physical preservation. Long-term, hypothetical, even ethical problems tend not only to become largely irrelevant but fade altogether from the mind, in the said last resort. Concentration on survival of necessity becomes basic.

So it was with Robert Bruce and certain of his comrades in the month that followed. Certain only, because, in the test, some inevitably fell by the wayside, one way or another. Some were not of the stuff of survival, mentally or physically; some were unfortunate; some came to conceive that anything would be better than a continuation of these conditions, and opted out; some, quite simply, died. Four weeks after the Glendochart debacle, ten men only remained with the King — his brother Edward, the lords Douglas, Hay and Campbell, an obscure knight named Sir William Bellenden, and five common soldiers.

Not that there was now any observable difference between the men; indeed, if there was any ranking amongst the ten, leadership was frequently taken by a squat and uncouth Annandale mosstrooper named Wat Jardine, whose sheer powers of survival and self-help exceeded all others. All were equally filthy, unshaven, lean, brown and weather-beaten, half-naked in ragged tartans. Not once in those weeks had they slept under a roof. They had eaten raw meat more often than cooked, from stolen cattle and hunted deer and wild-fowl — even raw fish, although it turned their stomachs — but more often had to fill the said stomachs with blae-berries, fungus and wild honey. They had been hunted like brute beasts — and like beasts they had rounded and rended and slain, when they might. They had come to look on all men as their enemies, and the empty wilderness their only friend, night and storm their occasional allies.

They had never reached Argyll. The Campbell's territories which stretched from Loch Awe to the Western Sea, were hemmed in unfortunately from the east by part of Lorn, Mamlorn and Nether Lorn, as well as the lands of the Macfarlanes, MacNaugh-tons and MacLachlans, chiefs allied to MacDougall. In conse-quence every glen and pass and access they found held against them, with the whole country roused. Each shift and attempt they made ended in failure — and the diminution of their numbers. Moreover, Neil Campbell now feared that even if they reached his lands, they would there be invaded by forces too great for him to withstand.

So they had at length turned back. Malcolm Earl of Lennox was believed to have escaped after Methven, and now represented the only major noble free, and committed to the King's cause. South towards the Lennox they had turned, therefore, avoiding all the main glens and making their indirect and secret way around the lofty shoulders of the great mountains. Ben Lui, Ben Oss and Ben Vorlich, and many lesser peaks.

Now they were on the dark edge of long Loch Lomond, near the north end. It was a mid-August night, and for two days they had been in hiding in Glen Falloch to the north, resting up by day and prospecting the possibilities of escape by night. For they were still in Macfarlane country, enemy territory, and their presence in the area known. They were being sorely hunted. Just across the loch was MacGregor land, where they would expect to be com-paratively safe — for though MacGregor was not necessarily a King's man, at least he was at permanent feud with Macfarlane, Macnab, and to a lesser degree with the MacDougalls. The Camp-bells also, as it happened — but that probably would not seriously affect the issue. Moreover, south of the MacGregor lands lay the great country of Lennox, the first of the West Lowlands. Somehow the fugitives must get across the mile-wide and twenty-five-mile-long loch — for the valley-floor to the north, in Glen Falloch, was watched for every yard of the way by the Lord of Lorn's minions, as they knew to their cost. Search parties were scouring the area for them, and Falloch had become too hot to hold them.

Unhappily, Macfarlane had obviously decreed that all the many boats of the small lochside communities should be put beyond the reach of the refugees. Bruce and six of his companions now sat silent, in a cranny amongst the rocks above the black lapping waters, having each pair covered their allotted search-area, at great risk, even as far as half a mile inland, but without the least success. All boats on the west side of Loch Lomond, that night, were evidently securely hidden or under lock and key.

The silence was grim rather than dispirited or despairing. These men were long past that. They were now fined down to surviving from hour to hour. Disappointments, failures, losses, reverses, were but incidental, to be accepted and absorbed into the pattern of survival. Any who indeed survived this prolonged ordeal would emerge very different men, men of steel, tried, tested, tempered. And ruthless.

James Douglas and Dod Pringle, one of the men-at-arms, emerged like silent shadows out of the gloom, and squatted down beside the others.

"Nothing," the young lord said briefly, flatly.

"No," the King acknowledged.

"A raft. Of driftwood. Tied with ropes of twisted bracken," Campbell suggested.

"For ten? To sail a mile?"

"Two can swim. They can draw it."

"It will be dawn in two hours. No time. We would be seen."

"Tomorrow night, then."

"If we live."

"Some will. *You* must."

The use of titles and honorifics had long since been given up.

Edward Bruce, always highly strung, a man like a coiled spring, had become almost half-crazed these last weeks, in glittering-eyed tension, his hand seldom far from his dirk-hilt. One of their number he had already slain, in a sudden fit of rage. He was a killer now, and even in that fierce company men eyed him warily and kept their distance. He spoke now.

"Back there. A mile. There are two cot-houses. At the lochside. Women in them. I heard them. A boat they will have. Somewhere. I will make them talk."

"No," his brother said. "Not women."

"I say yes. Cross this loch we must. Squeamish folly will serve nothing."

"I do not make war on women. I have enough on my mind." That was final.

There were mutterings for and against — for no man's word was law in this company now.

They were interrupted. Another little group emerged from the

31

shadows of the alder thickets on the left, the remaining pair, Sir
William Bellenden and the Annandale mosstrooper, Jardine. But
there was a third figure, whom Jardine had gripped in a savage,
arm-twisted hold, and bent forward almost double. At first Bruce
thought the prisoner was an old woman, hung about with rags.
Then he perceived the long grey beard.

"Found him by the lochside," the mosstrooper jerked. "Spying
on us, for a wager! Jabbers nothing but his heathenish Irish."

The King, leaning closer to peer, distinguished even in the darkness the dull sheen of gold at approximately the waist, the en-
twining serpents of a magnificent belt.

"Fools!" he cried. "This is the Dewar! The Dewar of the
Coigreach. Unhand him. He is a friend."

"Then why does he lurk here? At this hour?" Bellenden asked.

The old man launched into a flood of Gaelic, furious, vituper-
ative, outraged, however unintelligible. Jardine would have
silenced him with a buffet, but the King caught his arm.

"Say on, Master Dewar," he directed. "But in the tongue we
may understand, of a mercy!"

The other obliged, and eloquently. "Spawn of the devil!
Offspring of Beelzebub!" he declared, with a sibilant vehemence
that lacked nothing in venom for all the Highland softness of intonation. "To lay their foul hands on the Dewar! To defile Saint
Fillan! May they roast on the hottest hob of hell everlastingly! May
the cries of their torture ascend eternally!"

"To be sure. To be sure," Bruce agreed. "Their offence will
receive due punishment, undoubtedly. But — what brings you here,
my friend? To Loch Lomondside?"

"You do. Who else? You, Sir King. I came seeking you." Evidently Bruce's totally unkinglike appearance did not confuse the
Dewar.

"Here? In the dark? How knew you to look for me here?"

"Much is known to the Dewar."

"It is? Then, not only *you* will know we are here?"

"To be sure. All the Highlands know that you are on the wrong
side of Loch Lomond. But only I know how you may win away
from here."

"Ha! You do?"

"I have brought you a boat, see you."

They all stared at him, and then at each other.

"How can you have brought a boat?" Edward Bruce demanded.

The other did not trouble to reply.

The King rubbed his unshaven chin. "My friend — I am grate-

32

ful," he said. "But the lochshore is watched. All Glen Falloch is watched. We fear that all boats will be denied us. Even yours."

"You know not what you say," the Dewar replied scornfully. "Come — I will take you up to it. But quietly."

"This could be a trap," Bruce's brother jerked. "Leading us into our enemies' arms."

"Aye. Belike they sent the old man to cozen us," Bellenden agreed. "To betray us. Once more."

"I think not," the King said. "This Dewar of the Coigreach gave me Saint Fillan's blessing. He would not betray me now."

"I would not trust him. I would not trust any of these Highland savages," Edward asserted, hand feeling for dirk.

"You would not?" Sir Neil Campbell, Highlander himself, asked thinly.

"Enough!" the King snapped. "The decision is mine — and I trust the Dewar. Sir — we will follow you, and gladly. But — where is your boat?"

"You shall see. So be these fools go quietly! Come."

The old man, despite his stooping shuffle, could move surprisingly quickly. Turning, he led them away from the lochside, through the shadowy junipers and scattered birches, up and down amongst the knolls and hummocks, muttering to himself in seemingly disgusted fashion, but nimble — and not so much as glancing behind to ensure that they all followed. He twisted and turned, and sometimes actually doubled back on his tracks, so that his mutterings were echoed by some of those behind. And once or twice he stopped still, and waited, almost as though sniffing the air, before moving on at a tangent. In the dark, and without landmarks, it was difficult to say what general direction they were taking; but Bruce had the impression that they were going southwards and roughly parallel with the loch.

For perhaps twenty minutes he led them on this roundabout progress, without word or indeed glance at his companions; but however irritating and mystifying a process this was, at least he led them to avoid contact with others, their enemies or the cot-houses of local clansfolk — though once they heard voices at no great distance.

At length they emerged at the waterside again — and after the constriction of the trees and knowes, visibility seemed to be enhanced. At least they could see that they were opposite a small tree-clad offshore island. It was difficult to say, in the gloom, how far off it was — possibly only two or three hundred yards.

From out of the lochshore boulders at their very feet a figure rose — to the hasty indrawn breaths of the fugitives and reaching for dirks. But the old man threw a brief word at him, and was as briefly answered; and Bruce, peering, perceived that this was in fact the younger Dewar, the custodian of the saint's arm-bone.

Almost without pause the old man waded straight into the loch, not so much as troubling to hitch up his trailing rags. He did not beckon them, though the younger Dewar gestured them on.

Bruce, following fairly close behind their guide, was surprised to find the water rising no higher than his knees, as he waded out. Nevertheless, in a few moments, there was a smothered yelp and some splashing behind him, and he turned to find one of his colleagues in the loch almost up to his neck. He could have sworn that, amongst the objurgations and exclamations behind, he heard the old Dewar sniggering in front.

Their guide had not, in fact, seemed to be heading directly towards the island, but slightly to one side. Then he suddenly changed direction, turning almost at right angles, as it were back on course. Bruce realised that they must be on one of the hidden under-water causeways, of which he had heard, dog-legged or zigzag, allowing access to certain islands by those who knew the secret. He turned to James Douglas, immediately behind, to warn the others to keep close and to turn exactly where he did.

They reached the island safely, and the old Dewar consented to explain. This had been a former sanctuary of Saint Fillan, where he retired for contemplation, and there were still remains of a cell and altar amongst the undergrowth. It was the Dewars' duty to tend this, and other shrines, and for this they sometimes required to use a boat. This they kept here.

He showed them the craft, in a little creek at the far side of the islet, with some pride. But it was tiny, little more than a coracle, only large enough to hold two, or at a pinch, three.

"By the Mass — is that all!" Edward cried. "That cockle-shell!"

"It is a boat!" Bruce declared. "Which is the great matter."

"It will carry the King across the water," the old man said. "For the others of you, I care not!"

"I am the King's brother, fool!"

"So much the worse for the King!"

Bruce intervened. "Peace, my friends. Here is much to be thankful for. It but means that we must cross two at a time. So that we have not long to spare. Before dawn. Let us waste none of it."

It seemed that the younger Dewar was to act boatman. He declared that a patrol of Macfarlanes had passed along the shore shortly before their arrival, heading north. He thought that there would be no more, for some time at least; though there might also be patrols in boats beating up and down the loch.

Though Bruce would have drawn lots for it, all others agreed that he must go across first — moreover the elder Dewar all but had apoplexy at any other suggestion. The King elected to take Sir James Douglas with him.

They climbed cautiously in — for it was quite the smallest craft either of them had ever been in, and moreover gave the impression of being half-rotten in its frail timbering. The water slopping about in the bottom could have been caused by rain, of course. The King expressed his thanks to the old man, as the younger inserted himself beside them — but their saviour maintained his peculiarly mocking and ungracious attitude to the end, even though the valedictory flood of Gaelic he sent after them might conceivably have been an addendum to the Blessing of Saint Fillan.

It made an alarming voyage. The coracle was grossly overladen, with three aboard, and Loch Lomond made itself all too evident. Indeed quickly it became clear that too much of the loch was coming inside with them, and the two passengers were soon as busy as the paddler, scooping the water out with their cupped hands, since bailer there was none. The possibility of enemy boats out here watching for them was never far from their minds.

The actual crossing was probably less than a mile — but it seemed to take an unconscionable time, with the craft heavy and sluggish to a degree and, whether from its construction, inexpert paddling or overloading, seeming to sidle and move crabwise rather than straight forward. But at last the far shore loomed in sight, dark and apparently thickly-wooded. Their escort deposited them on a shingly beach and, surprisingly, considering the course followed, seemed to know exactly where he was. He told them that a little way to the right and up the steep hillside, beside a waterfall of the first burn they came to, was a cave where they could hide. He advised that they hide there all the next day and only move south by night — for though this was now MacGregor country, it was only sparsely populated, and the MacDougalls, Macfarlanes and the rest would not hesitate to come raiding across if they suspected that their quarry had won over.

Bruce was anxious about the boat on the return journey, with the Dewar unable to paddle and bail at the same time; but the other assured that with only the one in the craft, the intake of water would not be nearly so great. He launched away again with the minimum of delay.

Leaving Douglas at the waterside, the King went in search of the cave. Once he had found the burn flowing into the loch over an apron of whitened pebbles, it was not difficult, entailing only hard climbing for some 300 feet up a steep braeface of scrub-covered rock and scree. The waterfall splashed in a drop of about thirty feet near by. It was a fair-sized cavern — although ten would tax its accommodation — formed out of a deep crevice over which a great flat rock had fallen. It was dry and secure, and better than many of their recent refuges.

Back at the shore, Bruce found that the second boatload had not yet arrived. Indeed they had to wait for some time before Edward Bruce and one of the men-at-arms were delivered. At this rate it would be dawn long before the ferrying was done.

In the event, dawn broke with only six of the party across. Fortunately it was a still morning, and the mists that rose everywhere on the surface of the water might serve to hide the little boat. When, after what seemed an endless wait, the watchers on the east shore did spot it again, certainly the craft was quite close inshore before it emerged from the vapours. Moreover it looked so low in the water, so lump-like, that it could almost have been a floating log. This impression was caused, it turned out, not only by the fact that the coracle was at least half-full of water, and that the three passengers were leaning forward almost flat and paddling that way with their hands; but that Wat Jardine, one of the two who could swim, was actually in the loch behind, clinging on with his hands and kicking out with his feet. This was the entire company, for since the boat did not have to be returned after this trip, the young Dewar had remained behind and would come for his property on some other occasion.

He and his elderly colleague had sent a message, however, by Gilbert Hay. The King and his party should not move from the cave; not until nightfall. Not until a guide had been brought, to lead them southwards.

"The fools! They think that we must be led like bairns!" Edward exclaimed. "That we cannot find our own way here. As we have done before."

Campbell nodded. "Our own guides we will be."

"We owe these Dewars much," Bruce demurred. "This at least we can do."

"To what purpose? We are our own best guides. And if Mac-Gregor is indeed loyal, what need . . .?"

"'I have said what we shall do, my lord," the King observed evenly. "Saint Fillan's blessing I will honour."

"As you will, Sire." That was the first sire, or my lord either, to have been heard in that company for days.

Emptying the waterlogged boat, and hiding it amongst the loch-side alders, they climbed to the cave.

All day they lay hidden up there on the stony face of Creag an Fhithich, the Raven's Crag, and though they slept, two were always awake, on watch. And, intermittently, there was much to watch. A mere mile away, on the far shore of the loch and on the hillsides beyond, frequently activity was evident, by groups large and small. In the afternoon, boats appeared on the loch, searching shore and islets. And later, a strong company actually came down their own side of the water, only a few hundred feet below them. That they were not MacGregors seemed evident by their wary and heedful attitude; they were watching as much as searching. Fortunately they were not concerned with the steep stony braeface directly above.

All the King's party were awakened for this — and few felt disposed to sleep again thereafter.

By dusk all were fretting to be off, but Bruce insisted that they wait. Besides, to move before it was fully dark would be folly. But it was long past dark, and tempers strained, before a watcher reported movement up the burn-channel. The fugitives crept out of the cave, to crouch and hide amongst the rocks around. They were not going to be caught in any trap.

Two men materialised out of the shadows, panting heavily. One was recognisable as the stocky person of the Dewar of the Main; the other was much larger in every way, a tall and massive figure, gasping the more in consequence.

"Sir King," the younger man said hoarsely, "is it yourself?"

"I am here, yes. We were fearing that you were not coming. It is late, man."

"Late, yes. We dare not come sooner. To be seen . . ."

"*Dare* not? Watch your words, man!" That was his large companion.

"Lest we be seen. To come here . . ."

"You have brought us a guide?" Bruce said. "To lead us south to Lennox."

"In a way of speaking." The younger man gestured. "MacGregor."

The big man inclined his head. "MacGregor," he repeated.

"Yes. That is well. Think you there will be enemies — MacDougalls and Macfarlanes — on this side of the loch? Still? Some passed below us early!"

"It may be so," the Dewar nodded. "They may well now fear that you have crossed. Your boat, therefore, should hold well to mid-loch, see you . . ."

"Boat! No more boats, by God!" That was Edward. "We had enough of your boats, last night."

"By boat, yes," the MacGregor guide said shortly. "It is my decision."

"*Your* decision, by the saints! We make our own decisions, fellow!"

"Quiet, Edward . . .!"

"On MacGregor land, *I* make the decision, whatever. Mind it, Southron! I am Malcolm, son of Gregor, son of Hugh."

"I care not whose son you are! I am the King's brother, now Earl of Carrick . . ."

"Fool! Think you such new kingship is of any moment to a son of Alpin?"

"Alpin!" Bruce exclaimed. "Malcolm, you said? Son of Gregor, was it? Son of Hugh. You are not . . . MacGregor himself? Of Glenorchy? The chief . . .?"

"I am MacGregor, yes. Himself. And my race is royal. None so royal."

"MacGregor is come to take you to the great Earl, Sir King," the Dewar explained. "The Earl of Lennox. His friend . . ."

Bruce scarcely heeded. That this, one of the proudest men in all the Highlands, in all Scotland indeed, should have come in person to act their guide, was significant, whatever way it might be considered. The MacGregors were not one of the greater clans, as far as numbers went, but they had an importance far beyond their size. They claimed to be descended from Gregor, brother of King Kenneth MacAlpine, and if so, were the most direct representatives of the original Scots royal line, a dynasty lost in the mists of antiquity. Their main territories were Glen Orchy and Glen Strae, at the head of Loch Awe, but there the Campbells had been encroaching and there was bad blood between the two clans. This area on the east side of Loch Lomond comprising Glen Gyle and Inversnaid was of minor importance, and the chief's presence here was a surprise. Was it for good or ill? This could mean a welcome accession of support — or, equally, it could mean more treachery.

Bruce glanced quickly at the Campbell chief. In these Highlands, clan feuds mattered a deal more than national wars. Sir Neil, never a diplomatic or forthcoming individual, could precipitate immediate trouble. But would he do it, on MacGregor territory?

Apparently not. "I am Neil, son of Colin Mor, of Lochawe, of the line of O'Duin," he said briefly.

"I had heard that you were of this King's company," the MacGregor returned, equally cryptic.

"We are honoured, much honoured, MacGregor, to have *your* company," Bruce said hurriedly. "We had not looked for so notable an escort."

"You are on my lands," the other returned simply.

Bruce was afraid that his brother might blurt out that, in theory at least, all the land in this realm was the King's; it was the sort of thing that Edward would do, in his present frame of mind. Fortunately, he forbore.

"The Earl of Carrick has made himself known to you. Here now is Sir James, Lord of Douglas. Sir Gilbert, Lord of Erroll. Sir William Bellenden. And other friends . . ."

"Let us be done with this talk," Edward jerked. "This of the boat? Do we hazard this?"

All knew what he meant. MacGregor could be leading them into a trap.

"I have the blessing of Saint Fillan," Bruce said slowly, carefully.

There was silence, while men considered that.

"None could be more potent, at all," the Dewar observed. "MacGregor will agree."

"That is truth," the chief nodded. "That saint is patron to my name and line. At his call I am here. For this, and because you are the friend of my friend."

If the King thought that MacGregor should rather have come out of loyalty to his liege lord, he did not say so, content that these other loyalties should ensure his good faith.

"That is well," he acceded. "My friend, and yours? Do you mean the Earl of Lennox?"

"The same. Malcolm, son of Malcolm, son of Maldwyn, son of Aluin, son of Aluin, of the Levenach. To him I can take you. And only I."

"Only . . .? Why so?"

"Because he is in hiding."

"Hiding? The Earl? In his own Lennox?"

"Even so. His castles are all occupied by *your* enemies. He pays dear for supporting King Robert Bruce!"

"Aye. Nor Lennox only." Sombrely Bruce nodded. "We are in your hands, then, MacGregor. Take us to Lennox. If you will."

They left the cave, not to clamber down to the waterside again, but to climb upwards by a steep and difficult ascent amongst the rocks and slippery screes — this apparently because just a little farther to the south, almost sheer cliff overhung the lochshore, which would have forced anybody travelling down it to traverse a very narrow strip between water and cliff, providing a perfect site for an ambush. If their enemies suspected that the fugitives were on this side of the loch, that corridor would be closely watched.

At length they reached a long ridge, about 600 feet above the water. It seemed much lighter up here, and the sense of constriction which had oppressed them for days lifted somewhat. Along this bare ridge they moved, for about two miles, before they began to slant down half-left over smoother grassy slopes into a parallel valley formed by the Snaid Burn. Here cattle grazed, and it was a strange sensation for the fugitives to pass close to cothouses without skulking and creeping. Presently they came down to Inversnaid, where a sizeable township clustered round the seat of one of the MacGregor chieftains. Men were astir here, and quiet salutes greeted the chief; but no attention was paid to the others, King or no King.

Turning west again, on a well-trodden track down the steep ravine of the Snaid, here practically a prolonged waterfall, they emerged once more at the loch. But it was a very different beach. Here were more houses, and from them a stone jetty thrust out into the dark waters. Not a few boats were moored or drawn up thereabouts; but tied to the jetty was one the like of which the visitors had never seen — save only Campbell. It was long and narrow, high of prow and stern, with a single central mast on which hung a great boom with furled sail. At bows and stern were raised platforms and double-banked along each side were the black ports for many oars.

"A galley!" Bruce exclaimed. "A chief's galley! Yours, MacGregor?"

"'Mine."

"But how, a God's name, comes a galley on Loch Lomond? A sea craft. On an inland water?"

"Where MacGregor goes, there goes his galley."

"But how, man? You come from Glenorchy, in the north, do you not? Above Lorn."

"My galleys ride on Loch Etive, of the Western Sea," he said. "When I would come to these southern lands of Clan Alpine, I sail out into that sea, and down through the isles, to Tarbert at the head of Kintyre. There my Gregorach draw my galley out, set it on round tree-trunks, and pull it across the low neck of land one mile to Loch Fyne. I sail down that loch, to Bute Kyle, and then up Loch Long. Only two miles divide the head of Long from this Lomond. Again my oarsmen draw the galley across the land. On this Lomond, then, my galley is supreme."

"I' faith — here's a wonder . . .!"

"You learned that trick from the Northmen's king," Neil Campbell observed sourly. "Magnus, Hakon's goodson, did the same, before Largs fight. When he burned the Lennox."

"You mistake, Wry-mouth," the other gave back. "Hakon learned it from MacGregor. Clan Alpine has been so doing since before there was ever a Campbell to defile Argyll!"

"God's patience . . .!"

"And we sail in your galley?" the King intervened.

"What else? When you sail with MacGregor."

Now there were men all round them, fierce-looking — but no fiercer than themselves — bristling with arms. To one, MacGregor gave a command. He blew loud and long on a great curling cattle-horn, the whooping, moaning ululations echoing and re-echoing amongst all the enclosing hills. Bruce and his companions, after weeks of hiding, could scarcely forbear to demand quiet, secrecy, abashed at this blatant drawing of attention to themselves. But clearly they were now in the company of no skulkers. MacGregor of MacGregor, on his own heather, was not the man on whom to urge discretion.

The horn had been the signal for the galley to be manned. Men poured aboard in surprising numbers, equipped with their great rawhide and studded targes, circular shields, which they proceeded to hang over the sides of the vessel, forming a sort of armour-plating thereon.

"Where were all these when we needed them?" Edward Bruce growled. "These past days, when we were hunted like beasts, just across this loch! The MacGregor is something tardy in his duty, I say!"

"Better tardy than never. Or against us," the King murmured, lower-voiced. "Indeed, I think he is not here for *my* sake, even now. He is doing this because the Dewars besought him. And for his friend Lennox's sake. Let us be grateful for such mercies as come our way, brother."

The chief ushered his visitors aboard, the lesser men to the bow platform, the greater, with himself, to the stern. Bruce was surprised to see how many oars the vessel used, twenty on each side, in two banks, long powerful sweeps, each worked by two men seated on cross thwarts. With a relay of swordsmen standing by to take their turn at the sweeps. MacGregor must have had nearly 200 men aboard.

They cast off immediately and efficiently, and the huge square sail was unfurled — with all that oar-power, and since there was little wind, Bruce imagined more to display the MacGregor arms of crossed oak-tree and sword, painted hugely thereon, than for propulsion. With surprisingly little splash and fuss for so multiple a

41

motive-power, they moved out into the night-bound waters, and swung southwards, down-loch.

It made a very strange sensation for Bruce and his party to be sailing openly, indeed dramatically, on the great sheet of water which had for so long been their bugbear. Especially when, presently, the helmsman began to chant a lilting haunting melody, rhythmic and repetitive, in time with the beat of the oars, which the rowers took up in deep pulsing power — one of the many boat-songs of the West. To the surge and thrust and ache of this they thrashed down Loch Lomond, sweeps flashing, spray flying, at a speed which none of the Lowlanders had believed possible on water. Greyhounds of the sea they knew these galleys to be called, but this headlong progress was beyond all their imagining, exhilarating, challenging.

This aspect of challenge preoccupied the fugitives. MacGregor might be puissant and redoubtable, but the MacDougall Lord of Argyll and Lorn was still more powerful. This shouting aloud of their presence might be magnificent, but it was surely foolhardy.

But when Bruce indicated as much to their host, he was met with scorn. "Who will question MacGregor's galley?" he asked simply. "Besides, there is no other on the loch."

"At least they will know where we go."

"Where MacGregor goes," the other amended. "Why should they believe King Bruce with him?"

Loch Lomond broadens out to the south, and at its foot it is almost five miles wide, and dotted with islands. Ten or so miles down towards this the galley drove. Whether or not the chief was right and none dared to interfere with MacGregor's galley, they saw no other boats throughout — although their passage must have been entirely evident to any who watched.

After perhaps an hour, with the widening of the loch, the looming black shadows of the great mountains drew back and dwindled as they sailed out of the Highlands and into Lennox. Bruce had quite expected that they would be conducted to one of the many islands. These, after all, would in the main belong to the Earl of Lennox, and might provide refuges. But, no. The galley drove on through the island area without diminution of speed, MacGregor himself directing the helmsman. The regular splash of forty blades meeting the water in unison, the creaking of oars, and the gasping pant of the men, dominated the night with purpose. The smell of sweat was like a miasma that travelled with the ship.

The foot of Lomond spreads out into flat level country, ranged only distantly by low hills. The galley, in fact, was making for the very south-east corner, where the River Endrick flowed in through farflung marshland. Now MacGregor slowed his rowers drastically, peering ahead keenly. Soon a leadsman in the bows was shouting soundings, as the water shoaled.

The chief pointed suddenly, and the helmsman nodded. Posts could be distinguished rising out of the water. Three of them were visible, obviously in a line.

"The mouth of the Endrick," MacGregor mentioned. "Deep water channel."

They eased in towards the posts, and soon it was apparent that there was a long line of them. The galley was edging along very slowly now, following the posts closely. It was not long before there was a low black belt at either side of them, darker than the water — reed-beds. The channel, twisting now, was narrowing notably.

At length the chief called a halt and, oars raised upright, they nosed forward to one of the posts. The helmsman used a steering-oar to manoeuvre the craft round, across the channel. Two men jumped down into the reeds and shallows. The water came barely to their middles.

MacGregor nodded. "Sir King," he said, "Come you." And with no more ceremony than if he were dismounting from the saddle, leapt down into the water.

Bruce could not but follow, and his colleagues after him, with but a word of farewell and thanks to the young Dewar — who apparently was coming no further. The water was not cold, but the muddy bottom was unpleasant.

MacGregor was already wading strongly in an easterly direction, parting the tall reeds and rushes before him as he went. In a stumbling, slaistering, cursing line, the others trailed after.

How far, in actual distance, they went, it was difficult to compute. It seemed a long way in the blanketing, featureless reed-sea, so difficult of passage, with wild-fowl exploding into alarmed flight continually, and somewhat heavier creatures, roe-deer perhaps or even cattle, splashing away into deeper fastnesses. Possibly they covered no more than a mile, however indirect their route — and how the MacGregor knew where he was going was a mystery. But he seemed never at a loss — and none had sufficient breath to question him.

At length a new sound, from the splashing and splatter, the quacking of ducks and the whistle of pinions, rose from the marshes — the sudden baying of hounds, and from no great distance ahead. Their guide halted, and responded promptly with great hallooing cries of "Gregalach! Gregalach!"

43

The dogs continued to bark, and the chief ploughed on directly towards the sound.

Soon the water began to shallow, and the dark mass of scrub or woodland loomed ahead. Then they were climbing out on to firm grass-grown ground — but now armed men, restraining snarling wolfhounds, were milling around them. MacGregor demanded to be taken to their lord.

They appeared to be on a fair-sized island in the marshes, a hidden place of scrub and bushes and open turf, many acres in extent. There were tents here, camouflaged with fronds and branches, forming quite a large secret encampment.

A man of middle years, slightly built, of narrow head and fine features, was standing before the largest tent, staring. Him Mac-Gregor approached, shaking water off him like a dog.

"I disturbed your sleep, friend?" he cried. "But you will forgive me. See you whom I have brought you."

"I heard your Gregalach. Have you brought me news . . .?" The other was scanning the newcomers in turn, in the gloom of near dawn. He showed no sign of recognition — and little wonder.

"Malcolm!" the King exclaimed. "My lord!"

"I am Malcolm of Lennox, yes. Who speaks me so?"

"Save us — do you not know me?"

"My lord — is this your greeting to the King's Grace?" young Sir James Douglas reproached.

"Grace? The . . . the King?" the Earl faltered, peering. "What mean you? The King is dead . . ."

"Not yet, Malcolm my friend — not yet!" Bruce said, and went to him.

Lennox, a curiously sensitive man to be a military leader — though he was that by birth rather than by inclination — was quite overwhelmed. He could find no words; indeed he wept on Bruce's shoulder — to the embarrassment of most there. Not of the King himself, however. Bruce had learned to despise no man's emotions, confronted with the stresses of his own.

"My good lord," he said.

"I believed . . . you slain . . . at Methven," the other got out. "I have mourned you. Wept for you. Since. Aye, and mourned this Scotland with you!"

"I was wounded. As I heard were you. Led off the field . . ."

"Thank the good God for it! This night I shall for ever praise! The night my liege lord returned to me. And my hope. Returned. For I had lost all hope. Here, in this desolation of waters . . ."

"Aye, my friend — I also. Almost I lost all hope likewise. Until it, and I, was saved. Saved by my Elizabeth. And the Dewars of

44

Saint Fillan. Now, I think, I shall not again lose my hope. While life is in me. And if I, excommunicate, who spilled blood on God's altar, can have hope — why then, I say, hope should be lost for none!"

To make amends for this display of emotion, Lennox offered his guests food and drink. Despite the remote and primitive nature of his refuge, he appeared to be well supplied, and the fugitives ate well, hugely indeed, for the first time for weeks, wolfing cold meats and fish, oatcakes and heather honey, washing it down with wine and the potent spirits of the country.

Their own spirits rose in consequence, their host's with them.

It was obvious that Lennox had been very depressed, deeming all his cause lost and himself a broken man, a mere fugitive on his own broad lands. Not that his state had compared in any way with that of the royal party, for though a refugee on this strange secret island in the reeds, he was in the midst of his own people and vassals, and lacked for little. But his castles and houses were denied him, occupied by supporters of the Comyns or the English. Assuming Bruce dead and further resistance useless, and living thus in winter out of the question, he had apparently decided on betaking himself off, first to the Hebrides and thence to Ireland, where he had links, there to await better days.

Bruce took him up on this, over meats. How had he intended to reach the Isles? Or Ireland? For if this had been a suitable progress for Lennox, it was the more so for himself, and urgently so, with his enemies only a jump or two behind him.

The Earl, clearly alarmed at this intimation of imminent pursuit, said that he had made no arrangements as yet — but that his notion had been to sail by small boat from the Clyde to the Isle of Bute, where the High Steward, he hoped, would provide him with a sea-going vessel to reach the Hebrides. They were only a dozen miles from the Clyde coast, at Dumbarton.

The King found no fault with that — except that the Governor of Dumbarton Castle was still the same Sir John Stewart of Menteith who had delivered up William Wallace to the English — and Dumbarton dominated all the upper Clyde estuary. He might well seek to repeat the process with Bruce.

That gave them pause, until Sir Neil Campbell announced that he had a younger brother, Donald, who had married a Lamont heiress and gained a rich property at Ardincaple, farther down the coast from Dumbarton. If they could reach Sir Donald at Ardincaple, he could provide boats for Bute.

"We must cross Macfarlane and Colquhoun country to get there," Lennox pointed out.

"Where lie Colquhoun's sympathies?"

"Humphrey de Colquhoun is a vassal of my own," Lennox said. "But he was wounded at Methven, and like me, lurks in hiding . . ."

"I will get you to Ardincaple, through any beggarly Macfarlanes or Colquhouns whatever!" MacGregor interrupted briefly, disdainfully. "So be it you may trust the Campbell when you get there!"

"I have a higher opinion of my friends than have you, sir," the King declared, before Sir Neil could rise in wrath. "But I thank you for your promise — and trust MacGregor to perform it."

"Tomorrow night? It must be done by night."

"Tomorrow, yes." Bruce looked at Lennox.

"I will be ready," the Earl said. "To come with you. Tomorrow night."

The King eyed him keenly. "My lord — no need for you to come. We are hunted men. Dispossessed of our lands. Knowing not where we will next lay our heads. Not so yourself. You have still great possessions. Lord of a whole province. Your castles may be occupied, but you need not become a hunted man. Thousands would take you into their houses . . ."

"And think you, Sire, that I could sleep of a night in any house, mine own or other, knowing my liege lord homeless, hunted? No, Your Grace — where Bruce goes hereafter, there goes Lennox, God willing!"

Much affected, Bruce gripped the other's hand, wordless. The earl might shed easy tears, but he lacked nothing in manly resolution.

So it was decided, MacGregor would leave for his galley forthwith, and return early after dark the next night. Meanwhile Campbell would slip off alone, like any cateran, with a Lennox guide, to reach his brother at Ardincaple, so that boats could be assembled for the voyage to Bute.

The MacGregor and the Campbell left almost simultaneously — but not together.

CHAPTER THREE

ALL in that little ship, heaving on the long Atlantic swell, were used to seeing impressive castles. Bruce himself owned a round dozen of them, at least, as Earl of Carrick and Lord of Annandale and Galloway and Garioch — even though all were now in English

46

hands and of no use to him. Lennox had almost as many. But none of the vessel's passengers had ever seen the like of this, as, rounding the jutting headland a bare half-mile out from that wicked shore, they stared upwards.

To call the place an eagle's nest, a sea-eagle's nest, was the feeblest inadequacy. The headland of Dunaverty itself soared sheerly hundreds of feet above the crashing waves, and the thrusting narrow bastion or stack, linked to the main cliff by the merest neck, rose higher, a dizzy pinnacle of rock. And on the very apex of this, a mere extension of the beetling stack, the castle was perched, clinging unbelievably to the uneven summit and precipitous sides, itself tall, narrow, almost incredible, an arrogant challenge not to man but to sea and sky. A great banner flew proudly from the topmost tower, and though this was dwarfed by height and distance, it could be seen to bear a simple device of a single black galley on white, undifferenced, the emblem of the Isles.

But impressive as it might be, it was not the castle nor this fluttering galley which held the watchers' gaze, in the end. Farther west than the castle-rock another headland reached out, considerably lower but farther into the sea than the other, to curve round southwards in a crook and to act as a mighty breakwater. And in the sheltered anchorage thus formed, protected from the ocean rollers and the prevailing winds, was a sight as strange as the cliff-top castle. Row upon row of true, long, low, lean galleys lay there, their masts and great slantwise spars a forest — but a disciplined forest — their white sails furled like a flock of sea-birds' folded wings, their tall carved prows upthrust like the heads of a host of sea-monsters. Someone counted twenty-seven of these killer-wolves of the Western Sea, another thirty. Lying tethered there, motionless but menacing, they made a startling impact.

"I' faith — Angus Og himself must be at Dunaverty this day!" Bruce exclaimed. "None other could have that pack of hounds in leash! And, unless I mistake, that is the undifferenced Galley of the Isles flying above yon hold."

"Does it bode good? Or ill?" Edward Bruce demanded.

"God knows! But Angus Og MacDonald hates Alexander Mac-Dougall of Lorn!"

"The Steward sent word of your coming here, to the captain of this castle, Sire," Campbell said. James the High Steward of Scotland, from Bute, had provided this ship. "So they know that we come."

"And this MacDonald has come in person to receive us!" the King's brother snarled. "I'd sooner lack him! I trust none of these Highland savages."

Sir Neil Campbell, although he himself had no love for the Mac-Donalds, stiffened. One day there would have to be a reckoning.

"My Highland subjects are no more savage, neither better nor worse than most of those nearer home, Edward," the King reproved. "And, it seems, we are in their hands now. Do not forget it."

Nevertheless, Bruce drummed fingers on the hilt of his great sword. What they were seeing undoubtedly represented a complication, and a drastic one. Dunaverty Castle, at the very tip of the great peninsula of Kintyre which thrust out towards Ireland, was in fact, save for the Isle of Man, the southernmost outpost of the former kingdom of the Isles, and most strategically situated to dominate the sea-lanes between the Hebridean north and Ireland, Man and England. On his assumption of the crown, Bruce had sent Sir Robert Boyd here, to make sure of Dunaverty, one of his first acts. And Boyd had, somehow, taken the castle, and left it in the care of a captain. Now, it seemed, Angus Og of the Isles had taken it, in turn. What did this imply? Were they running their heads into a noose, here? Not that they could turn back now.

And even if the self-styled Lord of the Isles had decided that Dunaverty should be his, why was he here in person? Impressive as this outpost was, it was nevertheless a very unimportant corner of the vast and farflung territory of the Isles, which included not only the Inner and Outer Hebrides, but great portions of the West Highland mainland, not excepting this seventy-mile-long peninsula of Kintyre. That Angus Og, its lord — or prince, as he still called himself — should happen to be at Dunaverty this day, was highly significant, whether by chance or otherwise.

"Those galleys are not long in from the sea," the experienced chief of Clan Campbell pointed out. "See — men work on them, wash down decks, coil ropes. I would say that they were not here last night." He did not sound overjoyed.

None commented.

Turning into the bay, the King's ship made for necessarily humble and inferior moorings at the tail-end of the tethered fleet.

Campbell and Edward Bruce were for once in agreement that it would be wise to send an emissary to the castle, first, to test the climate of welcome; but the King would have none of it. No skulking and standing off could avail them anything here. Their vessel, however stout, could neither outsail nor better in fight even one of these leashed greyhounds. They had come to Dunaverty as the nearest secure hold which their enemies would be unlikely to challenge. For better or for worse, here they were. There was nowhere they might flee from the Lord of the Isles.

Bruce himself led the way ashore — perforce across the decks of three or four galleys, where tough, bare-torsoed and kilted clansmen eyed them grimly, and pointedly returned no greetings. On dry land, staggering slightly after the rolling and pitching of the notoriously hazardous sea passage round the Mull of Kintyre from the sheltered waters of the Firth of Clyde estuary, the royal party proceeded round the bay beside the crashing lace-white combers, to where a long, zigzag flight of steps was cut sheerly in the naked face of the cliff, a dizzy ascent but apparently the only access from shore to castle.

The climb, on worn and uneven steps, without so much as rope as guard or handrail, was not for the light-headed. There was not a little pressing against the inner rock wall and keeping of eyes steadily averted from the outer drop. In the dark, or in a storm of wind or rain, the thing would have been nothing short of suicidal. Fortunately the King had a good head for heights — and where he led, none could decently refuse to follow.

At the cliff-top these stairs evidently led to a tiny postern-gate in the soaring castle walls, the start of whose masonry was barely distinguishable from the living rock. But since the steps were on the cliff proper, and the castle crowned the almost detached stack, it was necessary to bridge the gap. This was achieved by a lengthy, sloping and removable gangway which reached across the yawning abyss at a somewhat acute angle, some forty feet long by not much more than three feet wide, this again without handrail. A less enticing approach to a house would be hard to imagine.

The landward access appeared to be by drawbridges over three deep water-filled ditches across a narrow neck of ground. But the outer of these bridges was up, and men were clearly waiting for the visitors at the narrow postern across the ghastly gangplank.

Bruce did not hesitate. Without even a backward glance at his companions, he stepped out on to the sloping spidery planking, and strode up. It was at least ribbed with cross-bars for the feet to grip — though equally these could cause the feet to trip. He did not once look down but kept his gaze firmly on the group who watched and waited beyond. Nevertheless he was far from unaware of the appalling drop so close on either side. Was this typical of Dunaverty's reception of guests?

Certainly the appearance of the men so silently awaiting them was fierce enough, off-putting. Half a dozen of them stood in or beside the narrow doorway in the beetling wall, big men made bigger by the tall pointed helmets they wore, mostly furnished with flanking pinions of sea-eagles, or curling bulls' horns, in the antique Norse style. These did not wear the stained and ragged tartans, but saffron tunics, belted with gold, some with chain-mail jerkins and some with piebald calfskin waistcoats, great swords slung from every shoulder, dirks at hip, and hung about with massive silverware and barbaric jewellery. None were bearded, but all save one had long and heavy down-turning moustaches which hid their mouths and produced a distinctly menacing impression.

The man who lacked the moustache was different from the rest in other ways also. He was younger for one thing, in only his mid-twenties, very dark, almost swarthy, and though not short — indeed well-built — the least tall of the group. He wore no helmet or mail, only the plain kilted saffron tunic, and carried no sword but only a ceremonial dagger. It may have been in contrast to those fiercely down-turning moustaches, but his lips, visible where the others were not, seemed almost to smile. He stood in the centre of the party, and there was no doubting the authority with which he held himself, however careless.

"Wait you!" a voice rang out, while Bruce was still only two-thirds across that alarming planking. It was not the young man who spoke. "Who comes unbidden to Dunaverty? Is it Robert Bruce, who calls himself King of Scots?"

Bruce halted — although it demanded all his hardihood on that grievous perch, and he knew that those behind him must be equally preoccupied. "I am Robert, King of Scots, yes," he answered, "Come seeking the love, protection and hospitality of Angus, Lord of the Isles. Do I find it at Dunaverty?"

"I am Angus of the Isles," the young man agreed. "How can I serve Robert Bruce?" His predecessors had been careful never to admit specifically allegiance to the Crown of Scotland, even when Alexander the Third had bought the alleged suzerainty of the Isles from Hakon of Norway.

"By holding out the hand of friendship, my lord. And . . . and by letting me off this accursed tree! I vow I grow giddy!"

Angus Og laughed aloud at that frank avowal. "Well said, Sir King!" he cried. "Come, then. Myself, I near grow ill but looking at you all!" And he held out his hand.

Bruce's sigh of relief was drowned in those from behind him. He waited for no further invitation.

Angus Og's hand-grip was that of an equal and no vassal, but Bruce did not find fault with it. Sufficient that it was strong and frank.

"Well met, my friend," he said. "Your fame is known."

"As is yours. *And* your misfortunes."

"Those, yes. But they will pass. Here is good fortune, at least — to find *you* at Dunaverty."

50

Introductions followed, in the crowded narrow court within the postern, the King's party impressive only in their names and titles — for though Lennox and the Steward both had sought to rig them out in better clothing, the fugitives still were less than well and appropriately clad, the King himself little better than the rest. Their martial-looking opposite numbers turned out to be the chiefs of Jura, Gigha, Ardnamurchan and others of the great Isles confederation. By and large they were civil, but no more than that.

It seemed that Angus Og MacDonald's presence here was indeed something in the nature of a coincidence. He had called in Dunaverty some days previously, on his way to a meeting on Rathlin Island with one Malcolm MacQuillan of Antrim, an Irish kinglet who had in fact been occupying Dunaverty when Boyd had taken it for Bruce just before the coronation. MacQuillan was now demanding back the castle, and Angus, who had sent his minions to eject Boyd's captain, had had a look at it before meeting MacQuillan. When the Steward's courier, therefore, had come to Dunaverty two or three days before, he had been sent straight on to Rathlin which, although off the coast of Antrim, was only fourteen miles from Dunaverty. Angus had interrupted his conference with MacQuillan, and come back to receive Robert Bruce — for good or ill.

The implied question was clear. What did Bruce want with the Prince of the Isles?

The King was frank. "Two things I seek of you, my lord," he said. "First, refuge. Shelter for me and mine, who have been hunted men for too long. While we rest. Regain our strength. Plan our course. None may give us this better than yourself. And second, your support. In arms."

"Against whom, Sir King?"

"Against those who occupy my kingdom. Against Edward of England. And against the Comyns and their friends, who support him. Such as MacDougall of Lorn and Argyll!"

The younger man looked at him from under down-drawn brows. "You have many enemies. And Comyn, I think, has many friends. Are these all yours?" And he gestured towards the little group with the King.

Bruce drew a deep breath. "These represent thousands. Many thousands. My lord of Lennox can field six thousand. My lord of Douglas four thousand. Campbell of Lochawe as many — more, it may be. My lord of Erroll, a thousand. The High Steward two thousand. My own lands of Carrick, Annandale and Galloway . . ."

"*Can* field, Sir King! Can. But do not!"

"My lord — all these *have* fielded their men. And will do so

51

again. For eight years we have been fighting the might of Edward . . ."

"And losing!"

"And losing, yes. Though not always. When we fought aright. And in unity. Pitched battles we do not win. Against many times our numbers. Edward's chivalry, and the English bowmen. But a different kind of war we can win. Wallace taught us that. Small actions. Castle by castle. Using the land against him. Burning all before him. Starving him and his hosts. Edward may win the battles. But he grows old. Sick. Tired. *I*, God willing, will win the war!"

"With . . . help!"

"With help, yes. Yours, I hope, my lord. With others. Since I thought to count you my friend."

"Some friendships may cost a man dear."

"Well I know it. And I have nothing to offer. Meantime. One day, I hope . . ."

"The friendship of Angus of the Isles is not to be bought."

"I know it. But a King, his kingdom won, can and should reward his friends and helpers."

For moments they eyed each other. Then the Islesman nodded.

"It may be so. We shall see. For the first, for refuge, shelter, you shall have it. In my islands. For the other, for men and swords and ships, I must needs think. And consult with *my* friends. We shall see, King Robert Bruce. Meantime, my house is yours. For as long as you will . . ."

With that they had to be content.

*   *   *

The windy, lofty house of Dunaverty was not Bruce's for long, despite its present lord's assurance. The very next day a visitor arrived, having come hot-foot across Kintyre after sailing from Arran — Sir Robert Boyd of Noddsdale, no less; the same who had taken this castle, for Bruce, six months before, and whom the King had last seen after the rout in Strathfillan, wounded, and leaving to escort the Queen's party northwards to Kildrummy. Boyd, of course, was taken to Angus Og before he saw the King — but that young man was not long in bringing him.

"Trouble," he said briefly, gesturing.

The veteran Sir Robert sank on his knee before Bruce, and took his hand to kiss it. He brought startling tidings. An expedition was assembling at Dumbarton, under Sir John Stewart of Menteith, the governor thereof, and Sir John de Botetourt, Edward of England's bastard son. It was known already, somehow, that Bruce had sailed for Dunaverty, and sea-going ships were being requisitioned all up and down the Clyde to carry this expedition in pursuit. The Steward had heard that de Botetourt alone had 3,000 men. They might have sailed from Dumbarton by this.

Angus of the Isles looked as thoughtful as did Robert Bruce, at these tidings.

It seemed as though they had been betrayed again. Treachery haunted Bruce. It had never occurred to the King, even though his enemies discovered where he was, that they would pursue him into these island fastnesses. Edward Plantagenet must be very determined indeed to have him — and very angry. This was grievous, in more than just the renewal of pressure on hunted men; it meant that Angus Og would be forced to come to some sort of decision about his attitude before he was ready. Bruce had hoped to be able to work on the man. This could hardly fail to be to his disadvantage.

It did not take the Lord of the Isles long to make up his mind as to immediate tactics, at least. Eyeing his fierce-looking chiefs, he turned back to Bruce.

"Sir King," he said, "I fear that you cannot remain at Dunaverty. My sorrow that it is so — but your Englishry leave me little choice. Either you must go, or I must fight them. And I do not know that I am prepared to go to war with Edward of England!"

"I understand," Bruce nodded. "This I feared."

"Do not mistake me," the younger man went on. "It is not that I am afraid to fight Menteith and this Botetourt. They have many more men than I have here present — but my galleys, I swear, would tear their ships apart, like eagles amongst lambs! But that would be to challenge Edward. War. This I may do. One day. But then it will be *my* war. Not another man's."

As men drew breath, the King bowed stiffly, silent.

Angus Og shrugged. "I speak plainly, friend — for I am a man of plain speech. But what I say I mean. And I have named you friend. My friend you are. I will not leave you to be taken by your enemies. We sail with tomorrow's dawn. I return to Rathlin, where I have business to finish. I promised you refuge. You shall sail with me to Rathlin. And from there go whither you please. All my isles are open to you. Or you could go to Antrim. Ireland. The Irish coast is but four miles from Rathlin. *I* go thither, to Antrim. Yours is the choice. A galley of mine shall carry the King of Scots where he will." A long speech for Angus Og.

Bruce raised his head. "For that I thank you, my lord. If I

cannot be your suzerain, I can and do at least accept your friend-ship!"

Their eyes met, and each smiled slightly. These two at least understood each other, however their respective supporters might glower.

When the Islemen had withdrawn from the King's apartment, Boyd, grave-faced, asked that he might speak to Bruce privily. They moved together out on to a parapet-walk that hung ver-tiginously above the wrinkled sea.

"Your Grace — forgive me," the knight said, "but I have more grievous tidings for your ear than these you have heard. My sorrow that it is I must bear them."

"Grievous? What, man? Out with it."

"Sire — your brother. The Lord Nigel. He is dead. And not only he. Your good-brother, Sir Christopher Seton. And his brother John . . ."

"No! Dear God — no! I'll not believe it . . .!"

"It is true, Sire, God's truth. Kildrummy Castle fell. We reached Kildrummy, with her Grace and the ladies. In time. But de Valence, Earl of Pembroke, knew it and was there within a day or two. Besieged us. And the castle was betrayed. Set fire to, from within . . ."

"Betrayed again! Will it never end?" Suddenly Bruce gripped the other's wrist. "Elizabeth? My wife. The Queen. She is . . .?"

"The Queen, Sire, is escaped. And your daughter. Won safe away. When the Lord Nigel learned that Pembroke approached, he sent them away hastily, secretly. With the Earl of Atholl. For the North Isles . . ."

"Thank Christ-God! That Nigel would do. But . . . Nigel! My brother — my dear brother? He died? At Kildrummy?"

"No. Not at Kildrummy. He was captured. Wounded. With the others. As was I. In the burning castle. Traitors set afire the stores of food and grain in the great hall. And then, in the smoke and confusion, opened the postern to the English. We were all captured. But I escaped, on the way south. I and Lindsay. All were taken south to Edward. At Berwick. And there they were slain. As Wallace was slain. Hanged. Cut down while still alive. Disembowelled. And their entrails burned before their eyes . . ."

"Ah, no! No!" A sobbing groan escaped from the King's lips. Abruptly he turned away, to stride some way along that dizzy walk and stare out over the isle-dotted vastness of the Western Sea, gripping the stonework of the parapet, knuckles gleaming white. Of his four brothers, Nigel had always been the favourite. "Nigel!

Nigel!" he moaned. "What did I do to you? What did I do to you when I grasped this accursed crown?"

Boyd stood where he was, silent, waiting, askance.

At length the King turned back, his features set. "Forgive me, friend," he said. "You say . . . Christopher Seton also? My friend. My sister's husband . . ."

"Aye, Sire. Drawn, hanged, and beheaded. At Dumfries. With his brother, Sir John."

"He . . . he was the first to swear me fealty! And here is how I rewarded him!"

"The others also. All who were captured at Kildrummy. Sir John de Cambo. Alexander the Scrymgeour. Sir Alan Durward . . ."

Bruce raised his hands, almost beseechingly. "Have mercy! Have mercy on me! It is more than I can bear. All my brave, true, leal friends . . ."

"Leal, Sire — but King Edward hanged and beheaded them as traitors! And the Steward said to mind you — he will do the same to yourself, King or none. And to all with you. His young son — the Steward's only remaining son, Walter — is with you here. He urges Sire, that you send him home. Then flee the country. Not to Ireland — for Edward's arm is long. But to the North Isles. Orkney. Where my lord of Atholl takes the Queen. And thence to Norway, where Your Grace's sister is queen. This I was to urge on you. The Steward prays you. His prayer and his advice."

"And yours, my friend?"

The veteran knight looked down. "Who am I to advise the King?"

"Robert Boyd has more knowledge of war than ever had James the Steward, I think. He is a good man, but no soldier."

The other nodded. "Myself, then, I say — do what is in your own mind, Sire. Mind — not heart! For you have a King's head on your shoulders, I swear. And never did Scotland need it more!"

For a long moment Bruce searched the man's rugged features. Then he drew himself up. "It may be that you are right. God's will be done, then — for I am God's anointed, for this Scotland. But God's will, I say — not Edward Plantagenet's! I will tell the Steward that . . ."

*   *   *

Bruce did not, in fact, go to the North Isles, nor yet to Norway, great as was the temptation. That he had the means, in one of Angus Og's galleys, and might be with his wife and daughter within a few days, all but overbore him. But he steeled himself with almost the last words Elizabeth had spoken to him. "Go, and do your duty." And whatever his heart said, his mind knew where lay his duty.

So, at Rathlin Island, where Angus of the Isles took him, and they looked across the narrows to the shores of Ulster, Bruce decided that, as King of Scots, however ineffectual, his place was in his own realm of Scotland. He would not even go to Ireland with Angus Og — for it transpired that the real reason for the Lord of the Isles' presence on Rathlin with almost 2,000 men, was to co-ordinate, with Malcolm MacQuillan of the Glens of Antrim, a great joint raid on the territory of the Bissets, an Anglo-Norman family whom Edward of England had made lords of much of Antrim — and indeed of this Rathlin, also — over the heads of its native chiefs. Such raiding was typical of Isleman employment — but of no interest or use to Bruce. So he would take Angus Og at his word, borrow a galley, and sail northwards through the Isles and along the West Highland seaboard. Who could tell, he might find support up there, as well as refuge. The Earl of Ross, that far-away potentate, was as yet uncommitted in the struggle for Scotland. He might be convinced that the advantage lay with Bruce and independence, in the long run.

This was a shrewd blow at Angus himself, for the Earl of Ross was in fact the Lord of the Isles' rival for almost complete hegemony in the North. But the younger man did not rise to the fly, apparently content to tackle one project at a time. He stood by his promise, however, and allotted the King and his party a twenty-six-oar galley under the command of one MacDonald of Kiloran, and wished them well. If the Bruce was still in his territories when he got back from the Irish expedition, they would forgather again.

On the 20th of September, therefore, one of the great fleet of galleys turned its back on Rathlin Island and the Ulster coast, and set off northwards into the Sea of the Hebrides. It was significant, however, that the banner which flew at its masthead, like that painted on the great square sail, was the black Galley of the Isles, not the red Lion Rampant of Scotland.

CHAPTER FOUR

THE slanting golden afternoon sun of early October, playing on the isle-dotted, skerry-strewn sea, brought out a depth of colour, of light and shade, of sheer breathtaking beauty, such as Bruce, for one, had never before contemplated. In the weeks that he had spent in the Isles, beauty had become commonplace, part of his life. But this of the level rich autumn sun in its flooding of the Sound of Eigg, was beyond all telling. The sea, blue and green and amethyst, picked out with the sparkling white of breakers on the multi-hued, weed-hung skerries, was no more than a setting for the jewelled islands that rose in aching loveliness all around, the turning heather of their flanks stained crimson, their cliffs slashed with violet shadows, their cockle-shell sands dazzling silver against the refulgent gold. Without ever having been greatly concerned with natural beauty, the King's trials, disappointments and sorrows had made him receptive to many influences which once he would have failed to perceive. And beauty such as this might put even his troubles into perspective.

But shouts came from near by, as he leaned on the poop rail in contemplation. They were sailing northwards towards the majestic purple peaks of the Isle of Rhum, with Eigg and Muck on their starboard bow, so that he had been gazing half-right. But others had been looking in the opposite direction, half-astern to port, into the dazzle of the westering sun. And now MacDonald of Kiloran, up in the bows and shading his eyes into the golden glare, was calling back to the helmsman, near whom the King, Douglas and Lennox stood. His shouts were in the Gaelic, but the pointing hand drew all eyes.

In all the glitter and eye-hurting brilliance of the westerly prospect, it was difficult at first to discern anything to account for the shouting. But presently, with many gesticulating, it became evident that there were solid shapes amongst all that dazzlement, even though these themselves seemed to be gleaming.

Kiloran came long-strided down the narrow catwalk between the rowers. "Three galleys, two and one," he informed. "And, if I mistake not, the two fly the red and gold of Ross."

"Ross?" Bruce echoed. "And that concerns you?"

"When they chase a birlinn flying the Galley of the Isles — yes!" the other replied shortly. Then he was shouting again to the rowers and helmsman.

57

Immediately that galley was transformed. From voyaging quietly northwards on its colour-stained way from Coll to Lochalsh in the narrows of Skye, with the oarsmen pulling almost idly at their long sweeps, to the gentle chanting of a haunting melody, it became of a sudden a ship of war again, braced, tense, determined. Round in a great foaming half-circle it swung, the sail-boom creaking, the canvas shivering and flapping, the rowers straining fiercely, the blades churning the blue water white.

Kiloran soon was seen to be steering an intercepting course. The relief crew of oarsmen were as obviously arming themselves.

"What do you intend?" Bruce asked of the MacDonald.

"To teach Ross whose seas these are."

The other might have pointed out that, since this was still Scotland, these were the King's seas. Also that Angus Og had lent him this galley for *his* purposes, not for challenging all comers. A few months ago he would undoubtedly have said so. But Robert Bruce had been learning in a hard school. He held his peace.

His eyes were now able to cope with the glare and glister, and he could make out, perhaps two miles away, the three craft, the two larger most evidently pursuing the smaller, and overhauling it fast. They were heading in an almost due easterly direction, towards the mainland, just north of the great peninsula of Ardnamurchan. How Kiloran could declare that they bore this colour or that device, Bruce did not know.

What quickly became clear, as they themselves swept across the sea at a speed unprecedented as far as the Lowlanders were concerned, was that the hunters, from the earldom of Ross or elsewhere, were not going to be diverted by the intervention of a third party; and also that they would have closed with their quarry before the would-be rescuers could reach the scene, fast as the latter were moving.

"It is another of your lord's galleys? Angus Og's?" Bruce asked, of Kiloran. "The Earl's ships are far south, are they not? I would not have thought they would have dared such piracy against the Lord of the Isles."

"Not one of Angus's, no. See you, there is a fish below the Galley. On sail and banner. That is for Garmoran. MacRuarie. Christina, of Garmoran. But of our Isles federation. Of the kin of Somerled. The Rossmen would scarce have dared attack one of Angus of Islay's own. So we go teach them!"

They were still almost a mile away when they distinctly heard, across the water, the crash and clash and yells as contact was made, and the two larger vessels bore in close on either side of the smaller, shearing off oars and skewering oarsmen in bloody chaos. Grappling-irons thrown in to hold the three craft together, men poured over into the birlinn from port and starboard, drawn swords flashing in the sun.

The rowers in the King's galley were now driving their sweeps in what almost amounted to a frenzy, the chanting, not to waste precious breath, superseded by the beating of time by sword on shield, in a rhythmic clanging which grew ever faster, punctuated by a sort of barking cough which was indrawn gasping breathing of fifty-two oarsmen — a curiously savage and menacing sound. The galley tore on in a cloud of spray.

Now, with the other vessels almost stationary, they overhauled them at speed. The devices on the flapping sails were clear — the black galley above a long black fish; and three red lions on gold.

"You intend to attack?" Bruce demanded.

"What else? I shall run in at the stern."

"You will be outnumbered. These are larger galleys than yours."

"What of it? Do you count heads, Sir King, before you draw your sword?"

"I do — if I may, yes!"

"So does not fight MacDonald! Bide you and yours in safety here, then, Leave this to MacDonald."

"I think you mistake me, sir," the King said quietly.

They drove in towards the sterns of the three ships. Hand-to-hand fighting was in progress in the well and after-parts of the birlinn, bodies dropping or being tossed over the side all around.

"What do we do, Sire?" Sir James Douglas demanded. "Join in? Or hold back?"

"This is no quarrel of ours," Lennox said. "It is foolhardy . . ."

"Perhaps. But these MacDonalds are our hosts," Bruce pointed out. "We live on their bounty. Let every man make his own choice. I, for my part, will pay the debts of hospitality."

"Sire — is it wise?" Lennox persisted, low-voiced. "If these are the Earl of Ross's ships. Ross is one of your earls. A most powerful lord. Needlessly to offend him, for the sake of this Angus of the Isles! Who does not even acknowledge your suzerainty . . ."

"Malcolm, my friend — apart from the sacred laws of hospitality, these waters are most certainly within the Lordship of the Isles. If these are Ross's galleys, then he is engaging in piracy. My duty, as sovereign lord of them both, is surely to uphold he who has the right of law . . ."

The laws of piracy or hospitality notwithstanding, Lennox — who in fact merely hated fighting — was the only protester; indeed the remainder of the King's company were all preparing themselves for the fray. Warriors all, they would have been grievously disappointed and resentful had their liege lord's choice been otherwise — as well Bruce knew. After months of skulking and frustration, all were in fact itching for a fight, their master not the least.

Their approach and run in did not go unnoticed, needless to say. Clearly a certain amount of disengagement was going on in the birlinn, with some warriors jumping back into the two attacking ships.

Kiloran's tactics were uncomplicated to a degree. He merely drove his craft straight for the assailed birlinn — and therefore in between the sterns of the two galleys which closely flanked it. As they ran in, the forward oarsmen raised their sweeps high, to avoid impact, and even before the crash of collision, lessened by the rear oarsmen backing water with the expertise of long practice, grapnels were being hurled into the enemy vessels and lines tightened. Yelling MacDonald slogans, the first boarders were leaping over, left and right, seconds later.

In the absence of any guidance from Kiloran, or anyone else, the King's party acted as each thought fit. They had all congregated at their own galley's high poop and they could not be amongst the first wave of boarders. They had to jump down, and press forward along the narrow gangway between the rowing-benches, where they were jostled and pushed aside by oarsmen shipping their sweeps and rushing to join the attack. Some flung themselves over into one or other galley as best they could, but most remained in a tight knot behind the King himself.

Bruce in fact followed Kiloran, who he guessed would make for the enemy leaders. He had clambered up over their own bow-platform and on to the raised stern of the birlinn. It was there that the most intensive fighting seemed to be taking place.

Bruce, like most of his Lowland colleagues, had chosen the short battle-axe as the most practical weapon for such close fighting, where the long two-handed swords would be at something of a disadvantage. Most of the Islemen were wielding claymores, but even these were on the long side for crowded decks. Some had already abandoned them for the handier and deadly dirk.

The King leapt down from the prow of his own craft to the poop of the birlinn, a drop of about five feet across a gap of six — and almost ended his personal engagement there and then. For only a tiny portion of the crowded deck was available for leaping on, and this was already slippery with blood. Bruce slithered on landing, and fell headlong. Only a desperate effort saved him from tumbling over into the sea — an effort which was not aided by the crash

60

of a writhing body across his own and its struggles thereafter to avoid the dirk-jabs of a third contestant, jabs which in the circumstances were just as likely to end up in Bruce as in the selected target. What might have eventuated had not James Douglas and Gilbert Hay jumped down, to all intents on top of the sprawling trio, there is no knowing. They despatched the dirker, and pushed his wounded victim off, with scant courtesy, in some uncertainty as to which side either belonged to.

There was no opportunity for niceties, even towards the fallen monarch. Before Bruce was fully upright again, the three of them were engaged by about half a dozen of the Rossmen, who left off their assault of a group at the head of the poop steps to attend to the newcomers. Bruce, aware of a red-dripping claymore blade slashing down on him, ducked and jerked aside urgently, cannoning into Hay, and almost overbalancing again on the heaving, slippery deck. But he had clung on to his battle-axe throughout, and now brought it up in an underhand swipe, more instinctive than shrewd — which however did make contact with the attacker sufficiently to knock him back against one of his colleagues — thus saving Douglas from a vicious thrust.

But now the superiority of the short-shafted axe over the long sword-blade was quickly demonstrated, for in-fighting. Moreover, Bruce was something of an expert with this clumsy-looking weapon. Unwieldy as it seemed, it could do major damage in minimum time, not requiring anything like the precision of sword strokes, the swinging circle, or the point-versus-edge decision — for, in fact, wherever it struck or at whatever angle, it was effective, whether it hacked, slashed, shattered or merely numbed.

Steadied back to back with Hay, with half a dozen short smashing blows Bruce had cleared a space before him, one man crashing to the deck, head opened, one disarmed and cringing a pulverised shoulder, and a third backing away, only grazed but suitably alarmed.

But this very clearance held its dangers, for it gave room for swords to swing and thrust. The axeman had to keep close or be outranged. And he had to remember his back. Hay, a seasoned fighter, would look to that last; and Douglas, though younger and less experienced, was trained to the tourney in France, and would support both.

So Bruce leapt forward, smiting hugely, while these strange tactics still confused the Highland sworders — than whom, indeed, there were few better. Some wore helmets, but more did not; and there was no armour, other than toughened leather jerkins and arm and leg paddings, save for a little chain-mail amongst the leaders.

Most indeed were bare to the waist, with only tartans and saffron and targes — small round shields — as protection. Plus their own agility, swiftness and great oarsmen's muscles.

Hay and Douglas, perceiving that Bruce had got into his stride, contented themselves with protecting his rear and flanks, backing up behind him while the King formed the driving apex of the triangle, lashing, thrashing forward with tremendous vigour and controlled accuracy. Robert Bruce, at his best, in action, was of a calibre few could rival, and few indeed would wish to challenge. He had not forced his way into the empty throne merely because he was his father's son and of the blood of the ancient kings . . .

How many went down before that deadly weaving axe he did not know, for apart from the disciplined determination of this close-set trio, there was great confusion aboard the birlinn — valour, yes, but little coherence or direction. The reason for this was probably the fact that MacDonald of Kiloran, having singled out the chieftain of the Rosses, had cut his way straight to him, to engage him in mortal combat — from which lesser men respectfully drew back. He had brought the other down, too, a thick gorilla of a man of middle-years and fiery red hair, with a claymore through the gullet. But he was himself thereafter slain, almost casually, by one of the onlookers, with a dirk in the back — this leaving both sides without effective leadership.

Bruce became aware of something of this when, tripping over a body and down on one knee, momentarily endangered, he perceived that it was Kiloran.

Recovered, thanks to his friends, he perceived something else hitherto unnoticed — that the group at the head of the poop steps, towards which he was driving, was in fact centred round a woman. This was sufficiently unexpected to disconcert him somewhat, slightly to put him off his stroke. But when a sword-tip ripped open his doublet sleeve, scoring a shallow flesh wound along his forearm — the first actual blood he had shed in this encounter — he very quickly retrieved his due concentration. The more fiercely vehement on account of his lapse — and of the stinging pain — he leapt in under the swordsman's dropped guard, and cut him down from shoulder to breastbone.

The fight, although it continued with unabated fury, was subtly changing its character. It was, in fact, becoming more coherent and meaningful, as lack of leadership was replaced by a more positive urge — at least amongst the Rossman. As though by some sort of telepathy, these began to accept that they had probably bitten off more than they could conveniently chew, and that a return to their own galleys would be the reaction of reasonable men. As yet there was no breaking off, no acknowledgement of defeat — for undoubtedly the attackers still outnumbered the others; but the climate of battle had altered. Possibly it was the advent of the Lowlanders, with their strange weapons and unexpected tactics, that disconcerted the raiders.

At any rate, the birlinn's poop quite quickly became a deal less crowded — even though there was not so very much more room to stand because of all the sprawling bodies on the deck. For the first time since jumping aboard, Bruce, gasping for breath, had opportunity to glance around him. The scene was confused, but only moments were required to establish the basic situation. Robert Boyd waved to him from the prow platform, giving the thumbs-up sign. Nodding, the King turned back.

The woman, four men with reddened swords and dirks close-guarding her, stood watching him, braced against some of the mast cordage. She was fairly young, he saw now, and darkly striking, with great eyes, long raven hair that blew in the breeze, and skin of an alabaster whiteness that gave the impression of transparency. But not for a moment did Bruce imagine that her whiteness had anything to do with fear or alarm. Every line of her bearing proclaimed a proud unconcern for danger or indeed bloodshed. There was blood on one forearm, raised to shield her eyes against the blaze of the sinking sun — but it was almost certainly not her own. She appeared to be concerned only with an inspection of himself.

In the circumstances, Bruce could do no other than adopt a similar attitude, leaving the final stages of the battle to others. Secure in his reliance upon the two stalwart knights immediately behind, he bowed, panting. Axe-wielding is breath-taking work.

"Who are you, sir?" the lady called, clearly above the din. "I am Christina MacRuarie of Garmoran. Whom do I have to thank for this deliverance?"

So it was Christina herself. A notable character, and in a sort of way, a kinswoman of his own. "You have to thank . . . our fallen friend, there. MacDonald of Kiloran," he told her, pointing down at the deck. "Myself, I am Robert of Scotland. The Bruce. I greet you warmly. And rejoice to name you cousin." He flattered himself that that was not bad for a man who had been laying about him with a battle-axe moments before, shortage of breath notwithstanding.

She was not really his cousin — no blood relation whatever, Christina of the Isles, as she still signed herself, was the only child and heiress of the late Alan MacRuarie, Lord of Garmoran. This Garmoran, which included the great mainland tracts of Knoydart,

Moidart, Morar and Arisaig, and the islands of Rhum, Eigg and Gigha of the Inner Hebrides, and Uist and Barra of the Outer, was one of the principal divisions of the Isles confederacy. Christina therefore was the great-great-granddaughter of the mighty Somerled, just as Angus Og was the great-great-grandson, their grandfathers brothers. The link with Bruce was only by marriage, for she had wed Duncan, younger son of Donald, Earl of Mar. Duncan had been Bruce's first wife's brother. He was now dead, and here was his young widow, married at fifteen and now ten years older.

"Bruce! The King! Himself!" she cried. "*Dia* — here is a wonder! Can it be true?"

"True, yes. Think you any but himself would covet Bruce's name and style, this day?" the King said wryly.

She pushed forward, between her wary guards. "Your Grace!" she exclaimed. "How come you here I know not. But you are welcome to my territories. And for more than this service you do me." She took his hand, dripping blood as it was. But she did not curtsy, nor raise it to her lips. Instead she leaned over and kissed him on the cheek. She was a tall, lissome creature, only an inch or so shorter than Bruce himself.

"You are kind," he jerked, a little taken aback, both at this gesture and her ability apparently to divorce herself entirely from the battle and carnage which still raged elsewhere than on this poop-deck. He himself was less detached, gazing round him and catching the eyes of Douglas and Hay.

"The day — it goes well, I think. They have had enough. They go back. These Rosses. If that is what they are. Back to their own galleys . . ."

"To be sure. They know what is good for them. Let them go. But . . . Your Grace's arm? You are wounded."

"A nothing. The merest scratch."

"Let me see . . ."

"Better that you look to Kiloran."

But she insisted on herself examining and ministering to his hurt, gesturing to others to look to the fallen MacDonald — who indeed proved to be dead.

Edward Bruce, Neil Campbell and Robert Boyd had taken charge elsewhere, and the situation was rapidly coming under control. Already one of the attacking galleys was sheering off, and the remaining Rossmen were fighting their way back to the other. The issue obviously settled, few contestants were now anxious any more to risk their lives on either side, and the final exchanges were more or less formalities. Some badly placed boarders jumped or were pushed into the sea, but by and large the retiral was effected with minimal opposition, the grapnel-ropes cut, and the second vessel pulled away. Cheers and jeers from the birlinn and the Mac-Donald galley proclaimed the end of the engagement.

None of the King's party had been killed, and of the few wounds none were serious. Undoubtedly the bloodiest part of the fray had been before they arrived. Nevertheless, Bruce and his colleagues found themselves deriving the greatest credit from the affair and, by Christina downwards, were acclaimed as the victors and rescuers — which was a little embarrassing, being scarcely true. Nothing would do but that they should all accompany the chieftainess to her house of Castle Tioram in Moidart — to which she had been making, from South Uist, when attacked. With Kiloran dead and his second-in-command wounded, it seemed a reasonable programme. Moidart, on the mainland just north of the great Ard-namurchan peninsula, was apparently little more than an hour's sail away. And Christina MacRuarie was obviously a determined and autocratic young woman.

*   *   *

Castle Tioram, which they came to in the blue October dusk, sat impressively on an abrupt rocky half-tide island almost stopping up the narrow mouth of the sea-loch of Moidart, whose heavily wooded shores rose high and dark on either side, shadowy in the twilight. The castle, though less spectacularly sited than Dun-averty, was larger, and clearly of considerable strength, built on the antique plan of a lofty perimeter wall of enceinte, some thirty feet high, that followed the irregular outline of the rock, topped by a parapet and wall-walk, with embryo flanking towers at sundry corners and no central keep. Within this embattled perimeter indeed, when their hostess had led her visitors in at the narrow and portcullised sea-gate above the galley-pier, it was not like a castle at all; but rather a village, consisting of a long low hall-house with thatched roof, a chapel, cot-houses, storehouses, stables, byres and the like, all scattered within the curtain-wall — more like a walled town in miniature. Resinous pine torches, lit by the score for their welcome, bathed all in a ruddy flickering glow broken by inky shadows, and the smell of wood-smoke, animals and roasting meats was highly acceptable to hungry voyagers.

The hall-house, however undefendable in itself, was infinitely more commodious and comfortable than any castle. Christina was obviously used to dispensing hospitality in a large way, and found room for Bruce's people with seeming ease. The King was given a large room which, he suspected, was the lady's own, and had certainly no complaints to make.

If any of the Lowlanders had had a notion that they would have to endure semi-barbarous conditions, they were speedily disillusioned. The feast that followed, considering the speed with which it had been conjured up, was on a scale and of a quality worthy of any great noble's establishment in the south, and the wines better than most could offer. Fully a score of Garmoran chieftains sat down with the visitors, in a sort of court — although Christina herself was the only woman present — their wolfhounds making up for their lack of womenfolk. But the behaviour of these was civil and orderly — indeed more so than many a hallful of belted knights and lords. If most were loud in their assertions as to what they would have done had they known of their lady's danger at the hands of the dastardly Rossmen, that was only natural. Taking their tune from her, they were all notably respectful towards the Lowland King, for Highlandmen.

Only the entertainment which accompanied the meal was somewhat strange to the visitors. Instead of minstrels, tumblers, clowning dwarfs or even dancing bears and the like, here were men, not all ancient by any means, who told endless stories about fabulous heroes and quite unbelievable deeds, interspersed with lengthy genealogies which seemed to be an integral part of the performance — and which were listened to, surprisingly, with evidently rapt attention. Since all this, however, was in the Erse, or Gaelic, which few of the newcomers understood — the Bruces did, since they had had a Celtic mother — and since it was not the southern custom to pay any close heed to mere background entertainment during a banquet, the King's people by and large tended to talk through it all — which clearly did not commend itself to their hosts, though there were no overt reproaches. Bruce, on Christina's right, grew uncomfortable; but his brother Edward, on her other side, was not affected, himself being fairly completely preoccupied by the lady's charms — and making it very clear. Edward was ever interested in the opposite sex.

Christina MacRuarie, who looked quite capable of telling guests at her table, or anybody else for that matter, to be quiet if she so desired, did not do so. She appeared to listen to Edward with one ear, while at the same time she did not neglect the King on her right, keeping his platters and goblets filled — yet managing also to seem to attend to the storytellers.

But presently, with a venerable, white-bearded seannachie bowing himself out, to unaccountable applause, and the youngest tale-teller of all stepping forward from halfway down the great table to take his place, the atmosphere began to change. Even Edward Bruce sat forward to watch and listen.

For this young man, although he had his head bandaged and one arm hung limply at his side, was an orator of a different order. Full of energy and fire, his words came out in rushes and spurts and flourishes, with dramatic pauses, and gesturings of his sound arm — and although the words themselves were still in the Gaelic, something of their import and urgency reached even to those who could not understand them.

Bruce listened keenly, especially when he heard his own name coming into it all — not as a king but as a renowned warrior travelled from a far country. The oration was in fact an extempore, vivid and highly stylised and elaborated version of the afternoon's galley-fight, with everything dramatised and turned into heroics, all noblest valour, fairest beauty, blackest treachery and haunting romance — a sort of instant saga. Thus, evidently, were the famed Celtic epics born. Bruce perceived that he was very much this one's hero, as his hostess was the noble heroine whom he had come so far to rescue. Somewhat embarrassing as this might be, he was not blind to the advantages it might have for his cause in these latitudes, amongst people at once so warlike, extravagant and histrionic as these.

All but exhausted, the young man finished on a telling note of the victorious Robert of Alba, the noble blood of his wounds being staunched by the beauteous Christina of the Isles, who then conducted him and his noble band to her ancestral halls amongst the fairest prospects of all the Hebrides. He was summoned to the head of the table to receive his lady's congratulations and thanks amidst the plaudits of all. Bruce did some swift thinking. The orator was introduced to him as Ranald MacRuarie of Smearisary, son of Christina's natural half-brother Roderick. He had, in fact, though young, been captain of the attacked birlinn. He was, therefore, of some consequence in the Garmoran polity. The King stood up.

"That sword?" he said, pointing to a huge two-handed brand which hung on the wall near by, beneath a tattered banner. "Whose is it?"

"That is the sword of my ancestor, Somerled the King," Christina told him.

"So much the better," he said. "I crave your permission?"

Assuming the said permission, he strode over and took the weapon down. Returning, he raised it high — with difficulty, on account of its weight and the stiffness of his now bandaged arm.

"Come, friend," he said to the young man. "I, Robert of Scotland, salute you. In your words and in your deeds." He brought down the great blade, more heavily than he intended, on one of the somewhat alarmed orator's shoulders. He should have tapped the other shoulder also, but feared in his stiffness that he was more likely to strike the already bandaged head in between, and contented himself, letting the weighty weapon sink to the floor. "I dub thee knight. Be thou a good and true knight until thy life's end. Stand, Sir Ranald MacRuarie MacDonald!"

There was a few moments of silence, and then exclamation and outcry from all over the hall. There was wonder, acclaim and criticism in it — the last from some of his own people, his brother included, shocked at this debasement of knighthood on little better than a young savage.

Bruce was not perturbed by the note of disapprobation, especially when it was so clearly overborn by the acclaim and even glee. He himself had no doubts that his impulse had been a sound one. He had, with a single stroke of a sword —, and Somerled's sword at that — not only made a notable impression on these people and given a unique impetus to a new-forming legend which might well prove extremely useful to his cause, but had established the fact of his kingship and royal prerogative before them all, doing something that no other could or would do. Moreover he had established a precedent, made a Highlander a knight — and if this was accepted, as it looked like being, it implied also the acceptance, here at least, of his suzerainty.

If the young man himself seemed quite dumbfounded, Christina at least was obviously delighted. She actually clapped her hands. "A King indeed?" she cried. "Here is a royal chivalry, honour. I thank you, Sire — on my heart I do!"

"This young man is your substitute and deputy, lady," he returned, bowing. "Might knighthood be bestowed on a woman, on your fair shoulders would fall this blade. In salutation."

"Your Grace is kind — and I am grateful. But perhaps there may be . . . other salute? More meet for a woman!" And she met his eye frankly.

Bruce inclined his head, but found this a good moment to make a display of handing over the sword to the new knight. They seated themselves again, and the banquet continued.

It was already late and Bruce, smothering yawns, was debating how he might, without offence to his hostess — who certainly gave no impression of weariness — intimate that his couch called, when an elderly man whom he had seen before, frail and stooping, came to whisper in Christina's ear. She raised her brows, and turned to the King.

"Sire — this Murdo Léigh is the physician who looked to your wounds, you will recollect. He now attends to others. Amongst whom is one of the prisoners from the Ross galleys. A man of some

68

substance, it seems. He talks of your affairs. Murdo fears that he is dying, but does not believe him deranged. He believes that you should see this man. For he speaks of your wife. The Queen."

Bruce rose at once, frowning.

Together they followed the old man out and across the court-yard and into a reed-thatched lengthy bunkhouse, but dimly lit by a few flickering torches. Here many men lay on sheepskin litters, some groaning. They were brought to one, huddled very still beneath a ragged plaid, grey of face, eyes closed. They feared that he was already dead.

But presently the eyelids flickered, and the old physician kneeled, to speak in his ear.

"I have brought the King. The Bruce. The Sasunnach King. He is here, man. Tell him what it is. What troubles you. Tell him."

The dying man stared up at Bruce. His lips moved, but no sound issued.

"Speak up, man . . ."

Bruce knelt on the rush-strewn floor beside the sufferer. "You have word for me? Of my wife?" he demanded. "What do you know?"

The other's eyes rolled up, and his lids closed. But after a moment he opened them again, and whispered. "The sanctuary. I . . . I swore . . . ill would . . . come of it. The sanctuary . . . violated."

"Sanctuary? What sanctuary? What do you mean? Tell me, man."

"Duthac," the other muttered. "The saint. It was . . . ill done."

"Of a mercy! What is this of saints? What was ill done?" Bruce gripped the man's arm.

The old Murdo signed to the King to wait. He spoke more gently in the other's ear. "Friend — heed you. Here is opportunity. To unburden your soul. You go to be with God. Soon. You said that your soul was heavy. A weight of guilt. I have no priest — but here is the King. You said it was God's judgement — that you should be cut down by the Sasunnach King. Here he is. Speak while you may."

In a fever of anxiety Bruce looked up at the woman. She touched his shoulder and shook her head.

The Rossman stared past them all, up at the shadowy, smoke-wreathed roof, unwinking. Then he spoke again, more clearly though no more strongly. "My lord commanded it. He cared nothing . . . for the sanctuary. We took the women . . . out of it.

69

This Queen. And the child. Slew their men . . . there at the altar. My lord commanded it . . ."

"Dear God — what are you saying? The Queen? And the child? My Marjory? Speak plain, man — for sweet Christ's sake! What lord? What sanctuary?"

"Saint Duthac's. At Tain. My lord of Ross. Chief of our Clan Aindreas. William, the Earl. The other earl — Atholl. He was fleeing, with the women. North. To the Orcades, they said. The English king's men after them. Fleeing through my lord's territories. My lord sought to take them. They took refuge in the chapel. Of Saint Duthac. At Tain. A noted sanctuary. We caught them there . . ."

"You caught them! Took them? You took the Queen? And my daughter? You slew . . . slew . . .?"

"Only the men. Who would have stayed us, lord. At the altar. God forgive me! Not the women. Atholl, the other earl, wounded. My lord William handed him over. To the English. With the women. It was ill done . . ."

"God! When? When was this?"

But the other seemed to be seized with a bout of agonising pain. Only groans came from him.

"Answer me, wretch!" Bruce cried, almost beside himself. "When was this infamy?" He shook the moaning man.

There was no answer, no further meaningful words, just the grievous sounds of a man in his extremity. With a fierce effort Bruce sought to take a grip upon himself, rising to his feet.

"So — Edward!" he panted. "Edward Plantagenet — he has my Elizabeth! And Marjory. By the damnable treachery of William of Ross. God Almighty's curse upon him!" On a gasping intake of breath he paused, eyes widening. He was staring at Christina MacRuarie, but he did not see her. "No — God's curse on *me*! Myself — it is myself that is accursed! Myself, I tell you. You heard? At the altar. Taken at the altar. At this Tain. As I took John Comyn's life at the altar. At Dumfries. Jesu God! It is *I* who did this. *I* who betrayed my wife and daughter . . ."

"Sire! My lord Robert — do not say so. You cannot blame yourself for this. For the villainy of Ross. Do not scourge yourself . . ."

Blindly he turned away, making for the door.

In the courtyard she caught up with him, reaching for his sound arm. "See — come with me," she urged. "We will speak of this quietly, privately."

He removed his arm, though not roughly. "I thank you. But I would be alone. I go to my room. I thank you — but this is for myself, apart. Go back to your guests. Say that I am wearied. That

70

my wound pains me. Goodnight. And . . . and say a prayer, lady, for Robert Bruce! Of your mercy . . ."

CHAPTER FIVE

THE days that followed were as grievous as any that Robert Bruce had had to bear, despite the comforts of his present refuge, the goodwill of his hostess, the sympathy of his friends and the beauty of his surroundings. He had thought that he was armoured now, hardened, against further fierce hurt and sorrow, that he had plumbed the depths of suffering; in ten years of war and destruction and Edward Plantagenet's malice and Comyn's hatred, in the ruin of his fortunes, the frustration of his hopes, the living with treachery and defeat; in the terrible deaths of his brother Nigel, his brother-in-law Christopher Seton and so many of his supporters and friends; in the torture of a whole people. But it was not so. His despair over Elizabeth was beyond all that had gone before, his agony of dread almost enough to send him out of his mind, his utter helplessness a crucifixion. Worst of all, perhaps, his sense of guilt, that never left him, day or night, the general background of guilt in that all surely stemmed from his murder of John Comyn before the altar at Dumfries; and the more immediate and personal guilt in that he had refused Elizabeth's pleas to let her remain with him, had sent her away — to this. While he himself remained safe, secure.

His heart ached also, of course, for his daughter Marjory, so young, at twelve, to be suffering for her father's sins, failures and ambitions. And for his sisters Christian and Mary, Isabel Countess of Buchan who had crowned him, and the rest of his womenfolk. What English Edward would do to them all, God alone knew — but chivalry and mercy played no part in either his warfare or his statecraft. Bruce had only one faint gleam of hope — in that Elizabeth was the daughter of Richard de Burgh, Earl of Ulster, Edward's closest friend and companion-in-arms. For de Burgh's sake he might conceivably stay his hand from the worst, from the most unthinkable atrocities. But, knowing the King of England, he did not delude himself with false optimism.

Bruce did not spend those days sitting in idle brooding, of course. He forced himself to activities in which he had neither satisfaction nor interest, grateful only when these tired him out sufficiently to dull the pain and fears that haunted him. Which was, indeed, quite frequently, for this was the season of the stags

71

roaring on all the mountain-sides around Castle Tioram, when the deer-hunting was at its best — and Christina MacRuarie determined that nothing which she might do to distract and entertain her guests should remain undone. There was great hunting almost every day, of wolves and boars and even seals, as well as deer; salmon-spearing in the river narrows; hawking for the multitudinous wild-fowl, and especially the long skeins of geese that ribboned the sky at dawn and dusk. There was feasting, music, story-telling, and the vigorous Highland dancing, until far into the night, evening after evening. Love-making too, for those so inclined — although Edward Bruce appeared to achieve no real success in his frank pursuit of their hostess herself. The King sought to act his part in all this, and not play the skeleton at the feast — though none were deceived.

Not that any there looked upon this sojourn in Moidart as any sort of holiday. It was only a breathing-space, wherein time fell to be filled in. This Hebridean interlude, though forced upon the King and his friends by sheer necessity, as the only area of Scotland where he could be safe from his enemies, and respite from being hunted fugitives essential, nevertheless had a positive and never-forgotten objective — the obtaining and marshalling of men, once more to prosecute the war. How these men were to be won, whether cajoled, bargained for or merely hired, was less than clear — but these Highlands and Isles were in fact teeming with men trained to arms, whose main delight indeed was to fight. Somehow, some proportion of them must be harnessed to the King's cause. That they were in theory all his own subjects was something of a grim joke. But any success in such harnessing depended upon information, tidings, knowledge in some measure of what went on elsewhere — otherwise, for Bruce to be isolated in these remote fastnesses spelt defeat indeed. So Christina of Garmoran was prevailed upon to send out messengers, enquirers, spies, north and south, by sea and mountain-track — and while her visitors waited for results, this entertainment.

In all this, Christina's attitude to Bruce himself was of a warm understanding, a care and concern that was noteworthy in so vehement and proud, not to say imperious, a young woman. It would be fair to say that she cherished him, who was scarcely of the cherishing kind. He sought nothing of the sort, of course, and, in his preoccupation with his anxieties and guilt, may have seemed less than appreciative. But he was well aware, too, that this woman might well be brought to play an important part in his eventual strategy, both as a supplier of men and as a link with other chiefs, even to work on Angus of the Isles himself. So he by no means wholly rejected her attentions. Besides, she was a woman, and handsome — and he not unimpressionable, even in these circumstances.

It was ten days after the arrival in Moidart, and the night of the return of the first of the Garmoran couriers, that Bruce, far from cheered by this man's tidings, made excuse to retire early from the feasting and entertainment, and went to his room. He did not immediately repair to his couch however, for unless very weary indeed, sleep did not come easily these nights — and it had been a wet and chill day, with no hunting. Part-undressed and wearing a bed-robe of the late Alan MacRuarie's, he paced the skin-littered floor of his chamber.

The messenger had come from the Comyn lordship of Lochaber and the MacDougall lordship of Lorn — useful listening-posts for spies, in that they were very much in the enemy camp. He had brought back word which no interpretation would make other than depressing. In Aymer de Valence, Earl of Pembroke, King Edward had obviously found a Governor of Scotland after his own heart. Terror stalked all the Lowlands. Not only in the south, below Forth and Clyde, where these past years terror had been more or less endemic; but in the north and east, or such parts as were not Comyn-dominated. Angus and Mar and Moray in especial were suffering — for in these great provinces Bruce had much support — and Pembroke was now wreaking his master's will on Inverness. His, it appeared, was an effective and methodical terror, not weakened by blind hatred, and he left little in his tracks to resurrect. With the Earl of Ross now committed to Edward's cause, the farther north was equally enemy territory, and Bruce's adherents being rooted out ruthlessly. The only hint of consolation was that the Bishop of Moray, loyalest of the loyal, was said to have eluded the enemy net and was thought to be making for Orkney, with some few stalwarts.

As to the Queen, the only word was that she had been taken, with her companions, straight to King Edward, who was settling down to winter at Lanercost Abbey, near Carlisle. There he had promptly hanged Atholl — and to protests that no earl had been hanged, in England or Scotland, within the memory of man, had answered by prescribing a higher gallows and a longer rope for Earl John de Strathbogie. What he intended to do with the women, none knew — but the rumours were many and dire.

That Edward had chosen to set up permanent headquarters at Lanercost, remaining on the Border and not returning to London or even York, for the winter, was as grim news as any. It implied that though Scotland was to all intents crushed, and Pembroke's campaign now no more than a mopping-up, the Plantagenet was determined to go further, and personally to superintend the process. Which could only mean that this time Scotland was to be ground into the very dust, and that the hunt for Bruce himself was to be continued, probably intensified.

That man, pacing his floor, was going over all this, when a knock at the door revealed Christina MacRuarie herself. She was dressed in a furred bed-robe not unlike his own, her long dark hair hanging free.

"Your Grace," she said, "My lord Robert — I heard you walking and walking. This will not serve. Not in my house. Not for the hero who came to the rescue of Christina of the Isles. Who shed blood for her." That was spoken as though rehearsed. She came in and shut the door behind her.

It could have been true that she had heard him, for this was a timber-built house within the castle walls, and her room was next to his — indeed this obviously had been her own bedchamber, and she was presently occupying its ante-room. She must have left the hall very early, however — soon after himself, presumably — for the noise of pipe-music and dancing still sounded.

He inclined his head, waiting.

"Sire — it is not good. For a man to fret and gloom so. Not right. Your burdens are sore, heavy — but they are not such as to unman Robert Bruce." She spoke a little breathlessly now, for her. "You hold too much to yourself, my friend."

"Perhaps," he acceded. "But that is part of my burden. Being a king is lonely work."

"Need it be so lonely? I think not. For a king is a man first, with a man's needs, a man's temper and person. You do not renounce your manhood in your kingship, do you?"

"You think that I do?"

"I think it, yes. In part. That is why I have come. I have sought to bring the man out, from behind the king — on the hill, in the hunt, the fast, the dance. With little success. Now I come to your bed-chamber, Robert. For I believe that you need a woman. Yet you have looked towards none that I have offered. So now . . ." She paused. "So now I have brought myself!" And she threw open the furred robe.

She was completely naked beneath it.

He stared, wordless, moistening suddenly dry lips.

The whiteness of her was startling, an alabaster white even in the mellow lamplight, only emphasised by the jet-black triangle at the crotch and the large dark circles which tipped her breasts. Compared with this woman Elizabeth was honey-coloured, almost golden, more rounded, more generous of hip and thigh and bosom. Not that the man was conscious of any comparison between his wife and this who was offering herself to him. But the distinction was there, unbidden, inevitable, the contrast of two proud and beautiful women.

For Christina MacRuarie had her own beauty, however different, of form as of feature. And that she was very desirable no whole man could have gainsaid.

She stood so, for a little, eying him directly, only her visibly heightened breathing hinting that perhaps she was less bold and sure of herself than she appeared. She held out one hand.

"Do I please you, Robert?" she asked.

He swallowed. "Aye. Yes, indeed. You ... you are very fair. Well-fashioned," he said thickly, hoarsely. He kept his own hands to his sides.

"And ... and do I stir your kingship's manhood?"

He further moistened those lips. "You could scarcely ... do otherwise! But, but..."

"Yet you stand abashed like any callow youth! Or less than a proper man. I vow your brother Edward would not be so backward!"

"Edward has not a wife. Whom he has brought to ruin. To dire danger, and sorrow. Would you have me further to betray my wife?"

She let the drawn-back folds of her robe fall together again, and shook her head. "Betray, no. Christina of the Isles is no betrayer of men, or women. Nor would lead others to betrayal. This is ... other."

"What, then?" he demanded, more harshly than he knew.

Holding her robe closed before her, she came forward to him. "Robert — how long since last you lay with a woman?" she asked.

Blinking, he ran a hand through his hair. "God knows! Two months. Three. I cannot mind..."

"Yet you are of a lusty habit, they say. No half-man."

He did not speak.

She seated herself carefully on the edge of his bed, her own bed. "Why think you that I have come here, this night? To your chamber?" She added, as an afterthought and almost tartly, "Sire!"

"You tell *me*, lady," he said.

"Very well. I have not come because I am panting for you! Neither for your manhood nor yet your king's Grace! Nor is this my habit. Nor even have I come out of my gratitude, that you saved

75

me and mine from the Rossmen. I came because I believed that you needed a woman. A woman's body, and a woman's comfort and tenderness. And since, it seems, you will not of yourself take a woman, I provide one. And since you are the King, and my guest, only *I* will serve. Christina. No other, I swear, would be sitting here, on your bed, putting all into words for you!"

"That at least is true!" he agreed, less stiffly. "What makes you think that I so greatly need a woman?"

"Because *I* am a woman, and have watched you. The signs are not lacking. Because a lusty man, and married, with time on his hands, is less than himself when deprived. And when the King is less than himself, many may suffer. More than those many should. Moreover, because in your fretting waiting in my house, you make but ill company. For me, and for your friends."

"You say so? For that I am sorry," he told her, stiff again.

"So are all who love you."

He stared down at her, frowning. What she said was true, of course — almost every word. He knew it, had long known it, without acknowledging it. Was he a fool, then . . .?

He flushed, as he realised that his man's eyes were busy, however sluggish his wits — for, leaning a little towards him, the woman's robe gaped open, so that both breasts were entirely evident, one exposed to the nipple. Her breasts were not large, but strangely pointed, firm, hard-seeming for a woman who had borne a child, as she had done. She had not fed the boy herself, it seemed. But if the breasts were not themselves large, the aureoles were larger and darker than any he had seen, and notably rousing admittedly. Moreover, the furred folds had fallen aside from one leg, and the white thigh and bent rounded knee were only a little less stimulating than the bosom. Indeed, sitting there, half-covered, she was altogether more tellingly desirable than when she had stood opposite him, wholly displaying her nakedness. More than his face flushed.

Probably she perceived something of these reactions, for she drew the robe back over her leg, though not very effectively, but raised her other hand to his sound arm.

"Come, sit, Robert," she said. "Tell me of your Queen. Your Ulsterwoman. Is she very beautiful? I have heard that she is."

He sat, since standing he was the more distracted. But to sit and discuss Elizabeth with this all-but-naked Isleswoman was less than suitable.

"She is, yes," he agreed shortly. "Beautiful, and leal."

"And she would have you monk, during this long parting?"

76

"Would not any wife?"

'Not any, no. Some, yes. *I* would not. With months, possibly years, between. My man's heart I would have cleave to me. His manhood, his body, denied me, I would not deny *him*."

For a moment that bedchamber of Castle Tioram in Moidart gave place to another room, darker, smaller and no bedchamber, whatever had taken place therein — the little rustic garden-house on the island in Linlithgow Loch where, four years before, Elizabeth de Burgh had yielded herself to him in passion and love. After that joyful, cataclysmic union, she had spoken to him very much as this Christina spoke now. What was it she had said? That she would be a jealous wife. That if she married him she would require him to be faithful. In his heart. That he might amuse himself with other women, even lie with them. But if he gave his heart to another, she would turn from him and never forgive him. Even might kill him, she had said. Those may not have been her words, but that was the gist of it.

And now, this.

"Your Queen and I, then, are of a different sort," she went on. "So be it."

"Different, yes. In much. But not ... but not ..." Absurdly, he felt that he had to be fair to Elizabeth in this.

Speculatively she eyed him. But she rose, pulling the robe close again. "I will go, then — since I cannot serve your need. Remember hereafter, Robert, that it was *your* need that brought me. Only that."

He looked up at her, biting his lip. They said that there was no hatred to rival that of a woman rejected. This woman's aid, co-operation, influence, he greatly required. And she was indeed beautiful ...

"Do not go," he said.

Their eyes met, and held.

"Do you not know your own mind, Sire?" she asked. "Or is it your body you do not know?"

"As to my body, there is no doubt, woman!" he told her. "Nor indeed in my mind, I think. It was my heart that gave me pause."

"We are not concerned here with your heart," she declared levelly. But she looked away.

He had a flash of insight there, that perhaps she lied. But he put the thought from him.

"Then give me ... what you came to offer. And find me ... grateful."

"Grateful?"

"Aye, grateful." He stood up, and stepped forward to her. "And more than that. Desirous. Demanding. Needful. Hungry." He reached out an ungentle hand to wrench back her bed-robe from her white loveliness.

"So — you are a man, after all!"

"Let me prove it, Christina of the Isles!"

"You have all night to do that, Sir King!" She flung the robe away. "Let us see if there is a saga to be made of this also!"

*   *   *

If thereafter Robert Bruce suffered twinges of a new sort of guilt, at least he made better company, and for more than just his hostess. None failed to perceive the change in the King — and few failed to find a reason for it.

It was a strange development, manifesting itself not in any new zestfulness, triumphant masculinity or obvious satisfaction; rather in a relaxation of manner and temper, a greater friendliness towards his companions, a kind of lowering of guards. Clearly he felt less cut off from his fellow men and women, more in need of what others had to offer in sympathy and personal support. Indeed, although humility was not a word that was ever likely to be associated with the Bruce, a sort of modesty grew on him. He had never been arrogant or overbearing but there had been perhaps a certain unapproachability, a reserve. Always there would be something of this, but now there was a distinct easement.

He even spoke frequently, to others, of the Queen and her perilous situation, as of his own helplessness, something that he had not done before. That she was much on his mind, whatever his current recreations, was evident to all.

Of course the affair with Christina did not limit itself to a single engagement. Living in such close proximity, occupying adjoining rooms, that would have been almost impossible. And there was no question as to their mutual physical satisfaction; neither had cause to complain of the other's adequacy or accomplishment. No coy teasings or lovers' tiffs were there to punctuate their association. Vehement characters both, once decision was taken, there were no half-measures.

Nevertheless, as time passed, Bruce recognised danger signals. He realised that he was becoming dependent on this woman, that not only was her physical presence becoming necessary to him but that her strong and vivid character was of growing influence upon him, upon his plans and his thinking. He was able to tell himself this way lay not only betrayal of Elizabeth but folly, the endangering of his cause. He accepted that it was not Christina's fault, or deliberately caused — at least, he thought not. But the conviction grew upon him that he trod on thin ice. It was time for him to break loose. Despite the onset of November gales, and the implicit assumption that the winter was upon them, when men drew up their ships and laid by their swords until the campaigning season returned, Bruce decided to make a move.

The couriers and spies had meantime been reporting back to Moidart, from many parts — although some there were who never returned. From their news the King was able to piece together a picture of the national situation as a whole. Basically all of Scotland was prostrated under the heavy heels of the English and the Comyn faction, plus those agile men who always looked to the winning side. But this was only a superficial impression. The enemy grip was tighter in some areas than others, just as the underlying Bruce support was stronger, manifesting itself in small revolts, rioting and civil commotion, ambushes of parties of occupying troops, night assaults on isolated garrisons, and the dumb non-co-operation of the people. The South-West, from Glasgow down to Galloway, centring round Bruce's own earldom of Carrick, was the most restive, aided by many small guerilla bands, relics of Wallace's great force, operating from the upland wildernesses of Ettrick, Merrick and Kells. Fife, where the Church influence was predominant, despite the Primate Lamberton's imprisonment in England, also was in a constant turmoil; as was South Angus, and Dundee said to be a hot-bed of revolt. There was significant word, too, from more than one source, of rifts between the Comyns and their English overlords, with actual fighting in Badenoch. The Bishop of Moray was reported to be recruiting men and ships in the Orkneys. The picture, overall, was of a nation defeated and held down but not subdued, seething with unrest — no satisfactory prospect for King Edward. A small surge of hope was renewed within the Bruce.

There was no further news, as yet, about the Queen or Marjory or of the other women in Edward's grasp.

While all this was encouraging in some measure, there was no blinking the one great ominous shadow — the Plantagenet's continued presence at the Border. Rumour had it that he was sick again — but still refusing to go south to the comforts of home life in London. Which could only mean his utter determination to destroy Scotland once and for all, and Bruce with it, in the coming season, once the days were long enough for effective warfare, the hill passes open for his heavy chivalry, and the coastal seas calm enough for his supply fleets. In 1303 he had let loose quarter of a million troops on Scotland. His present prolonged preparations probably meant an onslaught on a similar scale — and this time upon a prostrate foe and undefended land.

Anything Bruce could do, therefore, it became evident, must be attempted before the spring, while he still had men who might rise for him throughout the country — for nothing seemed more certain than that afterwards there would be no more such alive. Which surely meant that he should not be lying in idle dalliance at Castle Tioram, winter or no winter. Could he even make winter fight for him?

One maddening aspect of the situation was to be surrounded by fighting-men, in these Highlands and Isles, who would not fight for him. Or, at least, who would not unless their chiefs told them to. And what had he, Bruce, to offer the said chiefs — who looked on the Lowland Scots much as they looked on the English, and certainly accepted no sort of allegiance, or duty to support them. Offers of position and privilege, as reward, in the freed Scotland, should it ever be free again, would have little relevance. Yet these great numbers of fierce fighters were available. Angus Og indeed, like lesser chiefs, built much of the Isles economy on the hiring out his broadswords by the thousand, mainly to the ever-warring Irish princelings — as he was doing, and leading them in person, at this present. Bruce undoubtedly could hire them likewise — had he the wherewithal. But today, he had not two gold pieces to rub together.

Yet, apart from the empty Scots treasury, altogether, he was, in theory, one of the richest lords in Scotland, owner of vast lands and estates, whole towns, almost provinces. Carrick was his, and rich Annandale; much of Galloway; the lordship of the Garioch, in Aberdeenshire, and many other lesser estates. Moreover he controlled the great earldom of Mar, as guardian of his nephew. Riches indeed. And it was nearly the Martinmas Term, when the rents of all those lands were due to be paid to him. If indeed, most, or many, of his people and tenants and vassals remained loyal to him, even as lord, much less king, and if they would probably rise and shed their blood for him — as they had done in the past — might they not still pay their rents to him? Even in today's circumstances, and though almost certainly the English invaders would be mulcting them as well? It was worth a trial. He could send out rent-collectors, at least.

Then there was the position of his two remaining younger brothers to consider, Thomas and Alexander. Apparently the enemy had not managed to lay hands on them, and the rumour was that they were in hiding somewhere in Galloway, instigating much of the insurrection there. Alex was now a priest, in name at least

Dean of Glasgow, though barely twenty-five. Thomas, a year older, and long-headed, had been the stay-at-home of the family, content to manage the great Annandale estates. They should be found, and brought here to the Isles.

So Bruce borrowed a small galley from Christina, and sent his brother Edward, and with Sir Robert Boyd and Sir Robert Fleming, a Galloway man, to aid and also possibly to restrain him. They were to sail secretly to Galloway, seek out Thomas and Alex, then try to collect as much of the Annandale and Carrick rents as they might, and return to Moidart. He would meet them here again, God willing, for Yuletide.

For he himself was for the sea again, also. In Angus Og's lent galley, he would continue on his northwards travels, interview the northern chiefs, seeking men and support, avoiding the Ross lands. And on round the top of Scotland to the Orkney Isles, to link with the good Bishop David of Moray, there to draw up mutual plans. He hoped that when he returned to Castle Tioram, at Yuletide if possible, it would be in shape to take the first steps towards regaining his throne.

None knew better than he how many, how weary and how long-continued those steps must be. But at least a start would be made.

CHAPTER SIX

AFTER the spacious timber halls, the snug comforts, and much Yuletide feasting of Christina's hospitable house — to say nothing of her person's liberality — the small stone chambers of Kildonan's keep were bare, cramped and draughty, with the chill February wind finding its way in through a host of cracks and crevices. The crash of waves from far below was a muted thunder, as background for the whistle of the wind and the rattle of the timber shuttering of the small windows — ominous indication of the seas running in even these comparatively sheltered waters of the Firth of Clyde, and scarcely propitious sailing weather. But Robert Bruce and his friends were used to storms and high seas, these days, seasoned mariners. After the Sea of the Hebrides, the Minches in mid-winter, and rounding Cape Wrath into and out from the dreaded Pentland Firth between Scotland and Orkney, these Arran waters held little terror.

It was chillier, draughtier, less comfortable, in that tower-room than even was normal of a February night however; for the shutters of the lower unglazed half of one window were wide open, so that the night came in in blasts and buffets setting the lamps flickering wildly and gouts of choking wood-smoke billowing out from fireplace and chimney. The glass of the upper part was too thick to give any prospect, letting in only light and no view even by day.

Despite the chill, the King himself sat near the open window, a plaid round his shoulders; he and his colleagues had taken to the Highland custom of wearing plaids at most times, finding them the most effective protection by day and night, on shipboard, in the heather, as surcoat or as blanket. Indeed Bruce, now weather-beaten, curly-bearded and long of hair, looked entirely the Highlander, and a tough and fierce one — so much so that the captured English captain of this hold, whom Douglas had seized, still refused to believe that this was indeed the King of Scots.

Bruce's glance, though he listened to the talk of his friends, kept turning to that open window, as it had been doing since darkness fell. The others, James Douglas in especial, had offered many times to relieve his self-imposed, chill vigil and exchange a seat nearer the fire; but the King had shaken his head. So much of his hopes and plans could depend on what he saw from that window.

For, due south-east of this southernmost tip of the Isle of Arran, where Kildonan perched on a cliff above a tiny harbour, lay the Ayrshire coast of mainland Scotland. More than that, it was the King's own coast of Carrick. Only fifteen miles away from where he sat, his great castle of Turnberry, principal seat of the earldom, stood above these same heaving waters, his birthplace, now occupied by Englishmen. What was Scots in his blood, as distinct from Norman-French, stemmed from just over there, where his Celtic ancestors had ruled the South-West. These days, Robert Bruce was turning to the Celt in him, in more than his clothing. The ancient blood stirred.

But it was not just Celtic blood and wishful thinking that stirred the King tonight. He was looking for a sign, a signal. Sir Robert Boyd and Sir Robert Fleming were, if God was kind, over there now, spying out the land, secretly visiting key vassals, carrying the royal message. They had been gone for five days now. If conditions were not impossible for a landing, they were to light a balefire of driftwood in a place he had told them of, a corner of beach under small screening cliffs about a mile north of Turnberry, known as Maidens. Here the fire, facing into the north-west, would not be apt to be seen from landwards but should gleam clear across the firth to Arran. To be lit either this night, or the next — the timing was important.

So Bruce peered into the stormy dark till his eyes ached, scarcely aware of the cold, and listened to his friends' idle talk with only one ear. There were not many of them to chat, in that upper room — apart from Edward, only the Earl of Lennox, James Douglas, Gilbert Hay and Neil Campbell. The others of his company were far scattered — though he hoped, and would have prayed if he had dared, that his younger brothers were not so very far away at that moment.

Edward Bruce had been successful in his mission in November, duly finding their two brothers, Thomas and Alex, in Galloway; and thereafter managing to collect a sizeable sum in rents. Most rental was paid in kind, of course — in grain, beasts, labour and armed service; but many of the larger vassals elected to pay at least some proportion in money, and the Bruce brothers had brought back to Moidart gold and silver, little enough for a great earldom's rent-roll, but a large sum indeed in the Hebridean economy, where a gold piece was a rare sight. After their reunion at Yule, then, the three brothers had been despatched to Ireland with most of the money, to seek out Angus Og — who with his mercenaries was wintering in comparative comfort in Antrim, as seemed to be his preferred custom — there to hire as many gallowglasses, Highland or Irish, as the money would buy. Thereafter they were to bring their new host to Rathlin Island, where Sir Reginald Crawford, a kinsman of the late Wallace, from Galloway, would meet them and guide them to a planned invasion of the mainland, in Galloway itself, where insurgent support was awaiting a lead. This to coincide with Bruce's own projected landing at Carrick.

All this had gone more or less as planned, and ten days ago Edward Bruce had brought word from Rathlin that Thomas and Alex were there, with 800 men, had met Crawford, and intended to descend on the Galloway coast on the night of the 9th of February, in the neighbourhood of Loch Ryan — tomorrow night.

The final member of the King's former close company, Sir William Bellenden, had been left at Orkney with Bishop David, to aid in an invasion of the North, to coincide with these two attempts.

Bruce waited there at the window until after midnight, reluctant to concede that there would be no signal that night. At length, with Edward and Lennox already retired, and the other three dozing by the dying fire, he sighed, and stood up, stretching stiffly.

"There is still another night," he said. "And Robert Boyd will not fail me. If the thing is possible. And if he is safe. If he has not been taken . . ."

"Sir Robert is cautious and wise, Sire. He will be safe," Douglas said, rising hurriedly. "And if there is no sign, we can still go to Galloway. Join the others."

"Aye. But much would be lost. All would be the more difficult.

The English, once warned, could seal off Galloway. The Carrick landing could prevent this. By linking up with those who fight from the mountains, from Ettrick and Merrick. Pray you for Boyd's signal, then. A good night to you . . ."

Bruce had barely seemed to lay his head on his pillow in the small mural chamber that was all this stark hold offered him, when he was awakened by Douglas shaking his shoulder.

"The signal, Sire! It burns! It burns!" the younger man cried. "The watch saw it, from the parapet-walk. It still burns clear."

"Eh . . .? What hour is it, Jamie?"

"Near to four. Four of the clock."

"It is late. Late. To be sending the word . . ." But Bruce rose, and wrapped his plaid around him again.

Up at the tower-room window, there was no need for Douglas to point. In the windy dark, apart from the line of phosphorescence from the breaking waves on the beach far below, the only thing to be seen was the bright point of light, reddish-yellow, that grew and contracted, waxed and waned in brilliance, away to the south-east, as they watched. Obviously a fire.

"It is the right airt?" Douglas asked.

"Yes. That is just north of Turnberry Head. So be it. Boyd's signal, yes. But . . . so late. Why has he delayed?"

"He could have been prevented, Sire. From reaching the place. Forced to a long detour. Hunted by the English. In enemy-held territory, anything may constrain . . ."

"Think you I do not know it, man! Have I not spent weeks, months, in enemy-held territory?" That flash of irritation was unusual in the King, who kept a close watch on his tongue. "Boyd is an experienced soldier. He knows that it is too late, now, for us to embark our men, win across the firth, and land in Carrick in darkness. Four o'clock. It is but four hours to dawn. It will take two hours to cross, in this wind and sea. If not more. Not the galleys, but the small craft."

Hay and Campbell had joined them at the open window. "And we must have time, over there, for our dispositions," the latter pointed out. "Further darkness."

"May not Sir Robert have thought of that, Your Grace," Douglas suggested. "And thus be giving us plenty of warning for tomorrow night. Giving us all day to prepare. If he had waited until a safe time after dark tomorrow, it would have cut into that night. And if he had lit his fire earlier, we would have made the crossing *tonight*. This way he gives us time."

"It may be so, Jamie,' the King acceded. "We can well use that time, whatever else. To make our preparations. To eat well and

84

sleep well. We sail tomorrow evening, then, at first dark, and shall have a long night of it. Meantime we can sleep again. It may be we shall need it all . . .!"

*　　　*　　　*

The wind and seas had abated a little, but it was still an unpleasant crossing, the following night, especially for the smaller boats. Bruce had 300 men, 200 of Christina's Moidartach, granted free and for love, and 100 sent by Mackenzie of Kintail, not so much for love as for hatred — hatred of the Earl of Ross, Mackenzie's unfriendly neighbour. Christina had provided an extra galley too — indeed she had had to be dissuaded from accompanying the expedition herself; but even so, further transport was necessary, and the smaller, slower craft were scarcely adequate for the winter seas — especially as the incoming tide was racing up the firth from the ocean, south-westerly, the same direction as the prevailing wind, while the flotilla was proceeding on a course at almost right angles, south by east, with consequent rolling beam seas. Fortunately the men were Hebrideans and used to the sea, or they might have made but a doubtful fighting force at the end of it.

There had been some speculation that Boyd might have lit his beacon again tonight, to guide them in; but as yet there was no sign of it. The night was dull and cold, with occasional slight sleet showers, inclement for sailing in open boats but suitable enough for the activities ashore.

There were no stars to navigate by, but three-quarters of the way across Bruce decided that a cluster of lights that showed faintly must be from Turnberry Castle itself. In which case they were too far to the south. He shouted an order to the helmsman, in his leading galley.

Presently they could hear the thunder of the breakers on the shore, an ominous sound; and after some minutes of anxious peering into the mirk, Bruce thought that he could distinguish the long belt of white that would be the seas disintegrating on the savage reef of skerries that half closed Maidenhead Bay from the south. Another half-mile and they ought to be able to turn in, around the north end of the reef, and run into the comparatively sheltered corner of bay behind, the rendezvous where the balefire had blazed.

Soon they swung in, tossing violently as they passed the tail-end of the skerries, and thereafter quickly felt the sea's motion to abate. The re-entrant of the bay ahead was dark, under low cliff, giving no sign of life. The King remembered two salmon-fishers' cot-houses there, where he had played as a lad.

Cautiously, sail furled, Bruce's galley nosed forward, the sweeps dipping gently. There was no jetty or landing-stage, but an easy boat-strand of sand and pebbles, where three fishing cobles were already drawn up.

Skilfully manoeuvred, the vessel's forefoot crunched into the shelving shingle with a minimum of shock, amongst only small waves. Had the wind been northerly, or the landing unprotected from the south, it would have been a very different matter. Bruce himself was one of the first to jump down, caring nothing for the cold splashy shallows, and more affected by this stealthy return to the mainland of his kingdom than he would have been prepared to admit.

There was no one there to greet them. No movement showed on the dark shore.

Edward's galley moved in now, with the smaller craft, like a brood of ducklings, close behind. His brother came striding over the pebbles.

"Where is Boyd?" he demanded. "And Fleming. They should be here."

"I had looked for them, yes. Perhaps they do not expect us so early. Have not seen our arrival. They may be waiting in one of those cabins."

The King led a group up over the shingle and the sea-grass to where the dark low bulk of the cot-houses loomed. With sword-hilts they beat on the closed doors, demanding to open in the name of King Robert.

Only alarmed fishermen opened to them.

When these men's immediate fears were allayed, they declared that only themselves were in the hovels, no lords or great men. Sir Robert the Boyd had been here, yes — but that was four days back. He had sworn them to secrecy and had bade them gather drift-wood for a great fire. On the beach. Not to be lit until he returned. But he had not returned.

"Not returned, man?" the King burst in. "What do you mean? You lit the fire, lacking him?"

"No, lord. The fire is not lit. We await Sir Robert. As he said . . ."

"But — by the Rude! The fire *was* lit. That is why we are here. It was a signal."

"No, lord. Saving your lordship's presence. The fire is not yet lit. The wood still there. Down below the cliff . . ."

"Dear God! Then the fire we saw last night . . .?"

"Not here, sir. That would be the alehouse up at Shanter. Some drunken English soldier set it afire. Last night. Two of them died

86

in it, they say. And Mother MacWhannel herself. God rest her soul! A great blaze . . ."

"Christ's mercy! We have come then on a wild-goose chase!" Edward cried. "A burning alehouse!"

Appalled, they stared at each other in the darkness.

"Thank God we have learned it in time, at least!" Lennox said. "We can return to Arran, and little harm done."

"Oh, no . . .!" That was young James Douglas.

"There speaks a lily-liver. A craven!" Edward accused. "We have not come all this way to turn back now."

"My lord . . .!"

"My friends — peace!" Bruce intervened. "Here is matter for better debate than this. My lord of Lennox may be wise. We have made a grave mistake, it seems . . ."

"You would not turn tail?" his brother demanded, incredulously. "We have successfully landed. Unopposed. Is that not the great thing . . .?"

"It is important. But there are greater things. Robert Boyd is the most experienced campaigner we have. And an Ayr man. That is why I sent him. He was to light his fire if he deemed conditions at all possible for our invasion. It seems that he has not done so. Therefore must we not believe that he deems the venture impossible? Or too dangerous?"

"He may be captured, Sire. Or dead," Hay put in.

"It may be. Does that aid our decision?"

"Save us — we cannot turn back now!" Edward insisted. "Without so much as a sight of the enemy. That will not win back your kingdom for you!"

"I have so far shown the Scots people only defeat and disaster. My first attempt in this new campaign must be successful. Or at least no defeat. Or my cause is the worse served, greatly the worse."

"Yet, if we go back to Arran now, Sire, with no blow struck, is not your case equally hurt? When it becomes known." That was Neil Campbell.

"I would not turn back to Arran. Not now. I would sail south. To Loch Ryan. To join my brothers in Galloway. But . . ." The King paused. He turned to the fishermen. "Have you any notion as to how many is the English garrison at Turnberry?"

"Many, lord. Many."

"Aye, man — but *how* many? Are they in scores? Or hundreds? Or many hundreds? Only a mile away. Surely you have some notion."

"Hundreds, sir. Many hundreds. I do not know. Four, five hundred, it may be. So many they cannot mostly lodge in the castle. They fill every house in the Castleton. As in the Kirkton. In the kirk itself. And the mills and farm-touns around. So many."

"They are scattered, then? Lodged separate? In groups. Apart."

"Aye, lord. They needs must."

"And their masters? The knights and captains? Where are they?"

"Where but in the castle, sir. Where lords and knights would bide. With the great lord, the Percy . . ."

"Percy!" Bruce actually gripped the speaker's arm. "Percy, you say, man? Do you mean Henry Percy? The Lord of Northumberland?"

"The same, yes. He commands here now. As Governor and Sheriff."

"Lord save us!" The King swung on the others. "You hear? Henry Percy it is, who sits in my house. Rules my earldom! That smooth snake!"

Bruce was not the only one roused at the mention of the Northumbrian's name. They had scores to settle with the Percy.

"And his men are scattered!" Edward cried. "His captains with him in the castle. If this dolt speaks truth."

"As why should he not? Fearing no surprise assault, it is what they *would* do. And . . . the Castleton of Turnberry is a quarter-mile from the castle, no less!"

Suddenly there was no more talk of turning back. Percy's hated name, and the thought of his men dispersed, had changed all that, as far as Bruce was concerned.

"Henry Percy keeps but poor discipline, I think. If his men, drunken, are burning down alehouses at four of a morning!" he said. "It may be we could teach him a lesson."

"That is better talking, by the Mass!" Edward agreed. "How do we go about it? Isolate the castle, first?"

Bruce turned to the fishermen's spokesman, Cuthbert, by name, it appeared. "Friend — these English soldiers? Can you tell us where they are lodged? Besides the Castleton and the Kirkton. Each mill and farm-toun and place. All that you know."

There were six men in all, and between them they worked out a list of some eight separate locations where Percy's troops were billeted around Turnberry, some as much as a mile away from the castle — one indeed only a comparatively short distance inland from this bay, at Maidens Mill, where there was a troop of perhaps thirty horse and some archers. Practically all the locations the King and Edward knew, so that they could visualise the terrain and lay-out.

Bruce led his group back to their 300 Highlanders, who were now all disembarked and waiting on the shingle. He called for quiet, and spoke to them in their own tongue, his own mother's tongue.

"I have work for you, after your own hearts," he told them. "Quiet, deadly work. Not open battle, you understand, but quiet effective killing. Surprise. There are more of these Englishmen than there are of us, but they are lodged in small numbers, fifty here, seventy there. I need not tell you, surprise, quiet, speed — this is the heart of the matter. None must give warning to other. None must escape to raise any general alarm. Above all, no hint of it must reach the castle, where trumpets could sound to rouse the whole country. So, no fires. Is it understood?"

A fierce elated murmur rose from the Islesmen's ranks.

"Our first is a mill, quite near, where fifty or so sleep. We will surround it, closely, that none may break out. Then the killers will move in."

"Prisoners, Sir King?" somebody asked.

"We can afford no men to guard prisoners," Bruce answered evenly.

There was a sort of rumble from deep throats.

"After that, we divide into three companies. Under myself, the Earl of Carrick, and the Earl of Lennox. One will watch the castle. The others will find the rest of the soldiers' lodgings, and deal with them. If we lack success, if the alarm is given, we all come together at the Kirkton. The church stands on a grass mound midway to the point and the castle, and is easy found. Is all understood? Good. Come, then — and quietly."

With one or two guards left on the boats, Bruce and his brother led the way inland. They followed the course of a stream in its ravine, the Maidens Burn, almost up a waterfall at first, and then, away from the shore, through a winding tree-grown dean, where they must go single file, frequently leaping or splashing through the water. At length, they came to a widening of the little dell. And here, beside a dark mill-pond and swirling lade, were grouped four buildings — Maidens Mill itself, a tall granary, the miller's house and a double cottage with range of stabling. Silently Bruce motioned his followers to encircle all this.

There was no light or sign of guard or sentry. A faint stirring of horseflesh came from granary and stabling.

The 300 started to close in. Bruce had feared barking dogs, but none such sounded. The miller undoubtedly would have kept dogs in such a lonely place; therefore, either the soldiers had got rid of them, or the miller was no longer here.

When the ring was sufficiently tight, Bruce passed the whispered word round to halt, and the assault parties to move in. And to remember that the miller and his people were to be spared, if at all possible. About one third of the force soundlessly detached itself, forming four groups, two larger parties for the mill and the granary, two smaller for the millhouse and the cottages. At a given signal, they all advanced on their objectives together.

Bruce and his companions waited outside with the main body. By common consent this was accepted as no work for kings or those of knightly quality — and admittedly they would be less efficient at it than the Highland caterans. Tensely they stood, and the King, for one, had to steel himself to an acceptance of what he had ordained.

In fact, as a horror, it was less harrowing than anticipated, for gently-born watchers. The Islesmen were indeed experts. There was remarkably little fuss and noise. Only one actual scream rang out, high-pitched — and it was swiftly choked off. There was a certain amount of groaning, gasping, bubbling, some thuds and scuffling, the clatter of steel on stone flags, and a succession of bumps which was almost certainly a body falling down the granary stairs. Otherwise, apart from the sidlings and whinnyings of frightened horses smelling blood, there was little or nothing to intimate massacre to uninitiated watchers. No single refugee burst out from any of the buildings. In a remarkably short space of time, the shadowy Highlanders began to emerge, wiping their dirks and murmuring chuckled pleasantries to one another.

They left a strange sort of muffled and jerky stirring behind them, nevertheless, more seemingly evident of life than heretofore. Dead men lie less quiet, for a while, than do mere sleepers.

The Islesmen's leaders reported all done thoroughly, decently and in order. There had been no sign of anybody that had looked like a miller or member of his household — certainly no women; all appeared to be just Southron soldiery. There would be considerable pickings?

Bruce said that they must wait for that until the night's work was done. He did not question whether all were dead within, nor did he venture inside to see.

Forming up, they moved on up the burnside, with a new and feral menace about the Hebrideans that somehow communicated itself to the others, a sort of lip-licking anticipation and relish. Even the King felt it, and tried to put it from him.

Upon the grassy rabbit-cropped links, amongst the shadowy

gorse-bushes, they came to their next objective, a small farmery. Considerably before they reached it they perceived that this would be a less simple proposition. For here lights burned, and as they drew stealthily closer, the sound of uncouth singing, and a thumping beating of time thereto, reached them. It was not yet midnight, of course.

Bruce called a halt, while he considered. Caution suggested that they should perhaps leave this lively billet until later, in the hope that the Englishmen would quieten down and retire to sleep shortly, as was suitable. On the other hand, it would delay the programme to come back here, and this farm of Auchenduin lay between the Kirkton and the sea, so that its people, if roused, would be in a position to interfere with any enforced retiral on the boats. Moreover, the singing sounded distinctly slurred, and punctuated with raucous shouts, which seemed to indicate a fair degree of intoxication. Bruce decided to risk an assault. After all, making all that noise anyway, a few more shouts and screams would not be apt to be noticeable.

There was some low-voiced bickering amongst the Highlanders. It seemed that the previous killing party were assuming that they would continue with the good work, whereas the others wanted to share in the proceedings. Almost they were coming to blows on the matter. The King had sternly to order peace, and commanded that a new selection of dirkmen be given their chance.

The farmhouse itself was small and mean, little better than a cabin; but the associated buildings were quite extensive, barns, stables and byres, for formerly much cattle had grazed on these grassy links — Bruce's cattle. It was from these outbuildings that the singing emanated, where the troops were presumably quartered. The King's own party drew their swords this time, and moved close in with the rest of the encirclers, in case this proved to be a less tidy exercise.

It did — although the knightly swords were not in fact required. None of the enemy ever actually emerged from the buildings, but the process of elimination was clearly a much lengthier and noisier one, with shouting and yelling, the clash of steel and the crash and tumble of fitments and bodies. This went on at some length, so that Bruce was constrained to detach another couple of score of eager participants from the surrounding cordon, to send them in to aid and speed the work. He kept glancing over his shoulder, southwards towards the Kirkton, less than half a mile away. Admittedly all was dark in that direction, and the blustery wind was from the south-west; but an unholy noise was undoubtedly arising from Auchenduin steading.

At last the racket began to abate, and the Islesmen to emerge from the buildings. Some few were wounded now, and presently one was carried out dead. But there was no depression, most evidently. It seemed to have been a thoroughly enjoyable affair for the Moidartach, really more satisfactory than at Maidens Mill; these were of course professional sea-raiders and killers, however addicted to poetry, the sagas, music and dancing. They claimed that there had been all of four-score Englishry in there. None would trouble Scotland again.

This experience convinced Bruce that he was wise to leave the Kirkton and the Castleton until later. These were villages, or at least hamlets, with a number of houses, and the danger of noise, disturbance and resistance would be the greater, especially with the local people there to complicate matters. Much better to pick off the outlying billets first — and according to the fishermen there were still four more of these to account for.

So again ordaining that there was to be no plundering meantime, and that the horses were to be left in their stables, the King divided the company there and then into three parties of approximately a hundred each. Edward, with his overbearing and impetuous nature, did not get on well with others — with men, that is; he did well enough with women usually — was given Gilbert Hay as lieutenant, Hay being a quiet, level-headed but effective man. They were to deal with another smaller farm-steading to the north, and a second mill on the Morriston Burn. Ninety minutes was all the time they could be spared for this, and they would have the longest distance to travel — so haste was essential. Lennox was sent to watch the castle exits, with Neil Campbell, a hardened fighter, to stiffen him. Their task meantime was to avoid conflict if possible, avoid detection, but to ensure that the English leadership was prevented, if roused, from issuing forth to take charge of the situation. Bruce himself, with James Douglas, would tackle the castle brewery and the main kennels and falcon-yard. These being both close to the castle walls would demand extra care and quiet. They would all meet again at the Kirkton in about ninety minutes, for a joint attack.

Douglas, who had remained very silent until now, voiced his views to his monarch and hero as they moved off, southwards, with their hundred men.

"This is ill employment for a King, as for noblemen, Your Grace," he declared. "I never thought to see the day when I would skulk and steal and slay sleeping men, like any thief in the night!"

"It is not pretty work," Bruce agreed. "But necessary. How would *you* order it, Jamie?"

"I do not know," the other admitted frankly. "I have had but little experience of war." Sir James was just twenty-one, and had spent six years as a refugee in France, with Norman relatives. Tournaments and jousting had been all his military education. "But surely other than this."

"Aye," the King said heavily. "But if you are going to serve me and my cause, lad, you will have to be prepared to soil those white hands of yours. Oh, yes — you have done well as a fugitive in the heather, Jamie. Taken your part and complained nothing. I have watched you. But when ill work fell to be done, anything that went less than well with your honour, it was not James Douglas who did it. That I noted also!"

The younger man bit his lip and said nothing.

"See you — once I thought as you do. But I have learned in a hard school. Eleven years I have been a-learning. I have learned that a nation that fights for its very existence cannot always afford the luxury of honour. I have had two stark teachers, Edward of England and William Wallace. For long, the lords of Scotland prevailed nothing against Edward, who cares no whit for honour or chivalry or anything such. Only Wallace knew how to fight Edward. Against the overwhelming might and utter ruthlessness of the Englishman, Wallace alone made headway. He fought no pitched battles, made no knightly sallies, accepted no challenges. He slew by night, surprised, ambushed, outwitted. He burned a small castle here, took a village there, harried the flanks of armies, cut their supplies, wasted the land before them. And only Wallace did Edward fear. This, Jamie, is Wallace's kind of warfare. And it is the only kind Bruce can afford to wage today."

"Since needs must, some must do it, yes," Douglas conceded. "But . . . must the King?"

"The King? What is the King, man, but the representative and leader of his people? I have thought much of kings and kingship since that coronation-day at Scone. Would you have your King to stand back, not to soil his hands with what he would have others do on his behalf? That is not as I see the King's part, Sir James. Nor yet Douglas's part. Remember who you fight. Remember that day when first we met. Ten years ago, at Douglas Castle. Remember how the English then were prepared to fight, to win your castle. By hanging children before your eyes, so that the Lady Douglas's tender woman's heart would be wrung into yielding her house rather than see it done. Mind you that!"

"And yet, Sire, it was because *you* were so otherwise, because you threw aside all your position and safety, your credit with King Edward, to save those same children, that I saw Robert the Bruce as worshipful. Then, and have continued so to do. All those years ago I swore that, one day, I would be the man of this noble knight."

It was Bruce's turn to be silent. He could by no means refute what his friend had said. And at the back of his mind he was well aware that what he had been enunciating was as much to convince himself as Douglas.

They were nearing the Kirkton now, and must by-pass it to reach the brewery. There was no opportunity for further debate. The King frowned as he strode forward.

The castle's former brewery was situated beside another small stream, and with its maltings, brewhouse and stores formed a size-able establishment. No lights showed here, however, and it was unlikely that there would be dogs present. A couple of scouts, sent forward, came back to report that there were men in the maltings and storehouse, but not in the brewhouse. There appeared to be no horses — evidently these were footmen, archers perhaps, quartered closer to the castle than were the cavalry.

Bruce divided his party seventy–thirty this time. With only a third of the former manpower, he could not afford any close-knit outer cordon. Instead, the outside thirty were set to watch windows and doors for possible escapers. The seventy should be sufficient for what was required within.

"Your permission, Sire, to lead the killers," Douglas requested formally.

"Not so, Sir James. This is my part. You will command out here." The stiffness went out of Bruce's voice. "Though, God knows, I but go in with them — do not lead them. Since they know the task better than I do."

Accordingly the King did not announce his heading of the pur-suit, but merely slipped in amongst the last of the party of thirty or so entering the maltings, drawing his dirk like the rest. He did not know whether or not to wish for some return of the former animal elation that had swept the company after the first bloodletting.

Inside the building it was very dark, making even the outside mirk seem light. At first Bruce could distinguish nothing. But the Moidartach appeared to have cats' eyes, and moved with entire confidence. Before he began to achieve any real vision, however, he became aware that the Highlandmen were all in fact hurrying past and up a stairway, unseen but sensed, ahead. Making after them, he blundered into a stand of tall yew bows, which he saved from falling with a clatter only by a desperate effort. Evidently this was indeed an archers' billet, and they used the basement only for their equipment.

A choking, gurgling noise from above indicated that the slaughter had begun. It was followed by a scream quickly muffled. Thereafter the sounds were more like those of many dogs worrying rats. The Islesmen used their plaids to smother their victims at the same time as they stabbed and slashed. Reluctantly the King forced himself to climb those stairs.

He was only part way up when the sort of general scuffling above was punctuated by a sudden scrambling and slipping, involved with bitten-off Gaelic cursing. Swift movement, the padding of bare feet, heralded a running man at the stairhead. The merest hint of light came from a window up there, and against it Bruce was able to make out a figure, evidently dressed only in a shirt. This came hurtling down upon him in panting panic.

The King acted without hesitation, almost without thought. Throwing himself in the path of the escaper, he grabbed the man with an encircling left arm — the formerly damaged arm, now healed — and in the same movement raised the drawn dirk and plunged it deep into the other's breast. As the shocked gasp began to rise to a shriek, he released his grip on the dagger and raised the hand to clamp it over the open mouth. He was vaguely aware of teeth sinking into his flesh as the man slid down within his grasp and thereafter to the steps. He wrenched his hand free, and his victim rolled away bumping down the stairs.

A little unsteadily Bruce went after him. It was only the second time in his life that he had used a dirk on a man, many as had been his sword-thrusts — and that other had been John Comyn at the Dumfries altar, the deed that came between him and his sleep. The Englishman was twitching and making strange snoring noises, and the King knew that he ought to cut the throat, as his minions above were doing, but jibbed at it. He waited there, instead, retrieving his dirk, for other possible attempts at escape.

None developed. The first Highlandman down the stairs made short work of the King's victim, without any request. The brewery was won, without casualty to the attackers.

Bruce remained lacking in elation, as they pressed on towards the kennels and falcon-yard, a little way south of the castle walls and ditches.

He had been concerned about this last assault, leaving it late, for here had been kept his pack of hunting-hounds, and a great hullabaloo and outcry was possible. But not so much as a single sounded as they approached, and it looked as though Percy had dispensed with the brutes, or at least kept them elsewhere. This time, the King allowed Douglas to go in with the attackers to the silent, unlighted square of low buildings, without demur.

It was soon over, here, with the smallest number of sleepers so far, mainly cooks, grooms and servants apparently. James Douglas looked stiff and, somehow, even in the darkness, gave the impression of being very pale, as he came out. He made no comment to Bruce — who indeed sought none.

The programme now called for a return to the Kirkton, and a united assault upon it, with time in hand. But well before the King's party reached the hamlet they heard noise therefrom, which grew to uproar.

"A plague on it — they are roused! That is an attack," Bruce exclaimed. "Whose folly is this . . .?"

He had no need to ask that, of course. Lennox was not the sort to initiate assaults, out of turn or otherwise. This would be Edward Bruce demonstrating his independence.

At the run now, the King led his men on, with the din ahead continuing. One of the Islesmen's leaders presently tugged at the royal sleeve, to point away to the left, where he declared two figures had shown briefly, fleeing in the other direction. Even as he spoke, someone else called out that he had seen a man running off on their right.

"Damnation!" Bruce cried. "Escapers. These will warn the Castleton. The castle itself. Edward is a headstrong fool!" He ordered some of the Moidartach to race after the fleeing men from the Kirkton, to try to prevent them giving the alarm elsewhere.

At least, it meant presumably that Edward's people were winning in their premature attack. The noise was gradually lessening.

This reading of the situation was confirmed as they came to the Kirkton. There was a certain amount of moaning, and screaming of women, with many dark shapes lying around, but the fighting appeared to be over. The houses clustered round a grassy mound, on the summit of which the church stood, a notable landmark. It was up there that any remaining activity seemed to be concentrated.

Hurrying up the hill, Bruce found his brother inside the church itself — which apparently had been used as one more barracks. All seemed to be over here too, though the number of bodies lying scattered amongst the gravestones indicated that it had been a fight, not a massacre of slumberers.

"My lord of Carrick — a word with you," the King called sternly. "Over here."

"Ha — is that you, Rob? You came too late. It is all by with. Hot while it lasted. But more sport than knifing sleepers!"

"We are not here for sport," the other snapped. He jerked his head. "Those women skirling? More sport?"

"You would not grudge our caterans a little play, man . . .?"

"By the Rude, I would! Any women here are villagers. Our own people. Moreover, they are my subjects. Mine. I have come to free them, not to savage them. Jamie — see you to it. With your sword, if need be. Quickly." He turned back to his brother. "As for you, Edward, you are a fool. Witless! And worse. You have disobeyed my commands. I told you to await me here. For a joint attack. I told you plainly . . ."

"Save us, Rob — what's to do? We finished these other two billets quickly. They were no trouble. Arrived here early. Why wait, when I could take the place? Save time?"

"Because I *said* to wait."

"God in Heaven — I am not a child! Think you I need your guidance, Rob, for all I do . . .?"

"Enough, my lord! It is the King who speaks — not Rob Bruce! When I give my royal command you, as all others, will obey. Mind it, hereafter. You have like as not made ruin of this night's work. You had not sufficient men to surround all this village. You have taken it, yes. But some escaped. To warn others. We saw them. They will warn the Castleton. Percy himself, in the castle, it may be. Percy still has men enough to destroy us, probably. Armour. Horsed knights. Men-at-arms. You may have won me this Kirkton, but you are like to have lost me the night!"

His brother said nothing.

"Enough, then. Get your men assembled. And quickly. We move at once. For the Castleton. With all speed."

The Castleton of Turnberry, the main village which had grown up to serve the principal seat of the Carrick earls, lay less close to the castle itself than was usual — this because of the cliff-top position of the fortalice, with no sheltered or convenient area near by. More than a quarter-mile south-east, and as far from the Kirkton, its village nestled amongst the trees of a shallow valley.

The Bruce brothers' united company of 200 was left in no doubts but that the Castleton had been warned. Lights were glowing and shouts sounding, as they approached; even a trumpet neighed shrilly on the night. That trumpet would be heard in the castle, without any doubt likewise.

Despite Bruce's lecture to James Douglas, what followed was a much more acceptable instalment of the night's work than what had gone before, though undeniably more expensive and less efficient. Men emerged from all the houses of the Castleton. Indubitably many were more intent on flight than fight, while not a few were still bemused by sleep or drink, but none had left their arms behind them. Two hundred attackers were insufficient to employ any surrounding tactics, and the resultant battle, without any real line or focus, was incoherent in the extreme, no more than a confusion of individual tussels and duels in the darkness, running fights with leadership and direction almost impossible on either side. What advantage there might be was with the attackers, with surprise and the night tending to fight for them; but on the other hand, the assailed were fighting for their lives, and moreover had the feeling of the great castle's support near by to sustain them. Neither side knew how many might be arrayed against them.

Bruce suddenly found himself alone, and engaging two men simultaneously, one armed with a halberd and the other with a short cavalry sword. His own longer blade dealt with the halberd effectively, shearing through the wood staff with a single great slash, and then cutting down the bereft wielder with a swift backhanded stroke. But this left him open to the other man's stabbing rush, and he had to jump backwards and sideways urgently, blindly, to avoid the vicious thrust. There was an unevenness in the ground, only a group of tussocks but enough to send him sprawling — and with the recoil from his own swinging blow, he overbalanced and fell his length.

Possibly that fall saved him, for a stabbing thrust can be quickly extended and realigned. He fell away just in time from that darting point — and his opponent thereupon tripped headlong over the same obstacle and crashed to the ground likewise. Bruce was able to rise first, and though his sword had been jerked from his hand, he was able to whip out his more useful dirk. Still only on his knees, before the other got that far, the King drove his dagger between the bent shoulders.

This was his only contribution to the engagement, though, retrieving his blade, he went in search of further involvement. The fight was so scattered and fluid that he could find nobody he could usefully engage. And he was distracted by coming upon James Douglas standing leaning on his sword, dizzy from a knock on the head received from some sort of club — whose late owner lay near by. By the time that Bruce had ascertained that his young friend was not grievously injured, the battle was, if not over, at least in its final stages, with Highlandmen everywhere pursuing their fleeing foes.

Concerned lest his force become so scattered as to be out of his control, the King sounded the recall, on the fine curling horn of a Moidart bull which Christina had presented to him — even though this must be heard in the castle. It was that castle's probable reactions that worried him now. Lights were showing from many of its slit windows, but no fighting or uproar was as yet apparent, from that direction.

When at least the majority of his force was re-assembled — though with quite a number missing, either casualties or still chasing the fugitives — the King hurried them on towards the cliff-top castle itself. Half-way there they were met by one of Lennox's men, sent to discover progress and to report that the castle was roused, but that so far its occupants had not attempted to sally forth.

Bruce pressed on, with the sea-wind, laced with sleet, in his face now. Presently he reached the narrows of a promontory crowned by the great soaring fortress which had been his birthplace. The cliffs here were not high, but the castle walls rose tall and sheer, occupying every inch of the mound's summit. The only landward access was by the narrow neck of the promontory, across which the usual deep and wide ditch had been cut. Massed across this neck of land, just out of arrow-shot from the gatehouse tower, Lennox and Campbell waited, shivering, with their hundred men.

"Here's a devilish cold vigil, Sire," Lennox complained. "They have made no move, no attempt to issue out, as yet. The draw-bridge is part-lowered, in readiness. We can hear their horses' hooves ringing in the courtyard. So they could ride out swiftly and are prepared. But all they have done is shoot a few arrows at us . . ."

"Percy will not know, in the dark, how many we are," Campbell put in. "He is a cautious man."

"Have you men down on the shore?" the King demanded. "There is a small jetty there. Boats. And a postern gate, with stair-way down." At the others' silence, he frowned. "You have not? Damnation — then they may have already sent out men. By boat. To gain information. To seek help."

"I am sorry, Sire. We did not know . . ."

"The fault is mine, friends. I should have told you. It may be too late now . . ."

He directed a picket to make its way down to the beach, never-theless. And presently a man came hurrying back, with the word that they had been just in time to glimpse a boat pulling away from the little landing-stage under the cliff. Too late to halt it.

"A curse! So we *are* too late! Percy may be cautious, but he is no fool. He has got his messengers away."

"What matters it?" Edward demanded. "They will but learn, for him, that he has lost his men. All of them furth of the castle. Little joy in that, I say."

"And *I* say that is the least of it. Think you that is all Percy will

99

have ordered? He will have sent for aid. Ayr is but a dozen miles, with its garrison. Irvine and Cumnock have garrisons likewise. Even Maybole, five miles away. And there are a dozen castles, English-held, no farther. He could have a thousand men here soon after daylight — mounted, armoured men. What use our caterans and their dirks, then?"

None offered an answer to that.

"I fear our shaft is shot. For this night," Bruce decided. "We cannot take this strength. And if I know Percy, he will not come out. He will wait there, secure, for reinforcement. And for daylight. To see our strength. And that we can by no means afford."

"We go, then?"

"Yes, we go. It must serve. We have struck a blow that all Scotland will hear of. My folk will know that their King is back!"

"We retire on the galleys, Sire?" Lennox asked. "Back to Arran . . .?"

"Of a mercy — not that!" Edward protested. "Not after this. When we have made our landing, and struck the first blow."

"No, not back to Arran," his brother agreed. "Or, not myself, nor most of you. You, my lord of Lennox, will take the boats, and a small company, to Arran. There to assemble and send on to me the more men that Angus Og and the Lady Christina will provide. The rest of us will make for our Ayrshire hills, around Loch Doon. Base ourselves there, near to Galloway. Make contact with my brothers. Raid from there. And build up our strength."

"Thank God for that, at least!" Edward commented. "Let us be on our way, then."

"First, a word or two might not be wasted, here," Bruce said. He nodded towards the castle. He handed his horn to Hay. "Blow it loud and long, Gilbert," he directed, and strode forward, near to the ditch's edge.

When the curious moaning notes of the horn died away, the King raised his voice. "Ho — the castle!" he shouted. "Do all sleep sound in Turnberry this night?"

A voice answered him from the gatehouse parapet promptly enough. "Who is there? Who dares come knocking at my lord of Northumberland's door, at this hour?"

"One who has a better right to that door than Henry Percy! Get him, man. I would speak with him."

"Fool! Watch your words. Do you not know that this is the seat of His Majesty's Governor here? Sheriff of Ayr?"

"You have your Majesties awry, fellow! Tell your lord that Robert Bruce, King of Scots, whose territory he defiles, whose castle he usurps, demands his ear. And quickly."

There was silence from the gatehouse. But quite soon another and thinner voice spoke — proof that the Percy had been in fact standing by. "Henry Percy speaks, my lord of Carrick," it said. "What folly is this? Where have you come from?"

"Costly folly for you and your like, Percy. As you will find out. And the Earl of Carrick is now my brother, here. Mind it. Also, *he* is Sheriff of Ayr. I require your surrender of my castle of Turnberry forthwith. Yield it, and you shall go unharmed. Carrying my message to your master at Lanercost. That I require my kingdom at his bloodstained hands. And my wife also! Before every Englishman in Scotland dies the death of yours!"

They could almost hear Percy choking. "Are you out of your wits, Bruce?" he demanded, with difficulty. "Have your hurts, your defeats, turned your head? By morning, my men will have you cut to pieces . . ."

"Your men are all dead, Percy. Every one. They will not come to your aid. At the Castleton. The Kirkton. The stables. The brewery. Maidens Mill. And the rest. All dead. Cleansed. As all Scotland will be, one day. That message you will take to Edward Plantagenet."

There was no response from the castle now.

"Will you yield, then? And save your life?"

"No." Though that was hoarse, it was definite enough.

"Very well. You will regret it. I will find another messenger for Edward. Hide you there in my castle, Percy. I do not choose to destroy my own house, where I was born. But . . . your days are numbered. If I were you, my lord — which God forbid! — I would slip out of that postern, to the beach, while the dark is still kind to you. And take boat across Solway to your English shore. For they say you are a cautious man."

No word answered that.

Ordering Hay to sound a derisory blast on the horn to indicate that the King of Scots had spoken the last word, Bruce turned to Lennox.

"Keep your men here, in view from the castle, until I send for them. Then take forty, and back to the boats. Sail for Arran. Meantime, we go collect our booty. Horses. Food. Armour. Dead men's weapons. An hour should be sufficient. Then we head for the hills of Doon and Minnoch." He grasped the earl's hand. "Bring me more Islesmen and Irish, Malcolm, so soon as you may. I shall need every one. And God go with you."

"And with Your Grace . . ."

CHAPTER SEVEN

ROBERT BRUCE surveyed this his handiwork, at least, with some satisfaction — however otherwise his general frame of mind. The stag was a noble one, of ten points, and for the end of a long winter, moderately plump — which was not unimportant, with a score of men waiting to feed on it. And they were unlikely to get another that day. His arrow had taken it through the throat — even though he had aimed for the heart; but then, he was unused to these English long-bows and their cloth-yard shafts, purloined from the brewery at Turnberry. The Scots used much shorter and handier bows, if with correspondingly shorter range and less hitting-power. Still, none need know that he had aimed at the heart and hit a good eight inches to the left, since the stag was as dead one way as the other. At least he had done better than Gibbie Hay, who had missed his mark altogether.

Kneeling, he drew his dirk to blood the beast by cutting the jugular vein. They would have to cut it all up, as well as gralloch it, for the brute would weigh fourteen or fifteen stone at least, he calculated, requiring three men to carry it the couple of miles back to their cave. He might as well play the butcher now, while he waited for the others to come up.

Bruce had killed, eventually, in the narrows of a small side glen at the foot of Loch Doon, in the wild mountain country where Ayrshire rose to the Galloway border, under mighty Merrick, where they had spent the two weeks since Turnberry. Using his remaining score of Islesmen almost as hounds, he and Gilbert Hay had managed to have the three deer they had spied manoeuvred through the close country of steep hillsides, waterfalls, bogs and hanging woods, towards this trap of a narrow glen, the caterans spread out in a great semi-circle to windward, closing in to give the beasts just enough of their scent to make them uneasy and moving in the other direction, without alarming them so that they bolted off at speed. This was a tactic which Bruce had learned in Christina's Moidart, and very different from the traditional southern method of hunting deer on horseback. The two marksmen had waited in the throat of the glen for the stags to drift within bow-shot. The two younger beasts had in fact bolted off at a tangent, uphill, long before they were in range; but this heavier animal had come on, by fits and starts, into the trap, disdaining to be flushed and flurried. Bruce had seen Hay, from a somewhat higher position than his own, across the glen, shoot and obviously miss. His own shaft, of a minute later, at fully ninety paces, was, all things considered, commendable enough.

He was bending over to make the first belly cut of the gralloch when, out of the corner of his eye, he glimpsed movement. Across the glen, and up. It was Hay, standing and waving. And not the congratulatory waving of one hunter to another; an urgent beckoning, rather.

The King straightened up. Hay was no excitable enthusiast, to gesture to his monarch like that, without due cause. As the other continued to beckon, Bruce wiped his red blade on the stag's shaggy mane, sheathed it, and rose.

"Company, Sire," Hay called softly, at his approach, and pointed.

From this position it was possible to see down the main valley of the Doon below the loch-foot. And coming up the riverside track, less than a mile away, was a mounted party of about forty, arms and armour gleaming in the last rays of the sinking wintry sun.

Bruce rubbed his bearded chin. "Men-at-arms," he said. "I cannot think that they come to this remote wilderness looking for other than ourselves. Yet too small a company to be English sent to take us, surely. I believe they must be our first supporters, Gibbie!"

"And not before time, Sire!" Hay observed grimly.

That was hardly an unfair comment. Despite the stirring activities of the night at Turnberry two weeks before, no upsurge of support had materialised for the King of Scots, whatever might be the glee at Percy's discomfiture. No rallying to Bruce's standard had developed, even amongst his own feudal vassals of Carrick and Kyle. After waiting for ten days in these hills, he had been forced to the recognition that more positive recruiting was necessary, and had sent out his lieutenants, each with about four-score Islesmen, to try to raise fighting men. Edward had gone south, to the great Bruce lordship of Annandale; Campbell south-west into Galloway, to try to link up with the other two Bruce brothers; Douglas north-east to Douglasdale and the Moray lordship of Bothwell. This temporary dispersal of force was accepted only reluctantly; but apart from the urgent need for reinforcements, the food situation for even 300 men, in these empty fastnesses, had rapidly become a major problem, and the booty from Turnberry fast consumed. Hence the daily hunting on the part of the score who remained.

Bruce and Hay slipped discreetly down through the woodland thickets, making for a point where the newcomers must pass close and could be surveyed secretly. The Islesmen could be trusted to remain out of evidence until called for.

Unobserved they reached their vantage-point only a little while before the mounted party came jingling up. And quickly they perceived that there was in fact no need for secrecy. Riding at the head of the visitors' column was a youngish woman, and at her side Sir Robert Boyd.

The King stepped out into the track before them, holding up a hand. "Welcome, my friends," he cried. "Chris — you make a fair sight! Sir Robert — we feared you dead. Or at the least, captured."

There was a great to-do of exclamation, greeting, dismounting and hand-kissing. The woman was a cousin of Bruce's own, the Lady Christian of Carrick, of the old Celtic line; and the forty well-equipped men-at-arms her own contribution to his force. It seemed that it was on the women of Scotland that its monarch must rely.

Bruce embraced his kinswoman, with some emotion. "God bless you, Chris!" he said. "You are the first. The first of all the Lowlands to rally to my cause."

"Aye — we are become a race of mice, not men!" she declared vehemently, clasping him to her and bestowing great smacking kisses. "Fearful of every English shadow! Time indeed that you returned and shamed us into valiant deeds again. Would I could have brought you more than two-score, Robert my liege lord — but as you know, I have but small lands."

"You have brought me more than just two-score fine fellows, woman — you have brought me hope and faith again. When I needed them."

Boyd coughed. "Your Grace will need all the faith and hope you may muster, I fear," he said significantly.

"Aye. No doubt, Sir Robert. The more I have to thank the Lady Christian, then. But, man — where have you been? And how knew you that I was here? At Loch Doon?"

"I heard that you had landed, that night. At Turnberry. All the land has heard that! Despite that I had sent no signal. Deeming conditions to be unpropitious for a landing. In Carrick, at least. But I did not learn your whereabouts. Until I encountered Douglas, two days past, on his way to his own country. He gave me the news of Your Grace. And the error of the fire. Knowing that the Lady Christian had these men for you — she alone of all I approached — I went to her. So we have come here, secretly."

"Aye. That was right. There is little fervour for my cause, then?"

The other shook his head. "Men are leal enough. I think. And the common folk would rise for you. But the quality, the lords and lairds and knights, are sore afraid to move. They have suffered too much in ten long years of war, lost too much. Lost heart, most of all, I fear, Sire, that you have a sore hill to climb, ahead of you."

"Have I not always known it, man!" The King spoke shortly. "But, come — here is no way to treat a lady, who has journeyed long miles to see me. We are camped at a cave behind those crags. Up that small side glen. A mile. But you will have to walk your horses, to reach it . . ."

As they picked their way by deer-paths and difficult climbing tracks, leading the horses, Boyd contrived to draw a little way ahead, alone with the King. Picking his words, he spoke slowly.

"Back there, I said that Your Grace would have need of all the faith and hope you might muster. To my sorrow I did not say that lightly."

Bruce looked at him quickly. "You have more news for me than you have told?"

"I have, Sire — God forgive me! Grievous news. Once before, I brought you the like. The Galloway venture has failed. It is disaster. All there is lost."

"Christ's mercy — no! Not . . . not . . .?"

"Aye, Sire — the worst. Sir Dugald MacDouall and the Mac-Canns, Comyn vassals, fell on them the day after the landing at Loch Ryan. Unawares, it seems. How it was done I have not heard. Whose the blame. But it was a rout. And thereafter, massacre."

Fiercely Bruce gripped the other's arm. "My brothers?" he demanded.

Boyd moistened his lips. "MacDouall took them, alive. With Sir Reginald Crawford. And Malcolm MacQuillan, of Antrim, who led the Irish gallowglasses. Him he slew. But your brothers, and Crawford, he sent to King Edward, at Lanercost. Edward . . . Edward hanged and then beheaded them all."

For long moments there were no words, no sounds other than their passage through the dead brackens. Then a moan of sheerest desolation broke from the King's tight lips.

"Alex!" he whispered. "Tom! Oh, God — it is more than I can bear! First Nigel. Now Alex, Tom! Paying the price, all paying the price of *my* sin. The price of John Comyn's blood!"

"The price of Edward Plantagenet's savage hate, *I* say! The man is no better than a ravening brute-beast."

"Edward is . . . Edward. But I — I am accursed! Lost. Excommunicate, indeed! Forsaken of God and man . . ."

"Scarce that, Sire. You still have leal friends. Leal to their last breaths . . ."

"Aye — to die for me also! And so to add to my guilt."

The other was silent. He looked sidelong at his stricken liege lord as they went. "Sire," he said at length, his normally strong voice uncertain. "I have still more news."

Bruce strode on, set-faced. He might not have heard.

"It concerns your ladies. The Queen. The Princess. Your sisters . . ."

The suddenly indrawn quivering breath was more eloquent than any words. The King stopped in his tracks.

"They are not . . . not slain," Boyd went on hurriedly, almost gabbling for so slow and deliberate a speaker. "The Queen is sent, a prisoner, to a house in Holderness on the Humber. To be held close. Alone. The child taken from her . . ."

"Edward does that! To Elizabeth. His own god-daughter, whom he claims to love?"

"Yet that is the best of it, Sire. Hear me. Marjory, the child — she is sent to London. Alone. To the Tower. Not to be spoken to by anyone. There to be hung in a cage. On the outer walls of the Tower. For all to gaze at. Like an animal. In the open. A cage, of timber and iron."

"What . . .!" That was a strangled cry.

"The Lady Mary, your sister, also. She to be hung in a similar cage. On the walls of Roxburgh Castle. Day and night. In cold and heat. The Countess of Buchan likewise, who crowned you — she on the walls of Berwick . . ." The knight's voice tailed away.

Bruce was staring at the other unseeing, his features working strangely. Then he turned to stride on, at something near a run; and when Boyd would have hurried with him, flung round and pushed him away, violently. He stalked on alone up that twisting climbing path, not a word spoken.

"The Lady Christian, Countess of Mar," Sir Robert called after him desperately, as though he must at all costs be quit of the last of his terrible news. "Your other sister. To be confined to a nunnery, for ever . . ."

There was no sign from the King. Boyd turned and held the others back, duty done. At least he could gain him solitude for his agony.

But presently they caught up with Bruce, at the edge of the boisterous burn whose glen this was. It was near the foot of the tall crags of naked rock which had been pointed out from a mile away, with the valley now very narrow and steep, almost a ravine. Oddly enough the burn was actually wider here than it had been throughout; but here was the only place where it might be crossed, at a brief stretch of comparative shallows, perhaps thirty feet across, with a spray-spouting waterfall just above and foaming cataracts below.

Expressionless the King turned to Boyd, Hay and the lady, as they came up. "Cousin — let me carry you across," he said levelly. "The rest, follow exactly where I tread. A foot wrong, and you will be swept away. Lead each horse with great care. It is like a causeway, smooth rock, and slippery. And it is not straight." That sounded almost like a child's learned lesson repeated.

He picked up the woman in his arms, and now she found nothing to say to him, in the face of that granite-like sternness of expression. He stepped into the swirling water with her, and waded across with steady deliberate pacing, counting the steps until making a dog's-leg bend two-thirds of the way over. Setting his burden down, wordless, at the far bank, he paused, to watch the progress of the others. Gilbert Hay, eyeing him, thought that he had never seen a face so abruptly and direly changed. It was as though the living flesh had been overlaid and cast in hard, unyielding bronze, the lively eyes hooded and dull-glazed. No man sought to catch those eyes.

When all were across the hazard of the torrent, Bruce led on slantwise uphill, away from the water, to skirt the foot of the crags, amongst the rock-falls and screes. For perhaps a quarter-mile more they climbed, until they came to a single Highland sentinel beside a great boulder. Beyond was a sort of re-entrant in the cliffs, with a scooped dip before it and at the foot, the yawning mouth of a cave.

There was no room here for the horses, and Hay took them, and the men-at-arms, down to a hidden green hollow near by, amongst gorse-bushes and scattered hawthorns, where the few beasts left from Turnberry were hobbled. Bruce ushered his principal guests into the cave. Behind the lady, he paused, turning to Boyd.

"Cages, you said? In the open air? On walls? In winter? For a child! And women!" He spoke as though he used a foreign language, carefully, without intonation. "I did not mis-hear?"

"Cages, Sire. High on the outer walls of London Tower, Roxburgh and Berwick Castles." Boyd raised his eyes to his monarch's face, and quickly dropped them again.

They went inside.

*   *   *

Later, with Boyd and two men sent to escort his cousin through the night-bound hills back to her small property of Newton, south of Maybole, Bruce crouched at the back of the cave, where it bent and lowered to form almost a separate little chamber, hidden from the rest. A log as seat, he sat hunched, staring with unseeing eyes at the spluttering, smoking makeshift lamp, contrived from melted fat and a wick of cord in, strangely, a handsome silver quaich or drinking-vessel, one of the spoils of Turnberry though with the Bruce arms engraved thereon.

Alone he had sat there, for how long he knew not, facing the beetling dark walls and the hell of his own lot. He had been low before, all but crushed by the hammer-blows of fate, of treachery, of Edward Plantagenet. But he had never been so low as this. Before his tortured mind's eye had passed the long appalling procession of his friends and kin and supporters, those whom he or his cause had brought to ruin, shame, agony and death. Wallace, barbarously butchered. Andrew Moray, slain. The Graham, slain. Gartnait of Mar, his brother-in-law, assassinated. Simon Fraser, tortured and hanged — like his brother Alexander, like Hay's brother Hugh. Somerville of Carnwath, Barclay of Cairns, David de Inchmartin, Scrymgeour the Standard-Bearer dying the death of Wallace. William Lamberton, his closest friend and ally, chained a prisoner. As was old Bishop Wishart of Glasgow. Nigel, laughing, lively Nigel, hanged, drawn and quartered. And now Alex and Tom hideously executed also. Christopher Seton the same. His Elizabeth in solitary confinement. His little daughter like a caged beast for all to mock at. One sister and Isabel of Buchan likewise. Another, gay, lightsome Christian, walled in a convent. Randolph, his nephew, in prison. Others, countless others, suffering or past suffering. Because he had presumed to defy the usurper and put on the fatal crown. Or because he had stabbed John Comyn at God's own altar . . .

He had been King a year. And what of his kingdom did he hold? This cave, in his own lost earldom of Carrick. His strength? One remaining brother, the least loved, and a small handful of knightly friends. Less than 400 men. Nearly all wild Highlandmen, with him not for him or his cause but for love of their chieftainess. His lieges, the folk of his realm? They turned from him, stayed at home — as who would blame them! The invader was everywhere supreme, buttressed by unlimited power and numbers, sustained by traitors, egged on to consistent atrocity by the burning hatred of their lord, Edward. Edward, who would never relent, never for a moment relax the pressure. Edward the scourge of God on Scotland and on Robert Bruce.

There it was, the scourge of God! God had raised His hand against the presumptuous man who, a murderer, had dared to claim the holy anointing. Robert Bruce, the Lord's Anointed! Heaven help Scotland, with such for monarch! A King whom Holy Church had put forth, as anathema. To whom no priest dare offer the sacraments. The Bruce, outcast of God and man. Today a hunted, haunted fugitive. Tomorrow . . .?

Tomorrow — what betterment could be looked for tomorrow, in the name of truth? None. No least likelihood of improvement. The reverse, indeed. For after Turnberry, every English nerve and sinew would strain to punish and revenge, Edward's fury beyond all bounds. If forty men was all the response of Scotland to the night of Turnberry and her King's return — and these the gift of a kinswoman who had ever foolishly doted upon him — what hope of the future? A fool, he had said that she gave him hope and faith. Boyd and she, then, had taken such back with them again. For there was no hope, no faintest gleam of hope, in all the grim scene, in fact. And faith was not for such as Robert Bruce.

What, then? What remained for him? He was not yet old — though he felt ages old. He was but thirty-three. He was unlikely to die yet awhile, save by violence. He could seek that violent end, and find it no doubt, with little difficulty, many aiding. But would that not almost certainly involve the end of these last few who still trusted in him, his handful of leal friends? Douglas, Hay, Campbell, Boyd. And Edward, his headstrong brother? Would he have *their* blood also on his soul? Not that. Lead them back to Arran, then? Secretly. Thence to the Isles, where they could sell their swords to Angus Og for his Irish wars. A sad descent for such as these — but it would save them from the Plantagenet. He himself go on, alone, and lose himself in the greater world, beyond. Put all behind him, and go. Go where? Was there anywhere for him in all that world? Would he not be better to end it all, quietly, in the empty sea? The king without a kingdom, the earl without an earldom, the knight without honour, the friend whose friendship spelt death.

The knight without honour? He had vowed those vows of knighthood once — madness that it was Edward Plantagenet himself who had conferred that knighthood, heard those vows! Edward! Those vows he had taken before another altar. Amongst them, to take up his sword in the cause of the true faith, against the Infidel. Not to rest while the savage Unbeliever occupied Christ's holy places. His father and grandfather before him had both fulfilled that knightly vow — Edward, even — and gone on a Crusade. Was that at least not left to him? Was that not a better way to die? A single, simple knight again, to throw himself against the Saracen, and so make an end. Might there not just possibly, conceivably, be some small, faint glimmer of credit for him there? One drop of remission in the ocean of his guilt?

Thus far the man had got, in that dark hole beneath the crags of Doon, and thereafter lapsed into a state of almost mindless depression and stupor, when, out of it, he perceived that though his wits had sunk into dull vacancy, his eyes had not. He had, in fact, been heavily watching a spider which was striving assiduously to attach its slender thread to a point on the sheer rock wall of the cave. He realised that he had watched as four times it went through the difficult and involved process, without success. Its thread hung from the cave roof some three feet above Bruce's head, and the point on the vertical wall to which the creature wished to link its web was roughly the same distance lower and two feet to the left. The spider's method was to race down its line, from the ceiling, at such speed as to generate a strong pendulum swing, in the hope that this would carry it sufficiently far to the left to reach the lateral wall. In this it was successful twice out of the four attempts; but each time the contact with the comparatively smooth surface was too brief to gain a footing. Thereafter the spider had to swing back to the perpendicular again and then scramble up its long thread once more all the way to the roof, to repeat the process.

The man's lethargic watching grew to interest and a sort of actual concern, as the fifth attempt again ended in failure, and after a momentary hold on the wall the creature was dragged back once more, again to recommence its laborious upward climbing.

The sixth effort showed intelligence as well as determination. This time the spider swung itself at a slightly different angle, to reach a spot a couple of inches to one side and fractionally higher. It looked as though this might work, possibly giving a slightly better foothold — but no, gravity was again too great, and once more thread and spider fell backwards, frustrated.

"It is of no avail," the King muttered, shaking his head. "Can you not see it? Too stark . . ."

But the animalcule would not admit defeat. Undeterred, before even its line stopped swinging it was clawing up again to the roof, to launch itself downwards with unabated resolve. And this time, when its pendulum swing brought it to the wall, it managed to hang on. Almost breathlessly the man watched it, willing the creature success.

It remained on the vertical rock, its thread pulsing gently in the smoky, flickering lamplight.

"Now, by the saints — here is a wonder!" Bruce exclaimed aloud. "A sign, if ever there was one! If this creeping mite in a hole in the earth can so set its will to conquer, can Robert Bruce, crowned King of this realm, do less? Six defeats did not deter it. Shall I despair more easily?" He stood up, stooping since he must in that place. "Here is my lesson — from heaven or from hell! I shall not give in yet awhile. Nor yet awhile to seek my death amongst the Saracens! That can wait. Yet, I do swear to God, if He will hear me this once, out of this pit, that, my battle here in Scotland won, I *will* go to His holy places, and draw sword for His name. By all that is holy! But . . . first, this my realm's freedom!"

Filled now with a sudden access of restless strength and the need for action, or at least movement, Bruce strode out past the sleeping ranks of his men in the outer cave, out into the starlit night. A half-moon was rising to the south-east, washing the crowding hillsides in wan pewter and inky shadow. With a brief word to the two watchful sentinels, the King paced away along the track they had made at the foot of the crags.

It was not long before he realised that he was being followed, at a distance. He turned.

"Who is that? I would be alone," he jerked.

"It is but Hay, Sire," the Lord of Erroll called. "In case you need aught."

"Aye, Gibbie. Do not heed me. Go back and sleep."

He moved on until he came to the burnside, where earlier he had brought the others across. And there, with the moonlight glittering quicksilver on the dancing waters, he sat himself on a boulder, to stare out into the night, unseeing. But now his mind dwelt no longer on the past, on his sorrows, even on his wife and daughter in their extremity. He counted and assessed and planned.

Galloway, partly his own Bruce sphere of influence, had stabbed him in the back, yes. Because the MacDoualls, who claimed anciently to have been princes thereof, had seen opportunity to strike a savage, grudging blow for their long lost hegemony. That might be forgiven — but not the sending of Tom and Alex, wounded and bound, to Edward of England. That must be avenged. But, more important than any vengeance, a gesture must be made to show all Galloway, all Scotland indeed, that the royal cause was still potent, not to be flouted. That the King *would* avenge his own and strike down traitors. The English could wait awhile — if they would! This was between him and his own subjects.

Galloway was a great and wide province, and ill to conquer — as even Edward Plantagenet had found to his cost. No country for a handful of men to assail. But its mountainous north was different, fierce, empty, cut off by high passes, where a few, knowledgeable and desperate, could make the land fight for them. Not far from these Carrick hills — indeed, the one ran into the other. And he knew them well.

A limited campaign in North Galloway, then. Entice his enemies therein, to ambuscade, skirmish, attrition, raiding. Wallace's warfare again. Even these sixty men in such territory could, skilfully deployed and led, engage hundreds. Where, then? The Glenkens? The Rhinns of Kells? Merrick? Glen Trool?

Bruce was going over in his mind the North Galloway geography, visualising each stretch of that far-flung, lofty terrain, and the low-lying areas which might be successfully raided from each, when he started up, suddenly alert. Above the steady noise of the water, he had heard a different sound. It had seemed like the baying of a hound.

Tense, he listened. But the sound was not repeated. Could it have been only the call of some night-bird? Or a wolf? There were still wolves in these hills, though seldom seen now. Yet it was hound that his innermost mind had said, immediately — a hound baying in the night. And so far as he knew, there would be no hound within a dozen miles, with Loch Doon Castle in ruins.

After a while Bruce sat again, and sought to return to his possible strategies and tactics. But now he was listening all the time, his mind less wholly concentrated.

It was not a hound that he heard, presently, but the bounding clatter of a stone rolling down a steep hillside. From across the burn, some way to the left he thought, nearer to the main valley.

He cursed the noise of the waterfall above and the rapids below, which drowned all but higher and intrusive sounds. Rising, he climbed higher up the bank, in an attempt to rise above the rushing, splashing interference.

Suddenly movement close at hand made him jump like a nervous horse. But it was only Gilbert Hay again, coming down the track.

"Somebody comes, Sire," the other whispered. "I heard a hound, back there, I swear. As I sat."

This was no occasion for berating Gibbie for disobeying a royal command. "I heard," Bruce nodded.

"Could it be Boyd, back already?"

"Too soon, by far. But it might be some of our friends. Returning with aid."

They waited, staring towards the shadowy wooded hillside. Presently they thought that they caught the chink of metal against stone.

"If we can hear that, they are very near . . ."

"And come mighty quietly. Secretly! Would any of ours come so? I think not . . ."

"There, Sire! Movement." Hay pointed.

The hawthorns and scrub ended perhaps thirty yards from the water's edge, across there. Now there were darker shapes, and stirring, amongst the shadows of the trees. Peer as they would, the watchers could distinguish no details.

Then something about one of the foremost figures became plain. It was the strained backward-leaning gait of a man who restrained a dog from too hurried a pace. This, and two other figures, moved out from the denser shadows into the moonlight, cautiously. Obviously many more remained behind, hidden.

"So-o-o!" Bruce breathed out. "No friends would so come. Led by a bloodhound! They must have followed Boyd's and my cousin's tracks, back here."

"Quickly, Sire — back to the cave. While we are still unseen."

"No. They have to cross this burn. And it is not easy. Here is the place to hold them. Go you back for our people, Gibbie."

"You go, Sire. Allow that I wait here . . ."

"Do as I say, man. But, Gibbie — give me your sword." Bruce, for his preoccupied moonlight walk, had come away unarmed save for the dagger which never left his hip. Hay had been more circumspect.

Reluctantly the other yielded up his blade. He slipped away.

Sword in hand the King watched. The three men and the bloodhound were crossing the open belt of dead bracken to the waterside. One of the trio was very tall and massive, armour glinting. He clearly held the third man by the shoulder — and that man kept his hands behind his back in unnatural fashion, probably tied there. He could be seen to be wearing the short philabeg of the Highlands. Some others of the newcomers have moved a little way out from the trees. Bruce could distinguish only one horse. And no helmets gleamed in the moonlight.

The watcher deduced much from what he saw — and recognised more immediate danger than he had anticipated. These were no English soldiers. Probably Galloway men, under a tall chief. And they had a captive Highlander, which meant probably that they had ambushed Boyd's little party and taken at least this one prisoner. And here was the menace of it — this man would know the secret of this ford.

At the waterside it was obvious that the captive was indeed demonstrating the route across — no doubt it was the price of the poor devil's life. The newcomers would be all across the ford long before Bruce's people could arrive. How many they might be he could not tell. But they must be delayed, if at all possible. Nowhere else was there such an advantageous place to hold up an enemy.

The King raised hand to mouth. "Ho, there!" he shouted. "Stand you! Who comes? Like robbers in the night?"

There was a startled pause. Then a voice answered. "I am Roland MacDouall of Logan. Brother to Sir Dugald MacDouall. Who challenges MacDouall in these hills?"

A wave of cold fury came over Robert Bruce at the mention of that hated name. Here was the brother of the man who had delivered up Tom and Alex to shameful death. Come seeking *him*, now!

"Robert Bruce challenges you, traitor!" he called back, voice quivering. "The King of Scots. You have come to judgement!"

Again there was a pause, no doubt of surprise — as well there might be, at that answer. The Gallovidians would not, could not, know that he was alone, of course; but they could probably see that no large party awaited them.

No words replied, at any rate. For answer the big man turned with his prisoner and hurried back to the others. There, after a few words to his followers. he mounted the horse, and with two others now gripping the Islesman prisoner, led the way down to the ford, sword drawn. A great surge of men streamed after them, on foot — more than the watcher had anticipated.

The most elementary discretion decreed that Bruce retire hastily after Hay. But he was in no mood for discretion. Long-strided, he went down the bank to the burn again.

"Come, MacDouall!" he cried. "Come pay for my brothers' blood!"

King and horseman reached the water's edge at the same moment, ten yards apart. Bruce had tossed away his plaid, to free his arms. Even in that twilight he could have looked little the monarch.

MacDouall, with the hound-leader to guide him to the exact crossing-place, rode straight in. Bruce, a little downstream because of the dog's-leg bend in the underwater rock formation, went to meet him. A yard or so short of the actual bend, he halted, the cold water swirling about his knees.

The other was no fool, and the seeming confidence of the single royal defender would give him pause. He had undoubtedly been told of the narrowness of the causeway, and the fierceness of the torrent was obvious. In swordery the mounted man should have the advantage; but if he had no room to manoeuvre and so must make a direct frontal attack, his advantage was much reduced. And no horse is at its best in rushing water.

The chieftain made a hasty reappraisal. He pulled up, switched the sword to his left hand, whipped the short lance that flew his pennon from its socket at the back of his saddle, and almost in the same swift movement hurled it at his opponent.

Bruce, the moment he saw that transfer of the sword, guessed what was coming. He both dodged and ducked, but he had little more room for any change of stance than had the horseman. He all but overbalanced, his left foot actually slipping off the rocky platform. Staggering, he remained approximately upright only by a fierce effort and the use of his sword dug down as support. The spear-like lance-tip ripped along his right arm, tearing open his doublet sleeve, its pennon actually flicking across his face. With a yell, MacDouall spurred forward.

Bruce had only moments. Though still teetering unsteadily, he twisted round and, following the other's example, grasped his sword-hilt with his left hand. The lance had plunged into the water, and the current had swung its shaft round against his right leg. Quick as thought he stooped to grab it up and, raising it high, hurled it back — although the effort nearly overturned him again.

He would have had less excuse, even so, for missing his mark than had MacDouall; for it was at the horse that he aimed, and the beast was no more than eight or ten feet from him. The lance-point took the creature in the neck, full in the soft of the gullet, and drove in deep.

With a gasping, bubbling whinny, the brute rose high on its hind legs, spouting blood, forefeet beating the air. Side-stepping away to its left, it toppled over the edge of the causeway into deep water, in thrashing ruin.

MacDouall just managed to throw himself out of the saddle in time. But because of the way his mount collapsed, his leap to clear himself from those lashing hooves brought him down just beyond the causeway, at the other, downstream, side. Desperately he clutched down at the slippery rock for a grip, in the rushing torrent, weapon relinquished.

Bruce did not hesitate in any chivalric gesture. Sword back in his right hand, he brought it down with all his force on his attacker, where neck joined trunk. MacDouall's scream choked away to swift silence as his head went under, and the dark current swept him away.

The mass of the enemy had held back at the burnside, while their mounted leader opened the attack. Now, with yells of rage, they came on, struggling with each other as to who should be first, unaware of the full hazards of the crossing, its slippery narrowness.

Quickly they became better informed, as, right and left, men fell or toppled or were pushed into deep water. There was an interval of complete chaos before the situation became clear, with Bruce, in mocking shouted invitation, urging them on.

Somebody did take charge, ordering all back, and to advance again only two at a time, shoulder to shoulder. So they came on in a long line, not a broad front, feeling their way with their brogans' toes, out towards the defiant lonely figure in midstream.

There a situation had developed calculated both to aid and to hinder them. The horse in its death throes had got itself held across the causeway, its heavy saddle presumably having caught against the upstream edge of the rock. So that there it lay stranded, mostly under water, flailing and churning the stream in foam and spray. It made it fairly obvious just where the bend in the passage lay; but on the other hand it constituted a distinct barrier for men to advance past.

Bruce did not fail to perceive this last, and moved up as close as he dared to the obstacle.

The first pair reached the other side of the animal, yelling their hate. It is possible that they might have preferred a more wary approach, but they were pressed on by those behind. The leader sought to engage the King with his sword, over the horse's body, while his colleague scrambled past. Bruce acquiesced in this long-arm sword-play — but when the climber was almost over, drew swiftly back, and turning, ran the man through with the greatest of ease, heaving his sprawling person off downstream, before returning to the sparring.

Another man quickly took the casualty's place; and now, with the horse's struggles dying away, the first swordsman and self-appointed leader pressed closer, to give the climber better support. But not good enough yet, for no man could effectively get himself over a largely submerged horse in a swift-running torrent and engage someone standing behind it with his sword at the same time. The moment when he must ease himself down, to find a foothold again on the slippery stone beneath, was vital — or fatal. Bruce let this individual get exactly so far, them stepped back, and with a back-hand slash sent him sprawling after his predecessor.

The leader could not but perceive the insufficiency of this tactic, and tried an improvement. He himself, and another, plunged forward to clamber over the carcase at the same time, whilst a third moved up close behind and above them, sword swinging. Bruce crouched low, to be under the sweep of the blade, which could not be depressed for fear of flaying the others, and from this position jabbed a vicious thrust that took the first man over in the groin. The other got further, but while still floundering for a foothold and raising his blade, the King's swiftly disengaged steel swung sideways and upwards and knocked him staggering, a buffet rather than a sword-stroke, but one which, on that precarious stance, drove its victim over the edge into deep water. As despairingly he sought to gain a grip on stone, to save himself, Bruce had ample time to aim down a shrewd lunge that finished the matter off, and then to turn and put out of his misery the screaming agonised companion.

Two more were already struggling to take the places of this pair, and getting in each other's way in the process. These were the easiest victims yet. Panting, the King jabbed and hacked down on them. They fell away without contributing the least advantage to their cause other than the tiring of the defender's arm.

That was six disposed of — seven counting MacDouall himself. Bruce began to laugh aloud, although something gaspingly.

Now, the second leader gone, the attackers suffered a period of major confusion. They could be no means flee in the face of this one swordsman, even though he might be the King of Scots; but nor could they see a way to overcome him. Moreover more and more of their people were pressing on along the narrow causeway behind, unable to see what went on, in danger of pushing the foremost off into the river. Bruce's laughter, jeers and challenges scarcely helped.

As so often is the case in such a situation, all this frustration and lack of direction boiled up in a sudden, furious and disorganised rush forward — which, in other circumstances, by sheer anger and weight of numbers, might well have succeeded in its object; but on that cramped and unsure stance only precipitated further disaster. Yelling men crowded, jostled and impeded each other, were pushed this way and that, especially from behind and still were unable to get at their quarry, whose flickering, darting steel kept them at the far side of the horseflesh barrier — save for three who fell, pierced, across the horse, two remaining caught there and actually heightening the said barrier. The third was swept away in the current.

Somebody threw a sword, javelin-like. Bruce saw it coming and eluded it with ease, for such weapons make but unwieldy missiles. But others saw this as a preferable alternative to close-range death, and projectiles began to fly, clubs and daggers as well as swords. Few were effectively aimed, for of course on such a narrow front the men ahead got in the way. But Bruce was much preoccupied in dodging the hurled objects, and more than once all but lost his footing in the process. Once indeed he was struck, but only a glancing blow that did no damage.

He perceived that this development could change all, and urgently decided to risk a ruse. As another dirk spun past his ear, he produced a high yelp, as of pain, and went down on one knee in the water, steadying himself thus with difficulty against the pull of the river, and leaning forward on his sword as though stricken.

The effect was immediate. There was a great shout of triumph, and the long narrow column surged forward again to the barrier. Bruce waited until two men were almost across it, and at their most vulnerable, and then leapt up, sword flailing. Unready for this, the pair were disposed of in four slashing strokes. He was able to run through a third, behind them, before the others flung themselves back against the pushing tide of their fellows. One tripped as he did so, probably over a leg of horse or man, and the King managed to disengage his blade and make a wild, weary hack at the floundering man which, more by luck than skill, struck him on the side of the head and knocked him off the causeway on the downstream side where it was deepest. He disappeared.

Gulping for air and dizzy from fatigue, Bruce reckoned that was fourteen slain, or at least put out of action.

His pounding heart sank as more dirks now came whirling through the air at him — for this was the greatest threat, and it was surely only a question of time until one found its mark. And then, above the angry baffled yells in front, he heard other and more distant shouting behind, higher up the hill. Gibbie seemed to have been a long time about bringing aid — though probably that was only an illusion.

The enemy heard the shouting also — and possibly even on the whole welcomed it. They were by no means poltroons, but leaderless, out-manoeuvred, and perceiving no way out of their punishing predicament, they now had the excuse to turn tail and extricate themselves from a thoroughly unprofitable engagement — which they could scarcely have done in the face of just one man. At any rate, as with one accord, those on the causeway turned the other way and began to stream back to dry land again.

Hay and the Islesmen came scrambling down the bank, crying their slogans, with the Carrick men-at-arms a little way behind. Distinctly unsteady on his legs, Bruce waded back to meet them.

"After them, Gibbie," he panted, as his friend came up. "Before they can reform. No leaders now. Keep them running and they will not stop. For long."

"How many of them, Sire?"

"About 200. Less ... less fourteen! See — there is a horse to get over ..."

Somewhat light-headed, the King sat himself down heavily on the same boulder that he had used earlier, while his men surged past. He realised that there was a long score down his right fore-arm, dripping blood, but fortunately not deep. In something of a daze he heard the noise of conflict receding, across the burn, the wild eldritch whoops of the Islesmen sounding more like a hunt than a battle. The Gallovidians would, presumably, know that there were only some sixty to oppose them — since their prisoner would have told them — but failure is a progressive business, and lack of direction notably bad for morale. None evidently any longer were preoccupied with victory.

Presently Sir Gilbert returned, with most of the Carrick men and some few prisoners.

"They flee, Your Grace — they flee," he announced. "They make no stand. You, Sire? You are well?" He perceived the blood on the bare arm. "You are wounded? Dear God — Your Grace is hurt?"

"Nothing, Gibbie. The merest scratch. Of a lance-point. Thank heaven no others had lances, but their leader. And this small blood he paid for! One MacDouall. From Galloway."

"MacDouall? Not Sir Dugald ...?"

"His brother. A start is made in the payment of treachery also."

"The saints be praised for that! And that you are yourself again. . .

"The saints — and a spider, Gibbie. A spider, I say!"

CHAPTER EIGHT

IT was not everyone who loved Sir Neil Campbell of Lochawe, a dark, unsmiling, secret man, unforthcoming, alone. But Bruce, in these last testing months, had conceived a fondness for him, an appreciation of his unflinching quiet loyalty, as well as his de-pendability and courage. After all, he of them all was making the most immediate sacrifice in remaining with this small company round the King, the only Highland chief amongst them. His ter-ritories in far Argyll were in little danger from the English in-vaders. He could go home and live in security and at ease at any time.

Bruce embraced him now, heartily, when Campbell dismounted,

despite the mere score of men he had brought back, as a result of his long absence, to this beautiful wooded basin of Glen Trool amongst the mighty glooming Galloway mountains, however mocking Edward Bruce might look, and disappointed as were the others.

"It is good to see you back safe, Neil my friend," he said. "I feared that you might have come to ill in this Galloway. No place for a friend of mine, these days!"

"No," the other agreed. "Your Grace's cause scarce flourishes amongst these traitors. You . . . you have heard the evil tidings? Of your brothers?"

"I have heard," the King returned briefly.

"I am sorry. What may a man say?"

"Nothing. It is time for doing, not saying. And we have made a start."

"Aye — so I heard. Even in Galloway your doings are spoken of. The blows you have struck against the invaders and their minions. I had little difficult in learning that you were in these mountains. But finding you was none so easy. We have been in every valley of this land, I think, seeking you!"

"We have been on the move, yes. Seldom two nights in one place. Struck swift blows, and then moved away as swiftly. But . . . these are small blows. Pin-pricks, no more. Sufficient only to show our people that their King is active. Insufficient to serve our cause effectively. We must do a deal more than this — and soon."

"You have done sufficient to bring Pembroke here. Into Galloway. That at least. You have heard?"

"Yes. We know that he had been called to Carlisle, to suffer a tongue-lashing from King Edward. And now he has come back here. Up to the Cree. That he sits astride the Cree at Minnigaff. But fifteen miles away. And sends probing companies up these valleys. But he will not adventure his strength into the mountains. And we, with only 300, dare not challenge his thousands in the plains. We had hoped that you might have been able to bring us more than these, friend." Bruce glanced over at the score or so of mounted men Campbell had led in.

"I scarce thought I could gain even such few," the other said. "These are Bruce vassals of your own. From the Urr. It is hard to convince men that Your Grace's cause can succeed."

"Aye." That came on a sort of grim sigh. His brother Edward had brought back barely 200 from the great Bruce lands of Annandale — which a year or two before had raised 5,000. Boyd, who had been ambushed by the MacDouall party that day three weeks ago, on the Doon, and only escaped, with the Lady Christian, because they were fleetly mounted had managed to return in due course with Sir Robert Fleming and another two score — that was all. And Douglas was not yet back from Lanarkshire. There was still no surge to the King's standard.

"Until we strike a resounding blow against the English power itself, our folks will not flock to us," Edward broke in. "If they will not come to us — the English — we must go to them! Not against Pembroke — he has too many. But there are others. Clifford. Botetourt. St. John Percy himself — they say that he is now at Caerlaverock. Dumfries. We must choose one of these. Select the weakest, and strike."

"Clifford has now joined up with Pembroke," Campbell informed. "Or so it is said. King Edward's bastard, de Botetourt, is at Sanquhar. St. John holds Ayr and Irvine. They encircle you . . ."

"Three hundred lightly armed can do little or nothing against thousands of armoured chivalry. In open battle," the King insisted. "Our only hope is to make the country, the land itself, fight for us. So, by some means, we must coax these English out of *their* plains into our hills. There must be a way . . ."

"They are not fools," Boyd asserted. "They will not budge from Minnigaff and the Cree. Why should they? They can wait . . ."

"Some have already budged," Campbell interrupted him. "A company of them are none so far away. We had to make shift to avoid them, on our way here. Light horse, cantoned at Low Minniwick, in the Water of Trool."

"English horse! So near?" Bruce exclaimed. "We knew nothing of this. They must be new come. How many?"

"About 200, I would say. Sent out to probe for you, I have no doubt. By Pembroke."

"Yet camped . . .? In daytime?"

"I' faith — we could have these, at least!" Edward declared.

All round there was a stir of excitement, of anticipation, now.

"You say that they are cantoned, Neil? At Low Minniwick, down Trool? Settled, at least for this night."

"Yes. We were warned of them by the miller at Bargrennan. So we took to the hills. And looked down on them from the ridge of High Minniwick. They were camped — cooking-fires, horse-lines, pickets. Two squadrons, I'd say. They did not see us."

"Then why wait?" Edward demanded. "Why wait till this to tell us, man? We should be on our way — while it is yet light. Minniwick is but five or six miles away. Here is too good a chance to miss."

"Wait you, brother," the King said quietly. "Time enough. Let us use our wits before we do our swords. I have a notion that here may be the chance we have looked for. Not just to slay 200 Englishmen. But to draw Pembroke." He turned to Campbell. "If these are new come — as they must be, for they were not there yesterday, when we rode by — then they have been sent up from the main army. Yet only eight miles, into these foothills, from Minnigaff. And already camped. They must be making this Minniwick a centre, to send out patrols. Into all the side valleys, seeking us. Not to attack us — to *find* us. Some will be up here, at Loch Trool, by tomorrow, for a wager. Tomorrow, then, we must aid the English to find us! But not just a patrol — a host!"

They all gazed at him now, tensely, there by the lovely water of lone Lock Trool, under the frown of the Merrick mountains. It was the last day of March 1307, Passion Sunday.

By dark the entire party, mounted and on foot, was on the move down Trool Water in its winding wooded glen. Four miles they went, by the riverside track, then struck off half-right, to ford the incoming Water of Minnoch, and then start to climb, over slowly rising scrub-covered slopes. It was empty foothill country here, with the valley floors narrow and tending to be waterlogged. There were no villages or even houses, other than the occasional summertime shieling for herdsmen.

The company moved fast, for in that terrain the tough and agile Highlanders could cover the ground fully as swiftly as the horsed men-at-arms, and a deal more silently. In less than two hours they were fairly high on a long gentle whaleback of ridge that ran approximately north and south, flanking the Minnoch valley on the west, which valley, an extension of the Trool, had now widened out somewhat. The woodlands had dwindled away, and only the odd hawthorn dotted the ridge. There were cattle grazing on these rolling upland grasslands, shadowy shapes, that plunged off into the gloom in brief alarm at the approach of the purposeful party. Presently, below them a little way, a dog barked its own alarm from the small farmery of High Minniwick, unseen below the crest of the ridge.

Islesmen scouts went ahead, in case the English had posted sentinels on this high ground; but no warnings came back to the main body. Campbell accompanied Bruce in the lead, and at length brought him to a sort of escarpment on the east side of the ridge, where the ground dropped away rather more steeply, in a long consistent grass slope, down to the riverside flats. The dull red glow of a number of scattered and dying fires punctured the darkness down there.

"Low Minniwick and the English encampment," Campbell said shortly. "Half a mile."

Bruce gathered his leaders round him. "This is not just Turnberry again," he told them. "There will be sentinels here. Possibly pickets patrolling round the camp. And we do not want a complete massacre, see you. Sir Neil says there may be 200. I want fifty alive, at the least. But held. So see to it that your men understand. All must be under tight rein. This will be done exactly as I say." And he looked towards his brother significantly.

Men murmured acknowledgement.

"The Islesmen will go down first. Quietly. Take up positions around the camp. Their leaders will prospect the closer approach, for our cavalry. The lie of the ground. To inform us, when we get down. The horse will move down slowly, as silent as may be. To near the camp. Only when I give the word will you charge. If there is an alarm, we will attack only when I blow my horn."

These orders were transmitted to the men. In a few minutes the Islesmen melted away into the darkness.

They gave them perhaps seven minutes' start, and then the horsed men-at-arms, dismounted, with the two Bruces and the four knights, led their beasts slowly downhill, quietly picking their way, seeking to avoid the chink of hoof on stone, the rattle of harness and the clank of arms. They were by no means entirely successful in this — but they hoped that the fitful night wind and the rush of the headlong river would blanket the noise.

No alarm rang out, at any rate. Indeed it was hard to believe that a large encampment of soldiers lay so close ahead.

Bruce was becoming anxious that they were drawing altogether too close, in view of those fires, one or two of which were to be seen as more than just embers, when two figures rose up out of the shadows in front. They were Islesmen, and reported, in whispers, that all was well. There were about a dozen sentries, but they were clustered around two fires at either end of the camp, one at the bottom, near the horse-lines; the other, that looked brightest from here, up near this top end. While the Highlanders had been waiting, two of the guard had strolled round the perimeter of the cantonment, and then back to their companions. They had not made any probes into the darkness beyond the faint firelight.

Bruce nodded. "Half of your men to the horse-lines," he directed. "Cut the tethers. As quiet as you can. As many cut before the beasts stir, as may be. Their stir will bring the guard to see what troubles them. We will hear when that happens. I will sound my horn. You will drive all the horses you can in amongst the sleeping men. The rest of the Moidartach to attack from the left. We, here, will charge mounted. How is the ground, for a charge?"

"Fair," he was told. "A burn-channel to the left, with broken banks. Avoid that. Some wet, in front — but nothing that will hold you back."

"It is well. Off with you." Bruce passed the word for his own people to mount.

They waited for what seemed too long a time, thankful only for the noise of the river to drown the chinking bits and bridles and the stamping, scuffling hooves. They heard in fact no stirring from the enemy horse-lines. But presently men could be seen to rise from the dark huddle round the farthest-away fire, and start to move away, towards where the tethered beasts must be. But they did not hurry or sound any alarm.

Then there was a sudden shout, quickly bitten off. Then more cries. Bruce's horn was at his lips at the first yell, and the wailing hooting ululation of it rang out, even as he kicked in his spurs.

In two lines, on a broad front, the 200 horsemen drove on, down-hill, straight into a canter, then a gallop — though they had scarcely time for that before they were into the enemy lines. The beat of their hooves shook the slope, and the thunder of it was pierced by the cries of "A Bruce! A Bruce!" and the high yelling of Gaelic slogans from left and right, as the Islesmen raced in, swords and dirks raised.

In the event, it was all over in a ridiculously brief period. Most of the sleepers had little opportunity to do more than stagger to their feet before the fierce tide of slashing horsemen crashed down on them, and through, their confusion increased by the stampede of their own mounts careering in panic through their lines transversely, driven by yelling Highlanders. Bruce found himself beyond the last line of sleeping men and stacked arms, reining up his rear-ing mount at the very riverside, with only one effective sword-thrust delivered.

He had intended to turn his squadron directly round and plunge straight back for a second charge; but he perceived that in the chaos of frantic riderless horses, reeling sleep-dazed men and bounding cut-throat Highlanders, any such move would be folly, as likely to ride down their own people as the bewildered enemy. Instead, he shouted for some of his horsemen to divide and make sweeps round on either side, encircling the encampment, to spread terror and prevent escapes. He and his knights, with the rest, sat their restive mounts, waiting.

They were not required. It was entirely evident, before long, that the English were wholly demoralised and overcome, that there was no organised resistance and could not be. The Islesmen were in their savage element, and presently the King was blowing loudly on his horn again, to end the carnage, and leading his colleagues in, to enforce his will.

Fresh wood heaped on the fires revealed a ghastly blood-drenched scene of ruin and confusion. It seemed scarcely credible that such havoc could have been created in so few minutes.

Creating order out of the bedlam took a deal longer. A slightly wounded but wholly unnerved youngish man, in rich but bedraggled clothing, was brought before the King by Fleming.

"Here is their commander, Sire. He calls himself Sir Alan de Scrope. Do we burden ourselves with prisoners?"

"What say you to that, Englishman?" Bruce asked, sternly. "You, who sleep so sound on Scots soil! *Your* King only takes prisoners to hang and disembowel them, does he not?"

The other answered nothing.

With a semblance of order restored, Bruce called his leaders apart. They had almost 100 prisoners, in fact, and undoubtedly others had escaped in the turmoil and darkness. But this was as planned.

"Now," he said, "we set our lure. This English knight, with most of his people, we are going to send up Glen Trool. On foot. We shall cry this aloud. Say that we shall give them trial there, tomorrow, and hang them on trees at the loch-head. Make much talk of that sort. Naming Loch Trool. But a smaller number of the prisoners, perhaps a score, we will hold here, after the others are sent off. For a time. Then allow them to escape, with their news!"

Though Edward frowned, Hay chuckled. "To Pembroke! You think it will bring him?"

"De Valence is cunning as a fox," Boyd reminded. "Will he rise to our lure?"

"He cannot do nothing. And de Scrope, see you, is a notable name. You may not know it, but Sir Geoffrey de Scrope is Chief Justice of the King's Bench, in London. This puppy will be a son or nephew. I think Pembroke must attempt a rescue. When he hears that we intend to hang him. He must so hear, therefore. We have captured good supplies and wine and ale with these English — they do not stint themselves. We shall seem to make merry on it — and grow careless of our prisoners. And our talk. Insecurely guarded, and near some of their own horses. We will allow an escape. I swear they will not be backward! They will scurry down Minnoch, to Pembroke at Minnigaff. They will have him out of his bed before daybreak, I warrant."

"And we wait for him, here?" Edward showed more interest.

"Not here. We must coax him up the glen. Round the head of

the loch. There is a place there, I have seen, most apt for ambush. Of a large force. Pembroke may not come himself, but surely a large force he must send. He must think he has the King of Scots bottled up, penned in Glen Trool. His people careless, drunken — or near so. We must coax . . ."

Smiling now, they put their heads together.

So, by dawn, Low Minniwick was deserted — save for a ravaged farm-steading and a few Englishmen tied to trees, naked, heads shaven, and with scurrilous things daubed in blood on their white skins, including the names — Valence, Clifford, Botetourt, Percy. But they were alive — and would not die of cold yet awhile. If a punitive force came this far, these would give it information — and send it after the perpetrators, hot-foot.

Bruce's small host was now much split up and dispersed. Some few were up on the high ground again, watching, to signal any English approach. Some were no great distance up the riverside track to the loch, moving slowly, trailing their wings as it were, should there be any early pursuit, decoys. Boyd, with the main body of men-at-arms, held the mass of the prisoners up near Loch Troolhead. While the King himself, with the Islesmen, climbed a steep mountainside above the far, east side of the loch, with the first of the slanting April sunlight just beginning to blind them with its early dazzle.

This east side of upper Glen Trool was very different from the west. Where the other was thickly wooded and rose in great steps and terraces towards lesser heights first, and then to high frowning Merrick itself, on this side the land rose steep, stony and bare in an almost unbroken sweep to the towering summit of Muldonach, more than 1,500 feet higher than the loch. A single thread of narrow track crossed the face of this naked braeside, rising and falling, now near the water's edge, now many scores of feet above it. This track, the only one to lead southwards on that side, Bruce and his party had left, to climb steeply upwards, panting breath-clouds in the sharp morning air.

There was one sizeable break, or shelf, on the face of that long hill, a rough terrace about half a mile long some 300 feet above the water. This was their objective.

When they reached it, breathless, it was to find it deeper than the King had anticipated from a distance, more broken. But this was immaterial. It averaged perhaps 200 yards in width, was far from consistently flat, and was pitted with heather-grown hollows and aprons of trapped water and emerald-green moss. But mainly it was bare, backed by screes, and as well as surface-water it had trapped a great variety of stones and boulders, tumbled from higher. Bruce was well satisfied. The whole hillside was stony, of course; but this trap would save them much work and time. And from the low ground they could remain hidden save on the very lip of the shelf. And the view down the valley was not to be bettered, right down to the Cree, indeed across the Wigtown peninsula itself, to Luce Bay and the Solway.

He set his Highlanders to the collection, rolling and positioning of great stones and boulders, by the hundred.

With still no sign of movement from down the valley, and assured of progress here, leaving the Islesmen at work, and a look-out to signal any approach from the south, the King went long-strided downhill again, concerned to correctly position his few cavalry. In an operation of the scale he visualised, 200 was pitifully few. And a percentage of that had to be left to guard and accompany the prisoners.

He gave the impatient Edward the command of seventy-five, and sent them off along the narrow track above the lochshore, to the farthest-away position about a mile to the south-east, where a fair-sized stream coming down the mountain had carved a deep, steep ravine, which must serve to give them cover. At all costs they must remain hidden therein until signalled, especially from across the loch. Campbell was to take another seventy-five up the right-hand of the two narrowing glens into which the main valley split at the head of the loch, to hide around the first bend. Boyd and Fleming would retain approximately fifty mounted men, with the prisoners, waiting by the shore at the start of the east track, ready to show themselves and to move off south by east. Bruce detailed the signals, for each group, stressing the need for the most exact timing. More he could not do. Taking Hay for lieutenant, he set off once again to climb the hill to his Islesmen.

So commenced the trying, testing waiting, the enforced idleness. It was well enough for the men; they were all weary with the night's exertions and lack of sleep — though most of the Islesmen continued to add to their vast supply of boulders and rocks, now marshalled for a quarter-mile along the lip of the shelf. But Bruce himself could not rest, even though look-outs were posted to give ample warning of eventualities. He sat there in the heather, staring down the long fair valley, flooded now with sunlight, while the larks shouted above him, straining tired eyes for the first hint of movement, glint of steel.

An hour he sat, fretting, and half another, a prey to fears that he had misjudged, that Pembroke was not to be lured, provoked, coaxed. That, or else he was coming in great force, and taking an unconscionable time to effect it.

It was neither movement nor the gleam of armour which brought an end to his fretting, but a thin column of smoke rising above and behind the ridge of High Minniwick, almost three miles to the south, where he had posted a picket. That meant that the English were indeed coming, and were visible from there at least.

There was no need to strain the eyes, presently. Like a dark river alongside the silvery one, but flowing the wrong way, a dense column of men began to appear from round one of the far bends of the lower valley. It could not be a broad column, because of the constriction of the terrain; but that it was long became ever more evident. On and on came the ranks, emerging into view, seeming endless, too far away as yet for details, but by the pace, all mounted. There were brief breaks in the purposeful procession, but only between divisions and cohorts. New sections followed on monotonously.

"It is an army!" Hay cried. "He has sent a host, no mere striking force. I have counted twelve already — twelve divisions. And still they come. We cannot challenge such numbers, Sire!"

The King said nothing.

At last there seemed to be an end. At a conservative estimate that column was well over a mile long. Before the tail was much past the confluence of Minnoch and Trool, the head was reaching the foot of the loch.

"Fifteen, I counted," Hay declared. "What can we do, Sire? Fifteen divisions of the best soldiers in Christiandom. And we have 300. Mosstroopers and caterans!"

"We fight on our chosen field," Bruce pointed out. "That means much. Besides, what means fifteen divisions? Are they in scores or hundreds or five-hundreds, How many abreast do they ride? They can scarce ride more than three on that ground. Three files of three, mounted, would take up a dozen yards and more. That is . . . let me count it . . . say, 1,200 to a mile, no more. None so vast a host."

It was Hay's turn to remain silent, however eloquent he looked.

Loch Trool was more than two miles long but less than a quarter of that in width. By the time that the head of the English column was half-way up the west side, Bruce, from his elevation, could distinguish considerable detail, not much more than a mile away across the water. He reckoned that they did indeed ride in threes, a goodly array in the forenoon sun, standards, banners, pennons flying, the steam of horses, and everywhere the gleam of armour.

"I cannot think that there are more than a hundred to each

division, Gibbie," he decided. "Fifteen hundred in all, perhaps . . ."

"Five times our numbers!"

"Aye — but in bad country for cavalry. The standards at their head — can you make them out? The colours? The Leopards of England fly at this side, yes — but what of the other? Beyond. Not the azure and gules of Pembroke, I think."

"It is chequered, is it not? Blue and gold?"

"The azure and, or, checky, of Clifford of Brougham! By the Rude, he has sent Clifford!" Bruce's eyes had narrowed, in more than the glare of slanting sunlight. "Clifford, of all men, I would bring low! Once I challenged Robert Clifford to personal combat. After Stirling Bridge. He refused me. I swore that one day I would repay his insults. Pray God and all His saints for me, Gibbie, that this may be the day!"

The other mumbled something indistinct.

"He is worse than Percy. A black-hearted savage! For the challenge I made him, he crucified all Annandale. Slew 2,000 of my people. Burned Annan and a score of villages. Tortured, raped, trampled. And now he rides there!"

"Sire — he is an evil man. But a notable commander. If you will not retire, at least give the signal to move!"

"I said that I would let them come level with the Maiden Isle. They are not there yet. All depends on timing, man . . ."

At length the glittering head of the colourful array reached the vicinity of the islet, two-thirds of the way up the loch. Bruce turned and waved to the first of a hidden chain of caterans.

Reaction was not long in manifesting itself. From the woodland at the head of the loch, about a mile in front of the English, Boyd's party streamed out, in flight, heading south by east for the loch-shore track, a mixed company of some fifty mounted men herding about eighty dismounted prisoners.

Even at that distance, across the water, the watchers could hear the shouts of Clifford's men as they saw their quarry. Equally evident was the sudden increase of pace, as the leaders spurred to the chase. Bruce nodded grimly.

Now they must wait again, a tenser and even more taxing waiting, while they watched the drama unfold. Timing was indeed of the essence, yet so much was unpredictable and might go wrong. It demanded an iron resolution to sit there and do nothing, to withhold the next signal until the precise moment — which might well never come.

It was all a matter of pace and distance and ground; the contrasting paces of a fast-riding pursuit and a slow-moving huddle of dismounted prisoners; of a gap between, short enough to lure on the former beyond all hesitation, yet long enough to allow the latter to be kept ahead until the next stage of the programme; and this situation affected, complicated, by the fact that, in the woods which Boyd's party had just left, was the hidden barrier of the lock's main feeder-river to be got over bridgeless, and the marshlands of the loch-head beyond, difficult for horsemen.

So that, although the English van made up on the Scots at a great rate, reaching the loch-head trees while Boyd and Fleming were still ploutering with their charges through the bogs less than half a mile ahead, it was a little longer before Clifford and his knights emerged from the trees again, into view. And meanwhile there occurred behind them a great pile-up of the long English train, and not a little confusion.

The marshland forced Clifford to a walking pace and to practically single-file progress. Even so, he was into its emerald-green uncertainty before Boyd's party was out at the other side, no more than 500 yards separating them now.

But thereafter the going improved, as the Scots and their unhappy captives gained the firm though narrow lochside track. Driving the prisoners like a flock of unwilling sheep, shouting and beating them with the flats of their swords, the Annanadale mosstroopers hurried them along, while behind them the trumpets shrilled, neighing cavalry orders.

Sir Gilbert Hay could not keep still, in his alarm and concern, biting his nails and declaring that disaster was inevitable unless there was a miracle, that the English *must* catch up far too soon for their project to work. The King should blow his horn now, and let Boyd and his men save themselves at least and leave the damned prisoners. Clifford would still pursue . . .

Bruce did not so much as glance at him.

Clifford was no fool. When he and his nearest won out of the marsh and on to the start of the track, he was little more than a quarter-mile from his quarry. But behind him only a sparse, attenuated thread of men were picking their way through the quaking water-meadows as yet, most of his host still hidden by the woods, some even still in sight beyond, held up in the queue to cross the river. The watchers could almost see him fuming there, a splendid figure in colourful heraldic surcoat over shining armour, magnificently mounted, the blue-and-gold plumes of his helmet tossing, while his numbers so slowly grew.

Bruce and Hay could see, now, that the enemy was not so stupid as to make a wholly blind and headlong advance through this obviously dangerous country. A fair-sized column had detached itself, and now emerged from the trees to the northwards following the river up to where it split into the two tributary glens — obviously to stop any flank attack from that quarter. Clifford would well know that the fifty or so herding the prisoners was not all Bruce's force. Campbell was up there in the right-hand glen. But Campbell had his instructions — and at least he had hillmen as his little force, Annandale mosstroopers, not low-country heavy cavalry.

Boyd was now almost directly below Bruce and his waiting Islesmen. A few of the prisoners had fallen by the way, jumped or been pushed down to the shore or into the water, and had been left. But the great majority were still being herded along southwards.

Clifford was displaying exemplary patience. He could see, of course, the entire empty flank of Muldonach Hill ahead of him and of his quarry, and would reckon time to be very much on his side. Slowly his following was catching up with him.

When, at length, a trumpet announced the resumption of the advance, he still did not hurry off at a canter. The narrowness of the track meant that they could not ride more than two abreast, sometimes not even that. Any rush along it would mean only a few reaching the Scots unsupported. A slow trot would serve them well enough. .

Hay, in his efforts to report exactly how far both Boyd and the enemy had got, down below, was in danger of showing himself, and was sharply rebuked by the otherwise silent monarch.

"But they are within bowshot of Boyd now," he exclaimed. "Clifford is almost directly below. Almost upon them. Another minute or so and it will be all over!"

"Not so. Clifford and his knights do not use bows and arrows! Boyd knew his task — a sound veteran. He will draw them along until the last moment. Minutes yet. Even then he will put the prisoners between him and Clifford — a hold-up on that path." Bruce had drawn himself forward in the heather, to peer over and down. "Wait you, Gibbie. How much of a commander's task is but waiting!"

No more than 200 yards now separated the tail of one party from the head of the other. Boyd was stretching it manfully. The climax could not be long delayed now; but every second counted, with more and more English committed to that hillside path.

Boyd made his move. Abandoning the captives at last, he pulled out his men, past and through them, and trotted on beyond — but even now not at top speed.

The prisoners promptly turned to face the other way. But if they expected any rapturous welcome from the rescuers, they were disappointed. Clifford's shouts to them to get off the track and out of the way could be heard right up at the high terrace.

They did not do so with any alactrity, perhaps understandably, and there was a certain amount of delay and disorder as the pursuit reached them. More men went rolling down the steep bank, amidst curses and shrill cries of protest. Then Clifford was through, his pace increased to a canter, after the fleeing Scots.

Bruce was almost counting the yards now. Boyd was nearing the ravine where Edward was hidden. He was to ride straight on, over the burn and past. But the English could hardly fail to notice the hoof-marks of Edward's company turning off. Then would be the moment of truth.

Clifford was out of sight of Bruce's position now, his long tail of men stretched across the wide skirts of the hill. How to tell the precise moment? Whether he would in fact turn in, on Edward, go on after Boyd — or take fright, and send back warning, so that full surprise would be lost?

Thinly, the noise of distant shouting came from in front.

Bruce waited no longer. Rising, he stepped back, and raised his hand, to wave. Right and left he turned, waving.

All along the lip of that hillside shelf the Islesmen sprang into furious action. Within a few seconds of the signal, scores of boulders, great and small, had been tipped over the edge of the terrace, to begin their headlong bounding descent.

The King turned to Hay, at last, and threw the Highland hunting-horn to him. "Now, Gibbie!" he cried. "Sound! Blow you, loud and long!"

High and hollow, its winding, hooting belling never to be confused with the brassy blare of trumpet or bugle, the horn's message wailed and echoed amongst the thronging hillsides, far and near. Before it died away, the screams of men and horses were ringing out from directly below.

The first rocks were smashing down upon the English line, hurtling indiscriminately but in such numbers as to be utterly, comprehensively disastrous. There could be no taking action to avoid the bounding, crushing, erratic hail of them. The horsemen were totally without protection on that naked braeface, beasts and riders flung like skittles, in utter ruin.

On and on the fusillade of grey granite continued, each stone, even the smallest, a projectile of fierce velocity by the time it had plunged down the hundreds of yards of steep slope. The enemy cavalry was spread two abreast along that narrow track for well over a mile, and within a few brief seconds, practically all its central files, for almost half a mile, were swept clean away in mangled bloody chaos, down in flailing hooves and limbs to the water.

There was no need for all the collected rocks to be launched away, in fact. Indeed, Bruce, himself all but appalled by the scene of blind havoc he had conjured up, was in two minds whether to order the downhill charge planned, to complete the immediate debacle below. It was scarcely necessary, and the Islesmen's eager broadswords could be needed elsewhere.

"Gibbie!" he yelled. "Take a few. Two score. Down there. To finish the task. Then along, to aid Boyd and Edward. You have it?"

"Aye, Sire. And you?"

"I take most. Right. Campbell has the heavy end of this. And fewest men. Though not Clifford. Give me the horn . . ."

So, desisting in the rock-rolling, the Highlanders divided into two unequal companies, both surging over the edge, to go bounding downhill, shouting their slogans, broadswords out. The lesser number went straight down, though spread along quite a wide front, to finish off the broken horror of a column which now largely littered the loch-shore; the greater went racing slantwise, right-handed, northwards, down towards where the stone fusillade had tailed off, Bruce leaping at their head, thankful indeed for action.

Down there confusion enough reigned already. Utter disaster ahead, and cut off from their main leadership, the long files of horsemen were most obviously in doubt whether to press on to the aid of their fellows, and meet possibly a similar fate, or to turn back and get off this devilish constricting track and exposed hillside. The sight of Bruce's horde of charging caterans bearing down on them seemed to convince the majority, at least. Not without difficulty and delay, the truncated column turned on itself and began to hurry back whence it had come.

But now the noise of clash ahead became evident to them. Campbell had not led his seventy-five straight down out of the eastern-most side glen, which would have brought him into the soft marsh-land, but slightly uphill to the south, over the base of a shoulder of Muldonach. Now, in extended order, they flung themselves down at the vital hinge of the enemy line, where it left the solid ground of the track-head for the quaking water-meadows. His move, of course, would have been entirely evident to the detached English flanking party sent up to stop the mouths of the two glens; but these were on the wrong side of a rushing mountain torrent, and helpless to do more than hasten down again to the ford in the woodland, half a mile below.

Campbell's charge, with all the benefits of impetus and purpose, as well as surprise, swept another sizeable section of the enemy column into irretrievable disorder. There were still many hundreds of the English array disengaged, but they were strung out over a great area and on hopeless ground for cavalry. Pockets of resistance and discipline developed, but by and large panic took its fatal grip.

The sight and sound of Bruce's yelling Islesmen clinched the matter as far as the enemy south of the marsh was concerned. None who could get away awaited their impact. Some, rather than queue to take the winding marsh-path, plunged into the loch itself; but most risked the quagmires of the water-meadows.

Many got away, of course. But large numbers did not. For those green levels were treachery indeed for horsemen. And hunting the floundering cavalry like baying hounds came the leaping Islesmen, agile and light-footed. Great was the slaughter in that bog.

Bruce left the caterans to it. Campbell's mosstroopers, on the lighter garrons of the Annandale hills, were chasing what was left of the fleeing column, by the single marsh-track. It seemed obvious that there would be no English stand this side of the river — and possibly not beyond it. The King grabbed a riderless horse, and set off back along the hillside track.

He reached the area of shambles where the stones had done their fell work, to find only dead and dying there. Hay and his men had already completed their task, and hurried on towards the ravine. Bruce spurred his heavy English charger in their slippery, blood-soaked tracks.

He had not gone far when a single horseman rode to meet him. It was Sir Robert Fleming, a sallow, thin-faced youngish man with great brown eyes almost like a woman's.

"All is by with, Your Grace," he called out, excitedly. "They are fled. When the Lord Edward came out on them, from the rear, and we turned back on them, from the front. They were caught. In no formation. They fought for a while, as best they could. But . . ."

"Clifford, man?" the King interrupted. "What of Clifford?"

"He fought his way through us, Sire. We could not hold them. There were more of them than there were of us, even so. We in front could not do more. They cut through us, and on southwards. Fleeing . . ."

"You mean Clifford has escaped? A curse on it — I have lost him!"

"What could we do, Sire? When it came to close combat, they were better armed, armoured and horsed than we. Clifford and his knights. We went down before them. We lost not a few. Boyd is wounded . . ."

"Aye. I am sorry, Sir Robert. It is but that I sought him. Wanted Clifford for myself. A . . . debt of honour. A selfish whim!"

134

"At least, the Lord Edward pursues him hot-foot. I think he will not stop until he reaches Cree."

"Perhaps. Aye, perhaps, friend. Who knows, it may be as bitter a notion for Clifford to have to live with than if I had worsted him here in Glen Trool. But . . . that man will seek vengeance. And take it, as he has done before, on innocent folk, I fear." The King shrugged. "Another time, perhaps." He straightened in the saddle. "Go you back, Sir Robert. My compliments to Boyd. You have done well. I hope he is not sore hurt. And tell Gilbert Hay to send his fleetest rider after my brother. With my royal command that he is to turn back forthwith. Not to continue the chase. It is profitless, dangerous. Back with him. And Hay to bring on all able men to the ford at the loch-head. Quickly. We may need every man, yet. You have it?"

The two men parted, each to hurry whence he had come.

But back at the ford in the wood, nearly two miles away, Bruce found no battle either. Sir Neil Campbell, mud-covered from a fall from his horse in the bog, revealed that it was all over here too. The English flanking party, on meeting the refugees of the main body fleeing across the ford, had evidently decided that only fools threw good money after bad. They had not even waited to oppose the Scots themselves taking the ford, as they might have done successfully, but set off southwards, down the west side of the loch, at speed, still a disciplined if unblooded force amongst their broken and unhappy compatriots. Campbell had a picket trailing them — but he reckoned that they had seen the last of that squadron of wise men.

The King drew a long quivering breath. "So the day is ours, Neil — all ours! I thank God — and you all — for it. We needed it, i' faith! But . . . that is today. Tomorrow — what of tomorrow? Pembroke is not yet committed, did not come himself. And he has a mighty force. Tomorrow they will be aswarm in these valleys like a wasps' nest disturbed."

"Enough for today that we have won this battle, at least," the other grunted.

"It was no battle — only a skirmish. But we shall call it a battle, yes. Make much of it — for our own purposes. So long as we do not deceive ourselves. The battle of Glen Trool, no less — the first battle we Scots have won against the English in the field since Stirling Brig! So let the word go out, that men may take heart. All over the land. But *we* know better, Neil . . ." The King reined round. "Now — to work. I want to be far from here before nightfall."

CHAPTER NINE

IT was well over a year, not indeed since his coronation, that the King had sat at ease, or at all, under a roof of his own. That he should be able to do so now, even though the roof was a small and unimportant one, was perhaps a sign, an encouragement, however modest. That it should be back within a few miles of the point where he had made his February landing on the Carrick shore of the mainland, nearly three months before, could be another satisfaction — although it could also be the reverse, depending on which way the thing was viewed. Progress, or the lack of it. At any rate, Bruce did stretch before a hearth that he could call his own, that early May evening, and was moderately thankful — that is, for so long as he carefully kept his mind on the immediate situation and did not contemplate the appalling dimensions of the task before him.

Tired, after a long day in the saddle, he sat in the little hall of the Tower of Kilkerran, house of one of his Celtic vassals, Fergus son of Fergus, amongst the green foothills of the pleasant Water of Girvan, four miles south of Maybole, capital of his own Carrick, and only eight miles inland from Turnberry. Turnberry Castle itself was still held against him, and must remain so for the foreseeable future; he had neither the siege equipment nor the time for reducing powerful fortresses. But it was *only* the great castles which were held against him in Ayrshire now. Elsewhere he and his could ride at large, a month after Glen Trool.

Pembroke had been unexpectedly inactive since that affair. Not to be wondered at, perhaps, if it was true, as rumoured, that he had been summoned once more peremptorily to Lanercost in Cumberland to give an account of himself before the angry Edward Plantagenet. Bruce admittedly would not have enjoyed being in de Valence's shoes, in that respect; but by the same token, it could be assumed that it would not be long before he was back again, greatly reinforced and spurred on to mighty endeavours against the hated Scots — he or another.

But meantime the King's cause could be said to prosper, even though not spectacularly. With the main English army still at the Cree, holding that vital hinge between the Borders and Galloway, Bruce had moved north into Ayrshire. Daily men came to join him from Carrick, Kyle and Cunninghame, not in their thousands admittedly, not great lords and barons, but lesser men — a few knights, many lairds, and common folk. More important, perhaps, even than those who actually joined him, was the climate of opinion, the acceptance, at least in these parts, that the royal cause was no longer hopeless and to be shunned at all costs. Turnberry, Loch Doon, and Glen Trool had had their effect. Scots in more than Ayrshire held their heads a little higher.

None knew better than Robert Bruce, of course, how small-scale and ephemeral was such success. But at least it was a change from failure, from disaster and near despair. Even though that very day he had heard that Sir Philip Moubray, one of the Comyn faction — the same who had unhorsed him and nearly captured him at Methven eleven months before — was heading south from Stirling with 1,000 men, to try to drive him back into the arms of the English on the Cree. Bruce's commanders were summoned here to Kilkerran for a council on this, tomorrow, when his scouts should have reports for him.

It was not one of the commanders however who presently was announced as seeking audience with the King, but a very different sort of visitor.

"Master Nicholas Balmyle, Official of St. Andrews, craves word with Your Grace," Gilbert Hay informed, at the door. "Will you see him?"

"Balmyle?" Bruce sat up. "By the Rude — yes, I will see Master Nicholas!"

The man who was ushered in was small, neat, compact, richly-dressed in clerical garb, self-possessed and still-faced. He bowed slightly, but made no move to hurry forward to kiss the royal hand.

Bruce eyed him keenly, as well he might. Here, reputedly, was one of the cleverest men in Scotland, and one not hitherto notable for wearing his heart on his sleeve. He had indeed been Chancellor of Scotland for two years, under de Soulis' Guardianship — which made him the last Chancellor, or chief minister, the realm had had, before all Scots government was swept away. The two pairs of eyes met and held — Bruce's sterner than he knew, the cleric's level, emotionless but shrewd.

"Here is surprise, Master Nicholas," the King said carefully. "It has not been my pleasure to see you, for long. Even at my coronation!" The former Chancellor, Official of St. Andrews and Canon of Dunblane, had been one of the many notable absentees from that ceremony.

"That was an occasion for the great, Highness," the other returned composedly. "Not for lowly servants of Holy Church, such as myself."

"Lowly?" the King jerked. "You?"

"Aye, Sire. Younger son of a small Fife laird. A mere canon, an official in holy orders. And my good father-in-God's humble messenger and steward."

"Ha!" Bruce's somewhat suspicious glance widened. "You mean . . .?"

"That I have brought Your Grace a letter from my master. From the Lord Bishop of St. Andrews, Primate of this realm."

"From William Lamberton! From my friend!" That was eager.

"Yes." Balmyle drew out from within his dark cloak an unaddressed folded paper, battered and crushed but still sealed closely. "This reached me only days ago. By devious means. Within another, instructing me to convey it to Your Grace forthwith. And in person."

"From England?" Bruce took the letter.

"A friar in the train of Bishop Beck of Durham brought it. Secretly. My lord Bishop is held at Barnard Castle, on the Tees."

Opening the seals, the King strode to the window, to read. But he turned, and gestured to the table. "Meats. Drink, Master Nicholas . . ."

The folded paper contained another within it, this addressed to the High and Mighty Prince, Robert King of Scots, wherever he might be found. This opened, read:

My liege lord and good dear friend.

I have learned that there is occasion that this writing may be conveyed to Scotland in secrecy. I hasten to advantage myself, and pray God that it may in due course reach Your Grace.

My hope is that it finds you in good health. I think that this must be so for the word reaches this Durham, where I am held, of the works of no ailing man, of shrewd blows struck against the invader and those of your own subjects who betray their king. That you may prosper in these efforts is my constant prayer. And that I, held close here, may not aid you in your struggle is my as constant sorrow.

It may be that I can offer some small guidance even so, confined as I am, my lord Robert. I gain certain informations here from a source that you might not look to. That source is the Prince Edward of Carnarvon, styled as of Wales. His father the King loves him not, as you will know. I find this prince a very different man from his sire. He is much here at this castle, for King Edward mislikes to have him overmuch at Lanercost, preferring his bastard Botetourt. Yet the prince must be near for councils, since in name he commands part of the English host. He speaks much with me, being a man greatly confused and in need of spiritual guidance, yet wilful and petulant. And gets little guidance from Anthony Beck who the King makes all but his keeper.

But to the nub of it, Sire. King Edward is more ill in health than is told. His son believes that he will not see another winter, for he fails fast. His hatred for you and for Scotland fails nothing nevertheless, and he is mustering another great army of invasion for the summer. But he cannot himself lead it, that is certain.

When God takes Edward Plantagenet to Himself and England has a new king, it may be that I may be of some small service to you, my friend. For he esteems me in some measure, that I know. He will be beset around by hard and strong men, his father's men, and he loves not Scotland. But he lacks his sire's resolution and on that I may be able to play. So that I pray that this my captivity may not be all loss.

Of other tidings. I learn that your lady-wife the Queen is at Burstwick Manor, in Holderness in Yorkshire, no great distance from here. If I may I shall seek to get word to her. I have heard that King Edward has reduced his shameful command that your daughter the Lady Marjory should be hung in a cage on the walls of London Tower. His own Queen is said to have besought him for the child. She is to be held in the Tower, alone, but not caged, God be praised. Ill as that is. Others are less fortunate, at Berwick and Roxburgh, it is said. But of this wickedness you may know better than I.

If this writing reaches you, it will be by the hand of Nicholas Balmyle, my Official of St. Andrews. I commend him to Your Grace as an able and reliable servant whom you may use in my place, in my absence. Through him I seek still to guide Holy Church in Scotland, in some measure. I have asked him to bring you the tokens of that Church's support. You may trust Balmyle.

And now may God Almighty guard, keep and strengthen you, and His peace rest upon you, my son. I pray for you daily, and weary for the sight of your face.

I subscribe myself your father-in-God, true friend, and most leal subject.

WILLIAMW✝Episcopo Sancti Andrea.

Written in bonds at the Castle of Bernard Baliol in the County of Durham, this 12th day of April from our Lord's birth 1307 years.

Much moved, the King stared out of the window over the fair

139

green prospect bathed in the mellow light of the setting sun, before turning back to his visitor.

"Master Balmyle," he said, "I owe you much for bringing me this letter. From one who is close to my heart. It is of great value to me. And comfort. I thank you."

The other, from sipping wine, laid down his goblet. "I rejoice Sire, if I have been the means of bringing you solace. It may be that I may have brought you even more. Of other sort."

"You say so? My friend, I have learned the folly of pride. All your comfort and solace I will esteem. I am a glutton for it!"

The other nodded. "Below, in one saddle-bag, my servant guards gold to the value of 5,000 merks. From the treasury of the Diocese of St. Andrews, for Your Grace's needs."

"Five thousand merks! Of a mercy — here is generosity! Princely generosity to a penniless prince! Solace indeed, Master Balmyle."

"My lord Bishop's instructions."

"I scarce thought so much gold remained in this Scotland! That the English had not stolen."

"Holy Church makes shift, Sire, to protect her own. So that she may cherish her own, in need."

"Aye. But I had not thought to hear the name of Robert Bruce on that roll!"

The little cleric made no change of expression. "The Church is fallible and can make mistakes. But she recognises her own sheep. Even when at times they stray. So long as they are repentant."

"What do you mean?"

"I mean, Sire, that in my other saddle-bag below is different solace. More costly than any gold. Priceless. The wafer and the wine. That can be the Sacrament of our Lord."

"What . . . what are you saying, man?" That was little more than a whisper. "The Sacrament! Holy Communion! For me? You must know that I am excommunicate. From Rome . . ."

"We believe that the Holy Father was misinformed. Ill advised. In this matter. My lord Bishop believes that if he was free to visit His Holiness, or even to send an envoy, he could have the excommunication lifted. He is convinced of your penitence for the slaying of Sir John Comyn. Therefore, he would not have the misfortune of *his* imprisonment to limit the mercy of God towards you. By his command I am to dispense the Holy Sacrament to you. If so you will. After preparation."

"The mercy of God . . .!" The King stared at him. "The mercy of God indeed! Dear Jesu — I had not looked for God's angel in the person of Nicholas Balmyle!"

The other permitted himself a small smile.

"When?" Bruce demanded. "You speak of preparation . . .?"

"Your Grace lives amongst alarums and perils. Later tonight, if you will. An hour of prayer, perhaps . . ."

His alarums and perils must have seemed altogether too apt, for the sudden sounding of a trumpet, the drumming of hooves and the shouts of men halted the cleric in his speech. Bruce moved back to the window.

A large company of mounted men, some hundreds strong, was approaching at a canter from the north, with a stirring aspect of dash and élan, well-horsed and armoured. And at their head fluttered a large silken banner, white with an azure chief on which three silver stars stood out.

"Douglas!" the King exclaimed. "Jamie Douglas!" Swinging about, he brushed past his surprised visitor, out from the hall, and went down the winding turnpike stairway three steps at a time, in scarcely regal fashion.

Douglas came clattering into the tower's little courtyard just as Bruce reached it, and drawing up his splendid charger to a slithering, caracoling halt, with sparks striking from the cobblestones, flung himself down and strode, the few paces to the King, and dropped on one knee. He reached for the royal hand.

"My liege lord Robert!" he panted. "God be praised! For the sight of you again."

The King smiled. "Sakes, Jamie — am I so fine a sight? I'd not have thought it. You, now — that is a handsome mount you have there. You have me envious, I vow! And your fine armour — gold-inlaid, no less! Whom have you been robbing, lad?"

"The armour is my dead father's. And something big for me! And the stallion was Clifford's's. Yours now, Sire."

"Clifford's? You also have been crossing swords with that miscreant?"

"Not in person, to my sorrow. Although I heard that you had, Sire. But I have dented his shield, at least! He had been given my castle of Douglas."

"Ha! And now he is the poorer, eh?"

"Yes. He will not sit in my hall again!" Douglas's rather delicate nostrils flared a little as, narrow-eyed, he looked away.

Bruce searched his young friend's face keenly. There was something different about James Douglas. He had been away only some six weeks, but he seemed older by a deal more than that. Somehow, somewhere, those boyishly good-looking features had hardened, set, matured. He held himself differently too, with an assurance and command not formerly evident, to give balance to his eagerness.

"I perceive that you have much to tell me, Jamie," he said, taking the other's arm. "Come you inside. See, we have a roof above us! A table to sit at. Even wine to drink. Not only my Lord of Douglas is fine, this day! Come — tell me this of your castle. And where you got all those stout fellows . . ."

"That I shall, Your Grace. But there is other news that you should hear first, I think. More urgent. You have heard this of Philip Moubray? The dastard who struck you at Methven field. He is now keeper of Stirling Castle, for his treachery."

"I heard. He is moving south, with a sizeable force — 1,000, they say — to drive me into Pembroke's arms. If he can!"

"He was, Sire — he was. No longer is."

Bruce paused in the ascent of the stairway.

"By this, Sire, he may well be back at Stirling — since, to my sorrow I could not win at him, slay him. But he has few of his thousand with him, that I promise you!"

"You clashed with them, Jamie? *You* did?"

"If you, with 300, could rout 3,000 at Glen Trool — then I, with the same number, was not to shy from 1,000, on my own Douglas moors?"

"Not 3,000. Half that." The other stroked his chin. "Go on."

"It was last night. We were on our way here, by the Douglas Rig pass over Cairntable, when herds of mine brought us word that Moubray had come up from Bothwell and was camped in Kennox Water, making for the Shire Stone pass over to Cummock — only a few miles east of our route. It seems that he did not know that Douglas was back in Douglasdale! I waited for full darkness, then crossed the heather of Dryrigs and Kennoxhead, and attacked him from two sides, in his valley, without warning. While still he slept. As . . . as Your Grace taught me!"

"Aye." Grimly the King inclined his head. "That is the style of us, this year of grace! And you had them?"

"We had them. Some escaped, with Moubray. But not many."

Bruce touched the younger man's arm. "God forgive me that I must teach my friends in such school as this," he said. "I, who knighted you!"

Douglas raised a laugh, if a harsh one. "I did better than that at Douglas Castle!" he said.

"You did?" The King glanced back at Gilbert Hay and Neil Campbell, who, listening, were following them up the stairs. "Perhaps you should tell us here, Jamie. I have a visitor in the hall. A priest. Is your tale one for priestly ears? I would not have this one esteem us too ill!"

"Does any whey-faced clerk's esteem concern us, in this pass?" Campbell asked.

"I think it might do, yes. This once."

So, there in the narrow, dark stairway, Douglas told them stiffly, jerkily.

"When I left you that day, I came secretly to Douglasdale, by night. To find evil. Beyond telling. King Edward had given my lands and house to Clifford. My people were ground down. Harried, slaughtered, raped. What he and his creatures had done to fair Douglasdale! I counted thirty bodies, women and bairns amongst them, hanging in one wood. *My* people."

None spoke, as he paused.

"I understood then, Sire, what you had meant. When you spoke me that night at Turnberry. I saw how much honour meant, and the knightly code! In war. I vowed vengeance. For my poor folk. And took it."

The King gazed down at his feet. "It is need, sheer necessity, and expediency, that I preach, Jamie — not vengeance," he said.

The other might not have heard him. "Despite their savagery, these English were godly men, it seemed! Of a Sunday, they filled the Kirk of Saint Bride, at Douglas, it was said. Two days after I reached Douglas it was Palm Sunday. Tom Dickson, my steward, said he would attend Mass that day. With others. If there was room for them, with all the English. I said that I was less nice, and would wait outside. The garrison marched out, from the castle — a notable sight. A few of us watched them, from hiding. In the midst of the service, Dickson and his good fellows rose, and drew their steel, hidden till then. We rushed the door from without. We . . . we let none escape. Of the English. Save only their priest."

Bruce nodded. "I had a notion that this might not suit priestly ears!"

"Dickson died there. And others," Douglas went on, flat-voiced. "We went back to the castle. They had left it but little guarded. Even the drawbridge was down. With loads of hay for their beasts, we gained entrance, none suspecting. Said the captain had commanded it. Then we turned on them. It was easy enough. They had left a feast preparing. For Palm Sunday. For all the garrison. Such of my folk as were left in Douglas were near to starvation. I summoned all to the castle. To partake, with us. Before they left. For all must go. None could remain in Douglasdale after that. I took them away, into the Lowther Hills, to distant villages and shielings. They would have had me stay, to be sure. To hold the castle. But my place is with you, Sire, I told them. Aye, and I told them that

I had rather hear the lark sing than the mouse squeak. This you had taught me also — that holding castles is not for us."

"So you left your house again, Jamie? That must have hurt sorely. Even in your father's best armour!"

"I left my house, yes. My people took all they might carry that would not delay them. Then all else we took and piled high. In the Great Hall and the Lesser Hall, in the Armoury, the kitchens, in every room. In the gatehouse and every tower and watch-chamber. In the inner and outer baileys. The English had stocked Douglas well — stolen from better men. We took it all, meat and meal, fish and fowl, fodder and bedding. Every stick and stitch of plenishing and furnishing. Every beast that the folk might not take, in their haste, we slew and piled atop — cattle, sheep, swine, even some horses. And atop of these we put the Englishmen, Clifford's captain highest, with his cook. And fired all. Oil and fat there was in plenty, to aid the flames. Douglas burned well. For three hours we could see the smoke of my house, as we led the folk eastwards into the hills. Douglas's larder, they named it!"

For long moments after he had finished, none found words.

"Am I not, Sire, your most apt pupil?" the youngest of them grated at length.

The King reached out to grip his steel-clad shoulder, and then turned to renew the ascent of those stairs.

James Douglas did not avail himself of the Holy Sacrament, after his monarch, that night.

*   *   *

Bruce sat his horse, fretting — the same fine stallion which had been Clifford's and which Douglas had insisted his liege lord must use, along with the magnificent armour from Douglas Castle. He had schooled himself to patience and waiting, in his long struggle; but hitherto it had been waiting for battle to commence, then action. But this May morning it was a greater, sorer test — to sit, inactive, watching, while battle actually raged, battle on a scale unseen in Scotland since Methven, or Falkirk.

That was the point. This was battle, not raid, skirmish, ambush and the like. And he playing general today, not swordsman, warrior, even captain. As he had planned this, his place was here, on the high ground of Loudoun Hill, watching, a spectator. Not even directing — for it was past that stage. There might be work for him, and the small body of men who sat their horses behind him and Hay, some four-score mosstroopers as fretful as himself; but not now.

It was foolish to compare this with Falkirk in especial, where

King Edward had had so many scores of thousands that he could not bring them all to bear. Here there were only some 5,000 men involved altogether — for it was but the van of Pembroke's great army that was engaged, admittedly the cream of English chivalry, but no more than 3,000 in number, it was thought. And 800 or so flanking infantry, running at either side — MacDougall of Lorn's Highlanders, sent south in haste. His own force, though the greatest he had commanded since Methven, was but 1,200 all told.

Nevertheless, this was set battle, something that Bruce had set his face against, until now. And still would have avoided. But Pembroke, galled and frustrated by pin-prick defeats and his master's wrath, had issued a public challenge. He challenged the so-called King of Scots to stand, to act the man, the soldier, the knight, not the cut-throat brigand, to meet him in fair fight, and see how puissant he was then. All over the land this challenge had been trumpeted. Bruce was fighting a battle for his people's minds, as well as this physical warfare of flesh and steel. For that long-term and more abstract advantage, he felt that he must accept this English gesture, for once at least. And had chosen this Loudoun Hill, carefully, for his battle-ground, where Pembroke must pass.

All night they had worked, busy indeed, digging, cutting, carrying, the King labouring with the others. So that now, with battle joined, he could sit there, high above it all, with the morning sun streaming at his back, playing general, the King — and hating it.

Not that the battle was quite joined yet. Pembroke, the sun in his eyes, and riding slightly uphill at that, had formed his 3,000 into two great lines, with MacDougall's Lornmen racing along on the flanks. The van, with de Valence's own banner, blue and white with red martlets, flying beside the Leopards of England in the centre, charging forward shoulder to shoulder, at an earth-shaking canter, the fastest pace such heavily-armoured cavalry could achieve, in a blaze of colour and brilliance. Behind them, a quarter-mile back, the second line followed, meantime at a quiet trot, below Percy's standard. Gloucester, with the main English infantry, should have been behind that again — but Bruce, by a series of feints and stratagems, had delayed the great body of foot coming through the hill passes, and they were still miles off.

Facing Pembroke's charging threat, below in the level grassy ground that flanked the road — the main road, by the Irvine's valley, from Ayr to the east and north — 600 Ayrshire spearmen were drawn up, waiting in three schiltroms, or boxes, their friezes of pikes projecting like hedgehogs' quills. However sure and disciplined they appeared, their inadequacy in numbers was direly apparent. Jamie's silken Douglas banner flew over the central formation. Boyd and Fleming commanded on either side of him. The rest of Bruce's people, apart from his own group standing there on the hill, were disposed in no such tidy or military formations on the two flanks. They looked something of a rabble indeed, all foot — for these flanks were no place for horses, even mosstroopers' garrons. Edward commanded on the right with 300; Campbell with 200 on the left, the cateran Islesmen amongst them. Their ragged ranks seethed and were never still — for the best of reasons. Few of them stood on ground firm enough to hold them up for more than a few seconds.

Bruce, an Ayrshire man himself, had selected this battlefield after much thought. Pembroke, from Ayr Castle, had challenged the Scots to meet him, if they dared, at or on his way to Bothwell, in Lanarkshire, where he was to hold a conference of English local governors and sheriffs — no doubt to deal with the rising loyalist tide. The vale of the River Irvine, through which his route threaded, tailed out into the side of this Loudoun Hill, and thereafter the road climbed to cross high open barren moorland for many miles. Heedfully he had chosen. The ground below him was flat for some distance, open, and covered with fine sheep-cropped turf, ideal for cavalry. And broad, fully 800 yards of it, from the western approach on either side of the road. But this pleasing stretch was set between two peat-bogs of black and green treachery and great extent, plain for all to see. What was not so plain, at least from the lower ground, the west, was that the firm ground in fact narrowed, not dramatically but steadily eastwards; so that, where the three schiltroms were sited, there was not 800 but barely 500 yards between the quaking margins. And there was still more to the site than that — blistered hands and aching backs testified to it, that morning. Stretching from side to side across it, at hundred-yard intervals, deep and wide trenches had been dug — and then covered over lightly with scrub and branches thatched with turf. At a distance of more than a few yards these were practically indiscernible.

That front line of charging knightly might was a sight both to stir and strike terror.

Its ruin and disintegration was a shocking thing to watch, even for those it menaced. At first, only the keenest and most experienced eye could have perceived that something was amiss, as the extreme ends of the long line began to be forced inwards. In a charge of heavy cavalry, already close-packed, any major constriction can swiftly lead to trouble. The fine level front began to buckle and bend. At that pace and impetus it was not easy for the tight-knit ranks to give, to find room for their colleagues being pressed in on them. As a result, many on the flanks could neither draw up nor in, and were forced to hurtle on into the soft peat-moss — with immediate disaster. And along the line generally the enforced huddling together at speed began to tell, and there was some collision, horses and riders overthrown, with others crashing over them. And steadily the firm ground narrowed.

De Valence of course did not fail to see the danger, and the remedy. His trumpets sounded and his captains waved back the flanks desperately, to turn the advance from a straight line into a wide wedge, a great spear-head. At a thundering charge this, though simple in theory, was no easy manoeuvre to accomplish, with 1,500 men involved; but these were superbly trained and disciplined cavalry, perhaps the finest in Christendom, and the difficult adjustment began to take shape, although not without losses.

It was just as this transformation was taking place that the centre of the line reached the first of the covered trenches. Perhaps Pembroke and his leaders, had they been less preoccupied with changing their formation, might have perceived the slightly artificial appearance of the ground immediately ahead, carefully as the Scots had sought to camouflage it. As it was, they crashed into the trap headlong, and into utter chaos. The ground gave way beneath the heavy chargers' hooves, and down in hurtling ruin the flower of English chivalry fell, in a storm of flailing and breaking limbs, clashing armour and the screams of men and beasts.

Those ditches were a score of feet wide and a dozen feet deep. There was no jumping them or avoiding them, and with the impetus of the advance and the weight behind, no drawing back. Had it not been for the bodies piling in and filling up the gap, thus forming bridges, few would have got across.

As it was, probably more than half the van did win over that grim obstacle, in some fashion and in dire disorder. But it was the major leadership that had taken the brunt of it, and so lay lowest. Only the lesser knights and captains found themselves left to take command. That they led the survivors in only slightly abated attack, said much for their nerve and spirit. But it was a ragged charge now.

In only a hundred yards, of course, and in inevitable impairment as a fighting force, they hit the second trench. Complete confusion reigned, and all forward movement ceased.

Throughout, MacDougall's Highlanders had been leaping and bounding, light-footed, amongst the bogs and mosses on either side, Edward's and Campbell's motley companies awaiting them. At sight of the ruin befalling their main host, they faltered somewhat.

But they were fearless fighters, and pressed on, if with less assurance. In the slaistering mire of green slime and black peat-broth, they clashed with their own fellow-countrymen in fierce hand-to-hand fighting.

"Now, Sire — now!" Gilbert Hay cried, at Bruce's side. "Down on them now, and we shall have them before their rear comes up."

"No," the King said shortly. "Our horses would be of no more avail down there than are their own. Amongst the trenches or the bogs. Wait. The others know their tasks."

It was evident that none of the van was in fact going to get as far as the third trench, and therefore the schiltroms. For now, between the ditches, Edward's and Campbell's men were breaking off their contests with the MacDougalls and streaming in amongst the milling and disorganised cavalry and dismounted riders. James Douglas was breaking up the central schiltrom and sending its 200 men off round the flanks to assist in dealing with the MacDougalls. They cast away their pikes in favour of swords and dirks as they ran. The other two formations stood unmoving meantime, like their monarch above.

Possibly that steady waiting contributed something to the battle, nevertheless. The sight of it may have been the last straw, the final influence to convince the enemy, the van at least, that the day was without profit. At any rate, the tide turned — and once turned became a flood. In only a few moments, all who could escape were surging back. Many were unable to cross the horror of that first ditch, and fell to the Scots swords there. But the majority went streaming westwards.

And because the bogs restricted them to the firm ground, the horde of fleeing men and beasts could not do other than come into headlong confusion with the still advancing second line, under the Lord Percy. Perhaps with another leader the day might yet have been saved — for this reserve host still outnumbered the Scots. But Henry Percy was a cautious man, more of a schemer and administrator than a soldier. The sight of the disaster ahead, the still unblooded Scots schiltroms beyond those ghastly trenches, and the panic effect of the fleeing men on his own ranks and consequent disorder, decided him. His trumpets sounded the retiral.

After that it was devil take the hindmost. The Lornmen on the flanks saw themselves deserted, and broke away, to escape if they might through the morass. There was only the fighting of individuals, selling their lives dearly. Flight and pursuit were the order of the day. Bruce and his four-score remained unemployed, unnecessary.

"God's mercy — a victory, Sire! A victory!" Hay exclaimed. "Of a sort!" He sounded less than elated. "And we have not struck a blow!"

The King drew a great breath. "A victory, yes. A victory, not of arms and skill and courage, but of low cunning. Another brigand's victory, Gibbie. My answer to Pembroke's challenge. But ... I thank God for it, nevertheless. One day, perhaps, we will fight these English in the field, man to man, and beat them fairly. But that day is not yet — not for long. Come — we will go down and see if we can find de Valence. At least I have wiped out the shame of Methven. When he struck *us* by night . . ."

They did not find the earl amongst the slain. Someone said that he had been seen clambering out of that first trench, known by the blue-and-white of his handsome surcoat and helmet plumes, limp in his heavy armour to find a riderless horse, and ride back and away. Some notable men were amongst the dead, and more would be deep under the bodies in that ditch. None appeared to be amongst those with whom Bruce had personal accounts to settle. A report did spoil the muted triumph of the victory — the fact that more than one had seen his own nephew, Sir Thomas Randolph, his mother's grandson by her first husband, prominent in the English van, easily identified by his great height, as well as his arms and colours. He had been taken prisoner at Methven, and ransomed, one of the very few spared by King Edward. Now it was to be seen why.

Bruce gave orders to stop all pursuit of the fleeing enemy. The Earl of Gloucester, with the main body of English infantry from Galloway, was not far away. They were not finished yet. If these could be kept from joining Percy . . .

The hunting-horn sounded the recall, and reassembly.

Edward Bruce was, as ever, one of the last in. "We have them running!" he cried. "Running like whipped curs! Now they know who is master in Scotland!"

"Master, brother?" the King asked. "I am not yet master of this my own Ayrshire! And Ayrshire is but one county of Scotland. We have met the English in one field, and prevailed. By our wits. That is all. And Edward Plantagenet sits at Carlisle and musters his hundreds of thousands. Let us never forget that man — for he will not forget us!"

"He is dying . . ."

"I should still fear Edward, even were he dead! Such hatred will survive even the grave, I do believe . . ."

CHAPTER TEN

ALMOST against his better judgement Bruce was besieging the town and castle of Ayr — after a fashion. It was rather ridiculous in fact, with the numbers of properly armed and disciplined men he had at his disposal, and with no sort of siege equipment. But both the English themselves and his own subjects seemed to expect it, and he was in something of a quandary as to what to do next, anyway. So he made pretence of encircling Ayr — and was ready to be up and away at short notice.

After Loudoun Hill he had managed to trap his cousin's husband Ralph de Monthermer, Earl of Gloucester, and the mass of English infantry — the same who had timeously sent him the spurs and the shilling that night in London a year and more before, and so undoubtedly saved his life from Comyn's betrayal and Edward's vengeance. There, in the hills behind Cumnock, there had been a great slaughter, by night, when the English and Welsh archers could not see to draw on their foes. The darkness had aided escape also, of course, and Gloucester himself, with large numbers of his force, had fled here to Ayr, to join Percy therein. Pembroke had apparently fled from Loudoun Hill in the other direction, for Bothwell. But Clifford, somewhat in disgrace no doubt, had been bringing up the English rear and baggage, from Minnigaff and the Cree, and getting word of Gloucester's disaster, had avoided all engagement and likewise made hurriedly for Ayr. So that there was now a large if somewhat demoralised force in the town, many thousands strong, including two of Bruce's chiefest foes.

But there was more than these in Ayr. There were some thousands of townsfolk, as well as men thronging there from all Carrick, Kyle and Cunninghame. Their King's victories, small as they were, at last were beginning to rouse the people, to give them hope, to stir up young men to join their liege lord in arms. The hostility of these, with the citizenry, undoubtedly preoccupied the invaders, and added to the siege-like atmosphere.

Indeed daily the numbers of Bruce's force increased hearteningly. Few great men as yet committed themselves — although with so many of these dead, prisoners or in exile, this was scarcely to be wondered at; while many had always been in the Comyn camp. But the sons of this laird or that, with a dozen or a score of men, variously armed, came riding in every day, as well as great crowds of masterless common folk. Feeding, marshalling and controlling these was an ever-growing problem, and took up much of the time of Bruce and his little band of lieutenants. That this could better be achieved in the fertile and populous lowlands surrounding Ayr, than in the wilderness where he would have preferred to be, was another reason why the King lingered, though warily, in his sham siege — while he kept his rear free for quick retiral into the hills.

He had taken up his residence, meantime, in his cousin Christian of Carrick's house of Newton-upon-Ayr, Turnberry still being held strongly against him, and was able to live in more comfort than he had known for long. It was pleasant, of an evening, to dine well here, and to contemplate Clifford and Percy, only a mile or two away, tightening their belts — for food was known to be getting very scarce in Ayr's citadel these June days — although undoubtedly those two would be the last to starve.

It was in such frame of mind that Bruce and his companions, after a long day trying to lick into shape the heterogeneous collection of volunteers, lounged in the Lady Christian's apple-orchard, when the look-out from the tower's parapet shouted that ships were appearing from around the Heads of Ayr, to the south, many ships. Cursing, all lethargy banished in an instant, the King was up and running for the tower-door. This had been one of his fears — that King Edward might send up relief and reinforcements by sea to his beleaguered minions at Ayr. His bastard, Sir John de Botetourt, it was said, had developed a taste for seafaring, these days, and had earlier been savaging the Clyde ports and havens in a campaign of sheer piracy and plunder — a truer son of his father than was Edward, Prince of Wales.

When Bruce reached the high parapet, however, with the watch shouting that it was a great fleet, it was to know something of relief, at any rate.

"Those are galleys, man!" he cried. "Highland galleys — not English ships."

The watch, who had not said that they were English, wisely held his peace.

The King's relief was only partial. There were fully twenty large galleys out there, their hundreds of oars flashing with rhythmic motion as they caught the light of the sinking sun. Whose they were was not apparent. Not many Highland chiefs could muster such a fleet — but two who could were MacDougall of Lorn and the Earl of Ross.

Then, as the leading vessels turned directly into the bay, and their great square sails bellied to the westerly breeze, the vivid emblem of the Black Galley of the Isles stood out clear on each, undifferenced, unmistakable.

"Angus Og!" Bruce exclaimed. "Thank God it is he! Whatever may bring him here. Jamie! Neil! Down to the boat-strand with you. To wave them in. In case they make for the harbour. Take my banner." The English still held Ayr's harbour, dominated by the castle. "If it is Angus Og himself, pay him all respect. And bid him here, to me."

So presently, heralded by the shrill music of strutting, blowing pipers, a colourful company came up the north side of the River Ayr, across the water from the town proper, kenspeckle in saffrons and tartans, horned helmets and eagles' feathers, piebald calfskins and gleaming Celtic jewellery. Bruce awaited them before his cousin's gatehouse.

Angus Og, in full war panoply, and flanked by an almost over-whelming phalanx of chieftains in barbaric splendour, stalked in front — and he at least was smiling.

As they came up, James Douglas at his side, raised hand and voice. "Sire — here is the noble Angus Og MacDonald, Lord of the Isles . . ."

His words were drowned in the blast of a horn, and a much more powerful voice followed it, to shout "Angus, son of Angus son of Ranald, son of Somerled the Great, of Islay, King of the Isles and Lord of Kintyre. To Robert, King of Scots, greeting!"

Bruce swallowed. So they were back to that, again! But he smiled also — and when Robert Bruce smiled, the stern graven lines, in which his features had set these days, were transformed quite. He stepped forward, hands out.

"My lord and good friend Angus!" he said. "I rejoice to see you."

The other came to meet him, and they gripped hands and clasped shoulders, as equals and comrades-in-arms rather than as monarch and subject.

"I salute you, King Robert," he returned. "Here is a day to remember. Seannachies will sing of it."

"You say so?" Bruce blinked. "Then I am glad. You have brought news?"

"I have brought myself, and mine." That was simply said. "News enough, I would think."

"M'mm. Yes. To be sure. And you are welcome, my lord. All of you."

Angus Og did not actually frown, but his open boyish though swarthy face stiffened. "I am glad that I am welcome, sir. I had not expected otherwise, with one thousand broadswords!"

"I' faith — you mean . . .?"

"I mean, Sir Robert, that I am come to make cause with you. Against our enemies. With a score of galleys, two score chieftains and a thousand men. Straight from Ireland I have come."

"By the Rude — do I hear aright?" The King did not attempt to hide his surprise. "You have come to fight? Angus of the Isles joins my host . . .?"

"He comes to *aid* your host, shall we say?"

The other was not concerned to split hairs over the definition, there and then. He gripped the Highlander's arm. "Here is a great, notable day indeed. You have changed your mind, my friend, since that day at Rathlin Island?"

"You have changed it for me, Sir King. At Rathlin, I said that I would war with Edward of England for my own hand and in my own time. *Your* cause was scarcely hopeful. You have made it otherwise, these last months. The Glens of Antrim are not so far away that I have not heard of your doings. I have come to make your war mine. I have matters to settle with the English and their friends, over that sorry business at Stranraer. When your brothers were defeated. Many of the men slain then were mine, hired to you. Murdered, after the battle. And my friend, Malcolm Mac-Quillan, Prince of Antrim, beheaded. We can settle these scores together, you and I."

"So-o-o! Here then is the most sure sign of belief in my final victory, I swear! Of any I have received. That Angus Og should deem it prudent, worth his while to support me!"

If the Islesman sensed criticism in that, he did not say so. "Even so, it could be that I erred. Deemed wrongly," he said. "You are going to need my support sooner than I thought. As we came up the firth we spied and ran down an English craft, making for Wigtown Bay and the Cree. It bore couriers. Edward the King marches. Edward is on his way."

"What!"

"We took his messengers. With orders for Pembroke, Botetourt and the rest. Edward has risen from his sick-bed. He has given his travelling-litter to the cathedral at Carlisle, as a thank-offering for recovery, and mounted his war-horse again. He leads a host of 200,000, for the Border. To wipe Robert Bruce off the face of this Scotland!"

Stricken to silence, the King looked at him.

"I near thought again, as to joining you, then," Angus Og added, grimly. "But here I am."

"He is on his way? Now? He could be in Scotland by this?"

"Scarce so fast. It was at noon today we took his vessel. It had sailed from the port of Silloth only at first light. Edward was then making for the fords of Solway."

"Then we have a little time. To get away from Ayr. Into the high hills. It is back to the mountains with us. But tomorrow's dawn will serve. I will give orders for all to be ready to move with daylight. To a place where Edward cannot reach us. God's curse on the man — his spleen is as good as life to him! Will I never be free from his malice?"

The other shrugged. "He will die one day."

"His body, yes. But will his hate? Such all-consuming bitterness ...?" Bruce drew himself up. "But, my sorrow that I should hold you standing here, my lord. You and yours. Come — this is my cousin's house. But she keeps a good table. Tonight we can still take our ease. And tomorrow, march. What will you do with your galleys, friend?"

"Send them across to the Isle of Bute. To the old Steward, at Rothesay. They can await my summons there ..."

*   *   *

It was two weeks later, in the lofty lonely hills around Loch Doon again, on the Galloway border, before Bruce gained sure news of Edward, news that he could trust. Every spy and scout reported tales and rumours, not only his own but his various commanders' scouts — for the Scots host was now split up, inevitably, since none of these high narrow valleys could contain and support large numbers, and the royal force now totalled nearly 4,000. The tales said that King Edward was here, or there, making for the East March, or Edinburgh, or Galloway, or even returned to Carlisle. Pembroke, it was known, had come back to Ayr, with a Comyn army plus more MacDougalls; while Botetourt was lying off the coast, with shipping.

It was, as so often was the case, a friar who brought firm tidings — for, because of their cloth, these could move about the country more freely than other men, and their Orders were international. This one, a Benedictine, came to Bruce in his cave above Loch Doon — the same in which he had watched and taken heart from the spider — where he and Angus Og, Neil Campbell and one or two others who were not off with detached commands, sat round a crackling log fire and grilled venison steaks on spikes. He announced that he came from the Abbey of Melrose, across the Forest of Ettrick, sent by Master Nicholas Balmyle.

"The King of England is dead, Sire," he declared. "Edward is no more!"

Bruce laid down his steak carefully, features schooled, expressionless, and slowly rose to his feet. All around him men held their breaths. "Say that again, Master Friar," he got out, thickly. "And speak truth, if you value your soul!"

"It is verily so, Your Grace. Master Nicholas had the word direct from Carlisle. Sent by a canon there, who is kin to him. King Edward the First is dead. And his son proclaimed King Edward the Second."

Bruce's face worked strangely. Then abruptly he turned and stalked away, out of the cave-mouth. A babble of excited talk rose behind him.

It was a minute or two before he returned. "Your pardon, Sir Friar," he said. "Your news affected me. Have they offered you meat, drink, after your journey? Sit at ease, while you tell me all that you know."

"He died, Sire, at Burgh-on-Sands, but eight miles north of Carlisle. Still on English soil, making for the fords across the Solway sands, with his mighty host. He breathed his last, they say, facing Scotland. And cursing it."

Silent, the King nodded.

"His bile was stronger than his body," Angus Og said. "His black heart could not carry the weight of him, in armour and a-horse, after his sickness. He had too much blood, all men knew!"

"Yes, lord. But, as we were told, it was the news of Loudoun Hill, of King Robert's victory, that struck him down, rather than the journeying. He was stricken with an apoplexy."

A sort of choking groan came from Bruce. "So . . . so I killed Edward! In the end, I killed him."

None remarked on that.

"He recovered his wits before the end," the friar went on, eyeing the King doubtfully. "The Prince of Wales was summoned to his side. As was the Bishop of Carlisle — who told it to this canon. King Edward charged his son straitly. He caused him to swear an oath, to God and all His saints, in the presence of his lords and barons. That he would continue the fight to the death against the Scots. That he should not rest until he had brought down Robert Bruce to the dust, to die a felon's death. As had his brothers and the man Wallace."

Only the crackle and hiss of the fire made comment.

The speaker, a dark, youngish man, moistened his lips, his glance darting around uneasily. But he forced himself to go on.

"Further, the King required the Prince to promise that so soon as the breath was departed from his body, he would take that body and boil it in a great cauldron. Boil it until the flesh was separate quite from the bones. The flesh could be buried, where mattered not. But not the bones. These his son was to carry with him against Scotland, then and thereafter. To remain with him, night and day. And as so often as the Scots might in insolence rise in rebellion against England, he should assemble his fullest strength, and carry the bones against them. Not to be buried or laid to rest until that contumacious nation was totally subdued." The friar swallowed. "Only then did Edward Plantagenet yield up the ghost."

A long quivering sigh escaped from Robert Bruce's lips. It was many seconds before he spoke, none venturing to precede him. "Edward!" he said, almost whispering. "Edward — who once loved me as a son, he said! God pity him. God pity me, also! His mercy on that tortured soul — as on my own. I see it all. The knife turned in his heart. Satan laid his dark hands on each of us! Damnation — before the Day of Judgement!"

"Do not say it, Sire." That was Neil Campbell, harshly. "Edward is dead. The manner of his going matters nothing. We should be rejoicing, not glooming dark thoughts."

"He is right," Angus Og agreed. "No profit in such. Your chiefest enemy is no more. Thank God for it, and be done!"

Bruce eyed them, almost as though they had been strangers. "Little you know," he said. Then he shrugged. "Very well, my friends. Edward is dead. But Edward's might and his armies remain, his commands and his commanders. And his son. What of Edward the Second?"

"The word from Carlisle, Sire, is that the new King has a mind of his own. He has not obeyed his father over the boiling and the bones, oath or none. He is sending the old King's body back to Westminster for due and decent burial."

"Ha — he is? So that is the style of him! I' faith — he has long lacked love for his father. But never dared to show it, until now!"

"He has summoned all his barons and lords spiritual and temporal to come pay him fealty, at Carlisle, forthwith. Already he has made new appointments..."

"Aye, no doubt. But what of Scotland? What does he say of Scotland?"

"He has likewise summoned all Scots lords and landed men to come and do him homage. At Dumfries. Before this month is out. On pain of forfeiture."

"So! In this at least he is his father's son! What of his army?"

"Some of it he has already sent across Solway, it is said. They are marshalled on Your Grace's lands of Annon."

"Aye! They would be! The war, then, goes on, Edward living or Edward dead! To be sure, the son would have little choice in that.

All England is set to bring down Scotland. His lords will force him to go on with it, even should he lack the will."

"As to will or no, already he has appointed a new commander and Viceroy. In place of the Earl of Pembroke. The Lord John of Brittany, Earl of Richmond, his own cousin."

"You say so? John of Brittany again — that sour pedant! Aye, they were ever friends. So Pembroke is disgraced?"

"You have hit him hard, Sire," Campbell put in. "Caused him many defeats. Made him look a fool."

"Yet he is no fool. And a better soldier than ever John of Brittany will be — who indeed is no soldier at all. Which we must seek to turn to our advantage. All this will require much thought. Have you any other news for us, Master Friar?"

"Master Balmyle said to tell Your Grace that the King, the new King, has already put the Prince Bishop of Durham, Anthony Beck, from his Court. And is very close with John Stratford Bishop of Winchester — who is an old friend of the Bishop of St Andrews."

"Good! Good — that may bring some easement to my friend Lamberton. You will thank Master Balmyle for all these tidings. I shall not forget his good offices. He will have heard that the old Bishop of Dunblane has died. Tell him it will be my endeavour to see that he is elected in his place. And you also, my friend, I shall not forget. You have earned my gratitude. Your name . . .?"

"Bernard, Sire. Bernard de Linton. From Mordington, in the Merse."

"Then I thank you, Brother Bernard. One day I shall need able and trustworthy clerks . . ."

The friar withdrew, Angus Og spoke. "Fair tidings in the main, Sir King. What do you do now?"

"Nothing, friend. We wait. For Edward of Carnarvon. To see what *he* will do. He has still 200,000 men in arms. Not fifty miles away. To our 4,000. Besides many nearer still. In that respect little has changed. The English are still the English. Only now they are led by a weak man, not a strong."

"It may be so. But I did not come here to wait, to sit idly in these hills," the Lord of the Isles pointed out. "My broadswords like nothing less than rusting in their sheaths! My galleys are not for gathering barnacles in creeks of Bute. I came to fight. And I have debts to pay."

"You shall have your fighting, my lord, never fear! Your belly-ful! But not yet. I do not wish to force the new Edward's hand. He is no warrior — but he commands many of the finest warriors in Christendom. We shall await to see what he does with them. He is concerned now with homage-taking, not fighting, it seems. Let him have it, then. That will do us no hurt. And we shall see how many Scots lords hurry to kiss his hand at Dumfries. That will interest me, see you!"

"If few do, Sire — then he must needs march north," Campbell declared. "He cannot sit idle, after summoning them on pain of treason and forfeiture."

Bruce nodded. "That is as I see it. We will wait till then. Meantime gathering our strength . . ."

"In my country, one does not gather strength by waiting but by smiting!" the Islesman asserted strongly. "*I* do not wait patiently, to pay my debts."

"These debts, my lord . . .?"

"In Galloway. The MacDoualls. Five hundred of my men died shamefully at their hands. Time they were avenged."

This was obviously a large part of Angus Og's reason for aligning himself with them. "Aye. But I too have debts to pay in Galloway. Two brothers sent to Edward, to die! Think you I have forgotten, man? But I choose *my* time when to pay my debts. See you, Angus my friend, if we go raiding into Galloway now, not only do we provoke the English into action, but we cut ourselves off from the rest of Scotland. They could box us up in Galloway."

"My galleys could lift us out, by sea."

"Not 4,000 and more. When I punish Galloway, I shall do it in force. So that the MacDoualls will not forget. It will be no hurried raid. But . . . I will make you a promise. Hold your hand until the English show what they will do. And then, if we can be free of them for a space, I will come with you to Galloway. I want your thousand men close to my hand."

Angus Og shrugged.

PART TWO

CHAPTER ELEVEN

ROBERT BRUCE lay on his back and gazed up at the cobweb-hung rafters of the roof. It was a poor way to pass Yuletide, and a poor place — even though, in a fashion, the house was his own. Did that make it easier? He was long past caring greatly where he laid his head, or how lowly his couch — but this Mill of Urie was cold, draughty and moreover bug-infested. He was all too well aware of all three imperfections.

He lay still, however, motionless — apart from the frequent uncontrollable shivering, that is — not even allowing himself to scratch at the bug-bites. Though these were a minor irritation, compared with the other sores and grievous itching. He forced himself to forbear, not so much because the friar had advised it — he was not the man to set store by the instructions of any mumbling physician, however holy — but partly as a discipline for himself, and partly because he found that the least movement, the rubbing of the plaids that covered him, on his sores set them itching beyond all bearing. There were so many of them, his entire skin a red and angry patchwork, dry and flaking.

It required no little effort to hold himself still, not only on account of the itch and the cold, but because of the febrile restlessness that possessed every muscle of his body, urging him to toss and twist and jerk; but he did not cease to tell himself that if he could master his unruly spirit and errant emotions, and hoped to master a kingdom, then he could surely hold his body still. So he lay, as he had lain for seemingly endless days and nights.

No doubt he had been foolish. The sickness had first struck him some weeks before, when he had first reached Aberdeenshire. All of course, including the plaguey old monk, with the undoubtedly wholly unjustified local reputation for healing powers and piety both, that Gibbie had found for him, had urged him to take to his bed there and then. But he had not come all this way into the North to lie in bed and shiver. He had come to show the Comyns, and their allies, who was King in Scotland, up here in their own territory. So he had refused to halt in his Comyn-devastated lordship of the Garioch, to become an invalid, insisting on pressing on, up towards Buchan, to get to grips with John Comyn, Earl thereof, who still called himself High Constable of Scotland, and still was prepared to accept Edward of Carnarvon as Lord Paramount of Scotland rather than recognise Bruce as King — even with his own young wife hanging in a cage on the walls of Berwick Castle. Fevers and foolish weaknesses of the body could and must give place to the imperatives of rule and war. For over two weeks, then, in winter Aberdeenshire, in the great rolling lands of Mar, Cromar, Midmar and Formartin, he had hunted and harried the Comyns, in their enormous outlying domains, latterly carried in a litter. He had done great damage, burned many houses, hanged many men, but fought no battles — for Buchan himself lay infuriatingly low, allegedly in his great and remote castle of Dundarg on the far North Buchan coast, assembling his strength. At length, with no decision achieved, and his own weakness ever growing, shamefully, inexorably, until he was too limp to make more than feeble protest, his brother Edward ever taking more the command, they had brought him back here in his litter to this wretched Mill of Urie beside the burned-out ravaged shell of his castle of Inverurie, messuage-place of the once-great lordship of Garioch, how many days ago he could not tell.

A knock at the rough plank door brought a frown to the man's already set features, but only that. A second knock, and a third, went equally unanswered. He wanted no company, no chattering, fussing, pitying attentions, no gawping witnesses of his helplessness, however sympathetic. But the door opened nevertheless, and Gilbert Hay came in. And for as long as it was possible for that loyal uncomplicated young man to look apologetic, he did.

"Your Grace — the monk is here. Brother Mark," he said. "To attend you. Anoint you and salve your sores . . ."

"No!" the King said.

"But it is time, Sire. Past time, he says. Four times each day, the friar says, it is necessary . . ."

"No!" That was a bark, the voice strong if nothing else was. "Begone!"

Hay retired.

Bruce lay, muttering. It was hard enough to lie still, to master every itching, agonising, shuddering inch of him, without having to put up with fools and hypocrites.

He tried, for the thousandth time, to concentrate his mind on the military situation and its threats. He was direly short of men again, having had to leave James Douglas and fully two-thirds of his total force, to hold the South-West and watch the Border. It had been taking an enormous risk to dare this northern expedition at all, of course — but the Comyn threat had to be met before any progress could be made in Scotland. After spending weeks at Carlisle and Dumfries, holding fealty ceremonies and a parliament, the new King Edward had, in September, made a purely token advance into Scotland, with most of his vast host, perhaps 150,000 men. It had been a triumphant procession rather than any campaign for, since opposition would have been pointless, Bruce had made none, remaining deep in the Loch Doon mountains and restraining his brother Edward and Angus Og both, with difficulty. Moving only a few miles a day, the English had taken weeks even to reach Cumnock in Ayrshire. And there King Edward had halted, held court, made sundry proclamations to the effect that he was satisfied that his realm of Scotland was securely in his peace, knew its master and would hereafter be more kindly governed; and then turned his army round to face the south again, and deserting it, with most of his high nobles, hurried off ahead to far-away London for his coronation, leaving John of Brittany to rule Scotland. In these circumstances, after a brief punitive expedition into Galloway, to fulfil his promise to Angus Og — though it had scarcely satisfied that warrior — Bruce had turned to the North, to show his face and flag to more of his waiting, watching kingdom.

But he had gathered fewer troops on the way than he had hoped for. The English grip on the centre of the land was strong, with all the great fortresses in their control, with large garrisons at Edinburgh, Glasgow, Stirling, Dunfermline and Dundee. It was no part of the King's present intention to fight his way northwards county by county, and he and his small mixed force had had to go by devious ways, holding to the high ground, the marshes and empty areas and avoiding centres of population. This had produced very disappointing recruiting, and with a wet summer, very late harvest and winter approaching, the countrymen had shown little enthusiasm for military adventuring. The Lord of the Isles, disgusted, had been sent off on a parallel northerly course up the West Highland side of the land, to prevent any link-up between the forces of Buchan and MacDougall of Lorn, if possible. So, with only small contingents of men joining him in Perthshire and Angus, Bruce had come across Dee, to the Garioch and the start of the true Comyn country, with no more than 700 men — to find his lordship devastated and almost devoid of the manpower he had hoped to raise there. Few English were up here, but many Comyn bands. Fortunately, here Sir Alexander Fraser of Touch, and his brother had joined the royal array with 300 men; but even so it was a tiny force with which to face the Comyn country. But David, Bishop of Moray, had come south from the Black Isle of Ross to his own diocese of Moray, with a force of Orkneymen. It had been to link up with him that Bruce had pushed on and on, northwards, ill as he was. With Buchan himself keeping his distance at this stage, and Angus Og still not come over from the difficult mountainous terrain he had to traverse in the West, it had been only tip-and-run warfare hitherto, infuriatingly small-scale, time-wasting, with Edward Bruce making most of the running.

Of Bruce's band of close companions, only Gilbert Hay remained here with him at Inverurie, captaining a mere 200 men. Edward, fretting with impatience, had gone with the Frasers to show the King's banner in the coastal areas of Formartin, north of Aberdeen, as much to try to coax Buchan out of his strongholds as anything else. Neil Campbell had left them weeks ago, at Perth, with Angus Og, to slip home to Argyll, to see what the MacDougalls might have done to his patrimony there, and to try to return with a force of Campbells — although he was scarcely hopeful in this, for a Highland chief who deserted his clan territories for a long period, as he had done, could seldom count on much loyal support. Boyd was away recruiting in West Garioch, and Robert Fleming sent ahead northwards to make contact with Bishop David.

How to deal with Buchan himself, of course, was the problem which most agitated Bruce's fevered and at present ineffective mind. John Comyn, Earl of Buchan, in his person, his position and his influence represented the major Scottish threat to the King. That other John Comyn, Lord of Badenoch, had left a young son, and his kinsman, the High Constable, had assumed guardianship, and with it leadership of the greatest family in the land, a family which could field thirty knights and some 10,000 men, without calling on all the many and powerful allies and connections, such as MacDougalls of Lorn, the Earl of Ross and all the many Baliol branches. He had co-operated with the English, even while hating Edward Longshanks who had so shamefully humiliated him at Stracathro years before; how much more so might he be expected to aid Edward of Carnarvon, of whom he was said to approve?

The King had made little headway in his bed-bound strategy, when there was a further knocking at the door. Once more Gilbert Hay stood there.

"Sire," he said, "visitors."

"No."

"But these Your Grace will wish to see. I swear it."

"Be off, man! Think you I do not know my own mind?"

Hay was pushed aside, and Neil Campbell entered the cold and shabby room.

"Lord, Sire — here's a sorry business! I never thought to see you abed at this hour."

The King eyed him sourly, and offered no welcome.

"This sickness — how bad is it? Your stomach is it?" the other demanded. "Nothing that a flagon of *uisge-beatha* will not cure, I vow! Our good Highland spirits. Drive out these vapours, and make you a man again in short time. I have brought many flagons."

"Fool!" Bruce snarled. "Spare me your witless chatter, if that's the style of it! I hope you have brought me more than liquor from Argyll, since you are come? How many men?"

"Four hundred. The most I could raise, in the time. More will follow. MacDougall has borne sorely on my lands, curse him! But I have brought you more than men and *uisge-beatha*, Sire, From the West . . ."

The invalid was no longer listening to him, nor even looking at him. He was gazing past the man's shoulder. Christina MacRuarie stood there, behind, smiling at him.

All his resolutions about non-movement and bodily control were forgotten, as he raised himself on an elbow, to stare.

"Christina!" he panted. "You! How come you here?"

"With Sir Neil, as he says, my lord Robert. Grieving to see you so. I was in Lochaber, where I have lands, when I heard that Sir Neil was back on Lochaweside. I hastened there to gain news of Your Grace, learned that he was returning to your side, and prevailed on him to bring me with him."

Bruce bit his lip. "This is no place for a woman," he muttered.

She looked around her, mouth turning down. "Nor for a man! Any man, least of all a King! More meet for cattle." She came forward to the bedside. "You are not displeased to see me, Robert?"

He gave a jerk to his head, a gesture which might have been variously interpreted, but did not speak.

"I am sorry indeed to find you in this state," the woman went on. "As well that I came, I think. It looks as though I am needed here!"

"I will be well enough. Shortly."

'That we must ensure. But lying in this cold kennel will not help." Christina turned to Hay. "Is this the best you can do for him, Sir Gilbert?"

"He . . . His Grace would have it so," that unfortunate asserted. "The castle is but a burned shell. The steward's house likewise. This mill is the only roofed house left in Inverurie . . ."

"The more reason for making better of it, sir. Not so much as a fire . . . !"

"Let him be," Bruce intervened. "*I* chose this place."

"Then you must have lost your wits as well as your health!" she returned spiritedly. "Any hovel of a cot-house, with a fire and a woman's care, would be better than this. Are you grown men, or bairns?"

The King sank back on his couch, and turned his head away. "I would be alone," he said.

"Yes — leave us alone," the Isleswoman agreed promptly, "My lords — or your mercy, begone!"

The groan of protest from the bed was wasted on all. The two knightly cravens seized the opportunity to escape without delay.

The woman came round to the other side of the bed, to sit on it. "What is your trouble, Robert?" she asked in a different voice. "What has stricken you so? This is not the Robert Bruce I know."

"How can I tell? Some fever. It struck me some weeks back. Soon after Campbell left me. A weakening sickness. I am weak as a child. My joints ache. My skin burns. Yet I am cold, cold."

She put her hand to his clammy brow. "A fever, yes. How strange is your skin! Angry, broken."

"Is it so all over. Chafing, scaling. It near drives me mad!"

"I have never seen the like. Poor Robert — it is a grievous thing. But, 'fore God, this is not the way to mend it! Lying untended in this chill barrack."

"Not untended — the saints pity me! There is an old monk, a friar. One Mark, of Kintore. Reputed hereabouts as a physician. He would dose me every hour with his noxious stews, daub me with stinking brews made from the offal of toads and the like! The man's a pious hypocrite, forby . . ."

"Then we will be quit of him. I will be your physician now. A *cailleach*, my old nurse, taught me much of the art. It is time you were rescued, from monkish and knightly fools both! And from yourself, I think! Let me but restore myself, from my journey, and we shall make a start."

"No need . . ." the King began — but he might as well have spoken to the wind.

Christina MacRuarie was as good as her word, and better. It was not long before she had the invalid out of that millhouse altogether and into a nearby cottage whose occupants presumably got short shrift. Admittedly this was small, little better than a cabin, with earthen floor, turf roof, and walls of smoke-blackened clay; but somehow she had got the place cleaned up, arranged a more comfortable bed, and brought in some simple furnishings from heaven knew where. Moreover it was warm, with a well-doing fire of holly and ash logs.

Bruce, of course, did not admit that this was any great improvement; indeed he complained that the heat made his itch the worse. But that was an error of tactics, for Christina promptly declared that that would soon be put right. He discovered that she intended to wash him down with some salve of her own concocting. No amount of outraged protest had any effect on her — and the deplorable Gibbie Hay, not to mention Neil Campbell who had brought her, not only had deserted him quite but were completely in the woman's pocket.

The sufferer's resistance to this feminine assault on his integrity was vehement, but more vocal than physical. The strength just wasn't there, he discovered — and this was a young woman as vigorous as she was determined and unscrupulous. Neither royal commands nor appeals to her better nature were of any use. Taking shameless advantage of the situation, she stripped him naked and began to wash off the friar's medications from his shrinking body with warm water.

"*Dia* — but you are thin, Robert!" she declared, ignoring all that he was saying. "You are worn down to the bone! This is the work of no sudden sickness. What has happened to you?"

Bruce well knew himself to be in poor shape. Long months of privation, poor feeding, and sleeping out in all weathers had taken their toll. He recognised that his present illness was more probably a result of a general physical run-down, than the other way round.

"I have had little time for growing fat," he told her briefly.

"I know what you have been doing, and how you have been living. Sir Neil has told me much. And the word of your fightings and warfare has not failed to reach even Moidart. But this — this wretchedness of the body speaks of more than hard living. And this of the skin. So dry and red. It is grievous to see . . ."

"Then, of a mercy, cover me up, woman!" he exclaimed. He was acutely embarrassed by this open inspection of his shuddering cringing body. Even though he had lain with her not a few times and they were no strangers to each other's nakedness, to have Christina, or any woman, peering and poking and dabbing at him, was highly distressing, highly unsuitable — and not a little humiliating in the all too obvious feebleness of his shrunken masculinity.

Paying no attention to his requests, she went on with her ministrations. But perhaps she gave him her own comment. "We must make a man of you again," she said. "I swear this is not what I rode all the way from the West to see! Turn over, Robert — turn over."

Her washings and anointings, however to be deplored, at least produced some easing of his itch. Not that he admitted it. And he had to concede that she kept Brother Mark away, indeed kept everybody away. Moreover the food which she brought him presently was incomparably better than any he had been offered for long — not that he had any appetite for it. The fact that she sat by his bed and more or less forced it into him, of course, was cause for legitimate complaint.

In the midst of all this feminine attention, the Earl of Lennox arrived unheralded from the South, with 200 men. Even Christina MacRuarie could not prevent a belted earl from having audience with his monarch, and Bruce was enabled to pour a flood of his troubles into his old friend's ear. Unfortunately Malcolm of Lennox was altogether too much of a gentleman successfully to resist the Isleswoman's methods, and before long found himself on the wrong side of that cot-house door. The King more or less resigned himself to the inevitable.

Nevertheless that night Christina alarmed him in a new and major fashion; first by producing a pile of sheepskins and plaids over and above his own; and then by authoritatively allowing Lennox, Campbell and Hay, and one or two others, to come and say a very brief goodnight before shooing them out again like a henwife with poultry, and shutting the door behind them in remarkably final style. By the light of the flickering log-fire she laid out the sheepskins, one on top of another, on the floor at the side of his bed, and arranged the plaids on top, thereafter proceeding calmly to undress herself. The King eyed all this with mixed feelings; but even so he was quite unprepared when, standing in unabashed, complete and lovely nakedness, she threw back the covers of his own bed, and urged him to move over somewhat as she was coming in beside him meantime. The sick man's protest that he was in no state for haughmagandy or anything of the sort, met with no least response.

Settling in alongside him, she took him in her arms, not fiercely or passionately, but gently, comfortingly, her soft firm shapeliness enfolding him. He held his limbs stiffly — but that was all his reaction.

"You needed a woman once before, Robert," she murmured. "I think you need one again — only differently. The other will come, in time. But now you require some cherishing, some kindliness."

"I am not a child, a babe!" he mumbled, seeking to turn away.

But she held him strongly. And because she lay slightly higher in the bed than he, and her breasts warmly and caressingly encompassed his face, he found it scarcely feasible either to move or complain satisfactorily. Here was a struggle which apparently he did not sufficiently wish to win.

So he lay, and presently even began to relax. Sensing it, she gathered him a little closer, not to smother or constrain him but to soothe and cradle him. Gradually the warmth and smooth strength of her had its way with him, and he felt more at rest than he had done for long.

"Why do you do this?" he asked presently, not very clearly, from the hollow of her bosom.

"Because some woman should. And because of my love for you. One day, perhaps, your Queen will thank me for it!"

At that the man stiffened momentarily, but she calmed and quelled him with hand and voice, almost as a mother might.

"Hush you, hush you," she said. "Your Elizabeth will look for a man, will she not? When she comes back to you? Not a shrivelled gelding. Nor yet a corpse! *She* cannot cherish you. So I shall."

He did not argue the point.

"Have you had news of her? Of her state? Of late."

"Aye. Bishop Lamberton makes shift to send me word when he may. He is warded not far from her, has contrived to visit her. At Burstwick Manor, in Yorkshire. She is held secure, but less hardly than in Edward's days — the old Edward. She is well enough. But . . ." He left the rest unsaid.

"You did not give her a child?"

"Think you our state was such that she would have thanked me for making her pregnant? We have been on the move, hunted or homeless, almost since we were wed."

"She might have thanked you for it now, nevertheless! And your daughter? How is it with her?"

"I do not know. She was held, alone, cut off from all, in London Tower. But Lamberton, though prisoner himself, has some small credit with the new King. He said that he would seek his mercy on the child. I pray God for her, daily. For them both . . ."

"Yes, yes." Again the soothings. "This other Edward is not the mad tyrant that his father was. He will be kinder to a child. Your Marjory will be none the worse — for children throw off these hurts more readily than we fear. It is not good — but all might be worse, see you. One day the sun will shine again for them. And for you." She settled herself more comfortably, stroking the back of his head. "But now, rest you. Sleep. Is the itch troubling you?"

"Aye. But not as it was. I can thole that. It is the itch in my mind

167

that irks me most. So much to be done, while I lie here helpless . . ."

"Never fear but we will put that to rights. We have made a start to it. You are not shuddering and trembling now, at least. You are no longer cold, Robert?"

"*I* am not. But I cannot forget those who are. My sister Mary. And Isobel of Buchan. In their cages on Berwick and Roxburgh walls. In this winter cold. For my fault. I dream of them, hanging there. Weak women . . ."

"Women, I vow, will survive the like better than most men," she asserted. "We are none so fragile a tribe! But think no more of it now. Be at peace. Sleep."

But he had to get it out, now that he had someone to tell, someone with whom he did not have to maintain a pose of royal reserve and confidence. He poured it out, all the bottled-up agitation and concern which had been racking his mind as he lay helpless. He told her of the nagging guilt of his brothers' deaths; his fears of his surviving brother Edward's headstrong violence, excellent cavalry commander as he was; his disappointment that still no great men and no really large numbers were rallying to his banner — even the powerful Lennox had only been able to gather his paltry 200. He had money to purchase support, thanks to the Church — but still men held back. He told her of his fears that young James Douglas, in whose care he had left the South-West, would not be experienced enough, or strong enough, to hold it. He told of his own recurring doubts and near despair — but thereafter was moved to speak of the spider in the Galloway cave, his desperate resolve, his vow one day to go on a Crusade if only victory was granted him.

The woman listened without further chiding, perceiving his need. And presently something of the urgency went out of his voice, and pauses developed that grew more frequent and longer. At length he slept.

And after a while Christina of Garmoran gently eased herself away from the man's side and slipped from the bed. She covered him again heedfully, and for a few moments stood there, warmly naked in the dying firelight, considering him, before betaking herself to the couch she had made near by.

*   *   *

There was no doubt that Christina's arrival and ministrations were good for Bruce. In two days, indeed, she was having to change her attitude and urge care, restraint, when he sought to be on his feet again. Admittedly, while she was out of the cottage and he did venture over the side, it was to find himself a deal weaker than he had realised, light-headed and unsteady on his legs; so that he was safely back between the plaids when Christina returned. But even so this was a major advance, of the spirit more than of the body — though the itch was undoubtedly much lessened by the bathings, the red patches less angry, the shivering gone.

Oddly enough it was his brother Edward who was responsible for effecting the major cure. He came clattering into the Milton of Urie two afternoons after Christina's arrival, all shouts and clashing steel, demanding were they *all* asleep here, *all* sick men abed? Buchan was upon them, in force. Had it not been for him, Edward of Carrick, they would all be dead men, not sleeping, by now. Etcetera.

This brought Bruce out of his bed and reaching for his clothing, demanding details. "What do you mean? Have you clashed with Buchan? The earl himself? Hereabouts? In what force? Where is he now?" All weakness was for the moment forgotten.

"Not Buchan himself, no. It was Brechin. Our nephew Sir David de Brechin, one of his captains. But Buchan himself is not far off. At Oldmeldrum, they say . . ."

"They say! They say! Who says? Fact, man — I want fact!" The King was transformed, vehement, commanding again, with so little of the invalid about him that even Christina was astonished. "Oldmeldrum is but five miles away. Where is David de Brechin? Talk sense, my lord!"

Edward seemed about to expostulate, but a look at his brother's face changed his mind. "Brechin is now running. Back to Oldmeldrum no doubt. Like a whipped cur. I taught him his lesson — but not before he had wiped out your picket to the east, on the Bourtie heights. Making here from Udny, I found our dead near yon cairn on the Bourtie ridge. They had been surprised and cut down to a man. De Brechin, with about 200 men, was in the low ground making for the Souterford and here, when I reached him. He has not half 200 now!"

"The enemy so near? Dear God! Sir Gilbert — what of your sentinels? What means this, sir?"

Hay flushed. "I am sorry, Sire. I have heard nothing of it. No word has been sent to me. Of enemy approach. I have sentinels posted, scouts out, all around. But . . ."

"Aye! I have lain too long, by the Rude! When my foes can ride within a mile of me, and I know naught of it!"

The Lord of Erroll bit his lip, but said nothing.

Bruce whipped back to his brother. "Speak on," he jerked. "And tell it as it happened. But shortly."

Edward explained. He had been returning from his harrying of the low coastlands of Formartin, on the edge of Comyn territory, with his 350 men, when his scouts learned that the Earl of Buchan himself, with a large force, was marching south-by-west from the heartlands of Buchan towards Inverurie. The scouts could not tell numbers, but it was thousands rather than hundreds — too many for him to challenge. So he had made all haste here, but sent back men to find the enemy host, and report. Then, only an hour or so ago, he had come on the slain Bourtie outpost, and then on the advancing de Brechin — his banner and arms clear. He had managed to trap him against a bluff and a curve of the river. Brechin had managed to cut his own way out, with some few of his people, but left most behind him. He, Edward, had taken no prisoners — but before they died, one or two of the Comyns had said that Buchan was positioned on the south face of Barra Hill, just south of Oldmeldrum, with many men, one said 2,000, another 3,000.

"So! Buchan would cross swords with me. In person! Perhaps he had word that I was sick. Well, I shall not disappoint the High Constable of this my kingdom!" Bruce produced a smile, grim but the first for long enough. "You have done well, Edward. I thank you. But whoever commands our sentinels on that east flank hangs tonight — if he is still alive then! Gibbie — you will see to it. But not now. You have much to do, first. We all have. Out, and sound the assembly. Christina — aid me on with my harness."

"Robert — my lord King!" the Islewoman protested. "This is not for you. A sick man, you cannot go riding to battle . . ."

"I am no longer a sick man — thanks to you, woman! Besides, this has made me hale and sound. No medicine could have cured me as this news has done! I have four great enemies in Scotland, apart from the English invaders, four men who have earned my wrath more than all others — Buchan, the Earl of Ross, MacDougall of Lorn, and MacDouall of Galloway. One of them is now near, come seeking me. Think you I will fail him — or myself?"

She spread her hands helplessly, recognising the finality of his voice.

"Now, quickly. No more of talk. My lords — to your duty. Christina — that shirt of mail . . ."

So, within the hour, the royal army of just over 1,500 men marched out of Inverurie, northwards, the King of Scots at its head under his own great red-and-gold Lion Rampant standard carried by his armour-bearer, William de Irvine — even though the said esquire had also to prop up his royal master in the saddle. Only half a head behind rode Christina of Garmoran, no royal commands having been effective in holding her back at the Milton.

They crossed the Burgh-muir and thereafter splashed across the Urie at the same Souterford where the litter of dead bodies, men and horses, testified the accuracy of Edward Bruce's claims. The road to Oldmeldrum followed the far east bank of the river for a couple of miles before swinging away due northwards up the long gentle slopes of a flank of Barra Hill. This was a foothills land of green rolling hogbacks and smooth grassy ridges, almost devoid of trees, with wide waterlogged troughs between. Oldmeldrum lay, a grey village on the lip of one of these lesser ridges ahead, with a clear prospect in this direction — and obviously not to be attacked directly from the low ground in front. Bruce sent the Earl of Lennox off, with some 200 horse, to make a diversion to the left, to the west, skirting the boggy Loch of Barra, for the higher ground of Lethenty and Harlaw, from which he could circle round on firm ground towards Oldmeldrum and menace Buchan's flank. He him-self swung the main body, the majority on foot, sharply right-handed, off the line of the road, to follow the Bourtie valley round the back of Barra Hill itself. At this stage they were still out of sight of Buchan's position.

Barra Hill was no mountain, rising to little more than 600 feet, but it was the bulkiest and most prominent height in the area. Buchan almost certainly would have look-outs placed along its crest, and both his own and Lennox's progress would be only too evident from the heights. There could be no surprise, there-fore — but they might hope for some confusion.

Up the gentle green Bourtie valley, only a shallow depression in the grassy hills really, they advanced steadily north by east with protective screens of outriders right and left. Bruce could have sent parties out to clear the ridge above them, but deliberately did not do so. Now and then they caught glimpses of movement up there, and were satisfied.

The King, though distinctly light-headed and scarcely in full control of his limbs, nevertheless felt more like himself than he had done for long. Possibly Campbell's Highland water-of-life was indeed helping — though he insisted that it was that which made him dizzy. Christina watched him from just behind like a hen with one chick.

On and on up those sheep-dotted valleys they pressed, with the long bulk of Barra Hill hiding all to the left, and the land grad-ually shelving and opening to the north-east. In time, they had gone well past the line of Buchan's position, even past Old-meldrum itself, and the intervening hill was beginning to tail away into broken moorland. If some of Bruce's entourage, Edward in-cluded, began to fear that his sickness had affected his wits, they had perhaps some excuse; but the King's stern and jaw-clenched expression did not invite questioning.

At length, with the lie of the land forcing them ever eastwards into a wilderness of moorland hummocks, Bruce called a halt to this deliberate, almost leisurely progress. And now all was changed. As though he had suddenly wakened from some sort of trance, he had his whole force swing directly round on itself and head back whence it had come — but now at the utmost speed of foot and horse both. Back and up to the crest of Barra Hill, he commanded, with all haste. The foot he sent running and leaping across the soft ground, directly towards the whaleback ridge; the cavalry had to take the longer round-about route, for firmer going, before they could swing off right-handed to face the fairly steep ascent of the hill itself.

It was a ragged, scattered and breathless rabble that eventually reached the summit ridge of Barra Hill that late afternoon of Christmas Eve of 1307, as the light was beginning to fade from the overcast sky, Bruce himself reeling in his saddle, with Gilbert Hay positively holding him up at one side, and Irvine at the other. There was visibility enough left to discern the situation, however. And none on the ridge any longer doubted the sick monarch's wits.

The country was spread out before them, clear and open within a five-mile radius. And half-right, only about a mile away, a great host was streaming northwards, back through Oldmeldrum, in full retiral and some obvious confusion. From here it was evident that it had been drawn up in a strong position on the terraced south-facing shoulder of the hill below the village, overlooking the low ground, the loch and the road from Inverurie, its flanks well secured. But such position would have been of no avail in any attack from the rear, the north, from behind Oldmeldrum. Bruce's ruse had worked. Buchan's scouts, spaced along this dominant ridge, and now fleeing after their main body, had sent word that the royal force was making a great pincers-move to the north-east. Lennox's manoeuvre, plain to view on the other side, would give the same impression. The Comyn, concerned not to be trapped from the higher ground to the north, had abandoned his position and turned his whole army round, to make for a new defensive site further back. The King did not wait until all his array was drawn up on the hill-top He ordered his trumpets to blare the advance, the charge, and leaving Hay and Fraser to bring on the foot with all speed, plunged headlong downhill, in the forefront of his line, dizziness apparently gone. Edward led the cavalry on the right and Campbell on the left. Only a little way in the rear, Christina

MacRuarie maintained her position, black hair streaming like a banner in the wind.

Buchan did not fail to perceive the threat of this unexpected assault, and made swift dispositions to meet it — or tried to. But to turn a host of horse and foot round on itself, in any sort of order, is not a thing to be rushed. When the host is already strung out and scattered in some confusion by a previous sudden about-turn, and on the move to find a new position in the rear, the manoeuvre becomes little short of the impossible. Chaos developed on the northern flank of Barra Hill, as the royal array thundered down from the main ridge, trumpets braying, hooves drumming, armour clanking, with everywhere men yelling "A Bruce! A Bruce!"

Buchan was no poltroon, and he had stout and able lieutenants, notably Sir Walter Comyn of Kinedar, Sir William Comyn of Slains, Sir Alexander Baliol of Cavers, Sir David de Brechin — who arrogated to himself the title of The Flower of Chivalry — and the veteran Sir John de Moubray. They managed to rally much of their cavalry, but had less of a grip on the infantry. Indeed quickly the latter got completely out of hand, milling this way and that in disorder and in panic, so that soon their own horse were riding them down, led by the knights, in their desperate efforts to turn back and create a front of sorts against the enemy.

From the start of the charge the Comyns had only some five or six minutes to turn, reform and take up a defensive position, before the King's cavalry was upon them. It was not possible. While still the leaders were seeking to bring up and marshal their scattered men, the foremost ranks of the royal horse surged up in a yelling smiting tide. As might be expected, it was the right wing under the fiery Edward Bruce which reached them first.

Even so, Buchan's knights and chivalry put up a good fight, less than prominent as was their master in the business. But against the impetus of that charge, the lack of central direction, the utter chaos behind with the foot useless and fleeing, they were beaten before they started — especially when Lennox's squadron put in an appearance along their right flank. Moreover, almost certainly the fact that the King himself was seen to be leading the assault in person under his renowned royal standard, had a notable effect, not least on his High Constable. Bruce's reputation as a strategist had swept the country in these last ten months — and Buchan for one had thought him safely prostrate on his sick-bed.

At any rate, the Comyn line broke well before the loyalist foot reached the scene of battle — and once broken, Buchan himself was one of the first to be off. With Edward Bruce most evidently trying to hack his way through the press to him directly, he disengaged, leapt down from his heavy charger, grabbed a fleeter riderless mount, and clambered into the saddle with remarkable agility for a man of his years and bulk, in massive armour. He galloped off northwards. Many perceived it, and followed him — though Brechin and Moubray, scorning such behaviour, continued the fight.

But with the arrival of Hay and Fraser with the infantry, obviously it was all over. Most of the remaining armoured knights managed to draw together into a small, compact and fiercely effective phalanx, and so cut their way out and back. Had Bruce himself been in any state for serious fighting, it is probable that none would have escaped. But he was not, keeping upright in his saddle being his main preoccupation now; and Edward was of course in hot pursuit of the fleeing Buchan, despite the swiftly falling darkness.

Enough was enough, the King decided — especially with Christina MacRuarie at his elbow vigorously proclaiming the fact. The day was won, and with minimum loss. It was becoming too dark for effective tactics anyway, or any major pursuit. He ordered Irvine to sound the recall. Edward would pay no heed even if he heard it.

So leaving Hay, Campbell and the Fraser brothers to deal with the wounded, the prisoners and the battlefield generally, the King, with Christina and Lennox, not unthankfully returned to ride the few miles back to Inverurie, his couch drawing him now, in reaction, like a magnet.

It was late evening before Edward of Carrick returned, having pursued Buchan all the way to Fyvie, almost ten miles to the north, where there was a strong castle held by the English. He was hot that the victory had not been properly followed up — and since he could scarcely blame the King, he blamed Lennox and Campbell instead, the former in especial, who, he pointed out, had been fresh and with scarcely opportunity to draw sword.

His brother, sighing, called him over to his couch. "Edward," he said, low-voiced, for in that small chamber all might have heard. "You lack nothing in courage. And you are a good commander of light cavalry — few better. But let us pray God that my life is spared to me! For as King of Scots in my place you would not survive a month! Of a mercy, use your wits, man! Command, leadership, rule, demand more than throwing yourself at the nearest enemy like a bull, and berating all others for not doing likewise! You must have friends as well as defeated foes. Remember it, I charge you — for *I* need friends if you do not!"

That night Bruce was not content to be cherished and mothered in his cot-house bed. Later, after the man was asleep, Christina, beside him, lay and gazed up at the smoke-blackened but firelit roofing, and she frowned as often as she smiled.

CHAPTER TWELVE

"MEN," declared Christina MacRuarie, "are all fools! Greater or lesser in degree, but all fools. Even kings, it seems! And never so great fools as where women are concerned."

Robert Bruce kept his back turned, and wisely forbore to answer.

"You are the great ones. Under heaven, you rule all! All save your own silly wits. How think you would manage *without* women?"

"More quietly, at the least," the King said, and sighed.

He was gazing out of the window of his bedchamber, which was in fact the sub-Prior's room of the Blackfriars' Priory of Aberdeen, looking pensively northwards towards the Castlehill and the towering walls of Aberdeen's fortress, still held by a strong though beleaguered garrison of Englishmen. He was not really thinking, at the moment, about that symbol of the enemy's unrelenting grip upon his kingdom — although it, and so many others like it, was a constant preoccupation, a challenge, which one day would have to be faced and dealt with; but not yet; he was not ready for the expensive and time-consuming business of reducing major fortresses. His mind was more immediately concerned with the projected programme for that very afternoon of early April — if only the woman would be quiet and let him think.

But Christina was in no mood for quiet contemplation. She had a grievance. And a woman with a grievance is no aid to cerebration — especially one so masterful as the Lady of Garmoran.

"Am I not just as entitled to sit at your Council as any man?" she demanded, not for the first time. "I have supplied you with men and aid and shelter. I know as much of affairs in these parts as do any of your lords. I have given you better advice than most. I have even been at your side in battle. What do I lack for a seat at this Council-table? Tell me, Robert — what do I lack? Other than proud and arrogant manhood. And ... and its dangling equipment!"

He smoothed hand over mouth, at that, lest she saw the grin reflected in the window-glass. "Nothing," he admitted. "That only. Manhood. And you have other equipment that more than com-

175

pensates, my dear! But, see you — that is the nub of it, as I have told you. Because you are a woman the others would resent your presence. At a Privy Council. Never, I think, has any woman attended such — even a queen. I know their minds on this. They like you well, admire you. Edward indeed would bed you if he might, as you know! But a Council is men's business . . ."

"A Council is for counsel. And I can give better counsel than who will sit there. Than witlings like Gilbert Hay. Clerks like the Bishop of Moray. Nice fumblers like Lennox. Or fat lowborn burghers like this Provost of Aberdeen — a fellmonger, a tanner of hides!"

"Then give your counsel here, Christina. In my own ear. Always you have my privy ear. You can reach me when and where the others can not . . ."

"That is naught to the point, and you know it. This Council is for debate. Discussion. Hearing the word and advice of others, and to make comment, support, or discover error. For that I must be there. You are to discuss Angus of the Isles' plan to invade Lorn and Argyll. My lands flank Lorn to the north. Think you I do not know more of this matter than your Southrons? You will talk of a campaign against Ross. I and my clan have been fighting Ross for many years . . ."

"Christina — all that is true. And your guidance I shall value. As I have done hereto. But a woman at my first true Privy Council I cannot have. I know my fellow-men. This Council is all-important. Aberdeen is the first city in all my realm to fall into my hands — even though its castle still holds out. All the kingdom will hear what is done and said today. I have taken much thought to the style of it . . ."

"The more reason that a woman's voice should be heard. And be known to be heard. Abroad. Are not half your subjects women?"

A discreet knock sounded at the door — for which Bruce was decidedly grateful. He strode to open it, to find there young William Irvine, son of the Annandale laird of Bonshaw, who had joined him as esquire and armour-bearer after Glen Trool, relieving Gibbie Hay of certain such duties.

"Your Grace — my lord Bishop of Dunblane is new come. And seeks audience. He is below, in the chapter-house."

"Ha! Nicholas Balmyle? Here, in Aberdeen! Yes, he shall have audience. I will be down to the chapter-house forthwith."

Bruce turned back, to complete his dressing, belting the cloth-of-gold tunic with the splendid embroidered scarlet Lion Rampant of Scotland, and donning the purple cloak trimmed with fur, which was the gift of the citizens of Aberdeen. He was to be very fine today, part of the stage-managing of this his first real Privy Council, wherein he planned to act the monarch rather than just the soldier. Much would depend on this afternoon, and he was at least concerned to look the part. He had once, it seemed in another life, been something of a dandy in his dress, little as more recent appearances would have suggested it.

"You look a very picture of elegance," the woman observed sourly — which was strange, for partly this dressing-up had been her idea, the handsome thigh-length tunic made under her supervision.

"I thank you," he returned, smiling. "I am glad that I please you in this, at least!" And he escaped.

Downstairs he found the calmly self-contained person of Nicholas Balmyle, newly appointed Bishop of Dunblane. And with him the dark Benedictine friar Bernard de Linton, the same who had brought Bruce the news of the late King Edward's death, at Loch Doon. They bowed, the King greeting them warmly.

"Sire," Balmyle said, "we rejoice to see you afoot and all but yourself again, after your grievous sickness. We thank God and His saints for your delivery."

"Aye, my lord Bishop — do that. But also thank you the Earl of Buchan. Who contrived to effect my final cure, after his own fashion! At Barra Hill."

Balmyle looked mystified. "You say so? But two days before we came north from St. Andrews seeking Your Grace, I heard from a source you know of that my lord of Buchan has fled Scotland and is now in Yorkshire. To the displeasure of King Edward, who it seems had newly appointed him warden of Annandale, Carrick and Galloway."

"Buchan in England? I' faith — here is good news. After two small defeats, and with still a round dozen of his strong castles in his Comyns' hands, he flees the country? I had scarcely hoped for this. It should make my task the less sore. But . . . you had the word of it from my friend? From Bishop Lamberton? Have you also a letter for me? Is that why you have come here, my lord?"

"In part, Sire. Here is a letter. It was enclosed within one from the Primate to myself."

Bruce took the folded paper, bulkier than that he had received before, and still sealed. He did not open it, as Balmyle went on.

"I have come on other account also, Sire. Another letter has reached me. From Rome. His Holiness has approved of my appointment to the See of Dunblane. And summons me to the Vatican for consecration."

"Then here also is excellent news, my lord. For the Pope does not love me, or my cause, and I feared that he might refuse to confirm you bishop. To your loss, and mine. For you have proved my friend. And I need the support of lords spiritual as well as temporal. And few of either are prepared to give that support, I fear."

"They will, Sire — they will. In time. But while the English remain in possession of most of the land, is it to be wondered at? With death by hanging and disembowelling the penalty. Not all have Your Grace's strong courage . . ."

"But *you* have, my lord. And our friend, here." He looked at the friar. "To venture all this way, through enemy-held land, with this letter and your news."

The younger man, de Linton, inclined his head. He was sensitive-looking, gaunt, stringy and tall, with prominent bones. "My courage is but weak, Your Grace. But my conscience is the stronger."

"Aye. Well said, Master Bernard."

"I had to come to seek your royal permission, Sire, to leave the country," the Bishop went on. "To journey to Rome for my consecration. And while in Rome to seek to have the Primate's revocation of Your Grace's excommunication confirmed by the Pontiff."

"Aye. Though whether you succeed in that is more in doubt. My enemies will do much to prevent it. All the English and French bishops — aye, and some of the Scots! Yours will be a lone voice, my friend. But, yes — you must go. To Rome. And God-speed. Though I shall be the poorer for your absence."

"I thank you. And shall hasten my return. Meantime I have brought you Master Bernard. To remain with you, if so you will have it. To be a link between you and Holy Church. With myself, and with Bishop Lamberton, my father-in-God. That letters may still pass. As well, he is an able scribe, well versed, and I have found him both wise and true. He will serve you in many ways."

"That is well thought of. I' faith, I need a secretary. A King needs pen as well as sword. You will be my secretary, Master Bernard. And, by the Rude, you could not have come more aptly. For today, within the hour, I hold a high council. You shall act secretary thereat. And you, my lord Bishop, shall attend it, as of right. With Bishop David of Moray, who is here. It falls out most aptly, does it not?"

"Sire, I thank you," the Bishop acknowledged. "But may I trespass on your time a little longer? I have brought more than my news to Aberdeen. Two items. Another thousand merks in silver, for one . . ."

"Save us, friend — here's generosity indeed! Another thousand! You put me greatly in your debt. But I can use it, I'll not deny. Your last provision is near done — spent in the main in feeding and arming men. I thank you, from my heart."

"Thank not me. Thank my lord Primate. It is on his orders, and from the revenues of his See of St. Andrews, that the money comes. I still administer it for him, as best I may."

"Then thank God for William Lamberton and Nicholas Balmyle both, say I!"

"The other matter I am less sure of Your Grace's gratitude," the little cleric said, in his slightly pedantic, composed style. "I but serve my lord of Douglas in this. He sends loyal greetings — and a prisoner."

"Jamie? You have seen James Douglas, my lord? How goes it with him? Is all well?"

"Well enough, Sire. He is in health, but kept direly busy. He is a scourge to every Englishman not shut up safe within castle walls! He has become a notably fierce young man — as he must needs be, to be sure. But with something of innocence also. He seldom sleeps two nights in one bed, ranging the Lowlands from one end to the other, his sword never out of his hand."

"Aye. I laid a heavy burden on his shoulders, in leaving the South in his care. But of my close lieutenants him I could best trust with the task. And as lord of Douglasdale, and his famed father's son, he bears a name and style that men must respect. But my service has borne hard on him."

"As to that he makes no complaint, I think. But he has captured this notable prisoner, and sends him to you, by my hand. He waits without. Have I Your Grace's permission to bring him in?"

The King nodded. "I have not a few sins on my soul, other than the death of John Comyn," he said slowly. "You speak of James Douglas's innocence yet. But it is the rape of his innocence that bears sorely on my conscience. I taught him to hate. And to slay without qualm, without mercy. That sword you spoke of, I put into his hand. He was young, and good, and his heart gentle, and I made him killer..."

Bruce's grieving words faded as Friar Bernard ushered a fourth man into the room, a tall, darkly handsome, well-built young man, with a flashing proud eye and a noble brow, possibly the most handsome man that Scotland could produce in that age. He stared.

"Thomas...!" he whispered.

His own nephew, Sir Thomas Randolph, Lord of Nithsdale, bowed stiffly and remained silent.

"My lord of Douglas captured Sir Thomas in a fray in Ettrick Forest. Along with Sir Alexander Stewart of Bonkyl — who I understand also used to be Your Grace's friend. Their troops were English, however. Stewart was wounded. But this being Your Grace's own kinsman, my lord asked me to bring to you. For . . . for disposal!"

"Yes. To be sure. I thank you, my lord Bishop." The King, still eyeing Randolph, was frowning darkly in perplexity. He had liked this young man, spirited and talented as he was good-looking, and hitherto namely for being upright to a degree, his half-sister's son. Bruce's own mother, Marjory, Countess of Carrick in her own right, before she wed his father had been married to one Adam, Lord of Kilconquhar, of the ancient lofty line of MacDuff, Earls of Fife. A child of that marriage, a daughter, had wed Sir Thomas Ranulf of Nithsdale, another Celtic lord who had Normanised his name to Randolph. Here before him was the fruit of that union, a sprig of the most purely Celtic nobility, allegedly the soul of honour and the mirror of chivalry, whom Bruce himself had delighted to honour with knighthood at his coronation, Scot of the Scots, with no taint of Norman blood in him. Yet there he stood, a traitor caught in his treachery, a man who had, it seemed, bought his life at the expense of his honour. He had fought for Bruce at Methven, been captured, and almost alone of the long list of noble prisoners, escaped shameful execution, to fight thereafter for Edward Plantagenet.

"I have not seen you since Methven fight, nephew," the King said, controlling his voice. "Though I have heard of your doings. I believe you were at Loudoun Hill. At Pembroke's side!"

"I was," the younger man agreed, as carefully. "To my sorrow."

"Your sorrow? You regret it, then?"

"My sorrow is for this Scotland. And for you, my lord. That so sorry a travesty of battle should have been fought in the name of this realm. My regret for myself only that I had no opportunity to use my sword against your person."

The Bishop coughed, and seemed about to rebuke the young man, but Bruce held up his hand.

"You would have fought me, slain me, then? At Loudoun Hill? If you had been able?"

"I would have fought you there. Or otherwhere. In fair and knightly combat. To redeem, if I might, the honour of my mother's house!"

"Fair and knightly combat! Yet it was I who knighted you, man. At Scone. Four years ago. Have you forgot?"

"I have not forgot — and judge it my greatest shame, my lord."

Bruce drew a long breath. "You do not mince your words, nephew. It seems that you do not like me. Yet we used to be friends, as well as kinsmen."

"I used to deem you honourable, sir."

Again Bruce restrained Balmyle. "I see that you name me sir, not Sire. Lord not Grace. Yet you helped make me King, at my coronation, Thomas."

"You have besmirched that anointing and coronation. You have dragged the royal dignity in the mire of murder and brigandage. You have tramped the code of chivalry underfoot. I no longer recognise you as my King. And would God I need not admit you as kin!" The young man's pleasantly-modulated voice quivered a little, there.

As Bishop and friar stirred with disquiet, appalled indeed, Bruce's patience was heavy, iron-bound.

"So you took Edward Longshanks for King? Edward who disembowelled knights. Who hanged three of your own uncles and your aunt's husband. Who hung another aunt and your kinswoman Isobel of Buchan in cages on castle walls. You preferred his kingship to mine?"

"The old King's misdeeds do not wash out yours, sir. And in the field he fought fairly, honestly, at least. The greatest warrior in Christendom. But you — you slay by night, like any thief. You ambush, you trick, you deceive. You have become no better than the man Wallace. You have not once battled in fair fight since your flight to Ireland."

"Ireland . . .? What is this of Ireland?"

"After Methven, when I was captured, you fled your realm. Leaving others to bear the English yoke. That is what I mean. And then returned with a horde of hired Irish cut-throats, foreign savages, to gain by terror and murder what you could not gain by honest means . . ."

"So that is what they told you!" Bruce eyed the other with dawning comprehension. "You have been cozened, Thomas. Fed with lies and half-truths. Led by cleverer men than you are, so that you might be used as a stick for my back, a dagger under my armour. My own nephew! Do you not see it? I was never in Ireland. I never left my own realm. I was in the Highlands and the Hebrides. The men I landed with again at Turnberry, from Arran, and those my brothers led into Galloway, were my own subjects. Islesmen — when none in the Lowlands would rise for me!"

The other looked momentarily nonplussed. "They said ... they said ..."

"Aye, they said! And you believed. Did James Douglas tell you no better?"

"Douglas! He is no better than yourself! Trained in your school. His knightly vows forgotten. I would have no truck with him — though once I judged him honest."

The King sighed. He could have shaken this good-looking, headstrong son of his sister. Shaken him for the ignorant, self-righteous puppy he was. Yet, at the back of his mind, he knew a sort of relief, too. Relief that at least his blood, his mother's Celtic blood, had not after all apparently curdled to dastardly treachery as he had feared. Not in vile, craven self-seeking, at least. Whatever else he was, this young man before him was no craven. For if he believed that he, Bruce, was as he said, then his present defiant words and attitude could only lead to the rope or cold steel. It had been one of the hurts that nagged at him in many a sleepless night, that young Randolph should have changed sides, sold his King and his kinsman, in cowardice. Now he was at least beginning to understand.

After all, only a few years ago, even though it seemed in another life, when he was Randolph's age, he had thought much as this one did, filled with fine chivalric ideals, judging all by the knightly code, seeing war as only an extension of the tournament. Thus they had been brought up, to look on Edward Plantagenet, for instance, as the epitome of romance, Christendom's model, the crusading prince, the Norman-French influence all-important — even though Randolph was in fact pure Celt. Even James Douglas had been of this mind — until rudely taught otherwise. This other still lacked the teaching, that was all.

"Thomas," he said, with a major attempt at reasonableness, "you berate me for not waging fair fight, as you name it. For ambushing and tricking my enemies. Winning my battles by my wits rather than the strength of my right arm. You conceive this not to be knightly, or the kingly way. I agree with you that it is not knightly. But a king has more than chivalry to think on! But, at Methven — was that a knightly fray? When Pembroke, with whom you seem proud to fight, stole upon us by night, forced us to battle scarce awake. Did you conceive *that* knightly, that night?"

When the other made no answer, the elder went on.

"Pembroke so acted because this was war, not jousting. Not the lists and the tourney-ground. We are fighting now, not for honour, or glory; but for freedom, our very lives. And the continuing existence of Scotland. So I fight to win, lad, as best I may, using what weapons I have ..."

"*You* fight for a throne! A kingdom, for yourself. And would plunge all that kingdom in blood to gain it! Is that freedom?"

"Would you have the English to rule Scotland?"

"Once *you* did not find that so ill! When Baliol would fill the throne, not Bruce. Is Plantagenet any worse a king for Scotland than Bruce? Or Baliol? Or Comyn? When Plantagenet would spare the land the everlasting bloodshed, the fire and famine and devastation?"

They stared at each other for long moments, two strong men more like each other than they knew.

At length Bruce shrugged. "I have not time to deal with you now," he said. "You have drawn sword against your liege lord. You swore me fealty at my coronation. So you broke your oath and committed treason, both. For that, you know the penalty?"

"I do. I seek no mercy at your soiled hands, my lord."

"Yet I would show mercy if I might. For you are of my own blood. Nephew — let us start afresh." He extended a hand, open, palm upward. "We will talk of it more fully later. But meantime be reconciled. You have for a while forgotten your allegiance. Now, let us be reconciled."

"No, sir. I have been guilty of nothing to my shame. You arraign my conduct. It is yourself who ought to be arraigned. Since you have chosen to defy the King of England — to whom *you* more than once took oath of fealty — why do you not debate the matter like a true knight, in a pitched field? If you dare! Until you do that, I am no man of yours — whatever my blood."

"That may come hereafter, nephew. Who knows how long hereafter? *I* shall choose that day, not the invaders." His voice changed and he made a gesture of finality. "Meantime, since you are so rude of speech, it would be fitting that your proud words should meet their due punishment. But . . . for the sake of my sister's memory, I shall hold my hand. You will be put close in ward until you know better *my* right and *your* duty. Master Bernard — summon the guard . . ."

*   *   *

At the long refectory table of Aberdeen's Blackfriars Priory, the first Council of the reign sat in session. Bruce was at the head and his brother at the foot, and between them at either side were about a score of men, the King's close companions with an assortment of others, carefully chosen; Angus of the Isles, who had come from containing MacDougall in the West; the Bishop of Moray, ridden south especially for the occasion, leaving his force to watch the Comyns in the North; their host, the Prior of this establishment;

183

and the Provost of the Burgh of Aberdeen, a man much overawed by the company he was keeping. A notable absentee was Bishop Cheyne of Aberdeen, a Comyn nominee and supporter. The new Bishop of Dunblane sat near the King, and on his other side, at a small table of his own, Master Bernard sat with ink-horn, quills and paper.

Edward Bruce was holding forth, urgently, thumping the table in no council-chamber manner. ". . . And so first things first, I say! Let the Lord of Argyll and his MacDougalls wait, I say. We will deal with them in due time. They will do but little harm in the West, meantime. With Campbell to the south of them, the Lady of Garmoran to the north, and my lord of the Isles to the west, surely they do not threaten us unduly?" He glanced fleetingly at Angus Og. "Whereas, I tell you, the Comyns do! Still they do. Their defeat at Barra was not properly followed up. It hit their pride but left them but little diminished. My later defeat of Buchan at Aiky Brae, to the north, was more complete, with more men slain. But it was still only the remnants from Barra. The Comyn power is still scarce touched. And it is the greatest power in Scotland today, even yet. Their castles of Dundarg, Slains, Kinedar, Rattray, Kelly and Ellon — and these are only the great ones — control the country. The English, I say, are less menace than the Comyns, since they are more scattered and have to hold down the country-side. The Comyns have their force here concentrated, in Buchan and Moray and Badenoch. They must be dealt with first, and at once."

There was a murmur of agreement from the majority of those present.

"I support my lord of Carrick, Sire," Bishop David of Moray said, an unlikely-looking cleric, the church-militant indeed. "You say that you have word that the Earl of Buchan has fled into England. That may be good — or not so good. He is no longer young and they say he is ailing. A disappointed man. He has not led the Comyns with the fire and thrust of the late Lord of Badenoch, his kinsman. Now, if he is gone, another may take his place. In the leadership of the Comyns. He has a brother, Sir Alexander — he who holds the castles of Urquhart and Tarradale. And many cousins, fiercer even than he. I know them. I have lived my life amongst them. They are smarting now, from Your Grace's blows. But they are far from defeated. They could raise 8,000 against you, Sire. Perhaps 10,000, given opportunity. And they will, if you let them. We must strike them before they think to act without Buchan's palsied hand."

"The Bishop fears for his own fat Moray lands, I think!" Angus

Og declared. "These Comyns are licking their wounds. They may be all these lords say. But they have been twice beat, and will not seek another beating meantime, for a wager. But MacDougall has not been beaten. The old man, Alexander, son of Ewan, son of Duncan, son of Dougall, is also ailing, like this Buchan. But his son is not. I know John Bacach of Lorn — after all, we are kin. His mother was a Comyn, Badenoch's sister. He loves you less than does his father, Sir King. And he is strong. Strong as a man, and strong in men. These talk of 10,000 Comyns. I shall believe that number when I see them! But John of Lorn can field 5,000 broadswords at a snap of his fingers! And you learned their quality at Strathfillan, did you not? I have been fencing with them these past months, keeping your left flank. I believe John Bacach MacDougall is finished with fencing. That is why I am here. I say you must deal with him before all else."

"I agree with my lord of the Isles," Neil Campbell put in. "The Comyns may still prove a threat. But John of Lorn is a threat *now!*"

"I think that true, Sire," Lennox nodded. "The MacDougalls have allies right down the West — as you learned to your cost. Macnabs, Macfarlanes, MacLarens, MacMillans, MacAlisters. I know John of Lorn also. He is a different man from his father — and it is he we have to deal with now. If my lord of the Isles believes him set on battle, he could set all the West on fire, right down to the Clyde. And then the South-West lies open before him. With only young Douglas holding it . . ."

"The West! The West!" Edward interrupted scornfully. "These lords are all from the Highland West, brother. MacDougall is a rogue and a traitor, and must be taught his lesson, yes. But his thousands are but Highland sworders. Good at a tulzie, yes. I ask none better in an ambush or a night's raiding. But the Comyn's main might is in armoured horse. Cavalry. Such as win wars, not tulzies!"

The King opened his mouth to speak, then closed it again. This was a Council and he was here to be advised. He would let them have their say. He nodded encouragement to Aberdeen's portly, red-faced Provost, sitting on the edge of his chair and evidently eager to speak but diffident in the presence of all these great nobles and bishops.

"Your royal Grace," he began hoarsely, and faltered, looking round the table. "If it may please Your Highness, I . . . I would say a word."

"You have our ear, friend. Say on."

"Aye, weel. This toun o' Aberdeen. It has welcomed Your Highness right kindly, has it no? Right kindly. The folk favour you. But you havena' taken the castle. It's stuffit full o' Englishry yet. It's ower strong to be taken. And it can be supplied frae the sea. We canna stop that, for it glowers ower the harbour. And the English hae ships at Dundee. So, Highness, by your leave, I'd say dinna go stravaiging through to the West after thae wild Hielantmen and leave us to the mercy o' the Comyns and the English baith! Or it'll be the end o' us. Buchan is no' that far awa' — but twenty miles. If you dinna put doon the Comyns first, they'll be doon here chapping at our doors afore you're across the Mounth! And the English frae the castle in our backyards And Your Highness will hae lost Ab-derdeen. And we . . . we'll hae lost mair'n that!"

"Well said, Sir Provost. Your point is taken. I shall not forget Aberdeen and its good folk, never fear. Do any others wish to speak further to this matter?"

"Sir King," Angus Og said, "Malcolm of Lennox spoke of John MacDougall threatening the South-West. I say that he is more like to turn north. I have the word that he has been sending messengers to William of Ross. They were ever unfriends, until this. But since neither love you . . ."

"The Earl of Ross!" Bruce's voice actually quivered, with the fierce effort of suppressing the flood of emotion that name aroused in him — the man who had taken his wife and daughter from the sanctuary at Tain, to hand over to the English. "He . . . he . . . MacDougall joins hands with Ross?"

"So goes the word in the West. Any day now the high passes will be open, the snows gone and the floods subsided. Then, I think, John of Lorn will turn north-east, not south-west, to join up with Ross. And then, Sir King, you will be faced with trouble enough for any man!"

A shaken silence greeted his words. He did not have to underline the size of the threat for any man there. The Earl of Ross was second only to the Lord of the Isles himself in power in the North-West. The third most powerful man was MacDougall of Lorn. Ally these two in a joint campaign, throwing in their whole might, and there was nothing north of the Highland Line that could withstand them. Even Edward Bruce, for once, made no comment.

His brother drummed finger-tips on the table. "My lords," he said at length, "if this is indeed so, then the danger is great and we must take steps to meet it, somehow. Yet my lord of Carrick is right also, about the Comyns. As is the good Provost of this Aberdeen about the danger to his city. And *I* have scores to settle with the Earl of Ross!" He paused. "See you, in this letter I spoke of, sent me by my lord Bishop of St. Andrews, he says that the King of

186

England has betrothed himself. To the twelve-year-old Isabella of France. He is even now gone to France for the nuptials — you might think in some haste considering the years of his bride! He has planned a great coronation for the new Queen, when he returns. In May. He is much fond of such celebrations, is this Edward of Carnarvon. Moreover, he has much offended his lords by raising up his pretty favourite, the Gascon named Piers Gaveston, and creating him Earl of Cornwall. Now he has left all England in his charge, while he is abroad, a puppet of no stature, hated by all the nobility of his realm. So there will be trouble, my friends — that I warrant. What with Edward's absence in France, the coronation when he returns, and the offence of his lords. Bishop Lamberton believes, and I agree with him, that there is like to be no large invasion of Scotland this summer. So, at the least, we need not be ever looking over our shoulders to the south."

Satisfaction was voiced by all at this news.

"So now, my lords — here is my proposal. My brother, the Earl of Carrick, will take our main force and proceed forthwith to deal with the Comyns. Wait you — wait! I myself, with the Lord of the Isles, the Earl of Lennox and Sir Neil Campbell of Lochawe with a lesser force, will cross to the West, to join the Islesmen already there, collecting what more we may from the Lennox, the Campbells and other leal chiefs. We will be there, not to come to grips with MacDougall, but only to threaten him, at this juncture — since we have not the might to challenge him and the Comyns both. But if we do this, and I am there in person. I do not believe that MacDougall will risk marching north to join up with Ross, leaving me on his border. Moreover, I will seek to prevail on the Lady Christina of Garmoran to have her people make a similar sally along the eastern shores of Ross, to distract the Earl. And my lord of Moray, *your* men to feint at Easter Ross and the Black Isle. Then, my friends, when the Earl of Carrick has harried the Comyn country into submission, we will march north to meet him at Inverness — in three months' time, may be. To face Ross united again. And when we are finished with Ross, turn back to deal with MacDougall in earnest! How say you? We must use this campaigning season to bring all the North to heel, if we can, whilst the English are otherwise occupied."

There was a great storm of acclaim and approval, round that table, men almost unanimous in their enthusiasm and their recognition of the breadth and sweep of this comprehensive programme, this proposed solution of the deadlock. Even Angus Og was impressed; and Edward was of course highly delighted. His abilities were being recognised, at last.

Bruce let the exclamation and comment continue for a little, and then brought the Council to order again. "This is no light task," he said. "Let us make no mistake about what this course will demand of us. Of us all. Patience, discretion, the holding of our hands. For any major defeat, at either side of the country, would spell disaster for both. We must all fully recognise what are our objectives, and hold to them strictly. Going no step further, to endanger all. In the West we are there only as a gesture. We will fight no great battles. And this is equally so with you, my lord of Carrick. Your business is not to hazard my main force in battle — mind it! Your task is to subdue the Comyn country so that never again will that house threaten mine. Heed not their castles, unless they are easy. It is their lands, these vast lands from which they draw their men, the great masses of their men — these are your objective. So long as the Comyn threat, of mighty armed intervention, remains, the English have us by the throat. My throne remains insecure. And many in this realm, God knows, take their lead from Comyn. So — an example must be made. For the good of the kingdom. The whole province of Buchan must be taught its lesson, who is King in Scotland. You understand, Edward?" That was rapped out, Bruce's features graven grim, his eyes hard. "Your task is to harry Buchan, not to fight battles. For that purpose and that only, you shall have my main host. And with it the Bishop of Moray, Sir Robert Boyd, Sir Robert Fleming and Sir Alexander Fraser, to aid and advise you. I shall expect them all, and the host no less in numbers, at Inverness in three months' time. And Buchan laid low so that no Comyn shall raise voice or sword against me, ever again! You have it? All of you — you have it? Answer me!"

It was not often that Robert Bruce played the imperious autocrat. He did so now advisedly, deliberately, and with good reason. No man failed to be affected, and Edward Bruce for once was positively subdued.

There was some little remaining business, mainly concerned with the containing of the English in Aberdeen Castle, and defensive works to prevent any invasion by sea. Also the implications of Lamberton's letter that he had been now given a sort of limited freedom, on the payment to King Edward of 6,000 merks fine, and on the strict injunction that he did not return to Scotland, Edward indeed apparently believing that he could use him to help bring the Scots to heel. The Council agreed that, in the circumstances, Lamberton should seem to go along with the English in this, and at the same time, if possible, both serve as spy and encourage that King in his follies.

But the pressure had gone out of the conference, and all were eager to be away from the table, and at ease to talk, discuss and argue freely. The King drew the proceedings to a close, therefore — and rising, beckoned Gilbert Hay to his side.

"Gibbie," he said quietly, "you did not hear your name spoken in all that. Because I have an especial task for you. I think you used to be friendly with Thomas Randolph, my nephew?"

"Used to be, Sire — but not since he turned traitor!"

"There are traitors and traitors, Gibbie."

"This one the greater, in that he is your own kin. All should be dead! I heard that he had been brought here. What is Your Grace's will for him?"

"What would *you* do with Thomas Randolph, once your friend?"

"I would hang him. As *his* friends have hanged so many of us."

"If I was to hang all those who take part against me, I fear I would be hanging half of my subjects! No — I still have hopes for my sister's son. He conceives himself to be a man of honour — and myself otherwise! I want you to take him in hand, Gibbie. He is in close ward, yes. But we will take him with us, into the West. Get his parole — and, an honourable man, he will keep it! He will be in your charge. Entreat him kindly, but firmly. Work on him — as the English have already done. He is surprisingly innocent, I am convinced. He has much to learn. You are the best man to show him his error. Show him that I am not the brigand he takes me for. Show him that the knightly code will not win a war against ten times our numbers. Show him how the English really fight, behind their glitter of chivalry."

"If so you command, Sire. But I think you are too nice, too soft of heart. I'd take rope to him, and be done!"

"It is my head, not my heart, that commands in this, my lord of Erroll! Any fool can hang his prisoners. But there may be many who think like Randolph, many of my subjects. I may serve my cause a deal better by showing mercy and persuading that young man to be my living friend than my dead enemy! He is a man of parts, with great lands. And of the old race. I have not so many of these that I should hang them, when I might convert them. And Thomas Randolph converted would sound loud in Scotland. See you to it, my friend."

Less than convinced, Hay bowed.

At last, that evening, the feast given by the Guilds of Aberdeen for the monarch and Council over, Robert Bruce had privacy to draw from his doublet the unopened letter which had been contained within the other sent by William Lamberton. Even the sight of the strong and somewhat carelessly formed handwriting set his heart stirring. Feasting, drinking and dancing still went on below, and would for hours yet, if he knew his brother Edward; but he had managed to slip away, he hoped scarcely noticed, leaving the same Edward cavorting with a Christina who was at some small pains to show her liege lord a certain coolness. That suited the King well enough this night. He was as fond of gaiety as any — he had been accounted too gay, once — and had been starved of it, like the others, for too long; but that crushed unopened letter had lain over his heart for long hours, setting up its own vibrations within him. Now, in his own bedchamber, he broke the seals.

He read:

My loved lord and dear husband.

I have written you many letters these weary months, for my own heart's ease only, knowing they could not come to you. And so burned them in the fire, that in their very smoke some small waft of their love and aching might sail on an air kinder than men north and north over the long leagues to Scotland and my dear. Foolish woman that I am.

But now, I write in sudden gladness, so that I can scarce hold this quill from trembling, and you may scarce be able to read these feeble words for splutters of ink and tear-drops — I who am no weeper, as you know. Fool, indeed. But these are tears of joy, my sweet, in that at last I may write in the hope that you may read. For Bishop Lamberton is come to me, the first friend's face I have seen in more than a year. Who says that he has means to carry a letter to you secretly. I thank God for it.

I thank God also, Robert, for the tidings the Bishop gives me of you. Hereto they have told me only that you are a hunted outlaw, a murderer, a slayer of the innocent, harried and driven. Or else that you are fled the country, gone beyond the seas, in Ireland or Norway. Yet since you cannot be both, in truth, I have taken heart from their lies. And know at least that you were alive, and a trouble to these my captors.

Now, the saints be praised, I learn that you are indeed still your own true man, and mine, a scourge to your enemies, winning victories and waging war for your kingdom. So prayers are answered after all, and I rejoice.

I am held close prisoner here, but you must not deem me ill-used or woeful. I see no friendly faces, and live the plainest. But I have a garden to walk in and dwell, I swear, a deal more comfortably than does my lord. None treat me as Queen, but at least I am the Earl of Ulster's daughter. When I hear of what is done to the other women of our company, and to your poor daughter Marjory, I could hate my own betterment. But Robert, how I do long for you. Estate, and bodily wellbeing, these matter less than nothing when I have not you in company. Would that you had heeded me in Strathfillan, and allowed that I remain with you. No privations and wanderings and dangers, at your side, could have matched the sorrows of this long separation.

I heard, my dear, what King Edward, the old Edward, did to your brothers. To the gallant Nigel, and to Thomas and Alex. As to Christopher Seton. My heart bleeds for you. I pray nightly for the souls of them, as for the damnation in hell of he who did these monstrous things. It is almost beyond belief that a man could be so vile. Yet I thought not ill of my God-sire once. I believe that only a sickness of the mind could have served for this.

Who knows how the new King will deal with us. He is much other to his father and a lesser man in most things, I am sure. But I do not believe that he will relent in any degree towards Scotland or to yourself. And therefore to me. So I do not deceive myself that he will let me return to you, save you make him. And God knows how that is to be done, for I do not. Although I pray for it unceasingly. The Bishop, it is clear, thinks as I do, and he knows this King better than do we. Robert, my good Robert — how in Christ's sweet name are we to come together again?

Ah, forgive me, my brave lord, that I should write so. It is no wife's part to assail your eyes and ears with my woman's wails. Indeed, the fact that I can be no wife to you is the worst of me. For my body, as my mind and heart, does long for you. And you know that I am near as lusty of temper as you are. You wed no modest, gentle milk-white Queen, my lord King, no meek sufferer, so that sometimes I do fear for my reason . . .

These last sentences had been scored through with a spluttering pen, but were readable enough. And eloquent.

Heed me not, Robert. This is not my true self that writes so. I am but carried away by this so unexpected link with you. Somehow you have of a sudden seemed to come very close, so that I feel I must needs grasp out at you, to hold you, keep you, lest you go from me again. When indeed all there is, out there, is a patient Bishop waiting for this foolish paper. But it is too late to write another, better letter now. I have kept your friend waiting too long already.

Here is the truth of it, Robert. I need you. I miss you beyond all telling. But I can wait. Oh yes, I can wait, never fear. One day,

God willing, I will be wife to you again. But meantime, my love, I know your man's need. I know you to be a hot man. Meet your need for women as best you may, Robert. I wed you knowing that need. But of a mercy do not tell me of it. I am foolish. You have my understanding in this. But scarce my blessing. Take who you will my, Robert — but oh my heart, love only

your

ELIZABETH

That last line and signature was scarcely decipherable, a straggling scrawl, blotted and tailing away. The reading of it brought quick tears to the man's own eyes.

Long Bruce sat, on the sub-Prior's bed, with that letter in clenched hand, motionless, though sometimes his lips moved, and once or twice he groaned a little. From below, the sound of music and revelry rose faintly — strange sounds from a monastery.

Then he stiffened as another sound came close. There was a brief knock at the door, and Christina MacRuarie opened it. She stood there slightly flushed but looking very handsome.

The King looked at her, but scarcely saw her.

"You read your letter again, rather than dance? Or even sleep?" she demanded. "Are bishops' letters so much to your taste?"

"It is from my wife," he said slowly. "Elizabeth."

"Oh," She stared, biting her red lip. "Your pardon. She . . . the Queen? She is well?"

He inclined his head.

"Then, Sire, I think . . . that you will not be requiring me? This night?"

"I thank you — no," he said. "A . . . a goodnight to you, Christina."

She shook her head, and in those darkly vivid eyes was a strange expression, compounded of pain and pity, regret and a deep understanding. And something more. Without a word she turned and left him there.

CHAPTER THIRTEEN

THE singer's voice rose strong, clear, tuneful, yet with a haunting sadness, to pause on a rising, questioning note that was at once and strangely both plaintive and challenging, a note that was allowed to die away into the blue hush of the night and merge with the lap-lap of the wavelets on the lochshore and the sigh of air in the scattered Scots pines whose sturdy gnarled trunks redly reflected the glow of the camp-fires. Quivering, the composite liquid sound seemed to soar away over heather and water, for long breathless moments before the tremendous, fiercely positive refrain crashed out again from a thousand throats, yet in perfect unison and unbroken melody. Robert Bruce shivered, though not with cold, as his mother's Celtic blood responded to the ancient magic of it, even though he understood only a little of the distinctively West Highland Gaelic of the saga's wording. Words are by no means essential to emotion, especially of a summer's night amongst the endless mountains that throng long Loch Ness.

It was a young giant who sang, clad in saffron tunic, piebald calfskin jerkin and gem-studded harness, with strongly mobile features and shoulder-length tawny hair which, like the great ox-horned helmet he had laid by, spoke of the Norse influence which for centuries had permeated the Gaelic Hebrides. Only in the Celtic civilisation, with its emphasis on the arts of living, in music and song and poetry, design and beauty would a young man who sang thus, before all, not be considered effeminate; this singer need fear no such imputation, at any rate, for he was a renowned warrior, Seumas son of Donald, son of Ranald, of Oronsay, one of Angus Og's chieftains.

As the rich, vibrant tenor commenced yet another verse of the ballad — the tenth, or perhaps the twelfth — the King, asprawl on a springy couch of pine-twigs and bracken, gazed round at the scene with some measure of real satisfaction. For here, surely, was something that he had achieved, and only he. Never before, since the realm of Scotland became a unity, had a King of Scots been able to do what he was doing. Here was a wholly Highland host, only the Earl of Lennox — who was a sort of tamed Highlander himself — sitting at his right, and Gibbie Hay, with his charge Thomas Randolph, were Southrons, the former frankly asleep, the latter looking stiffly bored. All the rest, chiefs and chieftains, from Angus of the Isles and Neil Campbell of Lochawe, down to the running gillies and horse-boys, were clansmen, Highlanders to a man — Islesmen of the MacDonald and MacRuarie confederation; Campbells from South Argyll; MacGregors whom they had collected at Glen Strae and Glen Orchy, under their intimidating chief Malcolm himself; Macleans of Morvern; and most interest- of all, Macphersons, Cattanachs, Shaws and Mackintoshes from Badenoch, Comyn lands which they had passed through on their move north from Lorn — but which, unlike the true Lowland Comyn country of Buchan, had only been gained in conquest by its Norman lords, not married into, so that its Highland population showed no enmity to Bruce, and following the example of the West Highland chiefs contributed their quota to the royal advancing army. Hitherto no King of Scots would, or could, have entrusted himself to a Highland army, since the Lowlanders looked upon these people as barbarians, little better than vermin, not to be associated with nor trusted. Yet here he lay, secure and accepted, within a company of 4,000 and more of these Highlanders, on the southern shore of Loch Ness, hundreds of miles deep within their mountain fastnesses. Moreover, using them to counter another Highland army, just across the water.

The King turned his glance, as he had done frequently that early August night, away from the dramatic scene of blazing fires and flaring pitch-pine torches and the thronged colourful ranks of fierce-looking clansmen, lit by the glow of the flames, against the twisted silhouettes of the trees and the black outlines of the crouching mountains — turned to the north. Loch Ness, although all of twenty-three miles long, was little more than a mile wide here, between Dores and Inverfarigaig: and across that mile more fires gleamed red against black hills.

For what seemed leagues those points of light glowed and flickered, left and right, marking the north shore of the loch, though they were less bright to the right, the north, where Urquhart Bay curved deeply back at the mouth of Glen Urquhart. The sky was overcast and dark for an August night, so that the host of fires showed the brighter, where the Earl of Ross's army awaited them, had awaited them for days; indeed, from all accounts, for weeks, on the borders of his great territory. For all Scotland to the north of where they camped here was in the grip of William of Ross, since it consisted of but the two mighty earldoms, and Sutherland happened to be heired by a minor, whom Ross dominated. Caithness was a no-man's-land, disputed between the crowns of Scotland and Norway, but in fact its unruly clans were also under the thumb of Ross. How many men lay encamped across Loch Ness none knew for certain — though there were tales of tens of thousands. That was undoubtedly an exaggeration — but there was enough to give Bruce pause, at any rate.

His glance, as had happened before, tended to dwell upon a certain point over there, some way east of directly across the dark waters. Here the pattern of lights was different, the gleams smaller and feebler and clustered close together, some indeed one above another. And it was noticeable that none of the larger lights looked close to these, on either side. For these indeed were not fires at all, but lights from windows, candle lamp or torch — the lights of Urquhart Castle on its rocky thrusting peninsula to the south of Urquhart Bay. That was Crown property, a royal castle, strong and strategically placed at the mouth of Glen Urquhart, guarding the only road to lead into the north-east between Inverness and the Western Sea. And presently held by Sir Alexander Comyn, brother of the Earl of Buchan.

The King rubbed his chin, eyes narrowed.

The singing was succeeded by Highland dancing, seemingly wild but essentially disciplined nevertheless, with the wailing, shrilling, groaning music of the bagpipes bubbling and skirling to hills and sky, when Bruce suddenly came to a decision and rose to his feet.

Angus Og, from near by, looked up. "You join the dancing, Sir King?" he asked, brows raised.

"Not tonight. I think that I will make a call. Across the loch. The night being dark."

"Now? By night? You mean — in force?"

"No. A secret call. Private, very. Come you with me, my lord?"

The other hesitated. "If so you wish. And believe it worth the doing."

"I believe it worth the trial, at least, yes. There are more weapons than swords in a King's armoury, friend."

Though all there who could hear looked uncertain, many wished to accompany the monarch nevertheless. But Bruce declared that two small boats were all that should go, the second only as a precaution in case of trouble. For days the Highlanders had been collecting boats from all up and down the lochside for many miles, assembling them hereabouts; also felling trees for rafts, for the boats to tow over. The shoreline was a mass of craft therefore, for 4,000 men would take a deal of ferrying across that mile of water, should it ever come to that.

Ordering the dancing to continue, the King led a little group out of the circle of the firelight and down to the shingly beach. Angus Og, Hay and Randolph — who was religiously taken everywhere that Hay went — joined Bruce, with two gillies for the oars, in one boat; Lennox, Campbell and the young man whom Bruce had knighted with Somerled's sword at Castle Tioram, Sir Ranald MacRuarie of Smearisary, went in the second boat. Christina MacRuarie had returned to Moidart, meantime, during the recent Lorn campaign, but had sent her nephew, Sir Ranald, with 400 men, as her link with the King. A popular young man with the Highlanders, because of his story-telling abilities, he now rejoiced in the somewhat empty title of royal cup-bearer. At the last moment a long lean dark figure came scuttling down to the strand, and came clambering aboard the King's craft, all flapping black robes, much to the scorn of Angus of the Isles — Master Bernard de Linton, the secretary. Shrugging, Bruce let him stay.

The oarsmen were set to row half-right, north by east, and at their quietest.

Presently, above the creak of rowlocks and splash of blades, Bruce heard sounds at their backs, and stared astern.

"There are craft behind us," he jerked. "Following."

"More than one," the Lord of the Isles agreed grimly. "Think you I would allow the whole leadership of this host to risk capture over there? Without a sufficiency of broadswords at our backs to ensure our safety."

The King frowned. "I said two small boats," he snapped. Then he waved a hand, assenting. "So be they keep out of sight. And quiet, I told you, it is not swords I am concerned with, this night."

With their own fires become mere points of light, in turn, strung along the southern shore, and some of the enemy's seeming alarmingly near now, the oarsmen, pulling very gently, drew in towards the dark and lofty bulk of Urquhart Castle on its bluff of headland. From this water-level its high walls, battlements, flanking-towers and soaring central keep looked impressive indeed, daunting. It was after midnight now, and few windows showed a light.

About fifty yards from the rocks, Bruce ordered the oarsmen to be still, and raised his voice. He did not shout, but called.

"Ho, the watch! Hear me. Does any keep watch in Urquhart Castle of a night?" Only on an overcast night at this time of year could they have won thus close, unspotted.

Swiftly he had reply. "Hey — fit's that? Fa's there?" a broad Aberdeenshire voice gave back, from one of the flanking-towers' parapets. "Guidsakes, is't a boat?"

"It is your King, man. Fetch you Sir Alexander Comyn, who captains this my castle of Urquhart."

"Eh . . .? Guidsakes — the King? Bruce . . .?"

"Fat's to do, Tosh?" somebody shouted, from another tower. "I can see twa boats. Sma' yins . . ."

'Quickly, fool!" Bruce commanded. "Tell Sir Alexander that King Robert requires speech with him. And no outcry, or you will suffer for it."

"Ooh, aye. Aye, Wait you . . ."

It was nerve-racking for them all to sit there, swaying on the water, so close to their toes — for Ross's patrols assuredly would be on the watch along all that waterfront, save just immediately in the vicinity of the castle's promontory. Bruce was torn between thankfulness, after all, for the presence of Angus Og's supporting craft somewhere behind, and the fear that these larger boats would loom visible from the main shore.

It seemed a long time before another voice sounded from the castle — not from any flanking-tower this time but evidently from a window of the great keep, though there was no light.

"Who claims to be the Bruce?" it demanded, in very different tones. "At this hour?"

"I do, Alexander Comyn. Your liege lord, whose castle you now occupy. You know my voice, as I know yours. In whose name do you hold the castle of Urquhart against me, sir?"

There was a pause, as well there might be. For Comyn to admit that he held it by right of conquest was to put himself in the wrong, since there was no question but that Urquhart was a royal castle. To say that he held it in the name of King Edward would be something of a humiliation for the proud Comyn, who undoubtedly considered himself an ally of the English King rather than a vassal.

"I hold it in the name of King John," he replied, at length. "King John Baliol."

"Then you are the only man in Christendom, Sir Alexander, who still calls John Baliol monarch!"

The other made no comment.

"I have come for my castle," Bruce went on. "Yield it to me, Sir Alexander, as is your duty and right, and you may remain its keeper."

The gasps of those beside him in the boat drowned any reaction that Comyn might have made.

"You hear me, sir? Do your duty. Yield me Urquhart, and I will forget the past. I will confirm you as keeper."

Still there was no perceptible reaction from the castle. Bruce cleared his throat. This calling across seventy or so yards of water was trying on the vocal cords.

"I have always considered you a man of some understanding, Comyn. No hot-headed fool, to throw away life and fortune on a lost cause. You have too much to lose, for that. And your Comyn cause is lost, whatever happens here. You know that. You have heard what is done in Buchan?"

"I have heard of savagery and shame. Of destruction. A fair land made a desert. A whole province harried without mercy. Do you boast of that?"

"I am not here to boast, sirrah. I am here to offer you terms. Or to destroy you. Destroy you as Buchan is destroyed. That Comyn shall never again threaten Bruce. The choice is yours.

Make your peace with me, your liege lord. Or fall — not to rise again."

"I am not like to fall, my lord. This castle is strong. And my nephew, the Earl of Ross, has a greater host than yours, encamped around Urquhart. You will not easily win across Loch Ness to come at me."

"Ross and his host are not here to save *you*, Comyn! They are here only to prevent me crossing the loch and entering their country. If they are outflanked, as they will be, they will leave you, like a stranded fish! They love you not, a Southron." Bruce took a chance. "I warrant the Earl of Ross, nephew though he may be, is not with you in my castle, Sir Alexander! Nephews are not always strong in their duty." And the King glanced over at Thomas Randolph.

Silence from the castle. Ross's mother was indeed Sir Alexander's sister, who had married the second Mac-an-Tagart Earl; but the Rosses remained purely Highland in outlook, with little interest in the Lowland Comyns.

Summoning reluctant lungs to the task, Bruce proceeded. "My brother, the Earl of Carrick, has finished laying Buchan low. He has done it thoroughly, and on my command. Not a single castle or place of strength, not a single slated house, or town or village remains to Comyn therein. Now he marches to meet me here. He is not far off, Sir Alexander. To the east. It is for him I wait, for he has my main host. But I have sent the word for him to come by the *north* shore of this loch, not the south! He will cross the river at Inverness. That town will not, cannot, withstand him. I expect him here tomorrow, Comyn. How long, think you, will Ross linger round Urquhart Castle when my brother appears on his flank? And with Lachlan MacRuarie, of whom you will have heard, marching from the North-West. He will retire up Glen Urquhart, to seek a stronger line in Strath Glass, where he may not be outflanked. You know it."

The continuing lack of response from the dark building was very eloquent.

"I offer you better terms than you deserve, sir." Bruce's voice growing hoarse and tired, now. "But I have a realm to win and to govern, and require the services of strong and able men, whether they love me or no. I would have Comyn, if not my friend, at least not my enemy. Your brother, the Earl of Buchan, is a broken man, and ill. Now in disgrace in England, it is said. The Comyn power is broken quite. You are the last to hold out against me. Let there be an end to this folly, Sir Alexander. Why should more men die? *My* subjects. Yield me this castle, and Tarradale on the Black Isle, also a royal house but held by you. Come into my peace. Then, I say the past is past. You shall remain keeper here, and your lands shall not be forfeit. How say you?"

"I . . . I must think on it. I require time to consider. To consider well . . ."

"Then you are a fool as well as a traitor, Comyn!" That was Angus Og, who could restrain himself no longer. "This King is over-kind, I say. He offers you a deal more than would I. It is Angus of the Isles who speaks. Most of the men yonder are mine. I have taken and burned many a stouter hold than this. Myself, I would have no parleying. And *you* would hang on your own dule-tree tomorrow!"

Bruce smiled to himself, at that.

From the other boat, only a couple of lengths away, someone else spoke up. "This is Malcolm of Lennox. You know me, Alexander Comyn. Do as His Grace asks, I pray you. We have had enough of killing and hatred. The King is right. And he is a true man. He keeps his word. What gain to you now by withstanding him? This our country, our kingdom, needs to be built up — 'fore God it does! Not torn apart. King Robert is the man to do it. You were ever the best of the Comyns. Will you not aid him in it?"

"Well said, Malcolm," Bruce murmured.

"Would you have me betray my own kin?" the voice from the castle came back. "The Earl of Ross?"

Bruce answered. "I ask no man to betray other. There has been too much betrayal in this Scotland. I say that you will serve Ross well. He cannot win against the rest of Scotland. None come to his aid. He hoped for aid from John of Lorn. But *we* have just come from Lorn. MacDougall licks his wounds. He has not come north, nor will do. And yesterday we captured a courier from Ross. To King Edward of England. Beseeching aid. Saying that he was sore pressed. That he had insufficient men to protect all the North. That unless he received English aid soon he must retire into a closer country. Knew you of this letter?"

That elicited no reply.

"Edward will not aid him, Comyn. *You* know that. Has he aided Comyn? This Edward is not as his father. Ross will win aid from none. The sooner he perceives it, the better. I do not wish to fight him. Even he, who delivered up my wife and daughter, I will receive into my peace. Tell him so. He is my subject. And by yielding me this castle, open his eyes, man."

"I must consider it. Give me time to think on it . . . Sire."

Bruce caught his breath in his hoarse throat. That one reluctant word, from Comyn's lips! Sire! It might serve — the thing might serve!

"Very well, Sir Alexander," he called. "Think you. Think well. I give you until tomorrow's noon." Edward had sent word that he would arrive the next forenoon. "This is a royal castle. Somewhere in it will be its royal standard, the Lion Banner of Scotland. Tomorrow, fly that standard above this castle, and pull down your Comyn colours — and I accept you into my peace. Keep your own banner flying — and I destroy you. Is it understood?"

"It is understood."

"Very well. I bid you a good night, sir. And may tomorrow's sun shine kindly for Scotland! For us all!"

Thankfully the rowers dipped their oars, to pull away.

"You are a strange man, Robert Bruce." Angus Og declared, as they headed back into the south-west. "Both cunning and trusting. Fierce enough, yet too kind of heart. You truly would forgive the Comyn all?"

Bruce was staring at the dark shapes of fully half a dozen larger boats which now loomed out of the night ahead of them. "It is not my heart that is so kind, I fear, Angus, my friend," he said slowly. "My head, rather. I am cursed, or blessed, with a head that speaks different from my heart, in many matters. Or perhaps it is that a king must have two hearts? One his own, and one for his kingdom, his people. And the first must needs give way to the second — or his coronation vows are worthless. I do not say that I forgive Comyn — yet. One day, perhaps. But I will keep my promise to him. If he submits."

"Oh, he will submit," Hay said. "You heard that Sire? There spoke the decision he will make, I swear."

Out of the quiet that followed, another voice made itself heard, one that seldom spoke. "My lord," Sir Thomas Randolph said, "was it truth that you said? That you would accept even William of Ross to your peace? The Earl? He who betrayed your lady?"

"God helping me, yes. Even he. For the sake of this realm."

"This, I say, is too much!" Campbell put in, vehemently. "I say Your Grace will turn mercy into weakness. And as such, men will see it."

"Not mercy, Neil. Nor yet weakness, I think. It is policy. God knows I find no mercy in my heart for William of Ross. But if I am to rid Scotland of the English invaders, I cannot afford a single enemy at home that I may win over or disarm, by word or deed. And Ross has thousands, who would take much beating, in the field."

Randolph spoke again, stiffly, formally — and sounding very

young. "Then, my lord — if tomorrow Sir Alexander Comyn yields, and comes into your peace, I too will do likewise. He is an honourable knight. I can do no less."

"Did I hear a puppy bark?" the Lord of the Isles snorted.

"You heard a man with a notable conscience, my lord. An inconvenience which is not laid upon us all!" Bruce kept his voice grave. "Well said, nephew. We shall see."

"I fear there will soon be more traitors in Your Grace's company than true men . . ." Campbell was beginning, when the King interrupted, abruptly changing the subject.

"My lord of the Isles — you would hear me tell Comyn that Lachlan MacRuarie approaches from the north-west, to threaten Ross's right flank. He does — but we know that he cannot be nearer than Kintail, and so near three days' march. Scarce so near as I made him sound! I think we must . . . dissemble a little, tomorrow. Despite all our noble words and conscience! If my nephew will overlook it, this once! The MacRuarie host is too far away for my purpose — but young Sir Ranald here has 400 men — and a MacRuarie banner! If you gave him some men of yours, say 600, to a fair showing, and sent him round this loch, to approach from the west, he might well be mistaken for his bastard uncle!"

"Ha!"

"How long would it take, think you, for your swift Highlandmen to get to the head of this Loch Ness, across the Oich River, into the hills to the north, and so up this far again?"

"It is sixteen miles and more to the fords at Bunoich. Six to Invermoriston on the north shore. Then up into the hills of Balmacaan, behind Mealfuarvonie, another eight — a hard eight. Thirty heather miles in all. In eight or nine hours, if need be, my people could be where you would have them."

"I would not have believed that men could cover rough country at that pace — had I not already seen your Highlandmen doing as much! Good — then we shall have them away forthwith, this night. And see if young Sir Ranald commands men so well as he tells tales of it! You will lend him your hundreds, Angus?"

"You command this host, Sir King — not I. But . . . is this thrust for fighting? Or only to make your fair showing? For if there is to be battle over there, I shall want some of my own tried captains in command, and no stripling fireside knight!"

"They will fight only if they must. But send whom you will . . ."

Next morning, after early rain, the great camp by the lochside was astir with activity. Scores of boats, and as many rafts, were assembled, manned and marshalled into flotillas, and embarkation and disembarkation practised, with raft-towing exercises out as far as mid-loch. Bruce sighed with relief when the last of the rain lifted off the hilltops, and the first watery sunbeams lit up the Great Glen of Scotland, giving crystal-clear rainwashed visibility — for visibility was all-important today. He sent trumpeters and hornblowers off to sundry eminences and viewpoints up and down the loch, to sound their calls and assemblies intermittently, and ordered all troops not engaged in the boat and beach-landing exercises to march and counter-march over a wide area of the shoreline, with all banners flying and pipes playing — but only in places where they would be seen and heard from across the mile-wide waters. Some of the Highland chieftains grumbled and snarled at this folly of play-acting; but the King was adamant. The air of excitement generated, however artificial, grew none the less.

Then in mid-forenoon, Gilbert Hay called to the King, and pointed almost due west, across the loch. High on the long purple ride that ran north-eastwards parallel with the shore, from the fine peak of Mealfuarvonie, a dark crest had appeared, almost like a forest of young trees grown suddenly there. But the flash of steel in the sun told a different story, and by straining the eyes it was just possible to distinguish the square black-and-white banner that rose above its approximate centre.

"So, Angus," Bruce exclaimed, "Your Islesmen have not failed us! Eight hours, no more. Show me any other fighting-men who could cover thirty roadless mountain miles in such time! What will my lord of Ross say to that, think you?"

'He will have heard, hours back, that they approach, for he is no fool and will have had his scouts well placed."

"That alters nothing. So long as he does not know that they came from this side of the loch. Believes them Lachlan Mac-Ruarie's host."

"It is good that we can see them so clearly," Hay pointed out. "For if we can see MacRuarie up there, a mile and more back from the loch, then we need not fear that Ross cannot see our busyness here."

"As you say. How think you Comyn feels this morning?"

They looked towards Urquhart Castle, where the blue-and-gold Comyn flag still could be seen fluttering above the keep.

"I vow he bites his nails, and scans all that he can see from his topmost tower! If he has not already made his decision."

As the royal forces kept up there almost feverish activities, the leaders' eyes kept turning ever more and more to the north-east. Edward Bruce, the triumphant harrier of Buchan, had sent word that he would join his brother that morning, from Inverness a dozen miles away, and the King's urgent orders were that he should advance along the north shore of Loch Ness until he made first contact with Ross's left flank outliers. At first light that morning another mounted courier had been sent hot-foot to Edward, who was meantime laying tentative siege to English-held Inverness Castle, as to the importance of the arrangement, and its timing They could see for miles towards the loch-foot at Dochfour, from the knoll directly behind the main camp. He should have been in sight before this. Could the hot-head already have taken action against Ross, somewhere to the north, while he still had command of Bruce's main army? By the Bunchrew or Moniack valleys, perhaps, thinking to take Ross in the rear? It was the sort of thing Edward might do . . .

As time went on and the sun rose towards the meridian, the King grew agitated, pacing the turf of the knoll. He should not have relied on Edward in so ticklish an issue as this.

When at last a shout went up, the fingers pointed, it was not towards Dochfour and the foot of the loch that eyes turned, but along the wooded shore road on their own side of the water. Less than a mile away, towards Dores, there was a sizeable gap in trees, and there a mounted cavalcade could be seen, the red-and-gold Bruce banner at its head.

"God's curse on all witless headstrong dolts!" the King cried. "Why am I plagued with such a brother! My orders were clear. Clear enough for a babe. But not for Edward . . .!"

As the mounted party drew near, appearing and disappearing amongst the woodland at a round canter, it could be seen that it was a gallant company indeed, all splendid armour, new-painted heraldic shields, silken surcoats, tossing plumes, flowing horse trappings, waving pennons — and all superbly mounted. But it was not an army. There were not more than some fifty men, though most of them appeared to be of knightly rank.

The King eyed their brilliance from under down-drawn brows.

They came jingling up, Edward at their head, more magnificent than any had ever seen him. He wore black polished plate armour, engraved with gold, and even his chain-mail was threaded with gold wire; his black chased helmet bore scarlet and yellow ostrich plumes, his sword-belt and even his spurs were of gold. He raised a gauntleted hand in flourished salutation, as he pulled up a notable stallion richly caparisoned.

"Well met, brother," he called heartily. "I greet you right royally! Here's a good day for our cause. I hope, though, that I see you well? You look thin, Robert, thin."

The King moistened his lips. He looked by comparison shabby, in peat-stained clothing and rusty mail. He was always at his worst with this brother of his, and knew it. Nigel had been hot-headed too, and probably less able in some ways than Edward; but at him had not always felt the need to rail and contend.

"I am well enough," he said evenly, dredging for patience. "I scarce need ask how you are! I rejoice to see you so fine! But I had not looked to see you *here*, this morning!"

"I was so near, it were folly not to come. To bring you my good news in person. And to show you how we may best deal with this traitor Ross."

Bruce bit back hot words. He looked from his brother to the ranks of glittering chivalry at his back, not a man of which was not the picture of knightly pride and circumstance. He saw Sir Alexander Fraser and his brother Sir Simon, Sir Robert Fleming, Sir John Stirling, Sir William Wiseman, Sheriff of Elgin, Sir David Barclay and his brother Sir Walter, Sir John de Fenton and Sir William Hay, a kinsman of Gibbie's. It was as good as a court Edward had to ride with him. It was very evident that these had been conducting a very different kind of war to his own, and a profitable one.

"Where is my host, my lord?" he asked, carefully. "My main army?"

His brother waved from the saddle approximately north-easterly. "Back yonder. North of the river. Ten miles. Boyd has it . . ."

"North of the *river*? The River Ness? I said the loch. North of the *loch*, man!"

"What matters it? A mile or so more or less? So long as they are across the river. That Ross may not hold it against us. See you, brother — this notion you have of crossing the loch in boats is folly. You will lose most of your men. Even though they are only Highlandmen! Ross can defend the far shore with ease. Throw you back into the water. Have you counted the cost? I have a better plan, by far. Beyond Inverness to the north is a narrow plain, by the side of the firth. Off it open two valleys, the waters of Bunchrew and Moniack. These lead into the mountains of The Aird, behind Ross's position. Up these, and we can take him in the rear. I told Boyd to halt my host at the place called Dochgarroch. By the river. From there I can send the foot up a small side valley, and so through the hills to the greater one of Bunchrew. The horse will have to take the longer way round, by the Dunain. When they see a smoke signal from me, on some hill-top here. Your Highlanders would best go round the head of the loch and make a sally from the west."

The King, who had been holding himself in with difficulty, spoke curtly. "My lord — do I understand that you have taken upon yourself to countermand my express orders? That you have told Sir Robert Boyd to take my host — *mine*, not yours, Edward — no further than this Dochgarroch? When I commanded that you bring it along the loch until you made contact with Ross's left flank?"

At his brother's flinty sternness, the other lost a little of his fine assurance. "I told you — this way we can confound Ross. Save many lives ..."

"Dizzard! Think you Ross does not know Bunchrew and Moniack Waters? In his own territory? Think you *I* did not consider them? But ..." He cut his hand down sharply in a chopping motion. "... Whether you thought or did not think, is of no consequence. I commanded, and you disobeyed. How dare you, sir!"

For long moments the two brothers stared into each other's eyes, there before all. None thought to intervene.

Edward put as bold a face on it as he might. "I did what I believed for the best. For your cause ... Sire."

"In this kingdom none countermands the King's commands — none, I say! You hear? All hear?" Robert Bruce's voice quivered, but only with his attempt to keep under control the hot ire that boiled up within him. "I heed and take advice from all. I let my mind be altered, in debate. I do not claim all wisdom. But ... my orders are royal commands. And any who choose to disobey them are guilty of treason. Treason! Do you hear?" He paused, and swung his wrathful gaze on all who listened, before returning to his brother. "Any — be they the highest in the land or the lowest. Remember, all of you — if you value your heads!"

There was a complete silence from all near by, broken only by the jingle of bits and bridles, and the stamping of hooves. From further afield a trumpet brayed to the surrounding hill, its echoes a bedlam.

As though accepting that as a sign, an assent, the King drew a long slow breath, and changed his tone. "This Dochgarrach? I know the place. It is too far to be seen from Castle Urquhart, is it not? Eight miles? Does any here know the castle well? It stands high, on a rock out into the loch. But not to view as far as Dochgarroch, I fear."

"I know it, Sir King," Angus MacFarquherd Mackintosh, Captain of Clan Chattan, said from behind. "It is too far. Not to be seen. There is higher land between."

"Aye." That was almost a sigh. "Then, my lord of Carrick, you have destroyed *my* stratagem. I never thought to throw men's lives away by attacking Ross across the loch, in these boats. I am less fond than are you of killing. Even Ross and his thousands are my subjects — and a king does not slay his subjects unless he must. What I may gain by any other means than the sword, I will. I let you loose on Buchan for a purpose, as example. Today, I had no intention of fighting. And my main host, visible there at the foot of the loch, was part of my design. You have brought it to naught."

Edward shook his head, helplessly. "I did not know. You did not tell me . . ."

"No — I did not tell you. I *commanded* you!" The King turned roughly away. "Now I must think anew . . ."

"But, Robert — Sire! My news! You have not heard my news. Hear me. Last night, the English in Inverness Castle asked for a truce. They are willing to surrender the castle, if we will spare them their lives, let them sail away. They have not failed to hear of my doings in Buchan, I swear! They sweat for their skins! They must be short of provision, to offer this. So I sent their messengers back, with their tails between their legs — like whipped curs should have! They will surrender without terms, I told them. And they will, you see. Any day. So that there will be only Banff Castle in all the North, held by Englishmen — for it can only be taken by sea. Aberdeen has fallen. That Provost and his citizens have won into it — how I know not. *I* have taken Fyvie, Elgin, Forres and Nairn from the English, and Kinedar, Slains, Rattray, Cairnbulg, Dundarg and Inverallochy from the Comyns. The Bishop of Moray now threatens Tarradale in the Black Isle. If we but take our courage in our hands and beat Ross now, all the North is yours! Do you not see it?"

"I see, brother, that there is a tide flowing our way, here in the North. And I rejoice in it. And give thanks for what you have achieved, with my host. But I also see, across this loch, some ten thousand, it may be, of fierce clansmen, ready to fight to the death. On their own territory, where they fight best. And know best. In mountains, where our chivalry is at disadvantage. Here is no attacking small bands, castles, villages and townships. This is battle, on a great scale. It may be that in time we should beat them. At much cost, which I can ill afford. And MacDougall of Lorn remains in the West, undefeated. I do not fight battles until I have tried other methods."

Edward began to speak, but the King held up his hand.

"You talk of courage. I have never doubted yours, brother. Perhaps you have more of the quality than have I! It is your wits, your judgement, I doubt. Even in this of Inverness Castle. I say the English offer of surrender must be accepted. On terms. Ross will hear of it, and be the less assured. The sight of the Englishry marching of their own will out of Inverness and sailing south will do my cause more good than any prolonged siegery. Then we shall pull down the castle, like all the others, that it never again be held against me. I hope that you razed all these other yielded strengths as I ordered?"

As the other cleared his throat and sought for a judicious answer, someone else spoke.

"Sire — you have said wisely, generously. Like a true king. In all this. And none can doubt your courage."

"Ah, nephew — I thank you!" Bruce turned to bow, in only lightly disguised mockery.

"Our traitorous kinsman still with you, I see!" Edward said, thankful to change the subject.

Randolph ignored him. "More than castles may yield, Sire — when the time is come. Will Your Grace now accept me as your leal man? Your subject. Receive my hand and sword, as your true knight?" That was awkwardly, jerkily said, from stiff lips. "I submit me — as I promised."

The King eyed the young man's tensely handsome features, and then, as the significance of those last words dawned upon him, swung on his heel to stare elsewhere, much farther away.

There, across the water, Urquhart Castle glowed warm red-brown in the sun, against the blue loch and the purpling hills. And clear to see above its lofty keep floated a different banner now to the blue-and-gold of Comyn — the Lion Rampant of Scotland.

"God be praised!" Bruce breathed. "So it served. After all."

In the exclamations and chatter that followed, Gilbert Hay touched the King's elbow, and pointed farther away still, towards the loch-foot. He did not speak.

It was sun on steel again, glinting and flashing though far away, the tiny gleams reflecting over a wide area.

"Ha — by the Rude! So there we have it!" the King cried. "Praises be! Comyn saw that sooner than did we. Robert Boyd knows his duty, if others do not! My true veteran warrior! Brother — see you there. Sir Robert Boyd knows whose host he leads. He did not halt at your Dochgarroch, but brought them on right to the loch. As I commanded you. Mark it well. As Sir Alexander Comyn, in Urquhart, marked it. And has signified his capitulation to me by that Lion Standard. For this I planned. Here is more burden on the Earl of Ross than any blood-soaked attack." He jabbed a finger in the other direction, due westwards. "There, on the ridge of Mealfuarvonie, MacRuarie and a thousand clansmen stand. Here we marshal a host of boats. There Boyd threatens and Comyn yields. Ross will retire, *must* retire, north-wards. Up Glen Urquhart. Abandoning this line of Loch Ness and the Great Glen. He cannot make stand again until Strath Glass or Strath Farrar. So we gain a victory of sorts, and much country. Without a man slain!"

There was a great clamour of acclaim, with everywhere men surging forward to hail the King. The knights behind Edward, as with one accord, dismounted and came to make belated obeisance. But Bruce had turned away, towards Randolph again, who still stood with Hay, a pace or two behind. He held out his hand.

"Sir Thomas," he said, "you have keen eyes. A keen judgement in some matters. And a keen notion of honour. May they serve me and my cause well hereafter. This is an auspicious day. I receive you into my peace, and gladly. You are a free man, nephew. And all that is yours shall be restored to you."

Randolph sank down on knee before his uncle, and took that lean hand between both of his. "My liege lord," he said, thickly. "I thank you. From my heart. I pray your royal forgiveness, for past deeds done and past words spoken. Hereafter, none shall serve you more faithfully."

"So be it, lad." The King looked down, and felt — indeed looked — very old compared with the unlined and nobly handsome face upturned to his, despite his own mere thirty-four years. "But I warn you, my service may try you hard. As it does others."

He turned to receive the homage of the now thronging knights.

Presently he looked over their heads to Edward, who still sat his fine horse, set-faced. "Come, brother — enough of bickering and hard words. Perhaps I am too sore on you. You in par-ticular — since I am sore on all, I fear. This is too good a day to spoil. Come, you."

The other's face lightened, and he leapt down, his magnificent mail clanking, and strode to grasp the outstretched hand, word-less.

"You are mighty fine, Edward. Whose spoil is that you wear?" Bruce demanded, thumping the other's armoured shoulder.

"My lord of Buchan's. The spoil of Dundarg. And I have brought better for you. A whole train of it! The spoil of a province. And of the proudest, richest house in all Scotland."

"Aye. You will tell me of all your campaign presently. I have heard something of it, even in the West. All the land talks of the Harrying of Buchan. But meantime we make more play with these boats. Marshal them differently, farther down the loch a little, opposite Urquhart. With much show. As though we had changed our plans, and will pour all our forces in through the castle, now that it has declared for us. Instead of assailing the beaches, Ross could not halt our ingress to the castle, from the loch. So he will hasten his withdrawal, I think . . ."

Some time later, the cry went up that a small boat was coming sailing across the loch towards this position. Presently it was seen that what had looked like a sail was in fact a large white flag.

"So Sir Alexander Comyn comes to make his peace with me," the King commented. "Bringing the keys of his castle. We must receive him suitably. In some style."

"I *hanged* my Comyns," Edward mentioned briefly.

But in a little, the sharp-eyed Hay was calling that it was not Comyn in the boat. There were four occupants, two rowers and two others, both young and in Highland dress. Interested, the party round Bruce watched and waited.

As the craft beached on the shingle, and the two young men jumped out, one holding aloft the white flag, Angus Og drew a quick breath.

"Hugh!" he exclaimed. "Hugh Ross, himself. Son of the chief. Eldest son. He of the red hair."

"Ha-a-a! You say so? Ross would talk, then!"

The red-headed newcomer was an open-faced, freckled, pleasant-looking man in his early twenties, well-built and richly clothed. He and his companion came pacing self-consciously up the beach towards the silently watchful and impressive group.

"I am Sir Hugh de Ross, son of the Earl," the redhead declared, in a rush. It was of passing interest to Bruce that this Highlander chose to Normanise his name thus. "This is a cousin, Ross of Cadboll. We have a mission from my father. To Sir Robert the Bruce, formerly Earl of Carrick." He was addressing himself to Edward, not Robert, perhaps not unnaturally in view of the difference in their appearance.

"I am King Robert. I greet the son of the Earl of Ross. And his kinsman. But how is it that you style yourself knight, sir?"

"King Edward of England knighted me. The old king."

"Ah. So we have at least that in common, sir. For he knighted me also! You would seem to have served him better than I did!"

The young man looked a little disconcerted. "I obey my father's commands, my lord."

"To be sure. A dutiful son — if less dutiful subject! Were you at Saint Duthac's chapel, at Tain? When your father violated that sanctuary, and tore my wife and daughter from before its altar, to hand over to your English Edward?"

"No, sir. I was crossing swords with Angus of the Isles — whom I see now at your shoulder. In the Western Sea. I do not make war on women and children. My father must answer for himself. He was seven years Edward's prisoner in the Tower of London. After capture at Dunbar fight. And released only on terms, four years ago. I think that he did not relish another spell in an English prison!"

"So he sent my women there instead!"

The other did not answer, and Bruce beat down the hot anger within him which was always so liable to rise and choke him when he most needed to be calm and clear-headed.

"So the Earl of Ross sends you as his messenger, sir?"

"Yes. He sends you offer of truce."

The gasps with which this bald statement was received came not only from the King. Nearly everyone who heard gasped. A truce! Offered, not sought, even. The gesture of a monarch to an equal. Even Angus Og, who might have adopted the same line himself, was outraged that the Earl of Ross should do so.

"Here's an insolent dog!" Edward exclaimed. "A truce, says he! That, from an accursed rebel! And a Highlandman, at that!"

"What mean you by that, sir?" Angus snapped.

"I mean here's a treacherous rogue acting the prince. Expecting us to treat with him. A truce, he says. He *offers* it, by the Mass!"

"Sir — I do not know your name. But none speaks of my father in my presence, and thinks to escape my steel! White flag or none." The red-head took a pace forward, hand on sword-hilt.

"Peace, peace!" the King intervened. "In *my* presence, none quarrel and bandy words! This is the Earl of Carrick, Sir Hugh — my brother. He should not have spoken of your father as he did. I declare it as unsaid. But — this of a truce. Subjects do not make truces with their monarch, sir."

"My father does not accept you as his monarch."

With a hand raised, Bruce quelled the snarl of wrath that rose around him. "Whom *does* my lord of Ross accept as his liege lord, then? Edward of England? Son of he who imprisoned him?"

"No, sir. John Baliol. Who abdicated only under duress, and still lives."

"How could he be King of Scots, when he lives the life of a recluse, in France? Has not set foot in Scotland for a dozen years?" Bruce caught himself up. "But I am not here to debate my kingship with you, sirrah. I was duly and properly crowned king two years ago. And am so accepted by all save a few stiff-necked rebels, as your father. And the Comyns. The Comyns I have dealt with. Now it is your turn."

"No parliament has yet accepted you as King, sir," the young man persisted. "Until it does, no man can be proclaimed rebel who holds to King John."

"Dear God — this is too much!" Edward cried. "You will stand and listen to such impudence, Sire? For if you will, *I* will not!"

"Patience, brother — as I seek patience. Here is a young man of courage, at least. Who takes his stand on forms and ordinances. We must humour him with the forms he respects. You would have a parliament approve my kingship, sir? So would I. But it must be a true and free parliament. And while the English invaders remain in Scotland, none such is possible. You would not deny that?"

"A parliament can and should confirm the power of a new monarch." That was the Earl of Lennox, speaking with authority. "But it does not make the monarch. Nor can unmake him. Once duly crowned."

"And I was duly crowned. At Scone. By its abbot. On the true Stone. The Bishop of St. Andrews anointing. The crown placed on my brow by one of the line of MacDuff. Your father was summoned thereto, sir. He did not come. He could have come, and made objection. He, one of the seven great earls of Scotland. Indeed it was his duty, if he believed me usurper."

"Did the Lord of the Isles, here, attend your coronation? Or any other from the Highlands — save only the Campbell?"

"Have done with this folly of words!" Angus Og broke in. "Words and more words! The sword speaks truer." And he gripped his own. "Sir King — send this puppy whence he came, I say."

"Aye — so say I!" It was not often that Edward Bruce and the Islesman agreed. Indeed, now, led by Neil Campbell, most of the notables there raised their voices to like effect.

"Wait, my friends," the King insisted. "If we accept the sword as the truest speaker, then the strongest rules all, and the weaker must fall. Like right and justice. This Sir Hugh Ross has invoked forms and allegiances. So be it. We will show him that in these we are stronger also. For this is a realm I seek to rule, not a tournament, nor a bear-pit! You, sir — you say that your father denies recognition of my kingship, and accepts John Baliol's. You deny John Baliol's abdication. Who forced that abdication? The King of England. Therefore the King of England is John Baliol's enemy. And therefore your father's. Is he not?"

Wary, the other inclined his head slightly.

"Yet, I have here a letter from your father. To the King of England. Captured, two days back." Bruce turned. "Master Bernard — you have the letter? Aye — give it to me. This, Sir Hugh, is your father's signature and seal? He writes to the King of England asking for soldiers, money, aid, to fight against his own fellow-subjects in Scotland. This letter then, by your own showing, by every form and observance, is treasonable. The work of a traitor. To me — or to John Baliol! Deny it!"

The young man bit his lip, eyes darting, silent.

"So! Now — this your mission here? What does the Earl of Ross say to the King of Scots?"

Sir Hugh cleared his throat, obviously much put out. "He offers . . . he suggests a truce, my lord. In any fighting between you. For a time. Three months. Six months — as you will. Each side to swear no advance on present positions, or any armed conflict. Each side to yield hostage to that effect. As pledge."

"Why?" That was barked out.

"Why — in the name of God?" Angus Og burst out. "Need you ask why? Because he is outflanked and outwitted! Because he would hold Ness-side and not have to retire up Glen Urquhart to Strath Glass. Because he would give himself time to gather more men. To await the coming of winter, when the passes are closed against you and you cannot attack him. Save by sea. We can all see why!"

"You mistake me, my lord," Bruce answered coolly. "I asked not why there should or should not be a truce. But why he would have me yield a pledge. A hostage. Me, the King."

The young man blinked. "It was my father's word," he said.

"And your father's word requires such support, sir? It does not stand of itself? So — what pledge does the Earl of Ross offer me, to reinforce his promise?"

"Me," the other answered simply. "Myself."

"I' faith — you! You, as hostage?"

"Yes, sir. His eldest son. Heir. To remain with you. In token of his honest intentions that there shall be no breaking of the truce."

"I see." Bruce paused, and actually smiled slightly. "You have made something of a strange entry to my Court and company, Sir Hugh Ross! But — who knows, you may come to adorn it well! Like, I hope, Sir Thomas Randolph. You two should agree well together! But, see you — this may be my lord of Ross's pledge and surety. Mine is otherwise. My simple royal word. The word of the King of Scots. I give no other surety to any subject, or any man. So send you your cousin here to tell your father so. It is all the surety he will get — or require. You understand?"

The red-head bowed.

It was some moments before it dawned on the company what was here involved. The King was accepting the truce. Uproar broke out.

Bruce allowed his friends their head for a little, and then rapped out a stern "Silence!" Even so, the required quiet took some time to settle.

"This truce I will uphold," he declared strongly. "It may serve the Earl of Ross. It also serves me. We shall come to a conclusion another day. A three months' truce, Sir Hugh. As from this day. It is agreed."

"Yes, sir. Three months. That means until early November. Until then, each side holds its hand."

"So be it. And you, sir? I am prepared to accept your father's word in this. You may return to him."

The young man hesitated, and then jutted his chin. "No, my lord. I still obey my father's commands. To remain with you, as his hostage. That he ordained, that I will do."

Bruce eyed him directly, thoughtfully, for a few seconds, seeking to assess the reasons behind this. He conceived this young man to be honourable — which was more than he did of his sire. Was that it, then? Hugh Ross himself did not trust William Ross, and was seeking to ensure his father's good faith thus? It could be.

"Very well," he said briefly. "Send your cousin back with this word. Then put yourself in charge of Sir Thomas Randolph, my nephew. You will have much in common! That is all."

The Rosses bowed, and went back to the boat.

The King slowly searched the faces of those around him. "I see you doubt my judgement. All of you," he said. "I am sorry for that But the decision is mine, and I have made it. Rightly or wrongly."

"It cannot be right, Robert," Edward exclaimed. "To come to terms with the man who betrayed your wife and Marjory. And my sisters. I cannot understand how you could stomach it, 'fore God!"

"It is the King who stomachs it — not the husband and father and brother!" Bruce grated.

"Even so . . ."

"The King to accept an offer of truce from a rebel!" Campbell said, dark head shaking. "This I could not have believed, Sire."

"When you have Ross forced to retire!" Angus Og weighed in. "Of all times *not* to hold your hand! We are fighting-men, are we not? We came here to fight Ross. And now, when your stratagems have succeeded, and he sees that he is in trouble, you treat with him. If *he* needs this truce, you do not."

"I say that His Grace is right," Thomas Randolph put in, greatly daring, as all stared at him in surprise and offence. "This way much bloodshed will be spared. Time gained and no harm done. Ross holding the North behind this line will not hurt the rest of the kingdom, or His Grace's cause. For three months or six. So the King may turn his attention elsewhere."

"Thank you, nephew," Bruce nodded. "I see that you have more in that handsome head than mere notions of chivalry and honour!" He turned to the others. "See you — Ross needs this truce, as my Lord of the Isles says. He says *I* do not. But I can *use* it. Ross sent that letter to King Edward. He hopes for help from England. *We* know, thanks to Lamberton, that he will not get it. Even though he writes other letters which we do not intercept. Edward of Carnarvon is otherwise occupied. Ross no doubt still hopes for aid from MacDougall of Lorn. This we must see that he does not obtain. But — be sure that he wants help! That is what matters. If we ensure that he gets none, then three months will not save him. Nor harm us. And meantime, we can go back and deal with MacDougall! With all our power, this time — no gesture. When he least expects us!"

When no one found anything they could controvert in that, he went on.

"This truce allows me to come to grips with Lorn this year. Still time, before the winter sets in. Here is a great matter. If we can bring down MacDougall and the West before this truce expires, I cannot see Ross in haste to seek battle with us thereafter. This could save me a year of campaigning — as well as the much war and bloodshed Randolph speaks of."

Lennox nodded. "Here is good sense, true judgement. Thank God for your quick wits, Sire."

Angus Og, who much preferred to fight on the coasts rather than inland, so that he could use his great fleet of galleys, shrugged acquiescence.

"What do we now, then?" Edward demanded. "Between our two hosts, we have 8,000 men. And not to strike a blow!"

Bruce smiled, relaxing. "Never fear, brother — there will be blows aplenty for you. And before long. We march to Inverness forthwith. Receive the surrender of that castle, and demolish it — allowing the English to sail away. Leave the Bishop of Moray to hold that town and watch this line. We shall turn south-west. For Argyll and Lorn again. I would be knocking at MacDougall's door before he hears of this truce, if that may be! From now on, we move fast."

Even Edward could not complain of that programme.

"Master Bernard — before we march, prepare me a paper to send to Sir Alexander Comyn yonder. Appointing him my Sheriff of Inverness. To work with Bishop David. He is an able man. We must use him, keep him content in our service . . ."

CHAPTER FOURTEEN

DRAWING rein, Robert Bruce pointed, laughing heartily, easily, in more frank and honest mirth than his colleagues had heard from him for long. Bruce had been a mirthful young man once, too light-hearted for his father, seeing life through amused eyes wherever possible; if twelve years of war, sorrow, treachery and disaster had overlaid his high spirits, not with gloom so much as with a habit of sternness, of grim wariness, of self-protective constraint, it was all only an armour. The true man underneath was still sanguine, light-some, laughter-loving — if scarcely, any more, young of heart.

The occasion of mirth now was, as so often, the mild misfortune of another. Gilbert Hay's horse had stumbled in one of the in-numerable black peat-hags of the vast desolation of the moor, all but pitching its rider over its left shoulder. Gibbie, who had been dozing in his saddle in the warm afternoon sunshine of high August, had saved himself only by a major effort — but had over-done his sudden backwards and sideways jerking to such extent as to topple over the other side of the brute and into a little pool whose brilliant emerald-green coverlet was only a mossy scum to hide the thick black peat-broth beneath. Floundering in this gluti-nous mire, the unfortunate Lord of Erroll had covered himself more comprehensively in mud the more he struggled.

"Peace, Gibbie — peace!" the King besought. "Still, you. Float on it — do not swallow it!"

Similar unkind advice and comment came from all around, few failing to find amusement in the situation in that still fewer there had not been in something of the same predicament in these past days of mighty journeying across the rugged face of Highland Scot-land.

"A curse . . . on you all!" the bemired Gilbert spluttered. "This God-forsaken country!" He hurled a handful of the filth in the general direction of his monarch. "You are welcome . . . to your . . stinking realm!"

"Lese-majestie!" Bruce declared severely. And, as Thomas Ran-dolph jumped down to go to the aid of his friend, added, "Put him under, Thomas — under! Lese-majestie is a grievous sin. And to throw mud at the Lord's Anointed worse! Sir Hugh alone may do that — eh, my friend? Since you alone do not recognise me as King!"

Young Ross's grin faded, with his uncertainty as to how to take that. He made a cheerful hostage, and mixed well with the others — better than the more reserved Randolph ever had done; but he was always uneasy at the King's mild mockery and teasing. He in fact paid Bruce just as much respect as any of the company, while yet refusing resolutely to accord him the royal style and address. He got over his present difficulty by dismounting and aiding Randolph to extricate Hay.

While this was proceeding, Bruce turned in his saddle to look back, northwards, over the fantastic scene. In all Scotland there is nowhere quite so savagely and remorselessly desolate, so enormous in its waterlogged, rock-ribbed, peat-pocketed emptiness, as the Moor of Rannoch, so awe-inspiring in the sheer sullen immensity of its seventy square miles of brooding moon-landscape, and all only intensified and thrust into starker relief by the loveliness of its frame of distant blue mountains — Buchaille Etive and all the Glen Coe giants to the north the Black Mount massif to the west, the peaks of Rannoch and Glen Lyon to the east, and all the complex of Mamlorn to the south. Here is scenery, sheer territory, on a stupendous, daunting scale, and man the merest irrelevance.

Yet it was the men, the thousands of men, that Bruce considered, strewn over the face of the land behind him like ants on a forest floor. There were, of course, scouts ahead; but he, in the lead, had paused perhaps five miles out into the waste from the towering jaws of Glen Coe, Behind him, almost all the way back to those fierce mountain portals, his army straggled and spread. It seemed absurd even to think of it as an army, in the circumstances. After the long constrictions of the glens, where their 8,000 had perforce made a narrow column six miles and more in length, now men and animals spilled out and scattered far and wide, to pick a way for themselves across the wilderness of lochs and lochans, pools, runnels, burns, bogs and peat-mosses, as best they could, more like a plague of voles in migration than a royal and military force. The Highlanders took it all in their stride, of course; but the Lowland troops and cavalry were making heavy going, and the progress was slow indeed. If they were to be attacked now, on the verge of Lorn as they were, they would be helpless as a vast flock of stupid sheep. Except that no one *could* attack them effectively here, on any large scale, for the same conditions would apply to them. Bruce was not fretting, therefore, at their vulnerability, as he would have been almost anywhere else; nor even at the delay — though it did make nonsense out of his declaration that this descent upon Lorn should be swift and unheralded. MacDougall, in fact, could hardly have failed to be informed of their return, days ago. Although he could not be sure, of course, as yet, that they intended to turn due west and attack him; they could be on the way south, by Strathfillan and Loch Lomond, to Lennox and the Lowlands.

Something of all this was in the King's mind, when men's attention was diverted from Gilbert Hay. Two of the forward scouts were coming hurrying back, Highlanders mounted on sturdy broad-hooved garrons that coped with the treacherous ground as born to it. They were nearing Campbell country here, and the scouts were drawn from that clan. As usual with the Highlanders, ignoring the King, they carried their news directly to their chief.

"A company approaching, Sire," Sir Neil called. "Some two miles ahead yet. A small company, mounted. But armoured."

Armour never failed to reveal itself, even at great distances, in sunlight.

"How small?"

"No more than two score."

"They may be scouts of a larger force. Take a party forward, Sir Neil, to investigate."

When, a little later, the King's entourage topped one of the innumerable basalt ridges which ribbed that expanse, to view even more extensive barrenness ahead, it was also to perceive that Campbell had had no difficulty with the newcomers. He was quite close at hand, indeed, riding back with a little group of knights, handsomely equipped and mounted Lowlanders. And over these fluttered a silken banner showing a blue chief above a white field.

"Douglas!" Bruce cried, and dug in his spurs.

They met at no very salubrious spot, amongst reeds, tussocks and standing water; but careless of royal status or dignity, the King leapt down at the same moment as did the other, and strode to embrace the younger man heartily.

"Jamie, lad—here's joy! My good Sir James!" he exclaimed. "What brings you here I know not. But you are welcome, by the Rude! Welcome indeed. For I have missed you, Jamie."

"Your Grace ... my liege ... Sir Robert!" Douglas could not find words, shaking his head. "It has been long ..."

"Aye, long. But our joining again the sweeter. Let me look at you." He held the other at arm's length. "Aye — James Douglas as ever was!"

"Why should I change, Sire? But you — you are changed, to my sorrow! You are thin, wasted. I heard that you had been sick. You are not well, yet ...?"

"Well, yes — well again, lad. That is past."

"You drive yourself too hard, Sire. Too much campaigning, scouring the face of the land, hard living. You were not bred to this ..."

"Bred to it? No. I was not bred to it. Were you? Were any of us, save these Highland chieftains? Yet it is my blood and birth and breeding that has put me in the middle of Rannoch Moor this day, that set my hand to this plough. But . . . what brings *you* to Rannoch, Jamie? You, whom I left my lieutenant in the South?"

Douglas looked down. "No doubt, Sire, I should not be here. Should not have come, myself. Should have sent couriers, letters. But the news is urgent. And . . . and I hungered to see Your Grace's face again. It is a year and more . . ."

The King shook the other's shoulder, and his own head — but understandingly, not censoriously. "Aye, Jamie — we are flesh and blood, God knows! And God be thanked! Men, not graven images of duty and obedience and form. But . . . your urgent news?"

"Galloway has broken out in revolt again. Major revolt. Mac-Douall, once more. But with English aid. Too great a task for me. He had Umfraville aiding him also — Sir Ingram. And an English force under Sir John de St. John. I had not the men to face them — have not sufficient, in truth, to hold what I have."

"Galloway again! In Heaven's name — am I never to be free of Galloway's spleen? And not just Galloway. Umfraville — who was Guardian of the Realm, once! Still hating me. I' faith — hate dies slow in this Scotland . . .!"

"The English still hold all the line of castles from Lochmaben to Caerlaverock — Tibbers, Dalswinton, Dumfries. Cutting off Galloway. And Buittle in Galloway itself — a strong place. I dared not move against them, leaving the rest of the South bare. So I left Sir Alexander Lindsay and Sir Walter de Bickerton in charge, at Selkirk in the Forest which I have made my base, and hastened north. I believed you to be assailing the Earl of Ross, in Moray and the Great Glen. But I learned in Atholl that you had come to terms with him — which I could scarcely believe — and had turned south, by Lochaber, for the West. So I came hot-foot, by Tummel and Rannoch."

Bruce's expression had returned to normal — grim, guarded, narrow-eyed, calculating, the brief interlude of naturalness, of being himself over.

"So-o-o!" he breathed. "The Scots remain . . . the Scots! Preferring far to fight each other than the enemy! What curse is there on this people, what devil's seed sown in us, that we must ever stab our brother's back rather than our foe's?" He swung round to face the semi-circle of his leaders. "My friends — have you heard? My lord of Douglas brings ill tidings. Galloway is in open revolt again. With aid both Scots and English. Umfraville, no less. With the Comyn fall, he will now lead the Baliol faction. I had hoped him either tamed or tired! And Sir John de St. John — he who led me to Edward Longshanks at Linlithgow, and my wedding! One of the ablest of the English. This is no small MacDouall insurrection."

"Christ God's curse upon them all!" the Lord of the Isles exclaimed. "I told you! I call all to witness — I told you! At Loch Doon. That we should lay Galloway low. Not any petty ride around the place, waving a flag and hanging a few scoundrels, as we did. But with our fullest power, and no quarter. Fire and sword, to the whole accursed province! As you have done with Buchan. But you would have none of it. I had 500 Islesmen to avenge in Galloway!"

The King held in his own temper. Only Angus Og would have addressed him so. But Angus was Angus, and this no time to stress style and courtly manners.

"My lord, you did so advise," he admitted. "But it was not vengeance that was my great concern. It was the new King Edward's plans. Which we did not know. I had to think of all my kingdom, not just Galloway. I conceived that a light lesson would serve. I was wrong. It has not done so. And now we must pay for my error, and do what should have been done a year ago."

"It will be but the harder."

"True. But *we* are the stronger."

The Islesman looked bleak indeed. "I will take my galleys to Galloway!" he said, almost whispering. "They shall learn what it means to have insulted MacDonald!"

Eyeing him a little askance, the King said, "We shall see. This must be well considered . . ."

Edward Bruce had come up from a visit to Lennox in the rear, during the Douglas greeting. Now he broke in.

"We now abandon one savage for another? MacDougall for MacDouall! Leave Lorn and fall on Galloway."

"No!" Campbell cried. "That would be folly. Lorn is at hand, Galloway far . . ."

"And MacDougall a menace to your Campbell lands in Argyll! Have you thought of Carrick? Annandale? Which MacDouall and the English harass?"

"My lords — we are not fighting for lands or properties. Any more than for vengeance," Bruce intervened. "We fight for the freedom of a whole people, the saving of a kingdom. If *you* forget it, I do not. Let me hear no more of such talk. Win the kingdom, and all the lands therein shall be yours. But win the kingdom first!"

Sir Thomas Randolph spoke up. "Sire — my lands of Nithsdale are near to Galloway, and so menaced. But I say to strike at this Lorn first."

"You are uncommon noble, nephew!" his uncle mocked, as Douglas looked up, interested in his late prisoner's new role. "But then, we can well understand that you would rather fight Mac-Dougall's Highlandmen than your late friends the English!"

Randolph flushed hotly, caught the King's eye, and swallowed.

"You have other reason for urging that we hold to Lorn, Sir Thomas?"

"I have, Sire. Galloway stands alone. Even in successful revolt, it would not bring down all the South. But allow Lorn and Ross to join forces, and you could lose all the North again, truce or none."

"You have it, nephew! That is as I myself see it. MacDougall is still the greater danger. I proceed to Lorn, therefore, as planned. But Galloway — that wound must be staunched before it bleeds us white. I will think on this . . ."

So the great sprawling array straggled on across the Moor of Rannoch. And now the King fretted again, at the slow rate of progress.

They won out of that terrible wilderness, and down towards the wooded shores of lovely Loch Tulla, as evening fell, with the mountains closing in again and the going becoming firmer, surer. Bruce decided to camp here, where there was shelter and fuel, and the possibility of deer in the woods for skilled hunters to kill — for the feeding of so large a host in empty country was an ever-present headache. He had been preoccupied, thoughtful, since Douglas's appearance. Now he called his lords together, round him.

"I halt the main host here, early, although we have covered but little ground this day," he told them. "For tomorrow we shall be into Lorn, and it is best that the men be well rested and fed, in fighting trim. If may be. Out of this Loch Tulla flows the River Orchy, down to Loch Awe and the Western Sea. We follow it, tomorrow. Here then, we part. Most to camp for this night. But some to push on swiftly."

"Who?" Edward jerked.

"You, brother, for one. I have considered this thing well. In the campaign against MacDougall, the heavier Lowland cavalry will be of scant use. I fear. Wasted, in mountain warfare. I would have you take most of it — say 600 men — and ride hard for the South. By the mounth of Marlorn; Strathfillan, Loch Lomond, across Clyde, and so down to the Forest of Ettrick. And thence to Galloway."

"Ha!" Edward breathed. "So you have come to sense, Robert!"

"I have come to decision, my lord! You are strong for harrying and slaying! Here then is a task after your own heart. Collect what men Lindsay and Bickerton can spare you from Douglas's force in the Forest. Gain as many as you may from our own lands of Carrick and Annandale. You have my royal authority to call for all support wherever you may. Then descend upon Galloway with all speed. Waste no time on the English-held castles. Avoid set battles, if you may. But deal with Galloway!"

His borhter was grinning, fiercely. They were very different men. "It shall be so, by the Mass!" he declared. "Galloway shall pay the price, this time. I shall deal with Galloway as I dealt with Buchan."

"No," the King said. "Not quite that, Edward, I charge you. This war, not punishment. And glutted men fight but slackly. The English will always be at your elbow. This will not be Buchan again. But, see you — win me Galloway, and you shall be Lord of Galloway. Your province, brother."

There were moments of silence, as the significance of this sank in. It was a notable promise, of an enormous heritage, a princedom indeed — the first such kingly bestowal of the reign. It would spur on Edward, or any man. But also, of course, if Galloway was to be his own thereafter, Edward would not wish to destroy and harry it any more than he must. None there failed to see the meaning of this.

"I thank you, Sire," the other said, carefully.

"Aye. Sir Robert Boyd will be with you, as lieutenant. Heed his counsel. You shall have most of my knights. And hereafter, if I can spare more of my main host, I shall send it."

"Does Douglas come with me?" Edward undoubtedly was jealous of James Douglas's position in the King's esteem.

"No. Not yet. My lord of Douglas remains with me here." He turned. "My lord of the Isles — you also, if you will, to move swiftly tonight. Ahead, to the sea. Secretly. Your galleys lie off Kerrera isle, still? In the Firth of Lorn, threatening MacDougall? Yes — then will you make shift to reach them, and bring them to my aid? MacDougall lies in Dunstaffnage Castle, at the mouth of Etive. There I shall seek him. He will try to halt me before that, to be sure. But Dunstaffnage is my target. Will you menace it by sea? And bring your galleys up Loch Etive, to support my advance"

"I would sooner sail south. To strike at Galloway."

"No doubt. And so you shall. Aid me at Dunstaffnage and Etive, and then sail for Galloway. Your galleys will travel more swiftly than men and horses." He took Angus Og's agreement for granted. "How soon can you have your ships in Loch Etive?"

"If they are still in the anchorage of Kerrera, as I commanded, I can have them sailing up Etive in two or three hours. But I must get to Kerrera first. Through MacDougall country. Or skirting it. Forty miles. To Gallanach. Then a boat across to Kerrera island."

"Starting now, my lord? How long?"

"Riding through the night, I could be down Glen Orchy and crossed Loch Awe by sunrise. Through the Glen Nant and Glen Lonan hills to the Sound of Kerrera in daylight, Campbell country. I could be at the sea by nightfall. At this hour tomorrow I could be with my galleys."

"God willing," the King commented. "Good. Then the day following, can I look for you in Loch Etive?"

"Yes. When, depends on the tide. The mouth of that loch shoals badly. Only at high tide could we win through."

"Very well. Tomorrow this host will move down Glen Orchy, and along Aweside. Then through the Pass of Brander the next day, to Etive . . ."

"That pass will be held against you. It is the key to Lorn. A sore place to win through."

"Well I know it. But I cannot ferry thousands across Loch Awe, as you will go. So Brander it needs must be. There is no other route, is there? For an army. We must win through Brander, then. Your galleys threatening MacDougall's rear, in Etive, should aid us."

"It will be hard task, Sire," Campbell put in. "Remember Clifford in Glen Trool. Brander is ten times worse. It is like to the gates of hell!"

"It is Glen Trool that I *am* remembering, Neil. We must reverse Glen Trool."

Angus Og, like others, looked doubtful. But he shrugged. "So be it, Sir King — I ride for Gallanach and Kerrera. Tomorrow's morn I will have my galleys under Cruachan, at the far side of Brander. Wherever *you* may be! Let us eat . . ."

So, less than a couple of hours later, the two very different companies set out from the new camp by Loch Tulla, from the ruddy glow of fires into the wan shadows of the August late evening; Angus, with perhaps a score of his captains, on shaggy Highland garrons, to head south by west down Orchy; and Edward and his glittering knightly throng to lead his 600 jingling men-at-arms south, eastwards by the main drove road across the mounth of Mamlorn, for the Lowlands. There was no question but that Edward at least, went in high spirits.

Watching them go, with his much reduced little band of close companions, Bruce sighed. "Much Scots blood will be shed before we all forgather again, I fear. My sorrow that it must be I who ordains it."

"Do not blame yourself, Sire," Douglas said.

"Who shall I blame?"

"The dead Edward. Edward of England," Lennox averred. "On him alone lies the blame for all. One man's hatred and lust for power. All those years ago. A great man, a great king, turned sour!"

"Aye — so great a man consumed! By a worm at his heart. Why, Malcolm — why? I honoured Edward once. Esteemed, almost worshipped him. Loved him better than my own father. He was the greatest prince in Christendom, the finest knight, the best soldier, the ablest ruler. Edward Plantagenet. And yet — this! Destroyed and destroying. For what? For a notion, a false notion. Laced with spleen."

"He thought to play God," Campbell put in briefly. "And we all suffer."

"Aye. All men suffer when a king errs," Bruce nodded sombrely. "And the greater the king the greater the suffering. Here is a lesson for me, at least — however small a king! If ever I think to play God! Watch it, my friends — and save me from myself."

"With the Scots to rule, there is little risk of that, I think!" Thomas Randolph said — and for once brought smiles.

*   *   *

Another camp by another loch, a loch as great as Loch Ness, this one, one of the largest and longest in Scotland. Lying north-east and south-west, Loch Awe's club-foot thrust off a long toe north-westwards, into the narrows of the fierce defile of Brander, down which it poured its outflow, the brief but major River Awe, four miles, no more, to the arm of the sea called Etive. In the other direction the loch presented a mile-wide barrier for twenty-three miles, almost to the sea again at Craignish, a mighty moat guard-ing the country of Lorn. Trackless impassable mountains, in a vast semi-circle, sealed off the north.

It was early morning, and the lately risen sun was streaming rays slantwise down the valley of Glen Orchy at their backs, into the wide green upland amphitheatre which cradled the foot of the loch. Bruce was standing on a birch-crowned knoll above the shore, and staring due westwards to where the water altered all its character, exchanged all its blue-and-gold loveliness, mirrored amongst green and purple hills, for a narrowing smooth dark torrent that swept dramatically into the grim portals of a mighty gorge, there to disappear in sombre shadow. Brander.

The daunting place dominated all this north end of the loch, below the tremendous multi-peaked mass of Cruachan. It was unlike any pass the majority even of the Highlanders had ever seen, a huge, flooded, steep-sided gullet of the mountains, vast in scale, a barren rock-lined funnel with unbroken sides soaring from 800 to 1,200 feet before easing off into the normal hill-flanks above. All the floor of that long defile was deep dark green, deceitfully smooth but swift-flowing water, with no banks or shores. And there were three miles of it.

All night Bruce's scouts had been bringing in reports, and the King had scarcely closed his eyes throughout. The pass was held in great strength by the enemy. There was a single slender track along its north side, the only road, at wildly varying heights above the water, clinging like ivy to the rock-face. How consistently the length of this was held could not be ascertained, because scouts could not get past the first block. This was at a point about a mile along where, at a wooded cleft, a fairly strong party was stationed, guarding timber barricades. But high above, on the side of Cruachan itself, where the steepest walls of the defile levelled off somewhat, were large numbers of MacDougall clansmen, ranked all along the hillside. No doubt, beyond, at the far end of the pass, there would be more waiting.

Shades of Glen Trool indeed — save that here everything was magnified many times.

All the royal camp had been active since dawn, but for the last hour or so the King had stood alone, silent, apparently fascinated by that yawning chasm to the west, preoccupied to a degree, staring just staring. His leaders brought him reports, from scouts, of the readiness of the various companies, and he accepted these with mere nods, scarcely seeming to hear. Men eyed him almost as much askance as they eyed what Campbell had called the jaws of hell.

James Douglas came to speak, at length. "All is ready, Sire. Fourteen hundred of the youngest, noblest Highlanders, in four companies — under the MacGregor, the Mackintosh, MacDonald of Lochalsh and Sir Ranald MacRuarie. With 200 light bowmen. All stripped to the lightest. Waiting."

Bruce looked up towards the mountain-tops, still shrouded in the white night-caps of fleecy mist, tinged golden now with the early sun. "How long before those mists clear, Neil?"

"Two hours yet. At this season."

"And the wind? It will freshen?"

Campbell, whose castle of Innischonell was less than a dozen miles to the south, shrugged. "About the same time. I cannot give you any certain hour, Sire. But, with this weather, the mounting

224

sun draws the wind off the sea and up the hillsides. It is a thing we have to beware when we stalk the deer. It is partly this wind which blows away the thinning mists from the tops . . ."

"So the wind first?" Not a breath of wind now stirred the quiet morning.

"Yes. Or so is usual."

"Then let us pray this is such a day! So be it. Off with you both. You have only two hours — and this must be timed most closely." The King held out his hand. "The day depends on you both. Yours is the most dangerous part, Neil my friend. With no knightly glory! But all rely on it. Your people have all the flints and tinder? Jamie — your greatest task will be to hold back the rash. After your great climbing. Watch for it. Go, then — and God be with you . . ."

So back eastwards along the lochside the four companies marched off, into the dazzle of the sun; and any MacDougall scouts and look-outs posted in vantage positions to the west could not but assume retiral, or possibly some regrouping to attempt a crossing of the loch by boat farther south.

But, round a thrusting shoulder of the mountain, out of sight from the west, the Falls of Cruachan came crashing down in foaming white water, in a series of great steps and stairs, from the lofty and vast corrie cradled amongst the topmost peaks of the mountain. Through the centuries this cataract had worn a deep and steep ravine for itself. Up into this the eager bands of Highlanders turned, and began their tremendous climbing.

Bruce waited, anxiously watching the clinging mists that wrapped the summits above some 2,000 feet. If that cover were to lift too soon . . .

He gave them a trying, uneasy ninety minutes; and then, with the mists most evidently thinning and retreating, he marshalled his residual forces and gave the order to advance westwards, towards the pass, remaining armour at the front. They did not hurry.

The increasing narrowness of the track elongated the column grievously, inevitably. Gradually the towering jaws of the defile closed in on them. Word came back from forward scouts that small enemy pickets were retiring by stages before them. They would draw the invaders on, to the timber barricade a mile deep in the pass, as Bruce had drawn Clifford at Glen Trool.

The first stirrings of air reached them as they entered the gorge. In a little while there was a distinct breeze from the west, in their faces. With a sigh of relief the King halted his long column about half a mile in.

Men's noses caught the tang of burning before ever their eyes perceived the thin blue film of smoke ahead. Quickly that film darkened, however, and soon it was not blue but murky brown, until great billowing clouds of it, growing ever thicker, swept up the pass on the westerly wind. Neil Campbell and his company had played their part. Having climbed most of Cruachan, and descended beyond, they had fired all the heather and bracken hillside at the western entrance of Brander, and the pass was now acting as a vast funnel or flue.

Streaming-eyed, blinded and choking in the acrid flood, Bruce's force still waited. Now it was their ears' turn. All listened.

It was not easy to hear, for sound does not carry downhill so readily as up, and the sullen roar of the river was close at hand. But presently, high and thin, those keenest of hearing could discern the yells and shouts and clash of battle, far up above them. Douglas and his three companies had hurled themselves down from the very mountain-tops, out of the mists upon the waiting MacDougalls half-way up the hillside. Campbell would now be moving back to aid them. And Angus Og might well be making his presence felt farther west still.

The King again ordered the advance, slowly, into the smoke.

Soon they overran their scouts, who warned that the barricade was just ahead, around a bluff. Warily the armoured men moved in.

However bewildered by the smoke, and the obvious trouble above, the enemy here had not deserted their post. They had no warning of the invaders' approach however, with the smoke, and the first of the royal troops were clambering over the timber obstructions, swords and battle-axes poised, before the alarm was shouted.

Wild and bloody fighting followed, incoherent, unsophisticated to a degree. Tight-lunged, stinging-eyed men hacked and slashed and battered blindly, Bruce himself in the forefront, wielding a mace for this hit-or-miss warfare. But the defenders were massively outnumbered, and in only a few minutes the position was won.

The King's men pressed on along the pass, the smoke thick as ever.

One or two boulders and the occasional shower of smaller stones did come down on them from the obscurity above, but these were scanty enough to do little damage. Undoubtedly up there men were too busy fighting for their lives to concern themselves with the stone-rolling tactics. Sometimes, indeed, a body it was that came hurtling down — and these were not always MacDougalls. The Battle of Brander was being fought up on Cruachan, not in the pass.

There were two more barricades to negotiate. But the first w
deserted and the second but half-heartedly held, the defende
not unnaturally conceiving the situation to be desperate. For no
the sounds of fighting could be heard directly ahead, and lo
as the track level, presumably from the western mouth of the pass
The MacDougalls were looking as anxiously back as forward.

The smoke was beginning to thin. Sore-eyed, Bruce led his force
cautiously on.

That, in fact, for the main body, was the last of the fighting.
Presently they could sense the fierce sides of the defile to be drawing back, opening, even though they could not actually see it. Then,
where the track bent, to cross a spidery timber bridge over a
sudden narrowing of the river, they came across many bodies,
dead and wounded. The marks of axes on the bridge timbers
told the story. Some of the casualties were MacDonald islesmen — the crews of Angus Og's galleys. They had saved the bridge,
anyway.

Soon after, with an abruptness that was startling, and painful to
streaming eyes, Bruce strode out of the mirk and constriction, into
sunlight again and wide, colourful vistas. Blinking, bemused, he
and his stared around them.

They had passed the wide belt of burned heather hillside, which
now stretched upwards, to their right, in blackened, smouldering
ruination, the flames dying away as they reached the rocks of the
defile proper. In front, the wide basin of Etive, with its glittering
waters, opened out. Those waters were positively littered with shipping, galleys, some beached, some lying out, some manoeuvring,
some apparently fleeing down-loch with others in pursuit. And
along the south shore a running fight was proceeding westwards,
most clearly at speed.

Bruce turned his aching gaze uphill and slightly backwards. Because of the still-smoking hillside it was impossible to see what
went on up there; but men could be seen elsewhere, streaming
away over the various western flanks of Cruachan in large
numbers, scattered and without order. Douglas's people, had they
been defeated, certainly would not have fled in that direction.

The King, breathing a long sigh, relaxed for the first time for
hours. He sent young Irvine with a few hundred clansmen, to climb
up there, to see if they were required. The rest he led on towards
salt water, the smell of the tangle in their nostrils, instead of the
sharp tang of smoke.

"Another battle fought — or not fought — in no heroic fashion,
Thomas," he observed, to Randolph, who had been at his side
throughout. "But, I think, a battle won. How say you, nephew?"

227

"Won, yes. But against Highlanders, Sire. Not against armoured chivalry."

"It was against the enemy! Are your notions of knightly warfare only to apply to southron lords and the like?"

"No, uncle. I have learned my lesson. But I remind you that one day you will have to fight *my* way. One day come to grips with the armoured might of England, in true embattled war."

"One day, yes. I know it. When I am ready — not before. When I have a united realm behind me. Or as united as I can make it. Until then we fight *my* way! However it shames you! With my wits."

"It shames me no longer. I see that your wits can do great things. And save many lives, thousands of lives. Any other, to take that pass, would have sacrificed thousands. On both sides."

"You see that, do you? Good." He turned. "And you, Sir Hugh? What do you see?"

Ross, the hostage, inclined his red head. "I see, my lord, that I would never wish to fight, nor pit my poor wits against, King Robert the Bruce!" The word king was slightly emphasised.

"Ha! So the tide turns, indeed! I am glad of it . . ."

Two days later, the mighty and ancient fortress of Dunstaffnage, on the point of its green peninsula jutting into the mouth of Loch Etive, capitulated — the celebrated castle which had once been the seat of the early royal line whose latest descendant now hammered at its doors, where the Stone of Destiny had been enshrined before it was taken to the capital of the newly united Scotland, at Scone. Alexander of Argyll, aged, white-haired, stumbling, came out alone, bareheaded, barefooted, to make at least superficially humble submission to the monarch — and was received with stern dignity, decision and no recriminations. But he did not produce his son and heir Ian Bacach, John the Lame, of Lorn, who had commanded at Brander — who had indeed commanded at Strathfillan, that bloody day two years before. He had slipped away, by night, in a small boat, from a postern gate. The lack of him took something of the shine out of the King's victory.

But it was nevertheless a great and sudden triumph, achieved in infinitely less time than might have been expected. Alexander MacDougall yielded up Dunstaffnage, ordered the dispersal of his clansmen, and swore future allegiance. His Comyn wife glared daggers at Bruce, but said no word, as they were banished, under Campbell guard, to the small and remote castle of Gylen, at the southernmost tip of the island of Kerrera.

There was great feasting and much Highland jubilation that night in the lofty stone halls of Dunstaffnage — for the castle had not yielded through any lack of provisioning, at least. And next day Angus Og, with a much augmented fleet of galleys, the largest probably that even he had ever commanded, sailed south down the Sea of the Hebrides for Galloway. He took with him James Douglas, and many another, as passengers.

The King, in a strange mood of reaction, almost sadness, turned his face eastwards, once more. For the first winter in a dozen years there would be approximate peace in the North.

Chapter Fifteen

IF Robert Bruce has first turned his hand to stage-management, and what his brother called mummery, almost a year before at Aberdeen, for the setting of his first Privy Council, now, in the spring of 1309, he really went about the business with a will. While quite a number of his friends and supporters, as well as Edward, either disapproved of the entire proceedings as unsuitable, unnecessary and beneath the dignity of a monarch, or at least showed no enthusiasm, others again responded heartily, even gleefully. Of these the most useful and active were James Douglas, Gilbert Hay, Ranald MacRuarie, Bernard de Linton — and, strangely enough, Thomas Randolph. Also, of course, Christina of Garmoran, who had once again crossed Scotland to the east coast for the occasion.

The King had put as much thought and planning into the affair as into any of his military campaigns. For this was, in fact, no less a campaign than any, however different.

Bruce would have preferred to hold his first parliament at Scone, the ancient Celtic capital. But unfortunately the English still held Perth, near by, although two attempts had been made to dislodge them. Stirling and Edinburgh, with all the South-East, likewise were in enemy hands. But St. Andrews was the ecclesiastical metropolis of Scotland, and had been cleared of the invader. Moreover, the Church's share in what had been achieved for the freeing of Scotland fell to be recognised. So St. Andrews it was, thrusting out at the very tip of Fife into the North Sea.

The actual parliament was by way of being only the necessary excuse and setting for the entire programme. This was to be a show, a demonstration, a play-acting as Edward accused — but for a vastly greater audience than could ever crowd into the grey episcopal city by the sea. And St. Andrews was certainly crowded, that March, as never before.

It was a strange town, unlike any other in the land in that an actual majority of its population consisted of clerics and churchmen of one degree or another. Nowhere else was there such a concentration of abbeys, priories, monasteries, nunneries, churches, chapels, cells, shrines and colleges. While the huge cathedral, triple-towered and still a-building, dominated all architecturally, and the castle, which was the primate's palace, did so administratively, every street, square, wynd, lane and alley within the lofty enclosing walls was in fact a huddle of handsome ecclesiastical building, so cheek-by-jowl as to be bewildering, almost ridiculous, the close proximity tending to cancel out the frequently rival magnificence. Bruce, seeing St. Andrews for the first time, perceived something of how the extreme trait in the Scots character, and its fondness for religious and metaphysical argument, had led to this concentration; also, how it was that Lamberton, master of all this, had been able, through Balmyle, to continue to subsidise him so munificently — for here obviously was every indication of accumulated wealth such as even the nobility could only gape at with incredulous envy. The English had of course taken what they could, and done much damage to the city; but it was off the beaten track of invasion, and the churchmen were clearly much wilier at protecting their own than were the mere laity — and probably, so many of Edward's alien administrators being themselves clerics, had helped to save St. Andrews. At any rate, the King found here a city which seemed to belong almost to another world from that in which he had warred and campaigned for so long; and one with resources available to his hand, and for the moment freely granted — since it seemed that Master Bernard, who it transpired had succeeded Bishop Balmyle in the office of Official and Receiver, had a grip over central purse-strings much more effective than that of more highly-titled prelates.

The King, therefore, did not lack the wherewithal, the premises, or the personnel, to set his scene — for churchmen at this level were quite the finest organisers, showmen, pageant-masters and providers of good living. And they and theirs were here in abundance.

The session of parliament — to which all entitled to attend, throughout the realm, of whatever faction, had been summoned — was proclaimed to occupy the two days of the 16th and 17th March, with Lent ended — a matter of some importance in the circumstances. But the previous evening had been set aside for the more dramatic and significant if less constitutionally important events. These were to be staged in the largest available premises in the city, other than the cathedral, the Guest Hall of the Augustinian Priory, one of the greatest and richest monasteries in the land. The lead of its roof had been carried off by the late King Edward for his battering machines at the siege of Stirling, and other damage done, but temporary roofing had been improvised. To this huge hall, officially de-sanctified for the occasion by Bishop Balmyle, just returned from his consecration in Rome, the King made his way in splendid procession through the narrow crowded streets, from his quarters in one of the undamaged towers of the castle. He went on foot, beneath an elaborate purple-and-gold velvet canopy held above him on poles by four lords — Douglas, Hay, Campbell and Fleming — dressed at his most magnificent in cloth-of-gold and ruby trimmings, under the spectacular Lion Rampant tabard, a slender open gold circlet with strawberry-leaf points around his otherwise bare head. He was preceded by the cathedral choir of singing boys chanting sweet music; then by a covey of the fairest daughters of the nobility, dressed all in white and carrying garlands; and followed by no fewer than five bishops — Moray, Dunkeld, Brechin, Ross and Dunblane — and a great company of mitred abbots, priors, deans and the like, all in their most splendid vestments. Then came an almost more colourful cohort of Highland chiefs, chieftains and captains of clans, led by the Lord of the Isles, all in fullest Highland panoply, including Christina of Garmoran actually wearing a helmet and chain-mail for the occasion. An illustrious and unnumbered array of lords and knights, lairds and sheriffs and other notables, with their ladies, composed the central body of the procession; and the provost of the royal burgh, with the magistrates, brought up the rear, another contingent of choristers finishing things off. Happily the threatening rain forbore, although there was a frolicsome wind off the sea. More than 500 people took part in that procession — and all had to be got into the Priory Guest Hall, with sufficient space left centrally for what was to follow.

It took time for busy ushers, like clerical sheep-dogs, to marshal and arrange everybody approximately in position, while musicians played from the gallery and the King sat patiently on a throne — episcopal, but better than none — on the Prior's dais at the far end of the huge apartment, backed by his lords temporal and spiritual and a selection of the ladies. At length, at a sign from the door, trumpeters sounded a rousing fanfare, and Bruce rose to his feet.

"My lords and ladies, my friends, my people," he said, into the hush, "I greet you well, this fair and happy day, each and all. We have waited long for it, and many have died that it might dawn for us who remain — God rest and reward eternally all such. Few here do not mourn for some of these. As I do for three brothers, and friends beyond all counting." His strong voice quivered noticeably — and that was no play-acting. "With all my heart I mourn them. But likewise from my heart thank you all who have fought and survived to see this day."

There was a strange sound from the great company, that started as a mere murmur, swelled to a rumble, rose suddenly to a mighty shout of acclaim, and so continued until the King's hand rose to quell it.

"So I, and you, rejoice as well as mourn, and thank Almighty God," he went on, voice under control again. "But, though much has been attained, and we assemble here again in council and rule, as has not been in this realm for a dozen years, yet much is yet to be done. The invader still defiles parts of my realm and our land, lurks in many strong castles, and beyond our borders still turns malevolent eyes upon this kingdom. Today, my friends, is but a pause in the struggle."

The reaction now was a low muttering roar, like distant thunder.

"But at least we can now face our enemy squarely, eyes forward, like our swords. Not for ever glancing back over our shoulders. Hear you — I say enemy, not enemies! For that is the greatest joy and comfort of this day. Our enemy is now plain to discern. It is the English invader only, and no longer those of our own kin and people who were led astray, by error, offence or fear. That is past and done with. Today, my friends, the King of Scots is king of all Scots again — as has not been since the good Alexander died at Kinghorn cliff twenty-three years ago." That was something of an exaggeration, but perhaps permissible. "In token whereof I now call upon the Lord High Steward of this my realm to carry out his duty and service."

There was a ripple of exclamation at this, for James Stewart, the Hereditary High Steward, had of recent years been lying notably low on his island of Bute in the Clyde estuary. He had, of course, been one of the leaders of revolt against the old Edward once, but, an elderly man and no warrior ever, had sickened of war and come to terms with the English. He had used Bruce's stabbing of the Red Comyn at Dumfries as excuse to disassociate himself — as had many another — and had not attended the coronation at Scone although he had sent his surviving son Walter. His last service to the King had been surreptitious, provision of the secret vessel which had taken the fleeing Bruce from the Clyde to Dunaverty and the Hebridean interlude. The son of his brother John, who had fallen bravely at Falkirk fight, Sir Alexander of Bonkyl, had openly taken the English part thereafter, and in fact had been captured with Thomas Randolph, and since held prisoner.

A single blast of a trumpet cut short the murmuring, and a side door of the hall opened to admit two men, one old and one young. James, the fifth High Steward of Scotland, a tall, gaunt and gloomy man, dressed as usual all in black, but richly, had aged greatly of late. Always shambling and gangling of gait, he now moved forward stiffly, awkwardly, but with some dignity too, nothing hang-dog about him. Nor was there any sign of guilt about his son Walter, a good-looking youth, arrayed in most handsome style and carrying himself proudly. If the concourse was looking for any kind of dramatic public humiliation, these two did not offer it.

The Stewarts advanced a few paces, bowed low to the throne, and then turned to look back.

"I, as Steward of His Grace's realm, summon William, Earl of Ross, and his household, to pay fealty to his liege lord, Robert, King of Scots," the old man called. He was not a good speaker for his tongue was too big for his mouth and he dribbled continuously. But the name he slobberingly enunciated was clear enough.

Now the comment in the thronged hall was not to be damped down. Everywhere men and women turned to stare, agog.

They had something to stare at. The man who led in the group of half a dozen was eye-catching by any standards. Of middle years, huge, ponderous, fierce-eyed and heavy-jowled, clad in a curious mixture of Highland and Lowland garb, decked with flashing jewellery, William son of William son of Farquhar Mac-an-Tagart, Earl of Ross, chief of his clan and hereditary Abbot of Applecross, stalked heavily forward, a target for all eyes — and for vituperation also, for all knew well the part he had played in handing over the Queen and the royal ladies, and in the death of the Earl of Atholl.

Ross paced on towards the dais, looking neither left nor right. Behind him came his two sons, Sir Hugh and Sir John, the former looking embarrassed, the latter scowling. Then three young women, the Ladies Isabella and Jean Ross, the former notably beautiful, and Sir John's wife, the Lady Margaret Comyn, daughter of the Earl of Buchan. The King was insisting on women being very much to the fore this day; and since Buchan had no son, the presence of this heiress daughter was important.

The Rosses mounted the dais, and after a reluctant pause, the huge Earl went down stiffly on one knee before the throne.

"My liege lord Robert," he said thickly, jerkily. "I, William of Ross, and my whole house, name and clan, do seek your royal pardon. For deeds past done. I acknowledge error and seek mercy.

As agreed at the settlement of Auldearn, six months past. And desire to be received into Your Grace's peace."

If the older man was tense and strained, Bruce, sitting before him, was no less so. Although he had planned it himself, this was one of the hardest things he had ever had to do. He saw, instead of the basically arrogant and only superficially humble face bowed before him, the reproachful loveliness of Elizabeth de Burgh and the childish innocence of his daughter Marjory. And seeing, he could have lashed out at those heavy features with the foot that tap-tapped so close to them. Hands gripping the arms of the bishop's throne so that the knuckles glistened whitely, he sought to control the surge of sheer elemental fury within him.

It was his brother Edward's denunciatory muttering at his back that saved him, ironically. He drew a deep breath.

"My lord of Ross — since you chose to conclude our truce by making submission to my representatives at Auldearn in October," he said levelly, "I have well considered the matter. I then, through others, accepted your subjection on terms I conceived to be generous. Those terms still stand. But now you would make closer bond and fullest allegiance. Do you, my lord, and your whole house, swear to serve me as your sovereign lord, and my heirs on the Throne of Scotland, well and faithfully until your life's end?"

"I do, Sire."

"Then, Earl of Ross, here is my royal hand. It is my pleasure to extend it to you." And might God forgive him that lie, for it was only with an actual physical effort that he managed to bring forward that hand! "That I do so is in no small measure due to the good offices and noble bearing of your son, Sir Hugh, while he was hostage for you."

The Earl took the hand between his own two, and kissed it briefly. He stood up, distasteful duty done.

His eldest son knelt, on both knees this time, and took the King's hand. "Your Grace's most leal knight and humble servant — if you will have me, Sire," he said.

"I will have you, Sir Hugh — never fear." The you was slightly emphasised.

His brother, Sir John Ross, dropped only one knee and made his fealty only sketchily. Bruce eyeing him closely, silent.

The ladies dipped in deep curtsy — but the King did not miss the smouldering hatred in the glance of the dark-eyed, plain-faced Margaret Comyn.

"My regrets that your father died," he told her formally. The Earl of Buchan had died in England at Yuletide, disgraced and dejected.

She made no acknowledgement, as the Rosses moved over to stand at the side of the dais.

At a sign from the throne, the trumpeter sounded once more, and the Steward again raised his peculiar voice.

"Sir Alexander Comyn, Sheriff of Inverness and Keeper of Urquhart, to pay homage to the King's Grace."

Buchan's brother, a fine-looking soldierly man, grey-haired but upright, came in at the side door and marched firmly up. His bow was vestigial but when he kneeled to take the King's hand he did so as firmly, frankly.

"Your Grace's true man, from henceforward," he said crisply. "You will not rue your royal generosity to me, at least."

"I never doubted it. Rise, Sir Alexander — and play my friend as stoutly as you played my enemy!"

"That I will, Sire."

The Steward's next announcement drew more gasps. "Alexander, son of Ewan, son of Duncan, son of Dougall, of Argyll. And his son, John of Lorn."

The old man who came in now, white-haired, thin and stooping, looked notably frail to be the puissant chief of MacDougall who for so long had terrorised the Highland West. He was simply clad in saffron tunic, a belt of gold the only symbol of his rank. No son John came behind him, but only his hard-faced and somewhat overdressed wife. Bruce knew well that Lame John was still in England, and defiant, but had chosen this way of emphasising the fact.

MacDougall kept his eyes lowered in front of the King — although his lady did not. "I come to make my peace with Your Highness," he said thinly. "I offer my allegiance."

"You give it, sir — *give* it! As is your simple duty." Bruce looked at this man who had hunted him and his over so much of the Highlands, his English enemies' most active and consistent supporter. "That allegiance is belated. But . . . you acknowledge your error now?"

"Aye."

"And your son and heir? John of Lorn?"

"I cannot speak for my son. I do not know his whereabouts. Were he with me, I have no doubt that he would say as I do."

"But he is not here, sir. Despite my summons. So, although I accept your fealty, and that of your name and clan, I hold you responsible for John MacDougall of Lorn. Until he submits himself to me, in duty and service, I must hold some part of your lands and castles forfeit to the Crown. What part is for parliament to determine. You understand?"

235

The old man did not look up, but nodded.

"Very well, sir. Here is my hand."

Bruce looked into the eyes of the woman behind, the sister of the man he had stabbed to death at Dumfries. He saw no relenting, no hint of forbearance. The Comyn women would never come to terms with him. Were women always more implacable than men? Or was it only in Scotland?

The MacDougalls moved over to join the Comyn and the Rosses, as the Steward proclaimed still another applicant for the King's peace and mercy — Sir John Stewart of Menteith, uncle and guardian of the child Earl of Menteith.

For the Lowlanders present — the majority of the company, that is — though not to Bruce's own entourage, the announcement of this name held more significance even than those of the Highland Rosses and MacDougalls, or of the northern Comyn. For this was perhaps the most telling recruit of all to Bruce's side, the most clear barometer of the prevailing climate within Scotland, a prince of time-servers not conquered in war but choosing of his own judgement to change sides. This was the man who had handed over Wallace to King Edward, and death, in 1305, as Sheriff of Dumbarton; who was Keeper of Dumbarton Castle, one of the keys of the kingdom, for the English interest; who had been given, in name, the allegedly forfeited earldom of Lennox by King Edward, and who until a few weeks before had been calling himself Earl thereof. That he should be here in St. Andrews this March day, with the true Lennox standing just behind the King, was not only dramatic but very eloquent of the situation.

For so expert a fence-sitter, Menteith was an unlikely type, nervous, tense, ill-at-ease always. He came hurrying towards the throne, a swarthy, slight, youngish man, with strained anxious expression and great eloquent Stewart eyes. Whatever he gained by his changes of allegiance, it did not seem to be satisfaction. He faltered and halted below the dais, more like a hunted stag than a powerful noble.

Bruce was contained to encourage him. "Come, Sir John," he said easily, the mockery behind his voice fairly well disguised. "It is good to see you. We have not met since that day in Stirling Castle when we heard of Sir William Wallace's death, I think? We are four years older — and wiser, perhaps?"

"To be sure, Sire — wiser," the other said, in a rush of what seemed like relief. "I thank you — wiser." He came up the steps. "I crave Your Grace's favour and indulgence. And that you will accept my regrets for past misjudgements."

"Misjudgements you call them, Sir John? Well, it may be that

236

you are right. That all is a matter of judgement. And you judge, now, that my cause is worthy of your support?"

"I do, Sire. The support of all true men."

The snorting from behind the King was in chorus, though Edward led it.

"I am encouraged by that!" Bruce answered gravely. "I am sure that we all are. From so practised a judge."

Menteith dropped on his knees, holding out his arms for the monarch's. "You will accept me into your peace and company? And my ward, the Earl of Menteith? As you accepted the castle of Dumbarton from me?"

"A moment, sir. While I may judge such acceptance suitable, as King, there is another who is concerned, I think. My good and leal friend the Earl of Lennox." Bruce turned in his chair. "My lord Malcolm — how say you? Sir John Stewart has misjudged your interests, as well as mine! I seek your advice."

The kneeling man cast apprehensive glances around.

"My lord King," Lennox answered quietly, "I rest content that this man enters your peace. If you can stomach him. So be it he restores what is mine. I say receive him."

"As I do not!" Edward exploded.

The King ignored his brother. "I thank you, my lord. You are magnanimous. As a monarch must be also." He extended his hand, even though his lips curled a little in distaste. "Make your belated fealty, sir."

When the trumpeter blew another blast, Edward Bruce could contain his righteous indignation no longer.

"Brother! Sire!" he exclaimed, loud enough for all to hear. "Of a mercy, have done! No more, surely! No more forgiven traitors, received into your arms! Any more forsworn miscreants on this dais and there will be no room for honest men, I say!"

Frowning, Bruce cut through the murmur of support that arose from many around him. "Enough, my lord of Carrick. In the field your services are excelled by none. Within doors, they can be less valuable! A realm is not governed as by a charge of cavalry! Proceed, my lord Steward."

"Sir Robert de Keith, hereditary Knight Marischal of Scotland, to do homage to the King."

There was less stir over this announcement than there should have been — for the adherence to Bruce's cause of the stocky square-faced man of early middle-age, who came striding in, was of major importance, though not all perceived it. Keith had fought with Buchan and the Comyns in the old days of the Joint Guardianship, had been captured by the English in Galloway and imprisoned for four years. Released in 1304, he had been sent back to his own country, duly indoctrinated, as one of King Edward's four Deputy Wardens of Scotland. That he nevertheless was but little known by most of those present was perhaps an indication that he had served his new masters only modestly — indeed he had been relieved of his Wardenship before long. Now, voluntarily, he had taken this step. What was important to Bruce was not so much that he was by heredity the Knight Marischal of the Kingdom, but that he came from Lothian. Keith was a district in the north-western foothills of the Lammermuirs. All Lothian and the Merse of Berwickshire had from the first been completely under the thumb of the invaders; and still was. That so prominent and cautiously level-headed a Lothian man should have decided that this was the time to take an active part again, was encouraging. Others might be moved to do likewise.

Others already were, it seemed — for the next two applicants for the royal mercy were Sir Alexander Stewart of Bonkyl, the Steward's nephew, and Sir William Vipont of Langton, both from the Merse, and the latter an Englishman. Undoubtedly these submissions had the effect of turning men's eyes southwards.

A number of less important men came to make their peace. And if it was becoming a weariness to the great gathering, as well as an offence to those who thought like Edward, the King accepted them all patiently. So he had planned it, and so it was.

At length he rose to his feet. "My friends all," he said. "You have been patient, forbearing. Some may deem, like my brother, that *I* have been too forbearing, in this day's work. But if this realm is to regain its freedom, it is above all necessary that it should be united. Only so can we drive out the English from our borders, a more numerous people than we, and who act in unity. We have differences amongst ourselves, yes — but they are as nothing to our differences with the invaders who devour us. And who would keep us divided. For such is their policy, always. Therefore, it is my task, my duty, whatever my own feelings would have me do, to unite my people. Having taken the field against them, because I must, and shown my rebels who reigns in Scotland, I now must show that I am King of all Scots, not only those who supported me. This I have sought to do today. Some may accuse me of weakness. But is it weakness to know your enemy? I know my real enemy — and it is not my fellow-countrymen, my own subjects, even when they . . . misjudge!"

There was some applause then, some laughter, some murmurs.

"So be it, my lords and friends," he went on. "We have had sufficient of discourse and confrontation. And tomorrow, in parliament, we will have more — our bellyful of it! There is more to living than war and clash and wordy debate. For too long this land has been starved of mirth and gaiety, good cheer of body and mind. So now, to our due and overdue enjoyment! Thanks to my lord Prior of this great house, the refectory here is now set with meats and drink in abundance. For all are his guests, and mine. Let us regale and refresh ourselves, without stint. Let us make up for the many times when we have gone hungry and cold and in fear. And thereafter come back here, for masque and music, dancing and spectacle. Let us show all men that the Scots can laugh as well as fight, sing as well as suffer. And that, when this struggle is overpast, and my realm is free again, it will be a joyful, lightsome realm." He raised his hand high. "Enough, then — this audience is over!"

"God save the King!" Unexpectedly that cry came from the serious Sir Thomas Randolph. "God save our King, I say!"

In thunderous acclaim the entire concourse took up the refrain and so continued, until the Guest Hall rafters shook and showered down dust and cobwebs. To this clamant din, the King led the way out and across the cloisters to the monastery's refectory. On the way through the bowing, curtsying, shouting throng, he paused, beckoned, and offered his arm to the Lady Christina of Garmoran, and so proceeded.

* * *

Later, much later that evening, panting a little from his exertions in the wild Highland reel just finished — wherein not a few had had to drop out before the end, by reason of too much prior good cheer or sheer lack of staying-power — Robert Bruce shook his head at Christina MacRuarie smiling at his side.

"How you do it, I know not," he said, dabbing his moist brow. "You look cool as a . . . a water-lily, in one of your own Moidart lochans. Not even flushed. Yet you tripped that reel, as others before it, like any halfling laddie! Myself, I am more like a foundered horse! And look at the others . . . !"

"Perhaps I have drunk less deeply than some!" she suggested. "Than the King of Scots, even? Or it may be but that we women are differently made. Lighter of foot, as of head! With less weight to carry."

"Having eyes, and other parts, we all can see that you are differently made!" Bruce gave back, looking down with frankest admiration on the white bosom as frankly displayed. Christina was at her most handsome tonight, in a silken gown of black and gold, considerably more low-cut as to front than was the Lowland custom. "As to weight, I swear that you have more there to carry than have I!" And he brushed that swelling bosom lightly with his finger-tips as though only inadvertently in a gesture. "And, on my soul, it is only in your very difference that you display any sign of this crazed dancing, woman!"

She glanced down in turn. Admittedly her firm and pointed breasts were heaving slightly, and each stirring with its own individual motion in a rhythm intriguing as it was apparent. The jigging violence of the reel had rather disarranged the already somewhat precarious balance of her gown's bodice, so that on the left side fully half of the large and dark red-brown aureola was revealed at each quiet surge of breath.

"Does my . . . difference offend Your Grace?" she asked, making shift to adjust her dress, though by no means drastically.

"No, no. Let it be, Tina — let it be." He not exactly slurred his words, but spoke with a thickened intonation. He did not often use the diminutive of her name, either.

She looked at him sidelong, from beneath lowered lids, not coquettishly but thoughtfully. They had not slept together since that day in Aberdeen a year before, when Elizabeth de Burgh's letter had reached him from Yorkshire.

All around them the gaily-dressed crowd eddied and circled and swayed, laughing, calling, chattering — though some sprawled or lay on benches, even on the floor, overcome by too much or too sudden unaccustomed good cheer — while from the moment gentler music came from the gallery, and a hairy Muscovite with a pair of dancing bears paraded ponderously round the huge hall, the great shaggy brutes holding each other close, rubbing snouts, and occasionally pawing each other in obscene parody of human caressing. The smells of bear, sweating humanity, women's perfume, wine, lamp-oil, wood-smoke and horses — for one of the earlier masques had included white jennets bearing damsels representing the Graces — was heady indeed.

"What of a mercy have you as rod for our backs next?" the King demanded. "Any more of your mad Hielant cantrips and you will have all decent men on their backs! Like my lord of Crawford, there." He pointed to the recumbent Sir Alexander Lindsay near by, mouth open and snoring. "Even Angus Og and the MacGregor are far through with it! Worse than I am, i' faith!" James Douglas was in fact Master of Ceremonies tonight, but Christina had been largely responsible for compiling the programme.

"You have not done too much, Robert?" she asked, quickly concerned. "None intended that the King should dance all measures. You have been a sick man. You must not tax yourself . . ."

"Tush, woman — I am well enough. It is but your Highland

240

notions of dancing. A battlefield is kinder on the human frame, I vow, than your antic flings!"

"We of the Hebrides are of a lusty humour, perhaps," she conceded. 'Our blood not watered down with Sasunnach degeneracy! But, never fear — you shall have your wind back. There follows another masque, an allegory for the times. Demanding naught of you save open eyes . . ."

"Open eyes!" he took her up. "So long as certain eyes do not open too wide! In especial churchmen's eyes, in this house! Our Scots clerics are not inordinately nice, I think — but that last allegory of yours, whatever you named it, was scarce of monastic quality!"

"Save us, our Celtic churchmen would not have turned a hair at that! And your Master Bernard helped to devise it. Besides, most of the bishops and such-like are gone."

"But some are not. Nicholas Balmyle yonder. And David of Moray . . . though Davie, I swear, will shock hard! Did you see him dancing? Like a blackcock at a lek!"

"He is of good Celtic stock," she pointed out. "But . . . see you another of good Celtic stock, there. Of my own sex. And the fairest in this room, I judge. Have you noted, my lord King?"

He followed the direction of her glance, and nodded. "I have noted," he said shortly. "Edward was ever a lady's man. As you have reason to know, Tina."

"To be sure. But I can handle my good lord of Carrick. Can she? *Her* brother, I think, misdoubts it."

Over in a window alcove of the hall, hidden frequently by the circling throng, Edward Bruce had the beauteous Lady Isabella Ross, and was laying siege to her with the direct tactics and urgency which he used in the field — and apparently with some success. Clearly the contempt in which he held her menfolk was neither here nor there.

Bruce shrugged. "He is a man, is Edward — all man. And a grown man. In such matters I cannot harry him, as though a child. God forgive me, I harry him enough! And in this . . . in this he is not the only one, by the Rude!" That was true. In almost every corner and window-embrasure visible — and no doubt elsewhere likewise — similar activities were afoot. "Can you blame them? We have had little enough of this, for long years . . ."

"Far be it from me to blame any, in such matters. Your brother or other. You know that, Robert. But I think I see two who do!"

"Sir John Ross, maybe. That one is sour, and will bear watching, I agree. But not Sir Hugh, surely?"

"Not Sir Hugh, no. Hugh Ross has other concerns in mind! Has had, all evening!" And she nodded.

"Eh . . .?" He looked where she did, to see the Earl's eldest son, not huddling in any unseemly corner but nevertheless paying rapt attention to another personable young woman, and that the King's own youngest sister, Matilda Bruce. A mere child throughout most of the prolonged period of war, she had been sent for safety to the house of an aunt in deepest Galloway. Edward, after his recent successful campaign in that province, had brought her here to the Court, no longer a coltish gawky girl but a roving-eyed and attractive seventeen-year-old — and evidently one more problem for the King of Scots. "Aye," he said heavily. "So that is the way of it, now! It must be the spring, 'fore God!"

"Perhaps. But it is not the Lady Matilda and Sir Hugh that concerns me — for he is an honourable man, I think. Despite his father! But another lady, less fortunate. No gallant knight fondles Isabel de Strathbogie this night, you will perceive!"

Frowning, the King once more followed the percipient Christina's regard to where alone, neglected, the new Earl of Atholl's sister stood. The Earl himself was not present — for he was married to the Red Comyn's daughter and had taken the English side after Dumfries, remaining so even after his father's shameful hanging by King Edward. But his two sisters continued loyal. That they had turned up at St. Andrews was gratifying, for the earldom could raise many men — but perhaps more than loyalty had brought at least this Isabel. For Edward Bruce had been paying court to her for some time, off and on, as campaigning permitted. Now, it seemed, he had found alternative attraction.

"Would you have me play nurse to them?" he demanded.

"Not nurse. Midwife, perhaps!"

"What! You mean . . .?"

"Rumour has it that the Lady Isabel is with child. By your brother. She looks to be so, would you say? And he looks elsewhere."

"Damnation! You think it true? I had not heard of this. I knew they saw each other. But Edward plays with any woman. Here's a coil, then! Atholl's sister . . .!"

"A coil, yes. A woman is entitled to look heavy in more than body, earl's daughter or no! But when her lover shows his preference, before all, for the daughter of the man who betrayed her father to death, as Ross did old Atholl — then there could be trouble."

"M'mm. I will have a word with Edward on this. But not now. I cannot well reprimand him on such matter, in front of all. I will go speak with her. Though, God knows what I may say . . .!"

The King strolled over to the young woman, unhurriedly, exchanging a word or two with others on the way. He would not have noticed that she was pregnant for she was no sylph anyway, a strapping creature, high-coloured and comely enough but with no claims to beauty. She and her sister were notably good horsewomen, and many a hunt they had ridden with the Bruce brothers — for they were kin to the King in a sort of way, their mother having been elder sister to his own first wife, Isabel of Mar, after whom this girl was named.

"Will you dance the next measure with me, Isa?" he asked. "And save me having to trip another Highland reel with Christina MacRuarie! Or she will be the death of me!"

"I am not dancing, Sire," the other returned. "By your leave."

"No? You are the wise one, then! I should have said the same. I saw your sister dancing with Sir Gilbert."

"No doubt."

"Aye. I'ph'mm. You are well enough, Isa?"

"Well, yes. Over well, perhaps!"

"Eh?" Somewhat heavily he changed the subject. "Have you been at Kildrummy of late? We had good times there, did we not? It seems long ago. I have not seen it since . . . since the English took it. And Nigel with it." Strathbogie Castle was not far away from Kildrummy, at the junction of Bogie and Deveron, in Aberdeenshire.

"It is a sad ruin," she answered briefly.

"Yes. I will have to rebuild it. So much to do. They took young Donald of Mar south. To England. My nephew and your cousin. Have you heard aught of him?"

"If you mean, Sire, has my brother informed us of Donald, from England — then I say no. We have no truck nor communication with David. Do not reproach us with his treason!"

The King sighed a little. He had never thought of Isa Strathbogie as a prickly female. "I do not," he assured. "My lord of Atholl has a wife — and I murdered her father." Frequently he made himself use the word murder, lest he forget, a sort of penance. "Who am I to blame him? Blame is profitless, I have found, and men's passions not always subject to reason."

"Your Grace is magnanimous — as all do say today! Too magnanimous, I say! I am not! Towards my brother — or yours!" And she glared over towards Edward.

"M'mm. Well . . . Edward is Edward! You know him . . ."

"I know him! more to the point, he has known me! And seems to forget it. And with the assassin Ross's daughter, of all creatures! My poor slain father will turn in his English grave!"

Bruce shook his head wearily. "There is nothing in that, lass. A mere passing fancy . . ."

"And I a *past* fancy! Is that to be the way of it? We shall see! I promise you, we shall see . . ."

The King was grateful indeed for the sudden extraordinary noise which drowned his companion's bitter voice. It came from the minstrels' gallery. With the bears gone, the music had ceased, and now was succeeded by a high, wild moaning and whistling sound that rose and fell, rose and fell, for all the world like the gusting of a storm wind. Presumably fiddles and fifes, and the drones of bagpipes, were responsible. Then the splash-splash of water, slopped from pail to pail, was added. Everywhere talk died away.

At the foot of the hall the doors were thrown open, and the representation of a large ship moved in. It was handsomely made of painted canvas on a wooden frame, with three tall masts and sails. It held a crew of a dozen, who, although they actually walked on the floor, seemed to sit within. They wore breastplates and helmets, with the Leopards of England painted on them, and from the mastheads flew stiff banners, two red Crosses of St. George flanking another Plantagenet Leopard. They came in chanting, "Death to all Scots! Down with King Hob!"

King Hob was the English term of scorn for Robert Bruce.

This tableau produced the expected cries and groans of execration from the company, some of those who suffered most from liquor even advancing threateningly, fists raised.

Then, behind, emerged a smaller vessel, with only four occupants. These also were in armour; three with the white-on-blue Cross of St. Andrew painted on their breastplates, and the fourth, a handsome youth who stood amidships — indeed, none other than William Irvine of Drum, the royal armour-bearer — wearing the Lion Rampant and having a gold circlet round his brows. The supporting trio shouted "God save King Robert! Freedom or death!" while Irvine bowed graciously all round.

The loud applause that greeted this party was quickly drowned in violent shouting and war cries, as the larger craft swung cumbrously round and bore down on the smaller, its crew brandishing suddenly drawn swords.

A fierce and very noisy battle thereupon took place, a dozen against four, with much whacking and clashing of steel and the Scots taking some resounding knocks, the masts of their ship tending to come adrift realistically in the process — in fact, Irvine having to hold the mid-mast up. Sundry of the more excited spectators had to be restrained from forcibly joining in.

In the midst of this stirring if unequal contest a third vessel appeared on the scene, midway in size between the other two. This was skilfully represented as a galley, with a single mast, a great square sale on which was painted the device of three red lions on gold, and three oars pulling rhythmically on each side. Its crew wore Highland dress and bonnets, and its leader the eagles' feathers of a chief, with bunches of juniper as badge. Cheers shook the hall as the newcomers drove in towards the contestants.

But the cheers died away to shocked silence, and then changed to varied exclamations of wrath, jeering, abuse and laughter, as it became evident that the Highlanders were in fact attacking the Scots vessel, not the English. Only then it dawned on those sufficiently mentally alert at this hour of a gay night, that the red-and-gold colours, the juniper badge and the three lions device on the sail, were all the marks of the earldom of Ross; and that the leader with the eagles' feathers was a huge fat youth, made grotesquely fatter with pillows and the like.

Bruce, drawing a quick breath, looked over at Christina Mac-Ruarie — who smiled back at him unconcernedly. This was her doing, for certain, her way of hitting back at Ross for many things, but in especial undoubtedly for the attack on her personal galley that October day some thirty months before, in the Hebridean Sea, when Bruce had first met her. This was her method of showing that while the King might overlook and forget slights and injuries, she and others did not. The realisation of it grew on all there, and the noise was deafening.

Not a little anxious now, Bruce glanced across to where he had last seen the Earl of Ross drinking at one of the side tables. He was still there, but now happily had fallen forward, head on arm, goblet spilt beside him. Nobody was thinking to rouse him, apparently, to view the spectacle, much as he might hear of it afterwards. His sons however were not thus spared. Sir Hugh, beside Bruce's young sister, looked discountenanced and unhappy; while Sir John, with his Comyn wife, fumed and spluttered. Farther over, Edward Bruce laughed loud and long, his arm still possessively round Ross's blushing daughter.

"Your Isleswoman has a nice wit, at least!" Isabel Strathbogie observed. "Pay heed to what she is telling you, Sire."

The King said nothing. A policy of statesmanlike forgiveness and unity might be well enough for the monarch, but it seemed to be less than popular with his subjects. How to impose it, then? Of all his close friends only Lennox supported it, and that scarcely wholeheartedly. And yet, was there any other way to face the greater menace, the English?

These thoughts were temporarily banished by still another disturbance at the door. Into the hall swept a fourth vessel, and this quite the most eye-catching of all, magnificent indeed. It was all white and gold, another galley, everything — sail, mast, hull, oars, hanging shields — dazzling white picked out in gold. The crew were all in white also — but any insipidity in this was banished by the fact that they were all young women. There were a score of them in the galley, all but one clad wholly in diaphanous snow-white lawn or cambric, of a clerical fineness of quality that was only made for high churchmen's surplices — indeed, these were all surplices, only a little adjusted — almost transparent. That the ladies wore nothing else beneath was swiftly apparent to delighted male and scandalised female eyes. The glow of pinkish flesh, with darker patches here and there, through the white, as well as the arms and legs more frankly bare, was the only failure, if such it could be called, in the white-and-gold harmony. Each girl bore a gold-painted wand in her hand.

The one exception to this unwarlike company was a splendidly built, laughing-eyed young female who stood alone on the raised poop of the galley, holding a golden arrow. She wore a handsome white-painted helmet above her cascade of corn-coloured hair, the wings on either side golden. A steel breastplate, also white, only partly hid her otherwise unclothed upper parts, and the very obvious fact that it had been designed to fit other than a particularly pronounced and rounded feminine form only enhanced effect. The back, save for the armour's straps, was wholly bare. A sort of brief skirt of chainmail, and tall riding-boots, both whitened, completed the costume — though leaving notable stretches of delectable thigh uncovered.

Needless to say this boatload aroused a masculine enthusiasm far outdoing even that for the stoutly-battling but sadly outclassed royal craft, the King himself cheering heartily.

"Hussies!" the Lady Isobel observed succinctly, at his side, to choke him off. After all, it *was* a monastery.

The galley of the nymphs, or whatever they were, bore down on the other embattled three — and now the wild storm music sank and dwindled to a gentle melody. Out from the canvas craft the maidens rose, to step over into the other vessels, lightly waving their wands before the receptive faces of the sword-whacking warriors, or at least those opposing the four heroes in the royal barge, now in dire danger of becoming a casualty indeed. The breast-plated lady remained in the stern of her own galley, directing all

246

with her arrow-like weapon. With remarkable speed and unanimity the Englishmen and the Rosses alike collapsed before this potent assault — not so remarkable perhaps in view of the closing in of all this unusually underclad femininity. In a disappointingly short time, in the circumstances, Scotia's rescue was accomplished and the heroic monarch was safe — though he still was landed with the task of keeping upright the swaying mid-mast and sail, to his evident embarrassment. At this stage the nymphs' leader vacated her poop and, stepping over into the Ross galley, poked her dart approximately into the stomach of the stout chieftain, in formally dramatic fashion, whereupon he sank away out of sight below the gunwale, clutching his middle and howling horribly. The music rose to a triumphant crescendo. Evidently this belated *coup de grâce* had some especial significance.

The resounding applause was cut short by Christina MacRuarie, who stepped out into mid-floor beside the victorious galley, hand raised.

"Hear me," she called, in her softly lilting Hebridean voice, into the eventual hush. "Hear me, all you most noble of Scotland's race, Highland and Lowland. And others!" Her pause was eloquent. "Here is the Princess Aoife, of Skye, mighty heroine, and mother of Cuchullin's son, come to the rescue of the King of Scots, with her train of pure maidens and her mystic *gaebolg*, the dart of justice and truth, from which there is no known protection so be that it is hurled over water. Thus the King's saving and sure support came from across the water, the Western Sea, as the seannachies of old have foretold. So long as King Robert remembers the true Celtic origin and honour of his kingdom, so long shall he triumph and his throne be glorious."

There was more applause, but some murmuring too from the non-Highland part of the assembly, which saw this all as rather too blatant a piece of propaganda for the barbarous Erse and Islesmen. As undoubtedly it was, of course, a flourish, but a warning too. Bruce recollected something of the saga of Aoife of Skye, the semi-mythological heroine of many a Highland camp-fire, Lady of the Sea, Princess of the North, mistress of the legendary Cuchullin after whom the Skye mountains were named, and mother of the beautiful but ill-fated Conlaoch, whose invincible belly-dart was only effective over water. Bruce glanced round to seek for the Lord of the Isles. Angus Og would have had a hand in this, to be sure.

Christina, helping down the voluptuous dart-wielder from the Ross galley, and beckoning young Irvine from the royal wreck — so that he had to dispose of his wretched mast to one of his colleagues — led the two principals across to present them to the King.

"Here is Marsala MacGregor of Glenkinglass, niece to the Mac-Gregor," she introduced.

As the bold-eyed, high-coloured and excitingly-made girl sank in deepest curtsy before him, she might have been naked to the waist, as far as Bruce was concerned, her breastplate, by its very nature, weight and shape, being no protection to her in the least. Nor did the curtsy increase the efficacy of the chain-mail skirt. Clearing his throat, he leaned over to raise her up.

"Lady . . . Mistress . . . my dear," he said huskily, "I thank you. Indeed I do. We all do. You are most . . . superb! My felicitations. You are a credit to Clan Alpine, on my soul! A . . . joy to us all. I shall tell your uncle so." When she would have backed away, he held her arm and turned her, so that she stood by his side, flushed, radiant. The King was relieved to see that the Lady Isa had some-how removed herself.

He nodded to the young armour-bearer: "You wrought nobly, Willie," he acknowledged. "As who would not, knowing how you were to be delivered! You must act my tutor in some matters here-after, I see!" He turned to Christina. "As for you, my Lady of Garmoran — I am beyond words! Your talents are such that we all are left speechless. Which, it may be, is as well! It is my hope that my lord Prior will so remain. Equally my lord of Ross! But . . . you have delighted our eyes and our . . . sensibilities. You and all those who have so ably entertained us. I thank you all." He found that he was clutching the MacGregor girl's arm, made to loose her, and then forbore. "All shall be rewarded, as is meet, I assure you!" And Tina MacRuarie could make what she would of that.

Sir John Ross, with his wife, turned and stalked from the hall, without any of the required bowing towards the monarch. It was difficult to say who led who.

Save for the King's captive, the galley-maidens fled for their lives and virtue, not only their late victims in hot pursuit.

The hour was late, and this obviously had been the highlight of the evening. There followed more music and dancing, and there was still cheer of more solid sort for all who desired it. But all was now by way of anticlimax. When the King decently could detain his fair prisoner no longer, and yielded her to Christina, he moved over for a word with Hugh Ross, to soothe susceptibilities and to ensure that the old Earl was got discreetly off to bed. He advised his young sister, in the by-going, that it was time that she too retired from the scene. He looked for Edward, but was too late for

248

that active operator, who had already disappeared, and Isabella Ross with him.

Thereafter, commanding Gibbie Hay to see that all remaining guests obtained hospitality to their repletion, Bruce quietly slipped from the Guest Hall to make his way alone through the now deserted, night-bound streets to the Bishop's Castle and his own tower bedchamber. He was glad enough of the fresh North Sea air to clear a throbbing head.

It was William Irvine's duty, as page rather than armour-bearer, to attend at the King's chamber — but this night Willie would be otherwise preoccupied. After a word or two with the guard on duty, mounting the narrow corkscrew stair to his room at the tower-top, Bruce, at the door, paused, his nostrils catching the faintest whiff of woman's perfume. He smiled a little. He had a feeling that possibly Christina might seek him out, this night, for more than explanations. And, of a truth, he could do with a woman!

Entering the apartment, where a lamp was already lit and a fire burned brightly, the King was therefore not surprised to see the shadowy shape of a cloaked woman, back turned, over by the turret window. Small wonder the sentry downstairs had been rather more familiarly pawky than usual.

"Ha!" he said. "You should have allowed me to escort you here in person, my dear."

"Oh no, Sire. That would have been unseemly!" That was said with a giggle. And, though the voice was softly Highland, it was not Christina's.

"On my soul . . .!" Bruce stared, as the woman turned round. It was the MacGregor girl. She had discarded her helmet, but the long cloak, hanging open, revealed that she was still dressed approximately as before — if dressed is the word.

She sketched another curtsy. "I hope that I please Your Grace?" that was just slightly uneasy.

"Save us, girl — how did you get here?"

"The Lady Christina brought me."

"She did? And . . . where is she now?"

Again the giggle. "Gone, Sire. To her own chamber. In the Gatehouse. She said that she thought . . . that she would not be required further! Tonight."

"So-o-o!" Plunging, his mind sought for reasons. Why had Christina done this? They had not bedded since Aberdeen. Because of the letter from Elizabeth. He had indeed bedded no woman since then. A long time. Could it be . . .? She sensed his need — that would demand no Highland second-sight! But had divined also

249

that there was a bar between them in this matter, an obstruction to break down? And had chosen to break it down by means of a stranger, this MacGregor wench! A young lusty, compliant creature whom she could scarcely doubt had taken his eye, taken every man's eyes. Was that it? This Marsala was to prepare the way for Christina again. If he slept with her, could he deny the other his bed, once more?

It was the best that Bruce's somewhat bemused mind could do at this hour and with that piece of uncomplicated and quite distracting womanhood before him.

She had moved over to the fireside, and was holding out her hands to the blaze, though the room was warm enough, one booted foot on the raised fender — which meant that much of a white thigh and bent knee projected from the folds of the cloak, as well as the two bare arms. She smiled at him over her shoulder in simplest invitation, and shrugged the cloak a little, so that the cloth slipped further. Nothing could have been less subtle — or more effective.

Grinning, Bruce went over to her. "The Lady Christina is thoughtful and probably wise," he said. "We must not disappoint her! May I take your cloak? Marsala, is it not?"

She unfastened the clasp with alacrity, and stood revealed in her extraordinary but provocative costume. Her giggles were, in the circumstances, suitable, unexceptionable.

"You played your part well," he told her. "In the masque. But this heavy steel must irk your fair flesh sorely?"

"It does," she agreed, "I will be glad . . . to be quit of it!"

Nodding, he proceeded to unbuckle the strapping at her bare back — and found the contact with her soft, warm and firm skin set his fingers trembling; which, for a mature man, experienced and a monarch at that, was a sorry commentary on prolonged celibacy. Marsala MacGregor aided him.

The clumsy breastplate fell away to reveal breasts quite breathtaking in their shape and size. Too large, no doubt, in proportion to the rest of her, and likely in a few years to get quite out of hand and make her one of those top-heavy, quickly-ageing women. But that was no man's concern tonight. He found no fault as she turned towards him so that the thrusting points of her brushed his damnably quivering hands. It crossed his mind that she was better at this than he had been with Christina, earlier in the evening.

"You are . . . all delight," he said throatily. "This chain-mail? How is it secured . . .?"

She had anticipated him there, and at a little more than a touch from him the heavy if brief skirting fell to her feet with a satisfac-

250

torily solid crunch. Whatever may have been under it previously, there was nothing now save generous swelling womanhood, suitably framed and garnished.

Even as he looked down her white belly seemed to ripple and wave — or was that his own eyesight, affected by the liquor he had drunk? Or another symptom of his humiliating youth-like excitement and urgency?

She came close, to press all that undulating femininity against him, warm arms encircling his neck, red lips raised and open. The boots could wait. He would have picked her up in his arms and carried her to the bed, as the situation more or less prescribed — but the relics of sanity remained to him. She was after all a large creature, and would weigh more possibly than his dignity could survive. Moreover, he would be wise, almost certainly, to harbour his strength for his own immediate warfare. The priority now was to get some at least of his own splendid apparel off before the lower nature triumphed.

He strode for the bed, tugging off his magnificent tabard. She was not far behind, prepared to help in this also.

"It ... has been long," he panted, warning her. "I am not perhaps ... sufficiently a king tonight! Bear with me, girl. At first! And I will serve you ... royally!"

"I am MacGregor," she answered simply. "And my race is royal!" It was her clan's motto.

For a moment he paused, to stare at her — but only for a moment.

CHAPTER SIXTEEN

PARLIAMENT was to open at noon, and the King to ride in state to the cathedral where it was to be held. About an hour earlier, dressing for the occasion and going over in a mind which had in its time felt fresher, more alert, the projected programme for the day, Bruce made frequent glances at and out of the window. The smirr of thin, cold rain off the North Sea, with which the morning had started, could spoil the procession. Not that this was so very important; yesterday had been the time for the play-acting, and today's business was on a different level, serious, formal, but vital. Nevertheless, the thought of a lot of wet, chilled men in that great cold church, sitting hour after hour in debate, was not one to which he could look forward. Perhaps he was a little testy this morning. Gibbie Hay and young Irvine certainly gave the impression that they thought so, tip-toeing about and keeping eyes averted. That could be guilty consciences, of course. He had slept less than usual last night, admittedly — but so probably had they, and for similar reasons.

A brief gleam of watery sun, coinciding with a commotion down in the castle courtyard below, took him to the window once more. A small party of cloaked men had ridden in under the Gatehouse arch, horses steaming. The visitors were now dismounting stiffly as from long riding. There was nothing unusual about this, with the quality of most of Scotland descending upon St. Andrews these days; but that they should come straight to this castle was perhaps significant. And something about one of the travellers caught the King's attention.

This man was tall, gaunt seeming and stooping a little, but strongly-built, and by the skirts of his habit below the folds of his long travelling-cloak, dressed in the style of a Benedictine friar. Nothing extraordinary about that. Yet, something about the man, even viewed from this tower-top angle . . .

Suddenly Robert Bruce emitted a cry of astonishment, and dropping the gold belt he was in the process of donning, and brushing past the surprised Sir Gilbert, he actually ran to the door, threw it open, and went down the winding turnpike stairs two or three steps at a time.

Out in the wet courtyard, past the startled guards, the King hurried towards the travellers, who were now moving in the direction of the main keep. "William!" he cried; "William, my friend! My lord Bishop — God is good!"

William Lamberton turned, stern and bony features lighting up. He came long-strided. He seemed about to drop on one stiff knee before the monarch, but at the last moment thought better of it and instead threw his arms wide and took the younger man into his embrace.

"Robert! Robert my liege, my son, my most dear friend — here is joy! So long, so long it has been. Three long years."

They clasped each other for a little, too overcome for coherent words.

Then they stood back and looked at each other — and the marks of those years were only too plain to see on both of them. Lamberton saw a lean, purposeful, strong man of a great natural dignity and almost alarming if unconscious authority, with keen distance-searching eyes — yet with a gleam of humour about them. Gone were the last traces of immaturity, the relics of youthful uncertainty and indecision. Here was a man in his prime, of body and of mind, but chiselled, tempered, almost graven in both as by a sculptor of fierce conviction. And Bruce saw a worn, lined and ravaged giant, old before his time — for Lamberton was but forty-six, with only eleven years between them — grey-haired, weary, but though bowed of frame most obviously not bowed in spirit.

The King had been demanding how came the other to St. Andrews this March morning, but struck by the Bishop's evident fatigue, took the older man's arm instead and led him towards his own tower. "You are tired. Come to my chamber. Eat and drink, while I dress. For this parliament. We can talk then . . ."

But Lamberton gave him some information even as they mounted the stairs. "I am tired, yes — for I have been in the saddle since dawn yesterday and rested but two hours in the night. But that is nothing in my joy in seeing Your Grace. It more than makes up for any weariness of the flesh. It will be the leaving you again, the *going* that will tax me sorely — not this coming."

"Leaving? Going? What do you mean?"

"Only that I have not long with you, Robert. A day and a night, no more. At this hour tomorrow I must be over Forth again and spurring for the Border."

"Dear God — not that! Here is foolish talk indeed . . ."

"Not so, Sire. For what I have left of honour is at stake. You see before you a man forsworn. I have broken my word, my parole. All for love of you, my friend. I gave King Edward my word that I would remain in England. Only on condition that I did not return to Scotland was I released from my prison. I seek to tell myself that this means only that I would not return to abide here — not that I could not visit. But that is merest casuistry. I was not to leave Edward's realm. He trusted me. And I have done so. I must return forthwith."

"But if the damage is done . . .?"

"Perhaps not. I came secretly. I am thought to be making a pilgrimage of the shrines of Saint Cuthbert, in Northumbria. For my sins! I left Hexham Priory at dawn yesterday, supposedly to make for a cell in the hills of Upper Tynedale. Instead, I hastened across the Border passes of Deadwater and the Note o' the Gate, into Teviotdale. And so here, by secret ways we both know well. If I can return by the same route, and at the same pace, I may reach the Abbey of Lanercost two days hence. Where I am expected. And be thought only to have been travelling amongst the remote hill shrines. There is a Pilgrim Road. This I pray for — so shameless a deceiver I have become!"

"But your men? Your companions?"

"Only one, my personal servant, came with me from Hexham.

In England I do not ride the land like a prince of the Church! The others I picked up at my Abbey of Melrose, in Tweeddale."

In Bruce's bedchamber, after Hay had paid his respects to the Bishop, and provided meat and drink, he and Irvine left King and Primate alone — with reminders of the procession's timing.

"This parole of yours is a sore burden upon you, my friend," Bruce said, after a little, as he watched the other eat. "I am not one for breaking faith, as you know. But this was no ordinary demand upon you. It was the only way that you might regain freedom from prison, yes. But you were unlawfully imprisoned. You went to the English, before Methven, as an emissary from me. To imprison such emissary was a dishonourable act. And to hold captive for years a consecrated bishop of Holy Church, Primate of Scotland, to prevent him from ministering to his people — this is doubly unlawful, against the laws of God and man. In such circumstances is your given word to be held to? Is it not your duty, to your people, to *me*, to return to Scotland, by any means possible? You owe no duty to Edward of Carnarvon."

"Think you I have not turned over and over in my mind all such thoughts, Sire? I had ample time to do so! It may be so, as regards my episcopal duty. But I have my personal honour to consider, surely? My given word, as a man. God forgive me, I have indeed broken it to be here at all. For that I might convince myself of excuse. A visit only. But to *stay* in Scotland there could be no excuse. From my own conscience. It is my conscience that I fear, Robert — not King Edward's wrath."

"Aye. I understand. Probably I would judge as you do."

"Besides, I believe that I may indeed serve you best, my liege lord, by returning to England. Here I am Primate, Bishop, and your Chancellor, yes. But others can perform these duties, or represent me in them. Can any other do what I am in a position to do, in England? Here is why, after long thought, I gave my word. That young man, Edward Plantagenet, has a liking for me. Why, I know not. As he has a hatred and suspicion of his own bishops, Beck in especial. They were all his father's creatures — and all to do with his father he hates. He sends me letters, messages, seeks my advice, summons me to wait on him. He is a strange man, weak yet wilful, stubborn. And I can influence him. Have already done so. And can learn much of what is planned, against you and Scotland. To inform you thereafter. God knows, I have no liking for the task, to act snake, deceiver, spy. But I *can* do it. And I tell myself that it is to the eventual benefit of England also — an end to oppression, invasion, peace with Scotland. Judas's code, perhaps? But ...

254

I might achieve much. So my poor consience is torn two ways . . ."

"Yes. I see it. You may be right. Already you have sent me vital tidings. About Edward's wedding. This Piers Gaveston, and the nobles' resentment. You freed my hands, then, to deal with the North. That I can do with an ear, an eye and a voice at Edward's Court, there is no doubt. And you can . . . you can keep touch with my Elizabeth. Comfort her. That above all — although I should not say it! That above all." It came out in a rush. He had been urgent to ask about Elizabeth from the moment of their meeting.

"Yes, my son — yes. I know it. Elizabeth. God bless her! God bless you both. Being permitted to visit her is a great matter. I see her when I can. She is well. Brave. Proud in her sorrows. You chose wisely in your wife, Robert. Sinfully, I have ever begrudged Bishop Beck of Durham in that he wed you, not me."

"She is not misused? Maltreated? Humiliated?"

"No. She is not treated as a queen. But as the great Earl of Ulster's daughter she is respected. Young Edward does not love Ulster, his father's friend. But he does not vent his spleen on the daughter — save to keep her closely warded. A strange man, he has not his sire's savagery, but he hates almost as strongly. I think he hates the Scots little less than did Longshanks . . ."

"And his intentions, with Elizabeth? How long is he going to hold her captive?"

"That I know not. But I cannot raise false hopes for you, Sire. I would that I could say kinder. I think he will not release the Queen while ever you withstand him. Or your daughter. He uses them against you. Hoping your resolve will soften, your need and love for them bring you to terms. That is the English way . . ."

Bruce's groan was harsh.

Pityingly his friend eyed him. "It is an evil case. Here is dishonour indeed! But, at least, this Edward is less cruel. You heard that when I made representation to him, he ordered the release from their cages of your sister and the Countess of Buchan?"

"Yes. For that I am grateful. To you! Scarce to Edward, who kept them like cooped fowl for months after his father died. That any Christian prince could so act . . .! But — what is *my* duty, William? Towards my wife and daughter? I ask you — what is my true duty? I am a man, a husband and father, as well as a king. As *you* are a man as well as a bishop, as you have just said. I have set my throne before my wife. No — not my throne; my realm, my people. The freedom of Scotland before *her* freedom. And that of the child of my loins. And cursed myself for it every day of my life! What is my duty, man?"

"You know your duty, Robert. You have done it. And, I pray God, will continue to do it. You are King of Scots. I anointed you that day, at Scone. You are not as other men. This your burden you must carry, grievous as it is. All men know it. Elizabeth knows it, and would not have you fail in it. A king's is no mere title or honour, as is earl or knight. A king is wed to his people, first. You know it."

"I know it." Wearily the other nodded. "But, at times, I . . . I hope . . . weakly. That I might be spared this." Bruce straightened up. "But enough of this. You came because of today's parliament?"

"Yes. To support you in it. For I am still, in name, your Chancellor of the realm. And the Chancellor should conduct the business of a parliament, under the monarch's presidency. I cannot remain Chancellor — but at least I can support you at the opening of this, your first. This I had to do."

"It was kindly thought of. I am grateful. I had thought to use another acting-Chancellor. Nicholas Balmyle was formerly that. But now, as bishop, and administrator of your diocese as well as his own Dunblane, he is better as the realm's Treasurer. I had intended to appoint Master Bernard de Linton, my secretary, as acting-Chancellor. He is young, able, trustworthy, and of nimble mind. And loyal. Though of lowly rank. Shall I so appoint him, in your name, think you?"

"No, Sire. Not *acting*-Chancellor. Make him Chancellor of the Kingdom, in truth. An excellent choice. Better than Balmyle, indeed — who, though sound, has his limits. I wish to be relieved of this office. It is folly for me to remain in it, even in name. For too long there has indeed been no Chancellor. Give Bernard de Linton the seals of office. He will serve Scotland well."

"M'mmm. It is a big step, that. For one so humbly placed. There are those who will be envious. It is best to be a churchman, yes, a clerk and man of learning. But many others higher placed may demur. And since many must take instructions and even commands from the Chancellor, it would be unwise to offend such prelates. Taking instruction in *your* name, yes. But in the name of the Vicar of Mordington . . .!"

"True. Then we must use our wits. Between us, we can arrange it better, surely — King and Primate! Bernard is worthy of a promotion. It was on my suggestion that Nicholas Balmyle offered him for your service. He must be raised in rank." Lamberton permitted himself a wintry smile. "A mitred abbot? There is one abbey within my jurisdiction that is a thorn in my flesh — Arbroath! It is one of the richest in the land — yet Abbot John is for the English, as you well know. He cocks his mitre under the protection of the English garrison of Dundee! And refuses to pay his dues to my treasury here. See you how my mind works, Robert?"

"Ha! Appoint Master Bernard Abbot of Arbroath? In place of this John. One of the most senior abbacies in Scotland . . ."

"And let Master Bernard, who is an able chiel, and with his own ambitions no doubt, desire to get his hands on the revenues thereof, as well as the office! So, I think, we shall soon see notable efforts to oust the English from Arbroath and Dundee! To the benefit of all."

"Sakes, man — here is a ploy indeed!" Bruce chuckled. "Your wits have rusted nothing in your English prison, I vow! May I so announce to this parliament? The new Abbot of Arbroath to be Chancellor of the Kingdom, in your room? And Abbot John dismissed."

"When better to announce it, Sire? Although I had better have a word with Master Bernard first!"

"To be sure. I will send for him . . ."

*   *   *

So thereafter, when the King led the glittering mounted cavalcade through the rain-washed streets of the ecclesiastical metropolis, its own master, to the astonishment of all, rode at his side, clad in most magnificent episcopal canonicals hastily resurrected from secret storage for the occasion. If Lamerton's presence stole much of the limelight, in consequence, Bruce was the last to complain.

At the mighty cathedral, the largest in Scotland, all had been prepared with much care — though hardly for its own Bishop's presence. Certain damage had been caused by the English invaders but this was hidden behind evergreens and other decoration. The chancel-screens dividing the choir and high altar from the vast nave were further reinforced with more greenery and heraldic painted canvas, so as decently to shut off the holy parts from the rest. The nave itself, not normally seated, was now furnished with a great variety of chairs, benches, stools and forms, arranged in groupings and order to seat the varying degrees and status of the participating commissioners — and such was the scale of the place that there was still a large area at the west end available for onlookers. A dais had been erected at the chancel steps, for the throne, the Chancellor's table, the clerks' desks, and so on. Immediately below were seats for the great officers of state, and flanking them left and right were special stalls for the earls and bishops. Facing the dais were the three large groupings, already filled as the trumpets blared for the royal arrival — the estates of the Church, the barons and the burghs. Behind, the spectators' enclosure was packed. The lofty galleries of triforium and clerestories were today rivalling the splendour of such stained-glass windows as had not been smashed, in the kaleidoscopic colours of the ladies who thronged them.

Hidden choirs in the chancel sang anthems as the King of Arms and his heralds led in the King of Scots and his great entourage. Three men paced immediately behind him — James, the High Steward, Edward, Earl of Carrick, and William, Bishop of St. Andrews. Then, after an interval, came the Lords Spiritual — the Bishops of Dunkeld, Moray, Brechin, Ross and Dunblane. The earls followed — only Lennox and Ross, and the minors Sutherland and Menteith. Thereafter the Privy Council, followed by the provost and magistrates of the city.

At the dais the King halted, turned, and raised his hand — to some slight alarm on the part of the heralds, the masters of ceremonies, for this was unscheduled. When somebody had hushed the choirs to silence behind, the Bruce spoke.

"My lords spiritual and temporal, and all others here assembled — I require that the episcopal throne of this the prime diocese of my realm, be brought down from the sanctuary at the high altar, and placed near to my royal chair on this dais. For my well-beloved William, Lord Bishop of St. Andrews, Primate and Chancellor of this kingdom. Meanwhile, my lords — pray take your seats."

The gasp of surprise quickly grew into a chorus, a roar of cheering, as Lamberton stood, affected obviously, both nodding and shaking his grey head, and spreading helpless hands. In less orderly fashion than had been planned, the rest of the royal company moved to their places, guided by flurried heralds, while the gorgeously apparelled King of Arms sent scurrying servitors up into the chancel to carry down the Bishop's throne.

The King waited calmly throughout the commotion. Nobody else could sit down, of course.

At length, all were in their places, and with a certain amount of dislocation of decoration about the rude-screen, the massive chair with the high mitred back was manhandled down and on to the dais, men straining and panting with the weight of it. Bruce pointed exactly where it was to be placed, to the right and a little behind his own. Then taking the Primate's hand, he conducted him to it, with quite elaborate ceremonial. No one present had ever seen Lamberton look embarrassed, as now. As a tribute from sovereign to subject it was unique. It was also a highly significant gesture, creating a dramatic atmosphere, underlining the constitutional importance of the situation, and setting the scene and tone for the entire proceedings.

The King moved back to his own throne, stood for a few moments, and then sat. With a great sigh and much rustling and shuffling, the concourse took their seats and settled down.

The Scots regalia had been confiscated and taken south by King Edward in 1296, and never replaced. But after another flourish of trumpets, a gesture was made at representing these. Heralds brought up in succession Bruce's own long two-handed blade, as sword of state; a wand of office of the Silversmiths' Guild to serve as Sceptre; the golden spurs used at the coronation, and preserved jealously by the little Abbot of Scone; and the great and distinctly battle-worn Lion Rampant Standard. There was no Crown, other than the gold circlet the King already wore, and no Orb. These symbols should have been presented by the appropriate officers-of-state; but since only the Steward and the King of Arms were available, heralds brought them up, knelt before the monarch, holding the objects out for Bruce to touch, and then placing them on the Chancellor's table to the left.

This done, the King of Arms signed for another fanfare, and then called out, "I, High Seannachie of Scotland, declare this parliament and council of the kingdom and community of the Scottish realm, in the presence of the high and mighty Prince Robert, by God's grace King, with the three estates of that realm here assembled, to be duly constituted and in session. God save the King!"

After the bellowed response to this, which went on and on, Bruce raised hand again, remaining seated. "My lords and lieges here in session assembled — hear me, Robert. This day is a great day for this ancient kingdom, the most ancient of continuing subsistence in all of Christendom. It is the first parliament of my reign, the first for many bloody years. But more important still, it represents the resumption of rule and governance in this land, out of the blood-stained hands of the invader. Today, thanks to the courage and resolution, to the sacrifice and death of so many, and despite the error and folly of some, this Scotland stands a realm again. We are still invaded, our land defiled by the usurpers, still threatened by the might of England, Lothian and the South-East wholly occupied. But we are free men again, able to make our name and fame heard once more in the courts of Christendom. And especially in the court of the Plantagenet. To that end we must plan our strategies, muster our resources expend our energies, to the best of our abilities. Hence this parliament. Let us give thanks to God and His saints who have made it possible — especially the blessed Saint Andrew our patron, in this his city; nor forgetting the hallowed Saint Fillan, in whose especial care I have walked these many months. I, who sit upon a Celtic throne, the throne of one hundred monarchs, of Kenneth and Malcolm, Duncan and MacBeth, Canmore and David, and their predecessors and successors — I call upon two men to pray for God's blessing upon this assembly. The Dewar of the Coigreach, representative of the Abbots of Glendochart, in the Old Church, who gave me blessing when most I needed blessing. And Abbot Henry of Scone, who has served Scotland, and me, notably. I, the King, call these."

While from the benches of the clergy commissioners the small gnomelike person of Abbot Henry came forward briskly, a herald went to a vestry door opening from the south transept, to emerge again with the extraordinary hermit-like figure of the old Dewar, brought with some considerable difficulty from far Glen Dochart. It had been found impossible to part him from his rags, and he had blankly refused to don any of the Romish copes, chasubles or albs offered as a cover-up, plain or magnificent. However, the King had presented him with a fine black travelling-cloak, as a personal gift, and he had been persuaded to wear this, as showing suitable appreciation; and though the rags bulged out and showed very obviously beneath, at least the quite splendid and heavy gold-serpent belt of Celtic workmanship had been put on outside to hold the whole lot approximately together, looking strangely authoritative. Saint Fillan's famous crozier in hand, and venerable white locks and beard in tangled profusion, this eye-catching spectacle stumped over to the dais behind his superior-looking guide, scowling on all around — while the astonished murmur of much of the assembly grew and was shot through with widespread tittering.

Bruce stopped that promptly and effectively by rising from his throne and holding out his hand to the old man — an unprecedented mark of respect, which necessarily brought everyone else to their feet likewise, the noise and the scraping of chairs and forms drowning any remaining sniggers.

Abbot Henry, who was fortunately an unconventional cleric himself, and no formalist, as well as having a well-developed sense of fun, bowed to the Dewar, got no response, patted his shoulder nevertheless, and smiled genially.

The other raised his staff high, almost threateningly, and without waiting for any sign or cue, launched into a most vehement flood of Gaelic. Normally this is a liquid-sounding, misleading gentle-seeming language — but the Dewar of the Coigreach made it sound quite otherwise. Presumably what he was pronouncing was a prayer of blessing directed towards his Maker; but it sounded in fact more like a wholesale denunciation directed at the company present, delivered with quivering intensity. Fortunately it did not last long. Abruptly it ended, and as abruptly, without waiting to hear his Romish colleague's contribution, or making any acknowledgement to the monarch, the Dewar turned and stalked off as he had come.

Bruce kept a straight face throughout, and now inclined his head almost imperceptibly to the Abbot of Scone. His notion of bringing the Dewar here had been a gamble from the first. But despite this peculiar behaviour — which he had in fact anticipated — he was well enough satisfied. The gesture had been made. However comic or even unseemly might be the impact on the majority of Lowlanders present, on the Highlanders it would be otherwise. In two centuries the Romish Church had made only superficial headway in the West Highlands and Islands, and the ancient Celtic religious tradition still meant much, however inactive, latent. Bruce, above all, was concerned to rule a united kingdom, an idea almost totally abandoned since the Norman-French had come to Scotland. The Celic Church was a dead letter, of course, and could not be revived; but gestures such as this could greatly affect Highland sentiment.

Abbot Henry, a shrewd and practical man, saw what was required and, as the apparition disappeared into the vestry, staff thumping vigorously, made an equally brief but more conventional application for the Creator's blessing on their deliberations, and enduring mercies on the King, on the one Church, Holy, Catholic and Apostolic, and on all present, before bowing and returning to his place.

The monarchy, and all others, sat down with some relief.

"I now call upon the Chancellor to proceed with the business of this assembly," Bruce declared, in practical tones. "As is his duty and office."

Lamberton stood up. "Your Grace, my lords and commissioners," he said. "It is my great joy that I am able to be here for this great and memorable occasion. How I have achieved this, from ward in England, is not for me to explain to this parliament. Suffice it to say that I deemed it my prime duty to achieve this presence, at whatever cost — for two reasons. In order to support and acclaim our admired and heroic liege lord, King Robert, in his first parliament — without whom not only would there be no parliament but no Scotland today ..." He waited until the storm of applause had spent itself. "And second, that I might decently and duly open this session, as Chancellor, and then resign the office to

261

another more useful — as is right and proper. For I have to return to my ward in England tomorrow, and can therefore by no means serve in this important office further. His Grace needs an active Chancellor, not a paroled prisoner on foreign soil . . ."

There was an outbreak of groans and protest.

The Primate shook his head. "In this matter my mind is made up. The seals of office have been kept secure for me by my lord Bishop of Dunblane, during my captivity. For his good stewardship I thank him. Those seals and this office I now lay down before you all, for my successor." He paused. "Before I sit, I have one announcement to make, not as Chancellor but as Bishop. I hereby declare that I, for good and sufficient reason, have demoted and excluded the Abbot John of Arbroath, not here present, from the rule and supervision of that my great house; and have appointed Master Bernard de Linton, Vicar of Mordington, Official of this diocese and secretary to His Grace, to be Lord Abbot of Arbroath in his stead."

Lamberton sat down, to a stir of excitement.

Bruce spoke into it. "We receive my lord Bishop's resignation with regret but understanding. It is necessary that this realm, as this parliament, should have a Chancellor forthwith. I therefore here and now appoint Master Bernard, mitred Abbot of Arbroath, as Chancellor of the Kingdom, and require him to take up the seals of office, and to conduct the business of this assembly."

In absolute silence de Linton rose from his humble clerk's desk, walked to the Chancellor's table, bowed deeply to the King, less deeply to the Primate, touched the seals, and sat down.

There was no doubt about the sensation produced. For a young and unknown cleric to be appointed first minister of government was without precedent, however notable his suddenly enhanced rank. It was normal, though not automatic, that a cleric should be Chancellor, since few of the nobility were sufficiently learned in letters and Latin, the language of international correspondence, to cope with the duties. But there were many present who would have coveted the office, with all its influence — bishops, abbots, priors, of great seniority. Even Lennox himself, a scholar, Bruce suspected. But the King knew what he wanted from his Chancellor — and all recognised that this must be the monarch's personal choice. There were no formal protests, therefore, however much muttering.

"My lord Abbot — proceed."

Linton rose. "May it please Your Grace — first there are matters arising out of the recent wars, campaigns and truces. Certain matters fall within the authority of Your Grace's Privy Council.

But others require the decision of parliament. First, sentences of forefeiture. Such sentences have been passed against certain your subjects, and it is now desired that they be rescinded. Where these subjects hold the rank of earl or the office of sheriff, it is necessary for parliament to make the decision. To this rank and standing belong William, Earl of Ross, and Sheriff thereof; Alexander, Lord of Argyll and Lorn, and Sheriff thereof; and Sir Alexander Comyn, knight, Sheriff of Inverness. All now under sentence of forfeiture for rising in arms again the King's Grace. The Privy Council now requests that these forefeitures of lands and office be annulled. With the exception of certain lands within the Lordship of Lorn which shall continue in forfeiture. Is it agreed?"

Promptly, and on his cue, the Earl of Lennox rose. "My lord Chancellor — I so move, in the case of the Earl of Ross."

"And I in the case of the Lord of Argyll and Lorn," the Lord of Douglas added.

"And I in the case of Sir Alexander Comyn, knight," Sir Robert Boyd, knight, confirmed.

"All duly moved, each by one of his own degree," Abbot Bernard acknowledged swiftly. "Is there any contrary motion?"

With it all so obviously cut and dried, and by the King's closest associates, it required a bold man to question it. But such bold man was present.

"I know the warmth of His Grace's heart — none better!" Edward Bruce said, rising. "But I for one doubt the wisdom of these remissions. Traitors seldom cease to be traitors because they are softly used! Mercy is good, but may be overdone. At least some part of these forfeitures should be retained, to ensure future . . . loyalty!" He sat down.

All held breath, as the brothers eyed each other.

The King did not speak.

The new Chancellor cleared his throat, his voice less certain now. "My lord of Carrick — I am not clear. Do you oppose the motion? Or make amendment? Or but . . . advise? In general . . ."

Edward shrugged. "I leave that to you, sir. I am no clerk, no dabbler in words. I but speak my mind."

There was a ripple of undoubted approval and agreement over a sizeable proportion of the cathedral.

Bernard de Linton looked unhappily at the King.

Bruce, whose desire it was to intervene as little as might be, to have the day's proceedings appear as much as possible to be the true voice of Scotland, sighed — although not audibly. Indeed, his voice sounded easy, relaxed, as he came to the rescue of his embarrassed secretary.

"My lord of Carrick has made no counter-motion, nor yet an amendment, as I see it," he observed. "He but speaks his mind as he says. He also says, wisely, that he leaves the interpretation of his words to you, my Lord Chancellor. I advise, therefore, that you proceed."

'H'rmm. Yes, Sire. Is . . . is there any contrary motion, then?"

Edward frowned. "If so you must have it. Yes — I oppose the motion."

Almost with relief, since his own way at least was now clear before him, the new Abbot nodded. "The motion for remission of forfeiture stands proposed and opposed. Does any wish to speak further? Before vote is taken?"

There was a considerable pause, as all saw crisis, decision, yawning before them thus early in the day. Many indubitably felt as did Edward about the King's policy of forgiveness, of working with his recent enemies — for the Scots are not notably a compromising or forgiving people. Indeed, despite all the previous day's stagecraft and drama in the Prior's Guest Hall, and despite the comprehensive nature of the next two days' parliamentary programme, this issue was the basic one behind all. Could Robert Bruce do what none other had achieved, succeed where even Wallace had failed, and lead a united Scotland? Or must he merely be the dominant head of the strongest faction, keeping the others down? A vote now would count heads with a vengeance. For and against the King's policy. The King could not fail to note, and would certainly remember.

It was Lamberton who, unexpectedly, broke the tense silence. "My lord Chancellor," he said, "may I, who have attended many parliaments, make bold to advise you in this? That all be done in order. You say that this was a motion of the Privy Council, which now asks for the homologation of parliament? Very well. May I enquire — was my lord of Carrick present at that Privy Council?"

"He was, my lord Bishop."

"And did he move, by vote, against the decision to put this proposal before parliament?"

Linton blinked. "No . . . no, I think not. He argued against the policy of remissions, yes. But not . . . no, there was no vote taken."

"Then, my lord Chancellor, I see your duty as clear. This being a Privy Council motion, no member of that Privy Council may move against it, unless he has first given prior notice. By the rules of procedure you should rule that my lord of Carrick's contrary motion is out of order, and so falls."

Into the hubbub of exclamation the younger man banged his Chancellor's gavel, with waxing confidence. "I thank your lordship. I do so rule. Is there any further contrary motion? Which in this case can be put forward only by other than a Privy Councillor? No? Then, I declare the motion carried. Without necessity of vote. And the said forfeitures remitted. And move to the next business."

Few present, probably, were any less relieved than the Chancellor sounded.

'Item. Notice of forfeiture passed upon the following, unless they return forthwith to the King's peace. Or if they be outwith the country, they send written testimony, duly witnessed, of intention so to do. The Earl of Atholl — in England. The Earl of Angus — in English-held Dundee. The Earl of Dunbar — in Lothian. The Earl of Fife — in England. The Earl of Strathearn — whereabouts unknown. Sir Ingram de Umfraville, former Guardian of this realm, brother to the said Earl of Angus, Sheriff of Angus — fugitive in Galloway. Sir Alexander, Lord of Abernethy, English-appointed Warden between Forth and the Mounth — fugitive in Galloway. Others in like case but of lesser rank, not the concern of this parliament. All these to be received back into their liege lord's service, without any grievous penalty, if so be they submit. Otherwise, forfeiture of all lands and office. This also a Privy Council motion. Any contrary?"

There was silence, not only because this was obviously part and parcel of the former motion, with the same dangers; but in alarmed recognition of the power and significance of that resounding list. Five great earls, no less, still to be beaten down or won over. And a former Guardian.

While Linton had been reading this dire list, the King beckoned to young Irvine who stood behind the throne. "My advice to the Chancellor to move now to appointments," he said.

On receipt of the page's message, the Abbot was nodding when there was an intervention.

"Wait you, wait you!" That was the Lord of the Isles, from the barons' benches. "I do not, as of the Privy Council, oppose the motion — although, God knows I do not approve of receiving to our bosoms traitors, when they so choose to come! I but ask a question. Why is the Earl of Buchan's name not included in this list of ill fame? He whose treason is worst of all. And whose office of Constable should be placed on other and honourable shoulders."

Cheers greeted that.

"The Earl of Buchan's name has been deleted, my lord. The Bishop of St. Andrews has informed His Grace this day that my lord of Buchan, High Constable of Scotland, is dead. He died in England last month, rejected by King Edward as by King Robert."

This news produced the inevitable buzz of comment and speculation. Linton took the opportunity to look enquiringly at the monarch — who shook his head.

Banging the gavel again, the Chancellor won silence. "Appointments," he said. "Certain offices, lands and titles are vacant, as result of the passing of time and the casualties of war. All are in the appointment of the King, but some fall to be confirmed by parliament. Item. Edward, Earl of Carrick to be Lord of Galloway, and Sheriff thereof. Also keeper of all the royal castles therein, with the revenues thereof."

Edward rose, bowed briefly to his brother, and sat down.

Bruce raised his hand. "This is to redeem a promise made to my lord by the shore of Loch Tulla six months past," he said. "I promised him Galloway, the greatest single lordship in Scotland, if so be he would win it back to my peace. This he has done, most notably. His autumn campaign in Galloway was bold, able, skilful. He was not gentle — but sternness was required in that province. He was most ably assisted, in especial by my lord of the Isles and my lord of Douglas. But his was the command, and I know of no other commander in this Scotland who could have done as he did, with the numbers at his command. In one battle he used but fifty to defeat fifteen hundreds. I am grateful. I believe parliament should be also. Is the grant confirmed?"

There was no doubt about that. Loud and long resounded the acclaim. Edward was popular, his very impulsiveness an acceptable fault — which often coincided with the mood of the majority. Probably most considered the King to be too hard on him. Some said — perhaps Edward himself the source of it — that Robert resented that it was Edward who survived, when Nigel, his favourite, had been taken, with Alex and Thomas. Now, the King's tribute was applauded mightily. Men saw it as an olive branch. Edward grinned, shrugged, and examined his finger-nails, clearly embarrassed. Olive branches were not really in his line.

At a sign from the throne, the Chancellor proceeded. "Item. By the death of the Earl of Buchan, without male heir, the office of High Constable of the realm is vacant. Parliament's approval of the appointment thereto of Sir Gilbert Hay, Lord of Erroll."

Here was surprise. All expected a new Constable to be appointed, but few could have anticipated that it would be Hay — certainly not that modest individual himself, who looked quite dumbfounded.

The King spoke. "Sir Gilbert has served me with loyalty and devotion unmatched, my cause and my person. I know of none better suited for the important office of High Constable. Is it confirmed?"

There was no storm of agreement; but nor was there any voiced objection. As in a dream, Gibbie was beckoned forward by the King of Arms and invested with the sword of state from the table, as indication that henceforward he alone was permitted to wear a sword indoors in the presence of the monarch. As High Constable it was his duty to protect the King at all times. Carrying the weapon he went to sit in the special stalls for the great officers-of-state, beside the Steward and the King of Arms.

"Item. Office of Lord High Admiral," Linton went on. "Approval desired that it be removed from the Earl of Dunbar, forfeit, and appointed to the Lord Angus, son of Angus, son of Donald, son of Ranald, son of Somerled, of the Isles."

Tumult broke out. There were cries of delight from the Highlanders, and cries of shock and disapproval from many Lowlanders. None were objecting that Dunbar be deprived; but that so important a position be given to a barbarian Islesman was more than many could stomach.

"Sire!" James the Steward rose to his feet, gobbling. "This is not well done. My lord of the Isles is an able warrior. His services are namely. But . . . it is not suitable! His power belongs only to his own seas and coasts. The far Western Sea. All the other coasts of this realm require the protection of the High Admiral . . ."

Coldly the King interrupted him. "Address yourself, my lord, to the Chancellor."

Put out, the Steward floundered. "I . . . ah . . . yes, Sire. I . . . I move reconsideration."

"Aye! Aye!" came from various parts of the cathedral with opposing shouts elsewhere.

"My lord Chancellor!" James Douglas rose as the Steward sat down. "I ask — who has any shipping, not captured by the English, to defend our eastern coasts? Has my lord Steward? Has any other? Save Angus of the Isles. He displayed what his galleys could do, in Galloway. That campaign would not yet have been won, without his great fleets of galleys. Would the Steward appoint another to captain the Lord of the Isles' galleys? Would he? *Could* he? Yet those galleys alone can protect our shores. I say to the Steward — it is he who should reconsider!"

There was quiet, whilst men digested that. Then James Stewart half rose. 'Motion withdrawn," he mumbled.

"If there is no other contrary motion, the appointment stands

267

confirmed," Linton said. He waited. "Angus, Lord of the Isles, to be Lord High Admiral of Scotland."

Into the Highland jubilation and Lowland dejection he went on: "Item. The office of Warden of the Middle and West Marches is vacant. Likewise that of Sheriff of Teviotdale. His Grace proposes therefore Sir James, Lord of Douglas. To which he would add the Keepership of the royal Forest of Ettrick, with the revenues thereof."

This time there was no opposition, despite the youthfulness of the nomineee for such vital responsibilities. There was no doubt, of course, that his jurisdictions would have to be fought for; and although potentially the revenues of the vast Ettrick Forest area were enormous, it would be some time, in the circumstances, before they made of Douglas a rich man.

Thereafter, a list of further sheriffships, including that of Argyll to Sir Neil Campbell, and Ayr to Boyd, as well as other titles and appointments, went through almost automatically — although for Sir Thomas Randolph to be Sheriff of Moray, formerly a Comyn appointment, raised some eyebrows.

Bruce was thankful when this important but controversial part of the proceedings was over. It had, on the whole, gone better than he had feared.

The lords spiritual had sat patiently, if with some expressions of pious disapproval, through all this. Now Nicholas Balmyle rose.

"My lord Chancellor," he said, managing to make the new and lofty title of his late assistant and protégé sound slightly ridiculous. "I have declaration to pronounce on behalf of the bishops, abbots, priors and others of the clergy duly constituted in the realm, relative to the position, state and title of our Lord Robert the King. We have drawn up and written a full and sufficient investigation into the claim of Bruce, Lord of Annandale, known as the Competitor, to the throne of this kingdom; which writings, here under my hand, are of too great length here to read. But I make summary. That in the competition for the vacant throne before King Edward in 1291, that prince wrongously adjudged Sir John Baliol to be made King of Scots, when the Lord of Annandale had better title. That the disasters that have befallen this realm are in consequence. That the grandson of the rightful Competitor, having recovered and restored the kingdom, is now most undoubtedly our liege lord in right as in fact. And that any oppression to King Robert hereafter, by means of documents written or sealed in the past, such as were effected by irresistible force and violence, are null and void. We, the clergy of Scotland, therefore do proclaim the Lord Robert as of right the true successor of the ancient and unbroken line of our chronicled kings, and none other."

A little mystified by this statement of the evident, this gilding of the lily, most commissioners applauded politely. They were the more surprised, therefore, when, immediately the Bishop sat down, Lennox rose, also with a paper.

"My lord Chancellor — we, the earls, lords, barons and nobility of Scotland, do likewise make full and detailed affirmation that King Robert is the true and nearest heir of King Alexander last deceased. And declare, with the estate of the clergy and the whole community of Scotland, that the grandfather of our Lord Robert ought to have succeeded the King Alexander, and none other. This paper, signed and sealed, as witness."

"I thank you, my lords." Bruce, not making too much of this, inclined his head towards the speakers. "To further business."

"Item. Letter addressed outwardly to Robert, Earl of Carrick; and inwardly to Robert, King of Scots, from Philip, King of France. Received ten days past by the hand of one Oliver de Roches, ambassador, after travel by safe conduct through the realm of England. Wherefore the outer superscription. His Grace of France recounts his special love for King Robert. Reminds the said Robert of the ancient alliance between their realms, which he would see renewed. Declares that he has besought King Edward that there should be truce and peace between England and Scotland hereafter, promising his utmost efforts to that end. Promises further his representations with His Holiness of Rome regarding the position of King John Baliol. And does request and invite our Lord Robert to engage and join with him in a crusade against the Infidel in holy places. This parliament to consider reply to His Grace of France."

Men stared at each other, uncertain whether to applaud, to laugh, or to decry. Was the Frenchman mad? A crusade! At his time! A renewal of the alliance, after the French had so shamefully broken it? Peace with England, with the English still occupying part of Scotland? Reply — how could parliament reply?

Bruce enlightened them. "My lords, my friends — here is a matter of great import. More than might seem. And to our encouragement. The King of France sees Scotland, and my cause, as worthy of consideration, possibly support. As he did not, before. He writes to me — but the reply must come from parliament. Since only so will he, and others, know that it is not just Robert Bruce who speaks, but the whole community of the Scots. The matters his Most Christian Majesty raises are of varying worth — and folly! That we should be asked to consider a crusade is almost beyond belief. But His Majesty is concerned to earn that title of Christian. Moreover, to earn the Pope's approval — since they have been at odds for long. I suggest that parliament replies that we shall gladly join with him in such crusade, not only myself but many in my kingdom, when the last Englishman is expelled from Scotland, and we have good assurance that they will not come back . . .!'

Despite the sin of interrupting the King, loud cheering drowned his voice.

"As to the rest, I advise this parliament in its wisdom to agree that our ancient alliance be in fact renewed — since it is only against the English that it has any meaning. That we send ambassadors to France so to do. Also, to ask for French aid in men and moneys for our warfare. I think that Philip will not grant this. But it may serve to make him the more inclined to use influence with the Pope to recognise my kingship and right. This we greatly require. Without it the nations of Christendom will be loth to accord us our due. His Holiness, to my sorrow, scarcely loves me! Perhaps he has right. But he recognises John Baliol as King of Scots still. This is folly also — but such is the Vatican policy. Hence the declarations of the clergy and nobility just pronounced — for which I am grateful. These are scarce necessary for ourselves, who know the truth. But for King Philip and the Pontiff, that they may be informed."

Men nodded sagely to each other, lest any thought that they had not understood.

"Such reply to the King of France must be carefully considered. I suggest, my lord Chancellor, that you, with your clerks, and any other's aid you require, draw up such letter, for presentation and consideration at tomorrow's session. So that the rest of us, who have sat here sufficiently long for one day, may now betake ourselves elsewhere!" He paused. "If all so agree?"

Relievedly men rose, shouted, stamped and waved approval. Parliaments were all very well, but could go on for too long. Into the hubbub Linton, gavel banging, declared the session adjourned until noon next day. All commissioners, with their ladies, to partake of the hospitality of the provost and magistrates of this royal burgh and city of St. Andrews . . .

*   *   *

That night, after an evening spent together, when Bruce left Lamberton's chamber in the main keep of the castle, earlier than he might have done — in order that the older man should have opportunity for a good sleep, in view of his dawn start on the testing journey back to England — he called in at the Gatehouse

Tower on his way across the courtyard. In its upper room, allocated to the Lady Christina of Garmoran, he found only that lady's buxom Highland tire-woman in possession — although a scurrying just before his entry gave him the impression that someone less than light-footed might just possibly be hiding behind the arras in a dark corner. Christina herself, it seemed, had not yet returned from whichever of the many entertainments she was decorating, and with which St. Andrews was catering for its flood of distinguished visitors, that night.

"When your lady comes, tell her that I was grateful for her provision and forethought last night," he instructed the somewhat confused and costume-rectifying abigail, grave-faced. "She was very kind, and I have not had opportunity to thank her, this busy day. But if so be it she is not over-weary when she does come in, and she would have my poor thanks in person — then tell her that my door in the Sea Tower will not be locked! You have it?"

Blinking, biting her lip, and smiling all in one, the other dipped low.

PART THREE

CHAPTER SEVENTEEN

"ANOTHER hour," Bruce said. "We will give them another hour. Lest they are wakeful. And it will be darker." He looked up, sniffing the night breeze of the heather hills. "It will rain, I think. So much the better."

The Lord High Constable of Scotland turned to look in the other direction altogether, not westwards over the dark water to the darker castle on its tiny island, but behind them, south by east, towards the loch-head a couple of miles away, where red pinpoints of light marked the camp-fires of their enemies, their other enemies.

"I do not like it," he said. "We could be trapped here, all too easily. It is a bad position. If Atholl were to attack while we were assailing the castle, nothing could save us."

"Why should he do so? He has waited there four days. He awaits reinforcements, clearly. They have not come. He is young and inexperienced. He will not risk a night attack, I think. But, if he does, our scouts will warn us."

"Atholl may be young — but he will have experienced English captains with him, Sire," the third of the trio by the waterside put in — Sir Robert Keith, Marischal of Scotland. "If they had the least inkling that we would assault the castle tonight, they would advise him to advance. And they will have scouts on these hillsides, no less than we."

"I do not doubt it, Sir Robert. But why should they think it might be tonight? You have been here ten days and ten nights, and made no move. Why tonight?"

"They will have seen that *we* have arrived, Sire," Gilbert Hay pointed out. "They may not know that it is you, the King. But they know Sir Robert has been reinforced — though only by a small company. But they may look for action, therefore. I do not like it, Sire. We are less than their numbers. To risk yourself thus — the King! For this? A small unimportant place like Loch Doon . . ."

"Not so unimportant, Gibbie — to me!" the King said quietly. "This castle, though small, is a fist shaken in my face! Here in my own Carrick — or Edward's Carrick! From here, my good-brother

273

Christopher Seton was treacherously taken to his shameful death at Dumfries. And on this island, 500 years ago, died my ancestor King Alpin of Dalriada, father of the great Kenneth who united our realm — as I seek to reunite it now. I will have no Englishmen defiling Loch Doon Castle, I tell you."

His two companions were silent at that tone of voice. Nevertheless they were right — and Bruce knew it well. It was a kind of folly for the King of Scots to be here, in a dangerous position amongst the wild hills on the Carrick-Galloway border, with only a small force, besieging a strategically unimportant English-held fortalice. All over Southern Scotland, this summer and autumn of 1310, small or moderately-sized forces were besieging small and medium strongholds — not the great fortresses, such as Berwick, Roxburgh, Edinburgh and Stirling, for the Scots were almost wholly without the siege engines and trained sappers required to reduce such strengths. But the decision to drive the English out of the scores of lesser castles had been taken: Edward Bruce was investing Buittle in Galloway, Douglas was at Bothwell, Campbell at Livingstone, Boyd at Cavers, Fleming at Selkirk, Lennox at Kirkintilloch, and so on. The situation at large, on a national scale, was as awkward and incipiently dangerous as here at Loch Doon, with the loyal forces so grievously scattered. But it was something that had to be done, sooner or later — and this time of alleged truce was as good a time as any. The uneasy and purely tactical truce, engineered by the French King, between England and Scotland, had been in force for nearly a year — but latterly King Edward had broken it by sending shipping to reinforce and supply his garrisons at Dundee, Perth and Banff, as well as commanding general musters to arms in England. Two could play that game. Hence this campaign of the castles.

Sir Robert Keith, the Marischal, as yet untried in the King's service, had been given the Loch Doon assignment, with a mere 200 men. He would have been left to deal with it on his own, undoubtedly, had it not been for the arrival on the scene of David de Strathbogie, Earl of Atholl. The birth of a bastard daughter to his sister, deserted by Edward Bruce, had so enraged this proud young man that nothing would do but that he must at once take the field actively. From being merely a high-born exile in England, he became a man with a mission — to wipe out this affront to his name and fame. The English gleefully had given him a following assessed at 400, and truce or none he had marched north from Carlisle. Presumably Edward himself, besieging Buittle Castle deeper in Galloway, was too ambitious a match for Atholl's first sally; at any rate, he had made for this, the next nearest siege, and taken up a threatening position at the head of Loch Doon — but so far had not dared an attack.

The King had been holding justice eyres in Kyle and Carrick, based on his own house of Turnberry, only twenty miles away, when he heard of this situation. Instead of finding reinforcements for Keith from elsewhere, he had come himself, with Hay and a mere bodyguard of two-score men-at-arms. Now he had to justify it . . .

Superficially that was not difficult — for he knew the castle on Loch Doon as few did. Though an ancient strength, renewed and restored by the Baliols during the period when they controlled the Galloway lordship, it had been incorporated in the Carrick earldom and used by Bruce's father mainly as a hunting-lodge. As boys, the Bruce brothers had spent happy days here amongst the cradling mountains, with the giants of Merrick, Cairnsmore and Corserine all close by. If anybody could discover a weakness in that castle, the King could — for twice he himself had had it repaired from ruin and the effects of siege, the second time, but a year before.

Loch Doon was six miles long, but very narrow, and the island with the castle lay some 300 yards off the east shore at the south end — where it was in a position to dominate the drove road through the high passes from the Ayrshire lowlands south to those of the Galloway Cree, its sole strategic purpose. In the early days, after the Turnberry landing, when Bruce had lurked in this country, he had deliberately avoided the ruined loch-bound castle as refuge, preferring as so much less obvious his spider-cave five miles to the north, away from the road.

Like so many island castles, this one had an under-water causeway out to it, cunningly twisted. Keith had been told about this, but an early night attempt to progress along it unseen had resulted in a sad reversal and loss — for the English had cut a large gap in the hidden stone pavement some two-thirds of the way out, and within arrow-shot of the walls. Not unnaturally the Marischal was wary of a second such adventure.

Back at the camp, where all fires had been damped down, so that no movement would be visible from the island, their hour almost up, Bruce made his final dispositions, taking over entirely from Keith. He arranged that the force should be split, one party taking up position at the head of the causeway; the other placed to guard the south flank from possible attack by Atholl. Then he had the men gather round him closely, so that he could speak to the shadowy ranks without having to raise his voice. A thin rain had begun to fall.

"I want a score of good men," he said. "Only men who can swim a little. And who are not afraid of cold water! No small men, see you. Who offers?"

Out of all the murmuring, questioning and humorous comment, little more than a dozen stepped forward. There were no Islesmen or Highlanders in Keith's force, and the ability or need to swim was not a Lowland priority.

"I hope none may have to swim, in the end. But your lives may depend on it, nevertheless," the King went on. He counted. "Fourteen. It will serve. Now — off with your clothes. Then, ashes from the fires, to rub on your faces and shoulders. Bodies will show white, even on a dark night." As he spoke, he was unbuckling his own sword-belt and beginning to draw off his chain-mail tunic.

"Sire — not you!" Hay exclaimed, shocked. "Not the King . . . in the water! Naked . . ."

"Tush, man — am I the King because of my clothes? It must be I who lead, since only I know what I would effect. Moreover, I do not ask others to do what I will not myself do. You know that." All men indeed did know that. It was one of the secrets of Bruce's success, in his kind of warfare, with his kind of people. The Scots character was always such as responded best not to clear orders and discipline but to personal leadership and close contact, where there was affection and involvement with the men. As soldiers they had never excelled at siege-warfare, any more than in great impersonal battles, for this very reason.

So, presently, a very odd-looking and inadequate-seeming party of warriors made their awkward bare-footed way along the pebble-and-sand beach northwards for about 200 yards, to where a fair-sized burn flowed in from the steeply-rising flank of the hugely looming hill behind them. Completely naked save for belts and cords to tie weapons to their persons, they were daubed with wood-ash which made them so much less visible in the mirk. As well as their weapons they carried rope-ladders fitted with grappling-irons, and single knotted ropes with hooks attached.

Immediately below the shallows at the mouth of the burn, Bruce halted and formed up his people in single file. "Keep close behind me, and follow exactly as I go," he directed. "As I mind it, we should not have to swim. I was a laddie when last I did this. But I do not think aught will have changed. The burn will still bring down much silt and stones, and the flow of the loch is still northwards. There is a spit of this silt reaching out and bending down-loch, towards the castle. Perhaps that is how the island was made. The water gets much deeper than the causeway. But not over our heads, I think. It has been a dry summer. I used to be able to walk it as a lad . . ."

He paused, as a fifteenth naked and besmeared volunteer came hobbling up, and had to peer close to discover any identification.

"Ha, my lord High Constable!" he whispered. "You also? Man, your costume fair becomes you! Would that the Lady Annabel could see you now! Come, then — and slowly, silently. Pray that we do not have to swim — for that might give us away. And pray that the sentries watch best the front and the causeway."

Carrying a coiled rope with hook over his shoulder, and a cut hazel-stick in his hand, the King waded in — and gasped a little despite himself at the chill of the water. Even though it was only early September, the loch lay nearly a thousand feet above the sea, and was fed from giants 3,000 feet high.

Gingerly, carefully feeling his way at each step with both stick and toes, he edged out into the loch, Gilbert Hay immediately behind and the party following close. Bruce had toyed with the idea of having Keith stage some sort of demonstration at the causeway-head, or at the camp itself, to distract the watch's attention; but had decided against it as likely perhaps to rouse more of the castle's defenders. Better that all should seem quietly normal, and the beseigers' camp asleep.

Quite quickly the water deepened to waist height — where its chill made maximum impact. Thereafter the depth increased only imperceptibly until it was halfway up the men's chests. This gradualness did not imply a smooth and easy advance, however; continually Bruce came across uneven stretches, holes, or stumbled over boulders, waterlogged tree-trunks or other hazards. Fortunately the shoal or spit was fairly broad, and keeping to its crown was the least of the problem.

Bruce could not recollect just where the thing tended to bend northwards, with the main current of the loch — which was more like a widening of a river, with the Gala Lane entering at the head, near by, and the River Doon emptying at the foot. But some 200 yards out, slantwise from the shore, it became obvious that they were curving round. The castle loomed about another 150 yards ahead.

This second leg was the most testing — for from the direction of progress it looked as though the spit might have changed course during the years and be going to miss the islet by quite a margin, to the west. Also, at every step, Bruce feared a shouted challenge from the castle battlements. The men behind him seemed to be making an unconscionable splashing, and moreover puffing like stranded whales. It was now raining heavily. He had never been so thankful for cold, driving rain.

But at length he was under the lee of the island. He was brought to a stop, almost within stick-reaching distance of the bank, by deeper water. There seemed to be some sort of channel circling the isle itself. Taking a long breath he gently but strongly launched himself forward with a swimming motion. But almost at once his feet touched bottom again — sorely indeed — with the water only up to his chin. From there he could clamber carefully out on to dry land, with the dark masonry of the castle's outer bailey rising directly above him.

He whispered to Hay to stand aside and warn each man of the ditch-like channel, as he came up. And he held out his stick for each to grasp as he came over.

It took only a few moments — although with some alarming splashing — for the entire party to join him below the walls, unchallenged.

There was no need for any instructions now. Each man knew his task. They spread out along the few feet between water and masonry. At the signal of a pebble thrown into the water at each end, they went to work.

Their task was in essence entirely simple — but not necessarily easy to perform, and quietly, nevertheless. It was to throw those rope-ladders and single climbing ropes upwards sufficiently high for them to go over the walling and their hooks and grapnels to catch in the crevices and fissures of the masonry beyond, and so to hold. This was elementary siege-procedure, and all had practised it many times, even if they had not actually taken part in previous such assaults. For all that, hooks and prongs could not be guaranteed to catch and hold fast. And the noise of all that metal clattering on the stonework sounded like a carillon of cracked bells ringing to rouse even the dead.

Bruce's own hook caught at the second throw. Dirk between his teeth, jutting his bare feet against the walling, he walked up hand over hand, foot over foot, counterpoised between knotted rope and stone. Getting over the wallhead was the difficulty, where rope and stone came together. He barked his knuckles, but managed to hoist himself bodily, bare stomach on the coping, and uncaring of the scraping on tender flesh, vaulted legs over and on to the parapet-walk.

One or two figures were there — but they were naked, and therefore his own men whose ropes had held first throw. Bruce sighed with relief. The most dangerous moment was past, when defenders might have unhooked the ropes and sent the attackers crashing down. There was as yet no sign of any defenders.

"Gibbie!" he said, in a whisper — for though the ash had been washed off their bodies, faces were still daubed and it was almost impossible to identify individuals. Hay, in fact, was almost at his side. "Take half. Round that side. The gatehouse. I take this. Quiet as you may."

They split up. The castle consisted of a central square keep, surrounded by this high perimeter wall with its parapet-walk on top, with subsidiary lean-to buildings within the courtyard. At the far side of the perimeter, or outer bailey, nearest the shore and facing the unseen causeway, was the entrance, an arched pend with iron grille gate piercing the small gatehouse-tower which contained the watch-chamber and guardroom. In castles this was always the base from which sentry-duty was taken. The naked attackers now stealthily approached it from two sides, swords and dirks in hand.

This was a comparatively small fortalice, and was unlikely to have a garrison of more than perhaps thirty men. So no large number were to be expected on night-guard at any one time, and the sixteen assailants had no fears of being unable to deal with them effectively. The danger was that the dealing might be insufficiently swift and silent, so that the rest of the castle might be warned before the main keep could be reached.

In the event, when Bruce reached the gatehouse-tower, it was to find its door, opening on to the parapet-walk at this side, shut. It faced east, and there was an east wind, so this would be for the guard's comfort. Holding up a hand to halt his party, he put his ear to the planking, to listen.

What he heard was a gasping, choking noise, the crash of an upset form, and then a single high cry, swiftly cut off. Almost immediately, from down in the courtyard somewhere a dog barked twice, with yelping enquiry. Bruce cursed and threw open the door.

By the flickering firelight within he saw that Hay was already in control, the small warm chamber crowded with unclothed men. The men with clothes, three of them, lay twitching on the floor.

"Quick!" Bruce said, "Down to the courtyard. That hound . . ."

A voice called out thinly from higher — a Northern English voice. "What's to do, down there? What was that, Tom?"

Frowning, Bruce took a chance. That had come from the keep parapet — so there was another guard up there. "Tom burned himself. His hand," he called, trying to sound as English as the others, and hoping the muffling of his voice from indoors would help. "A burn only. The fire." He even produced a hollow laugh.

The man above still called down enquiries, but less concernedly. He must be ignored. The King gestured urgently towards the turnpike stairway. The dog had not barked again.

Down they all streamed, into the entrance pend. Across the courtyard, the keep door stood ajar. Detaching three men to look to the buildings in the yard, stables and the like, and to silence the dog if need be, he led the others at a rush across the paving-stones for the other door.

The basement of the keep contained arms, food and storage; but within the springing of its stone vault would be a timber sleeping-loft for men-at-arms. Racing on silent bare feet up the main stair, Bruce signed to Hay, at the first door, to deal with that loft. He himself took only three men, and hurried on.

The Hall, on the first main floor, was empty, a dying fire on the great hearth. But two deer-hounds lay thereat, now sitting up at the arrival of intruders, growling deeply in their throats. Bruce pulled the door shut — but not before the hounds began to bay. He dashed on upstairs.

On the next floor would be the master's chamber, the keeper of the castle's quarters. As he reached the door it was thrown open from within, and dimly seen, a man stood there, pulling on a bed-robe, a woman's querulous voice sounding behind. Bruce felled him with a single great flat-sided blow of his sword. The woman began to scream. Motioning his three companions higher, he rushed into the dark room, made for the bed by ear rather than sight, groped hands on a naked squirming woman until he found her open mouth, and shut it.

"Silence!" he ordered. "More noise from you, and you die! You understand? Die! Bide quiet here, and no harm will come to you."

He left her, choking and gasping and whimpering, but otherwise quiet.

There was only the one room to each floor. Above he found two of his trio coming out of the chamber, wiping their dirks and going in higher. Inside sounded more female cries and sobs. Silence was pointless now. He demanded information, in the darkness.

"Two dead ..." he was answered grimly, and, after a brief pause, "Three now, by God! These bawling doxies! Dirty bitches!"

"Leave them. Come higher ..."

But they were not required higher. Men were coming bounding up the stairs, naked men, shouting that all was over below. Leaving the remaining two storeys, and the guard on the keep's parapet-walk, to them, Bruce went down.

Hay had not had to kill more than a few of the sleepers in the main dormitory-loft. Now, in the light of a smoky lantern, he had about a dozen sleep-bemused or terrified prisoners, staring at the demon-like naked apparitions with the dripping swords.

Loch Doon Castle was taken, a bedlam of shouting, moaning men, screaming, weeping women, barking dogs and stamping, uneasy horses.

"Neatly done," Bruce commended briefly. "Now — lights, And let us find some clothes, a mercy's sake! And get word to Keith . . ."

They found a timber pontoon contrivance laid along the entrance pend and weighted with stones, obviously an underwater gangway to bridge the gap cut in the causeway. Forcing at dagger-point sundry of their prisoners who clearly knew how this contraption worked, to manhandle it out into position, shouts from the victors soon brought Sir Robert Keith, and others, on horseback, out over the causeway, from the camp. The Marischal was suitably impressed by the swift and effective capture of the strength which had defied his 200 for ten days; but he was otherwise preoccupied also.

"A messenger has arrived, Sire," he said to Bruce, now in the bed-robe of the knightly but unfortunate English captain. "From Turnberry. He came soon after you were gone. From England. From Bishop Lamberton. The English invade. They are over the Border, in strength. King Edward at their head . . ."

Before the words were out, Bruce had grabbed the nearest horse, pulled himself into the saddle, and went clattering out through the pend and splashing into the dark waters above the causeway, robe flapping.

* * *

Before the misty dawn, the King and the Marischal's force, leaving only a small garrison in the captured castle, were on their way northwards through the sleeping hills for Turnberry, riding as fast as the night would permit. The Earl of Atholl would have a pretty puzzle to unravel in the morning.

Bruce learned from Lamberton's courier, another friar who had been searching for him for two days, that the truce was indeed broken with a vengeance. He had known that Edward of Carnarvon was mustering troops — but that strange, unpredictable man had done the same before and then failed to use the assembled host, to the fury and despair of his nobles. Indeed, latterly his lords had been ignoring his summonses. Now, it appeared, he had acted with unusual haste and vigour, and made a sudden dash northwards from York — possibly to impress his notorious favourite, Piers Gaveston, Earl of Cornwall, who was with him. Bishop Lamberton was actually with him also, taken along as an adviser apparently. The Primate had managed to send off this friar from Alnwick, five days before. Berwick should have been reached by the army, of about 75,000, two days later. The Earls of Gloucester and Surrey, with the Lords Percy and Clifford, were with King Edward. Lamberton believed the English to be heading across Scotland for Glasgow, before going on to relieve beleaguered Dundee.

At Turnberry, Bruce sent out couriers in all directions, to his so scattered captains. All present operations were to be suspended immediately. Most groups were to rejoin him with all speed. There was to be no large-scale confrontation with the main English army. Harassing of flanks, rear and lines of support might be engaged in, but all the major effort was to be concentrated on laying waste the land in front of the advancing invaders, denying them supplies and shelter. Any stand to be made would be made at or near Stirling; but that was for the future.

Scouting parties were, of course, sent off south-eastwards to ascertain the enemy progress. Because of the delay with the news, they could be expected by now to be well into Scotland. From Berwick, if they were in fact making for Glasgow — as was reasonable, so that they could relieve besieged Bothwell and Kirkintilloch also — they would almost certainly move diagonally across country by Roxburgh, following the Tweed up through Melrose and the Forest to Peebles, and then over the mouth of Tweedsmuir and the high spine of Southern Scotland, to the upper Clyde valley. There was not much that could be done to devastate the land before and through the Ettrick Forest — where there was little to devastate indeed — so that Bruce's main attention must be to the grim, heart-rending business of destruction of the fair Clyde valley and its surroundings — Douglas country. He had done it before, more than once, and he could do it again — but it went even more sorely against the grain, this harsh and wholesale eviction and impoverishment of his own people. But it was the only way that he could eventually halt the mighty invader, since he refused utterly to risk all in a great battle — which was what the English wanted, with their preponderant power in numbers, heavy cavalry and hosts of archers. But a huge army of scores of thousands had to live largely on the country it passed through, and inevitably eventually ground to a halt if it could not gain food for its men and, above all, forage for its horses.

Keith was sent off, therefore, with a small contingent, to do what he could by way of delaying tactics in the Forest area, while Bruce headed for upper Clydesdale, calling for men from all quarters to aid in the terrible work. Once it was confirmed that King Edward was to come this way, across the watershed, they would start. And he called a council-of-war at Cadzow for five days hence.

Joined by Douglas, the King was at Lanark with just over a thousand men, when a messenger from Keith confirmed that the English were coming indeed. Roxburgh, Melrose, Selkirk and

Peebles were ablaze, and, on the fringes at least, the Forest was beginning to hang with dead men.

So the order was reluctantly given, and the great burning of fertile Clydesdale began, and Douglasdale with it, James Douglas acceding. The people were dispossessed and herded into the hills; all houses great and small, all barns, mills and other buildings, even churches, unroofed; all grain, hay and standing crops burned — and where the latter would not burn, trampled and flattened and wasted methodically; all bridges were demolished and fords made impassable; river banks and mill-lades were breached, pastures flooded, wells fouled with the carcases of all stock which could not be herded away. Inexorable, Bruce drove his man-made desert north by west, on a vast ten-mile-wide front. It took him back over the years to 1299, when he had first ravaged this same country, though in the other direction. And still they were fighting for Scotland's very existence. Eleven years! How long, oh Lord — how long?

Those days the King was bad company indeed, a savagely-fierce unapproachable man, black-browed, bleak-eyed, as he burned the realm he had dedicated his life to saving, made homeless the people he had vowed to protect. Even Gilbert Hay and James Douglas kept their distance, warily.

Lanark itself was soon overtaken into the pattern of desolation and left a blazing pyre. The council-of-war was put forward two days and called now for Rutherglen.

Edward Bruce arrived, the next day, from Galloway with 400 cavalry and the word that 1,500 foot was coming on, by forced marches, behind him. He brought more bad news. Another English force had crossed Solway from Carlisle, under the Earl of Richmond, and was ravaging and slaying its way up their own Annandale and Randolph's Nithsdale. As angry a man as his brother, if in a different, hotter fashion, he asked, demanded, permission to take the main force and give battle in the passes of Moffat and Dalveen and Enterkin — and was curtly refused.

Lennox was the last to arrive, from besieging Kirkintilloch — for Angus Og and most of the other Highlanders were meantime back in their own territories. The Earl was sadly depressed. Were they back where they had started, after all the years of bloodshed and sorrow? For once he got only short shrift from his friend.

The council at Rutherglen was a sorry one, difficult, rancorous, with disillusion heavy upon all. Edward led a strong group in a mood of hot defiance, urging attack, attack. If they had to go down, let them go down fighting, like men — not running, savaging their own people. Campbell urged a retiral forthwith to Stirling, there to stand to the end, at the narrow waist of Scotland, abandoning all the South as hopeless but making a stronghold of the North. Reluctantly Lennox, Boyd and Douglas agreed. But Bruce was sternly adamant that they continue to drive their slow way north-westwards. They could by no means defeat the Plantagenet — but they could starve and sicken him. And this Edward would sicken more quickly than his sire. Abandon the South to him and he would install his armies in Glasgow and Edinburgh, if necessary for the winter, supply them by sea, and so be in a state to marshal his fullest force against the crossing at Stirling when he was ready. That way lay ultimate disaster — whereas his brother's way was to make disaster immediate.

Timeously, during the council, another courier arrived from Lamberton, forwarded by Keith from Biggar. It was to report that King Edward was now aiming, after relieving Bothwell, not at Glasgow but towards the sea — or at least, the mouth of the Clyde, in the Inverkip-Renfrew area. John MacDougall of Lorn had been sent to Dublin to collect and captain a fleet of shipping and Irish galleys from the Anglo-Irish there, with their mercenaries, and to sail up the Clyde with them. On the Renfrew coast he would make contact with the King, and ferry over the main English force to Dumbarton and the Lennox, so that it could then turn east, bypassing Stirling, and make direct for Perth and Dundee, avoiding the natural bastion of the Forth and Clyde and intervening wilderness of the Flanders Moss. Thereafter, John of Lorn would take his fleet north-west into the Hebrides, to win back his father's Argyll and to deal with the Lord of the Isles.

Much shaken, the council listened to these tidings — which of course made nonsense of much that had gone before. But it only confirmed Bruce in his determination to wear down the English before ever they reached the sea. The devastation policy would go on. In addition, wrecking parties would make for all the Clyde ports and havens, from Carrick northwards, to destroy and make unusable all harbour facilities, so that, on the west coast at least, the invaders could import no supplies. And he would send swift Highland messengers north, by sea, to warn Angus Og, and to urge him to assemble all his galley strength to sail south and cope with Lame John MacDougall.

Even Edward Bruce was silent now.

*   *   *

Edward of England never crossed the Clyde estuary. By the time that, in late October, his huge army reached the Renfrew coast,

284

hungry, angry, soiled, frustrated and almost mutinous, the King had lost all taste for so inglorious an adventure — and Piers Gaveston with him. John of Lorn had not yet put in an appearance; the weather was bad, and there was famine in the land. Moreover Bruce was apparently prepared to burn all Glasgow and the West before him indefinitely. In petulant rage, he ordered a retreat by Linlithgow and Lothian, to Berwick, where they would winter. He did not trouble to try to inform John MacDougall.

That resentful man found Angus Og waiting for him at the mouth of the Firth of Clyde, and there was a great sea battle. It would be difficult to say who won — but MacDougall it was who broke off, and limped southwards, to vent his spleen on the Isle of Man for want of better target.

One more breathing-space gained — but at a price that could not continue to be paid.

CHAPTER EIGHTEEN

"THESE larks, I swear, must be traitor birds!" James Douglas cried, gazing up into the pale cold blue of the early April sky, laughing. "Hear how they shout for joy. They cheer us on."

"I say they are Scots larks, blown south by some storm," Gilbert Hay declared. "No English fowl could sing so sweet and true."

"Sweet, perhaps." It was Thomas Randolph who took him up. "But true? Who are we to talk of Scots being true! I think the English are truer than we."

"Well may *you* say so!" Campbell accused quickly.

"He means but that they breed the fewer traitors, I think," Hugh Ross said, coming to the aid of his friend. These two had grown close since that day on Loch Ness-side three years before.

"You should know — both of you!"

"Peace, dolts!" the King said, but easily, almost automatically — for this was a perennial dissension. "Every man in this host will depend on every other for his life, from here on. So who should talk of traitors? Gibbie is right. These are Scots larks, strayed a little. Like ourselves! Perhaps we should sing like them, now — lest we cannot sing hereafter!"

That brought them back to reality. They had, hitherto, been almost too carefree this sunny morning, blithe as any larks, apt to sing indeed, in a fashion highly unsuitable for great officers of state, sheriffs and the like. It was high time to adopt a more sober mood — though surely not a bickering, carping one.

In their lighter travelling armour, under colourful heraldic sur-coats, very fine, they sat their steaming mounts and looked back from the higher ground as the last files of their little army splashed across the ford of Esk near Kirkandrews. It was not in fact an army, but a hand-picked, tight-knit striking force of a thousand men, with a high proportion of them young knights, lairdlings or the sons thereof, superbly mounted, finely accoutred and armed. Here was indeed the cream of Southern Scotland — or such part of it as supported King Robert — selected thus for more reasons than one.

They stood, now, on the soil of England. It was five years since Bruce had last done that — and, as it happened, it was exactly here, at this remote and little-used ford that he had then crossed the Border, though then in the other direction, fleeing from Edward Longshanks' fury, a day or two before he had slain the Red Comyn. Now he was back, a king himself, and with a gallant if hard-hitting company.

It was against all his normal and cherished policy, a reversal to the old more brash Robert Bruce — or so it seemed. Yet he alone had decided upon it, and of a set purpose, just as he had carefully selected the men to take with him. This, in its own way, was in fact almost as much of a play-acting and demonstration as had been his St. Andrews parliament. Morale demanded that the risk be taken — the frustrated, angry morale of his own eager young cap-tains and leaders, the knightly class, whom he had held back from battle during all the English invasion in the autumn and turned baleful incendiary instead; and the sagging, uneasy morale of the Northern English, whose men made up the bulk of King Edward's army, still kicking its heels at Berwick after the idle winter. That army had waited for this spring for campaigning weather again, when the passes would be free of snow, the rivers crossable, the bogs somewhat drier. Bruce had determined to move first, taking an enormous but calculated risk. The larks at least commended him.

They rode on through the gradually rising empty grassy moors, scarcely high enough by Scots standards to be called hills, into Cumberland. Deliberately Bruce had chosen this lonely un-frequented route. One thousand men, however disciplined, are not transported through the countryside without attracting notice, and at this stage he desired the minimum of attention.

As well as the route, he had chosen his destination with great care. It must be remote enough to receive no warning of approach, far enough into England to be significant, yet large or important enough to cause considerable heart-burning amongst the English.

There should also be secondary targets in the area. Moreover, for preference, it should belong to Robert Clifford — or some of it! He had a long score to settle with the Lord of Brougham. The valleys of the Irthing and the upper South Tyne fulfilled all these requirements in general, and the Gillsland area in particular.

By noon, the long, fast-moving column was almost twenty miles deep into England, heading east, and leaving behind the empty moors for lower ground. They had passed one or two remote villages, inevitably, as well as shepherds' houses and granges; but they had left them all severely alone, and their occupants were not such as were likely to hastily send off messengers to Berwick, or even Carlisle. Crossing Bolton Fell they had had to negotiate a great drove of cattle, being herded south to Brampton market — and the drovers would assuredly tell what they had seen; but fortunately such herds moved very slowly over rough country, and by the time the drovers might give the news, it should not matter.

They came to the summit of Banks Fell, the last long rolling ridge before the Vale of Irthing, and from the shelter of scrub woodland surveyed the scene. It all looked notably fat and fertile, prosperous and peaceful, with flocks and herds grazing far and near, fresh green everywhere with patches of new tilth showing brown, many farms and granges and hamlets scattered wide, and in the centre the sizeable town of Gillsland, grey-walled and red-roofed, sending its blue chimney-smoke into the clear air. A little to the east rose the warm yellow masonry, tall and fair, of Irthing Priory, amongst spreading gardens and orchards. Yet it was in the other direction, westwards, that Bruce's own glance kept turning. Some three miles away, taller, handsomer, more splendid walls soared, amidst its own larger township — Lanercost Abbey itself. Lanercost, where the old Edward had so long made his headquarters for the subjugation of Scotland, and from which he had set out on his last journey of hatred, to die at Solway cursing Bruce.

"A-a-aye!" the King breathed. "There is Lanercost, where my ruin, Scotland's ruin, was plotted. And here," he pointed closer at hand, "Here is my lord Clifford's domain of Gillsland, with his priory of Irthing." Sir Robert had recently been created a Lord of Parliament. "He has burned Annandale of the Bruces four times. And your Nithsdale twice, Thomas. I promised him a reckoning, once. This is not it, since he is not here. But it could be a first payment! For both of them."

The rumbling growl from those who could hear his words was a frightening thing. There was an involuntary surge forward of urgent horsemen.

"Wait, you!" the King commanded. "This is to be done heedfully. *My* way. I will have no unnecessary slaughter, no women ravished, no bairns savaged, no men hanging from trees. If any there be, others of *you* will hang with them, before we leave! Wallace made three mistakes. To fight at Falkirk. To trust a Halyburton. And to fail to keep his men under good control when he raided into England. So that he created here not fear and panic and a refusal to invade Scotland again, but a burning hatred, the more set on vengeance. It is not for that we are here, see you. We have not come for vengeance either — although, God knows, I could wish we had! We are here for set purposes. To create alarm and unrest in the English camp at Berwick, so that they do not march north into Scotland. To show the rest of the North of England what is like to happen to them if they continue to provide men for the Scottish wars. And last, to gain treasure." He smiled slightly. "I will not deny that it displeasures me nothing that it is my lord Clifford's lands, and those of the Abbey of Lanercost, that we work our purpose on!" And as an afterthought, he added, "I said treasure. Only such treasure as may be carried conveniently. None must lumber themselves with booty. All else is to be destroyed. And, I charge you — such treasure is not for your pouches, my friends! But for my Lord Treasurer's coffers. That our warfare may be maintained."

Men chuckled at that, and a better temper for the business was engendered.

Bruce went on to make his dispositions. At this stage, the force would split. He would take half, to Lanercost. Douglas would lead the rest down to Gillsland itself, and Irthing Priory. They had not unlimited time. But seven hours until sunset. By which all this valley must be destroyed, and themselves over into the next and greater valley southwards — the upper South Tyne. There, seven miles beyond, lay the market town of Haltwhistle, as well as the castles of Bellister, Featherstone, Unthank and Blenkinsopp. Fleeing men from Gillsland would carry the tale of the hership of Irthing to these. They must not be given time to muster and prepare. Haltwhistle, therefore, must be taken before dark, and the castles isolated. Four hours only for the sack of Gillsland and Lanercost, and all on their swift way to Tyne. Was it understood?

"What of English forces from the garrison at Carlisle, Sire?" Campbell asked. "It cannot be more than a dozen miles from here. And Brampton nearer. There will be a garrison there?"

"Carlisle is too far to menace us before nightfall. And Brampton will not hold sufficient men to endanger us. That danger will come

288

tomorrow. Today's is that Haltwhistle and the Tyne will gain warning before we reach them."

"Sire," Randolph put in. "I know this land. I was here, at Lanercost, with King Edward." Not all men would have admitted that, there and then. "There is a way through from Irthing to Tyne. Through the hills. A pass, by way of the Tipalt Burn. A small company could hold it, near where the Roman Wall crosses. And so prevent any flight of folk to the Tyne and Haltwhistle. A score of men sent there forthwith would not be wasted. Going round by Thirlwall Common."

Bruce looked at his nephew thoughtfully. "Well said," he nodded. "You have the sort of head on your shoulders that I need, Thomas. So he it. Yourself take them and place them." He raised his hand. "Come, then — enough of words. Now we act. Gibbie — 500 men for me . . ."

So the two squadrons parted to turn, one west, one east, round the north base of Banks Fell, hidden from the unsuspecting Irthing valley.

The dual attack was indeed a complete surprise. As far as Lanercost was concerned, it was not even an attack. Bruce's party, emerging from the high ground behind the great Hadrian's Wall, had only a mile to cover in sight of the splendid Abbey, and their breakneck speed gave the Abbot's guard no time to assemble or even arm. Dispersing three-quarters of his force to deal with the large township of secular and domestic buildings surrounding the establishment, the King, with perhaps a hundred men, dashed up to the Abbey gatehouse, swept aside the dumbfounded porters, and rode into the precincts, calling loudly for the Abbot and Chapter. His men did not wait for any such formalities.

When the flustered and appalled cleric, a heavy moon-faced elderly man, was brought less than gently before the King, still sitting his horse in the wide courtyard, he was given no opportunity for protest, lamentation or plea.

"My lord Abbot — I am Robert of Scotland," he was told briskly. "Your abbey has in the past given much comfort to my enemies. Here was plotted my ruin, my death, my kingdom's devastation. The time has come for payment. I do not make war on Holy Church, unlike the Kings of England. But your treasure ought to be in heaven, rather than in your vaults! The late Edward, in gratitude, gave you much gold and silver and jewel, I understand. Plate, chalices, ewers, censers, lamps and the like. Much of it stolen from Scotland. I require it. All, mark you — all. And quickly."

"But . . . but . . . my lord! This is sacrilege!"

289

"It is war, sir. And retribution. Though not on the Church. On you. You have grown rich on the spoils of Scotland."

"I . . . I will not, may not, do it. You will not rob God's house? I will give you nothing, my lord."

"Address me as King, Englishman! And if God's house spills over with stolen treasure, should I respect it? I care not, priest, whether you give or I take. But all in this house is mine now. Choose you whether to deliver it up decently, or have my men pull your abbey apart to get it."

The banging and crashing and shouting that sounded from all around did not fail to underline his point. And looking up, the Abbot's pale prominent eyes widened as he saw the black smoke clouds begin to rise up from behind the precinct walls.

"You already . . . burn! Destroy!" he cried.

"Only barns, mills, gardens, my lord Abbot. Nothing sacred! Nothing that a man of God should set store by. But — your gold, now. Silver. Jewellery. Decide quickly, sir priest."

"Yes, yes. To be sure, my lord . . . Majesty. If you will spare the Abbey . . ."

"As your kings have not done in Scotland! In a hundred miles from my borders I have scarce an abbey, a priory or even a church with a roof to it! With doors to which abbots and monks have not been crucified! But . . . Sir Hugh. See that no chapels are damaged, no altars misused, no priests hurt. Sir Gilbert — go with my lord Abbot and take delivery of his treasure. All of it. And be not long about it." Abruptly Bruce reined his horse around and rode to supervise the destruction outside.

In ninety minutes the greatest, fairest establishment north of Durham was transformed utterly. The sacred buildings themselves remained entire, undamaged. But all else was smoking ruin, broken masonry, burning wood, trampled grain and garden and orchard, and the littered steaming carcases of slaughtered beasts. The Scots had had ample practice in the efficient spoiling of lands, their own lands; now they spoiled their enemies' with a will. In ever widening circles the devastation grew, until even the sun was obscured by the vast rolling pall of smoke which covered the valley of Irthing. Then Bruce, concerned with timing, and the fact that that smoke would be seen from Brampton, and far farther, called a halt. Detailing a score of men, under a young knight, to parcel up all the rich haul of the Abbey's treasure in emptied wool-sacks, and take it on a train of captured pack-horses quickly and secretly back to Scotland, he assembled his now smoke-blackened followers and headed off up the wide vale towards Gillsland without any leave-taking, abandoning Lanercost to its lamentations.

"At least they are alive, to wail!" he commented grimly to the somewhat doubtful Hugh Ross.

It was a westerly wind, and they rode, coughing, in the shroud of their own smoke that poured and billowed eastwards. But very quickly they were into still newer, thicker smoke, ruddy with fires and alive with fleeing folk, stumbling cursing men, sobbing women and wailing children, the sad exodus from blazing Gillsland, stricken to further abject terror and despair at the sight of this new looming host of grim horsemen.

Bruce found Campbell in charge at Gillsland, with Douglas superintending the spoliation of Irthing Priory a mile or so farther up the valley. The comprehensive burning, choking smoke clouds made all a chaotic nightmare, but Sir Neil declared that he thought there was not a single building left unburned in the town, or in a two-mile radius around. Catching and slaying the cattle had been the biggest problem. There had been no opposition worth mentioning.

Anxious about this vast pall of smoke being seen and interpreted from the Tyne valley five miles to the south-east, even above the hills between, the King ordered the trumpets to blow for disengagement and assembly. They rode southwards, out of the reeking, ravaged valley, almost an hour earlier than hoped for.

Now their route lay through the defile of the Tipalt Burn described by Randolph. The actual narrows of this comprised only the central mile or two; and well before this was reached the invaders found themselves having to plough through an unhappy flood of returning refugees streaming back northwards in renewed panic. Randolph's holding operation had served its purpose. When Bruce in due course picked up the little company strongly entrenched in the gullet of the pass, it was to be assured that no single messenger or escaper had got through to warn the Vale of Tyne — by this route, at least.

They were trotting through the final mile of the defile when, rounding a bend of its narrow floor beside the brawling burn, they came face to face with a mounted party of perhaps fifty, riding in the opposite direction. Bruce had not put out his usual scouting advance-guard on this occasion, no serious challenge being looked for, and as such would only be apt to offer prior intimation of something unusual happening. So this confrontation was a surprise to both sides.

However equal the surprise, reaction of course was quite otherwise, with so few facing so many — even though they would not see a quarter of them. Besides, these were not knights and men-at-arms, but looked like farmers and burghers on horseback. Almost certainly they represented a posse of Haltwhistle citizens hurrying to see what the great bank of smoke signified. At any rate, they behaved with commendable unanimity and expedition now, disciplined or not. With a great scrabbling, rearing and sidling of struggling mounts, they pulled round and went plunging off whence they had come, each jostling to be foremost.

"After them, Jamie!" Bruce commanded. "With our first ten files. Quickly! Head them off from the town. They must not warn."

Almost before the words were out, Douglas was spurring ahead, yelling to the front ranks of their company to follow. Pushing past the King's group, all but unseating some of them indeed, eager riders galloped in pursuit.

Bruce increased the pace of the entire host to a canter.

When they emerged, almost at right angles, into the open green vale, wider than that of Irthing, it was to see the better-mounted Scots dispersing the fleeing burghers left and right, like wolves amongst sheep, far ahead. The town of Haltwhistle showed grey beyond, its roofs and spires catching the glow of the sinking sun.

Ignoring the nearby castle of Blenkinsopp meantime. Bruce led his host directly and at fullest speed for the town, hooves drumming an earth-shaking, terrifying first intimation.

If many of the Scots were grievously disappointed at the lack of opposition they met, at the sheer anticlimax of the whole affair, the King was not. This was what he had planned and hoped for. By the time that they reached the first houses, the streets were quite deserted, no single face peered from door or window — although a few horses still stood tethered here and there. The host swept clatteringly through the town without meeting more than yelping dogs, squealing pigs and squawking poultry. It was not a large place, though larger than Gillsland; but it had a big and important church in its centre, with collegiate buildings attached. This church was a major reason for Bruce's presence here — for, oddly enough, it belonged to the See of Aberdeen, with considerable property in the town and surrounding country, a relic of happier days when the English were friends, and thus had been almost a detached part of Scotland. Holy Church was powerful and international, and Haltwhistle Church represented a useful excuse for the Scots incursion when the inevitable Papal fulminations began — for of course the Bishop of Aberdeen had been deprived of its due revenues for many a long year. Bruce, therefore, turned back for this church, to make it his base and headquarters, sending for the Vicar. Meanwhile he placed contingents of his men to dominate every street, lane and alley, with strong pickets to patrol the entire perimeter. But he gave strict instructions that there was to be no assault, pillage or burning here.

The terrified Vicar, when he was routed out of hiding and brought before the King, was assured that since Haltwhistle was as good as a Scots town, its people need fear nothing — so long as they co-operated and behaved discreetly. He was required to furnish a list of all Aberdeen property in the area; and then to go, under escort, and bring the principal citizens to Bruce, for their instructions.

So in due course these alarmed worthies were assembled to learn their fate — and could scarcely believe their ears. Haltwhistle would not be burned. Nobody would be hanged, beaten, ravished or otherwise molested. No hostages would be taken. The town would be treated as would a Scots town. The King of Scots and his force would occupy it for a few days — but they would pay for their keep and lodgings. Obedience and co-operation, that was all that was required. That, and the collection of the overdue and accumulated revenues for the Bishop of Aberdeen, which the King would take back to Scotland, as was suitable and lawful. For the rest, peace and goodwill. Only, the least hint of treachery, of attempts to communicate with other towns or areas, and there would be immediate and dire punishment, with no mercy shown. Was that understood?

There were no arguments, no questions.

That night the King, and most of his people, slept warm and comfortable, with minor detachments out guarding the approaches to the town, by the Tipalt Burn and both reaches of Tyne, while others kept careful watch on the small local castles. Bruce had chosen carefully in this, as in all else; Haltwhistle, placed as it was, was as good as a citadel for them.

*   *   *

Sunrise saw the Scots trotting in disciplined ranks down the broadening Tyne valley, leaving a small garrison, under Randolph, in Haltwhistle, with scouts carefully placed all around. The villages of Melkridge, Henshaw, Bardon Mill and Chesterwood went up in flames behind them, and by noon they were at the small town of Haydon Bridge, important strategically. There was a modest castle here, to guard the vital bridge over Tyne, but the word of the Scots advance had preceded them down the river and they found the castle abandoned, and town almost so. With the provisions of the whole missing community to sustain them, the invaders made their midday meal here. They moved on again in two sections, north and south of the river, under Douglas and the King respectively. They were seldom out of sight.

Newborough, Fourstones, Elrington and Wharmley fell to them, with many farms, mills and lesser places, without a sword drawn. All the vale behind was now hidden under a pall of smoke. The large town of Hexham, with its great and famous Priory, lay ahead, where North Tyne came in to join South.

Bruce had drawn up his contingent at West Boat, where there was a ferry by which Douglas came across to join him and receive orders, when scouts came to inform that a party under a white flag was riding out from Hexham. The King ordered the newcomers to be brought into his presence.

The white-flag party consisted of the magistrates and chief citizens of the town, looking very alarmed; and the Prior of Hexham looking magnificent, with even a silken canopy held over his head by four mounted acolytes on milk-white jennets, the stuff richly embroidered with a gold saltire on azure. Hexham had been a bishopric once, and its foundation in 674 by Saint Wilfred made it one of the most ancient and venerable fanes in all England. Undoubtedly the present incumbent was not disposed to forget it. Ignoring the genuflecting magistrates, Bruce addressed himself to the still-mounted prelate.

"You must be the Lord Prior of Hexham, sir, come to meet me. I thank you for your courtesy," he said gravely. "How may I serve you?"

Surprised, the other, a purple-faced, sagging-jowled man of strong features and intolerant eye, drew a much-beringed hand over his thin-lipped mouth. "If you would serve us, my lord — then come and accept of our hospitality, you and yours," he answered stiffly. "But spare our city." And he waved his plump hand towards the ominous smoke-clouds.

"Your hospitality it will be my pleasure to accept. But as to sparing your city, Sir Prior — tell me why I should?"

"Because it is a city of Holy Church. An ecclesiastical jurisdiction of great age and sanctity. As is all the country around — all Church land, Hexhamshire. Sacred to the blessed Saint Wilfred whom God loves, my lord."

"Sire!" James Douglas barked, at the Prior.

"Eh . . .?"

"I said, Sire. Not my lord. Address His Grace as befits a king, sirrah. And get down from that horse."

After a moment or two, the other slowly dismounted, frowning. He did not speak.

It was Bruce who inclined his head, not the other. "I have heard

294

of Hexham Priory's fame, of course," he said. "Its greatness. And all this goodly land is yours also? This Hexhamshire? How far does it extend, my lord?"

"All around you. You have been on my land these last miles Since Allen River. Church lands. Hexhamshire comprises 50,000 acres."

The King looked approvingly around him. "A goodly heritage indeed," he nodded. "Rich. Fertile. How much had you in mind, my lord?"

The other opened his mouth, and shut it again, purple deeper.

"Come, sir. You must have some notion of your city's worth? And your 50,000 acres of Hexhamshire? You, and these others, came expressly to me. Came with a proposal to put to me, I think? How much? Out with it!" That last was snapped in a very different tone of voice from heretofore.

The Prior blinked rapidly. "I . . . we would be prepared to make some small . . . tribute, Majesty," he conceded guardedly. "A token of . . . of goodwill."

"A token, yes. In order that your town and country be not destroyed. How much, man?"

"What can I say, Sire?" The clerical voice held a note that might almost have been anguish now. "I am but a poor priest entrusted with the pastoral care and oversight of God's flock in this place . . ."

"Your town, shire and treasure. How much?" And when the other only compressed already thin lips, Bruce jabbed a finger towards the chief of the magistrates. "You, then — how much?"

That was more than the Prior could in any way allow. "We have some few cattle," he jerked. "Wool. Grain. Forage . . ."

"And silver," Bruce added.

"But little, Sire. We are not rich in moneys . . ."

"Tush, man — the rings on your hand alone do belie you! Your cattle and grain and forage I will accept. Such as I require. But to save your town and lands, you will pay me 2,000 merks in silver. Forthwith. Is it agreed?"

A stricken moan issued from the cleric's lips. "You cannot . . . you cannot mean it, Sire! Not 2,000! It is not possible. It would beggar us. Indeed, I do not have so much . . ."

"Then find it, sir. Sell your rings, perhaps? Or do you prefer that Hexham goes up in flames? Like Gillsland and others?"

"No! No, Sire — no!" came from the magistrates, in a wailing chorus.

"On payment of 2,000 silver merks, Englishmen, or £1,300, if so you prefer it," Bruce went on sternly, "I shall sign you a decree declaring that the town of Hexham, with Hexhamshire, be free from all further tribute of reparation for English damage done in Scotland for the space of one year from this date. The Prior of Hexham to remain hostage in my hands until such payment is made. Agree to this now, or I command immediate advance upon your town, without mercy. Is it so agreed?"

"Yes, yes," the townsmen cried. All eyes were on the Prior.

Slowly, expressionlessly, that man inclined his head.

"Very well. Then we shall accompany you back to your Priory, my lord," the King nodded. "As your guests, to receive your hospitality, as offered. Hexham is safe . . . for a year. Come, to horse . . ."

As they rode towards the town, Douglas, at the King's side, shook his head. "I mislike this chaffering with the enemy, Sire," he said. "We came to punish, not to barter and deal! To cause the English army at Berwick to look back over its shoulder . . ."

"Spoken like my good brother Edward!" Bruce asserted, smiling. Edward had advisedly been left behind in Scotland to prosecute the siege of the English in Perth. He would have fitted but uncomfortably into this highly delicate campaign. "How do *you* know what we came to do, Jamie? We came to upset the Berwick army, without fighting it, yes. But much more. And that, I swear, is already achieved — or will be when the tidings reach them. Think you burning and hership the only way to cause the English alarm? It is their confidence, their pride, I would undermine. And this day's work will do that even better than yesterday's. Though yesterday's was necessary for today's."

"You mean . . . you planned this, Sire?"

"Say that I hoped for it. This Prior has served me better than he knows. Better than just by filling my purse! He leads the way for others to follow. Others will be prepared to do what the proud Prior of Hexham did not balk at — to buy their safety. For the moment! All over the North of England, let us hope."

"But . . . you could have had the wealth of Hexham — all of it — by but drawing your sword! Why this temporising . . .?"

"Do you not see it, Jamie? I warrant Thomas Randolph would have understood! He has a head on his shoulders for more than swordery. See you — my realm is direly impoverished. The governance of a kingdom requires much money. My treasury is empty, and I can by no means fill it from Scotland. If I burned Hexham today and took its treasure — that would be all I would win from it. This way, I have given it assurance for a year, for 2,000 merks. Think you that next year it will not think perhaps to buy more safety, instead of fighting? And others like it? Another 2,000.

Riches breed caution, James — and the English North has grown rich on the spoil of Scotland. We shall see to it that all hear of Hexham's bargain. There are many, many towns and abbeys and priories in these parts. After my burning of Gillsland, as was necessary, and sparing Haltwhistle and Hexham, I swear others will seek to make similar bargains. We shall, of course, burn here and there, to remind all! Hereafter, by constant raiding over the Border, I intend to see that Cumberland and Northumberland — aye, and even Durham and York — pay their taxes to King Robert rather than King Edward! Think you this will not trouble the English at Berwick — or at least, their leaders — as much as a few more towns ablaze?"

Douglas was speechless.

Hexham was situated at a most vital junction of ways and roads and rivers. In every direction valleys and routes radiated. Even as the crow flew, however, it was sixty and more miles to Berwick. They had four days, Bruce reckoned. And with the sort of men he had brought, a great deal could be achieved in four days, from a centre like Hexham. That very evening he split up his force into two hundreds, under eager captains, and next morning sent them forth, strictly commanded, wolves amongst scattered sheep — but careful, calculating, persuasive wolves, who intended to come back this way again and again, seeking sheep's fleeces rather than their blood.

Then he rode back to Haltwhistle, where all would rendezvous four days hence — unless, somehow, a major English attack developed sooner. From Haltwhistle he could keep a general's eye on Carlisle and the south-west — and could be back through empty hills to the Border in two or three hours.

Glory could wait on another occasion.

CHAPTER NINETEEN

THE King wiped the rain off his reddened, weather-beaten, deeply-lined face, and cursed the blustering showers — even though it was April and the season for such; two Aprils since his first English raid. It was not the discomfort that concerned him, for he was now so inured to discomfort as scarcely to notice it. What worried him was the effect of all this wind on the sea, and therefore on the ships he was riding to join — or, at least, on the stomachs of the men behind him who would sail in those open galleys. Seasick warriors were any commander's nightmare. Lowering his head into the wet south-westerly gusts he kicked his stumbling horse up the last soggy-peat-pocked, outcrop-strewn rise of the long heather ridge, muttering profanities.

The tinkle of laughter at his elbow was mocking, challenging and affectionate in one. Christina MacRuarie, as befitted a Hebridean, cared nothing for wind or rain.

"You are getting old, Robert!" she accused. "Near to forty, and beginning to cherish your comforts. Of which, to be sure, I am one! A chair by the ingle — I swear that is what you are dreaming of!"

"A chair anywhere, woman!" he growled. "Anything but this saddle. I am never out of it. Dear God — I rule Scotland from the back of a horse! From over the Border to Inverness. From St. Andrews to the Forest. From Galloway to Argyll. Year in, year out, I live in the saddle. I vow my rump is so calloused that I shall never sit aught else in comfort!"

"It does not incommode you in bed, at least!" she asserted. "Nor, it seems, in scaling walls! And sitting on judgement-seats and in parliaments!"

"And I so old a man!"

"Never heed. Soon you will be standing on a galley's poop, concerned only for your belly, not your bottom! If Angus Og has waited for you at Dumbarton!"

"He will be waiting. I am none so late. Four days? Five?"

"Angus is not the most patient of mortals. And would have preferred to sail for Man direct, without calling into Clyde. He told me so himself, at Inverness. He says he could, and should, reduce the Isle of Man to obedience, of himself, without the King of Scots' aid!"

"No doubt — and so claim Man as *his* thereafter! As part of the Sudreys, the South Isles. No — Angus is my good friend — but he must learn who is master in Scotland. Man is part of my realm, and must remain so — not part of the Lordship of the Isles."

At last they had reached the summit of the long lateral ridge of Rednock, last outpost of the Highlands, and were able to look out over the vast trough of the Forth, and all the wide waterlogged vacances of the Flanders Moss. Below, the isle-dotted Loch of Menteith gloomed leaden under the scudding rain clouds, and to the west the tall hills of Loch Lomond and the Lennox were part-shrouded by drifting curtains. But eastwards there was a break in the overcast, and, in the slanting yellow afternoon sunlight fifteen miles away, Stirling rose proudly out of the level plain, castle crowning its soaring rock in a golden blaze.

The sight, sun notwithstanding, did nothing to sweeten Bruce's temper. Indeed, he turned abruptly away from it, in his saddle, to look back over the long straggling columns of his host, which seemed to extend quite a lot of the way back to Perth.

"Keith!" he jerked, to the group immediately behind him. "Sir Robert — you are Marischal of this realm, are you not? Look there! I warrant it is time that you did some marshalling! Call you that a royal progress? More like a flock of straying sheep! See you to it, sir!"

"Yes, Sire." Keith, without demur, wheeled round his mount and went cantering back, others with him. When the King was in this frame of mind, such reaction was the only wise one.

Christina, of them all, chose otherwise, as often. "Stirling!" she cried. "Stirling Castle, there, arrogantly lording it over all. The key to Scotland! When will the King of Scots do to Stirling what he had just done to Perth?"

"God's sake, woman — Stirling is like no other fortress in the kingdom! Even Edinburgh," Bruce flung back, rising to her taunt. "It cannot be taken by surprise, or battery, nor any device. Only starvation can take it — or treachery. Besides, it is Stirling, the *place*, that is the key to Scotland — not Stirling Castle. Wallace won Stirling Brig fight, while yet the English were secure in the castle. I have no time to spend on that hold."

"Yet you spent four days in Perth. At risk of Angus Og's patience!"

"Days! *Months* it would take. Five months I would require, to take Stirling Castle. I have more to do, by the Rude!"

She laughed. "Your brother told me once that he could crack that nut quickly enough — if you would let him try!"

"Edward! Edward speaks loud. He tried to take *Perth* — but did not!"

Christina smiled, with her woman's guile. This would bring the King out of his black mood. Set brother against brother, and there would be no more glooming, at least.

Not that Bruce had any immediate cause for gloom. His recent capture of the town of Perth had been a brilliant feat, and all his own. Many, including his brother, had tried, these past years, to reduce the Tayside city, but all had failed. The late King Edward had fortified it as only he knew how, as the strategic centre in the Southern Highlands. Sir Andrew Fraser had been the last to take its siege in hand; and on his way south for his parliament in Inverness, Bruce had come this way to see how matters moved. Matters had not been moving at all, and on the second night the King in person had led an assault, first by swimming the Tay in spate, and then the outer moat; then by scaling the outer rampart by rope-ladder and grappling-hooks, at this, the least well-guarded flank, to swim the second moat and thereafter gain the parapet of the inner bailey, from whence he could storm one of the gates from the inside, open it, and let in the flood of more conventional attackers. So, after nine long years, Perth was in Scots hands again; and only Dundee remained English-occupied north of Forth. Two more days Bruce had spent in the town thereafter, setting things to right — and hanging the Scots traitors who had aided the English and mistreated their fellow-citizens during the occupation. The English he had allowed to go to their ships in the Tay, and sail for home. It was, however, those hanging Scots, decorating the captured walls, who had sent the King on his way in this black temper — for though Robert Bruce could be ruthless and inexorable where sternness was called for, such measures always left him a prey to conscience.

Frowning still, but no longer sullen, Bruce led the way down the south-facing slopes into the Carse of Forth, to turn west along it for Gartmore and Drymen.

Next day they found the Lord of the Isles' great galley fleet awaiting them in the Clyde at Dumbarton — though with Angus Og himself away hawking with the MacGregor on Loch Lomondside, and his Islesmen setting a scandalised area by the ears. Embarkation had to delayed for another day. It was the King's turn to wait patiently.

This expedition against the Isle of Man had been decided upon at the recent Inverness parliament — for two reasons other than the simple fact that it was an integral part of the Scots realm presently occupied by the English. Firstly, Edward of Carnarvon had granted it in gift to his favourite, Piers Gaveston — and Gaveston was now beheaded, a piece of judicial murder by the Earls of Lancaster and Warwick as much deplored in Scotland, where the favourite's demoralising effect on King Edward was appreciated, as it was gleefully acclaimed by the English nobility; therefore there would for the moment be a hiatus in the control of Man. And secondly, John of Lorn, whom Edward had made his Admiral of the Western Seas, was using the island as a base, and interfering with the Scots lines of communication with Ireland, important for the supply of grain, arms, horses and other sinews of war. There was also the advantage, of course, that any such attack on Man might have the useful by-product of distracting the enemy from full-scale invasion of Scotland this coming campaigning season.

They sailed from Dumbarton, still in squally conditions. Bruce embarked some hundreds of his own force but sent the majority eastwards to aid Douglas, who was engaged in punitive raiding into English-held Lothian. This expedition was something of a waste of his cavalry, admittedly, since the horses had to be left behind; but the Isles lordship had always been interested in winning the Isle of Man for itself, and it was important that the King and his own troops should be to the fore in any taking of the place. Angus was a sound ally and friend — if less sound a subject — but he was no more immortal than the rest of them, and a successor in the Lordship of the Isles, holding Man, could be a thorn in the flesh. Yet, of course, Bruce could nowise assail it without Angus's galleys.

They made an uncomfortable voyage of it down the Firth and along the Ayrshire and Galloway coasts. Half a dozen of the Garmoran galleys were included in the fleet — hence Christina's presence, the only woman in the expedition — and the King sailed in her own vessel. Fortunately he was an excellent sailor; a sick monarch and commander would have cut a sorry figure amongst those Islesmen. There was considerable discussion as to whether these gales would give any tactical advantage. They would certainly make any attack on Man unexpected; and they would be likely to keep John MacDougall stormbound — but whether at Man itself or in any English or Irish ports, remained to be seen.

As to that, the King hoped to gain some prior information. For the fleet was going to make a call up the Solway Firth *en route*, to where Edward Bruce was at present besieging Dumfries and Caerlaverock. Here he hoped to get the latest news from England, and to pick up some further reinforcements for the expedition — however much of a waste of time Angus Og declared it.

It was a relief to turn into the shallow, sheltered waters of the Solway, and thereafter into the narrow Nith estuary. They found the English flag still flying defiantly from Caerlaverock Castle and then, six miles farther up, at Dumfries. They also found Edward to be absent, with the siege of Dumfries maintained by Sir Robert Boyd, and that of Caerlaverock by Sir Thomas Randolph.

Edward, it seemed, was off raiding in Cumberland across the Solway sands. Word had recently been brought back from England that the Scots commissioners, sent secretly to collect the annual dues from subscribing towns, abbeys and the like, had this year met with trouble. In fact, more than trouble — annihilation. They had reached Hexham-on-Tyne, with some of the moneys collected, and there, instead of receiving the third of the Prior's payments-for-safety, they had been hanged, and their treasure confiscated. That proud churchman had presumably decided that he might spare himself further expense. Only one or two of the Scots party had escaped, to win back to Dumfries with the tale of it. Edward

Bruce, being the man he was, had promptly mounted a fierce sally into the flat lands west of Carlisle.

The King's anger was cold where his brother's had been hot. Dumfries had a bad effect on him anyway — the scene of his slaying of John Comyn nine years earlier, even though also of his assumption of the crown. He had shunned the place, since. Even now he would not sleep in the armed camp which surrounded the walled town, but removed himself the few miles back to Caerlaverock, and Randolph's camp. Here he detached himself from all, to pace alone, well outwith arrow-shot of the magnificent fortress in the marshes. It was a time not for wrath so much as hard decision.

He had made up his mind before he slept that night. Major changes of programme were called for.

The next morning brought the need for still further and quite unanticipated decision. Boyd himself rode in from Dumfries, bringing with him a young man, square, stocky, richly-dressed but uneasy of eye and manner.

"Sire," Boyd declared, "here is one, MacDouall. Fergus, son to Sir Dugald MacDouall . . . of whom you know!"

There, in the tented encampment, Bruce stared, his breath catching in his throat at the identification of this son of his hated enemy, of the man who had given up his brothers to shameful death. He did not trust himself to speak. Those around him were suddenly silent quite.

"He comes under a flag of truce, Sire. From his father in yonder Dumfries Castle. He would . . . treat with you, he says!"

"Treat! That blood-stained traitor's son? God's mercy . . .!"

"Treat, my lord King," the young man reiterated, tense-voiced. "In my father's name."

"Hang him!" Angus Og advised succinctly. "Also in his father's name! As you will treat the other — not treat *with* him!"

Many around the King growled their agreement.

"No! No — hear me, Sire," the MacDouall cried. "You cannot so do. I came under flag of truce. By all the laws of war you cannot do it . . ."

"Did your father observe the laws of war, wretch, when he took his liege lord's brothers prisoner, and then sent them to their deaths?" That was Gilbert Hay.

"That . . . that was long ago. When I was but a child. And my father could not know. That King Edward would slay them. It was Edward's orders. My father recognised Edward as King — not you, Sire. Still he does — the new Edward. He is King Edward's governor of Dumfries and Warden of the West March . . ."

Bruce held up a hand that trembled slightly, for silence. "Well?" he grated. "Say what you have to say."

"Yes, Sire. My father sends me to say that if you will promise him, and his garrison, their lives and liberty, he will yield Dumfries. To you."

"So-o-o! That is it? And he thinks that I will grant him such terms?"

"Your Grace's clemency is known."

"Aye!" Angus Og snorted. "And there you have it. Any traitor and dastard in this land now conceives himself to be safe! That he will not have to pay for his sins. You have let off too many rogues, Sir King. That is what your clemency means now!"

Even Christina joined in the chorus of declamation. "Your Grace will perceive that MacDouall did not offer to treat with the Earl of Carrick! Who has been besieging him these many weeks. Only when you come, and he is gone, does this man seek these terms. Because he knows your brother would have none of him! Save hanging on a rope!"

All knew that to be the truth, Bruce better than any. Yet he turned and paced away some distance, to stand staring over towards the strange shield-shaped castle that rose out of its complicated system of morass and water-barrier, unseeing. Once again he was fighting, fighting one of his own dire battles with himself, the King fighting the man. Dugald MacDouall, the treacherous Gallovidian he had sworn a great oath to kill, the man for whose blood that of his young brothers cried out. He had spared those other two, whom he had likewise vowed to slay — William of Ross and Alexander MacDougall. Spared and accepted to his peace, his very company, after all they had done. Must he do the same with this, this third especial offender? Was this sacrifice demanded of him, also . . .?

He turned back to the waiting company, set-faced. "Mac-Douall," he said, expressionlessly. "Go back to your father. Tell him that he may march out of Dumfries, he and his, with my safe-conduct. To England. This day. Tell him — for I will by no means see him — that he will be wise to bide in England hereafter. For if he sets foot in my realm again, I will take him and hang him. You understand?"

The other's response was lost in the uproar of the Scots leaders' disbelief, wrath and reproach. The King signed to Boyd to take the young man away.

"My lord Constable," he snapped, to Gilbert Hay, "you will go, in my name, to receive the surrender of Dumfries. You will ensure the safety of the garrison, and see them sent on their way to the

Border. Let there be no mistake, see you." He paused, to run his eye sobrely over the critical ranks of his friends. "You all blame me, I see. You all name me fool, or worse. Think that I forget the blood of my brothers and my friends. Do not deny it — I see it on every face. Thank you God, then, that you are none of you the King! That you can afford to judge scoundrels on their merits — where *I* must judge causes, results, policies, the realm's best weal. How easy your judgement! How difficult mine."

"You will win few to your cause by sparing MacDouall," Angus Og declared. "You will not win *his* allegiance. He will continue to fight against you, hating you no less for your gentleness."

"Gentleness, man!" Bruce's bark of laughter had no mirth in it. "Think you there was any gentleness in that decision? Or in my heart? You know me little, it seems, still. I spared MacDouall because it was the price to pay for Dumfries. With Dumfries ours we can starve this Caerlaverock. It will soon fall. But by no other means. And Buittle thereafter. The last English stronghold in Galloway. This is of greater worth than my vengeance on MacDouall. And I have not the men, nor the time now, to spare in further prolonged siegery. You have heard what has happened at Hexham and the Tyne. Let that remain unpunished, and all that we have done in the North of England will fall. All others will follow the Prior of Hexham's lead. For two years we have milked Cumberland and Northumberland, to our great gain. And kept the English from winning any great army from their North. We have won silver we direly needed. And time, precious time. All that will be sacrificed if I do not immediately deal with Hexham and Tynedale and the rest. My brother saw it, dimly, and went raiding yonder, in anger. I cross the Border otherwise, not in angry raiding but of set policy. Although my anger may have some play also, I think! And I need these men who have wasted their time, and mine, at Dumfries and Caerlaverock."

There was question on every face, now.

"You change your course then, Sire?"

"You do not sail for Man?" That was Angus Og, almost hopefully.

"I do not. I have other work to do." Bruce straightened up. "Now — leave me, my friends. For I have much thinking to do, first. We shall have a council later. Gibbie — off with you to Dumfries . . ."

That evening Hay rode back, with Boyd and most of the besieging host, to announce that all had proceeded smoothly at Dumfries. MacDouall and his garrison had marched out just after midday, and were now well on their way over the Border, under escort. Sir Robert Fleming was acting as governor of the town.

Bruce sent a trumpeter and herald to announce these facts, across the sunset-stained waters, to Caerlaverock Castle — whose present captain, it transpired, was no other than David de Strathbogie, the offended Earl of Atholl.

The council called for that night was more than usually formal, and deliberately so. It was not so much a council as an audience. The King was not seeking advice, but giving decisions. But he commenced proceedings, in Randolph's tented pavilion, with some ceremony.

"It is my royal will and good pleasure," he announced, "to honour in especial at this time two lords in whom I repose much trust and confidence. Step forward Angus MacDonald of the Isles, Lord High Admiral of my realm; and Sir Thomas Randolph, Lord of Nithsdale, my sister's son."

Surprised, and eyeing each other a little askance, the pair came forward.

"My lord Angus — your service and leal devotion is of the greatest importance to my cause. There has been dispute in the past between you and your brother, Alexander of Islay, now in Ireland, who has not supported me and has given aid and comfort to my enemies, in especial the MacDougalls. Your desire to reunite within your Lordship that part of your ancestor Somerled's heritage now dispersed to other descendants, is known to me. Therefore it is my will that hereafter Islay and Tiree be forfeited by your brother Alexander, and bestowed upon yourself. Also that the former MacDougall lands of Duror and Glencoe, and the Isle of Mull, likewise be so bestowed. And that the former Comyn territory of Lochaber be included in your Lordship. Thus it becomes the greatest in territory in all my realm. In return, apart from your continued loyal friendship and aid, I but require that you provide and build for me a royal castle at Tarbert, between Knapdale and Kintyre, for my use and garrison."

There was a pregnant silence in that tent, as everyone, not only Angus Og, weighed the King's words, and probed their significance. That this was a highly important pronouncement went without saying, infinitely more vital than any mere appointment such as the High Admiralship, which could be revoked at the royal will. Once the Lord of the Isles occupied and possessed these extra vast territories, dispossession would be wellnigh impossible. Yet Tarbert, that tiny isthmus of land between Loch Fyne and the Western Sea, was in fact the essential key to any attempt to bring control to bear on the Sudreys — that is, the isles and mainland coasts south of the Ardnamurchan peninsula, to which the territories mentioned belonged — clear evidence that the King intended to retain at least some hold on the area. And, as it happened, the Isle of Man was always reckoned to be a detached but important part of the Sudreys. And the Isle of Man had not been mentioned.

Angus Og took the careful part, and inclined his head, without committing his thanks, or his doubts, to words.

Bruce went on. "Sir Thomas Randolph — after previous error, mistaken but honourable, you have proved yourself most loyal, reliable and able. Your judgement I have found valuable. As my near kin, it is right and fitting that you should be ranked other than as a simple knight. It is therefore my royal pleasure that you shall be raised to the station of an earl of this realm."

The other did not hide his surprise, as he bowed low.

"One earldom stands vacant, with the forfeiture and death, without male heir, of the late Buchan. I cannot conceive that you would wish to bear that dishonoured title. But there is another ancient earldom, of the Celtic polity to which you belong, vacant since the death of Earl Angus over a century ago — that of Moray. Ancient, honourable and great. The lands of that earldom have in the main been acquired by the House of Comyn, and are now at my disposal by forfeiture. Lands from the Spey to the Ness, including much of Buchan; and west to the borders of Lochaber, including the great Lordship of Badenoch. I believe that you are the man to control those wide and important lands well and ably, recognising their consequence to my kingdom and rule." He paused, unbuckling his own golden earl's belt. "I do now, therefore, name and appoint, invest and belt you, Earl of Moray." And stooping, the King clasped the golden girdle about his nephew's — and erstwhile enemy's — waist.

The acclaim from the company was polite rather than enthusiastic — for the stiffish Randolph was scarcely popular, though Gibbie Hay and Hugh Ross had become his close friends. Also few there failed to notice that the new earl's lands marched with Angus Og's new Lochaber on the west, and the Earl of Ross's territories on the north. In other words, the King was inserting both a buffer between these traditional enemies, and his own watchdog into the Highland provinces.

Randolph was obviously overwhelmed by this totally unexpected honour and promotion. He shook his head helplessly.

But Bruce was not yet finished. He stepped back, and dropping the ceremonial tone, spoke more briskly. "Furthermore, my lord of Moray, you may make shift to add to your possessions! I go to

306

Tynedale, not the Isle of Man. You shall go there in my stead, with my Lord of the Isles. Commanding my land forces, as he commands the sea. And if you can win Man back from the enemy, it is yours."

There was a great sigh from the company, as all was now clear. Man was to be prevented from becoming a conquest of Angus Og's, and he was given much else, less strategically dangerous, instead. The vital Sudreys were to be divided. It was seen why Randolph had been chosen for this venture, and created earl so suddenly — so that the Lord of the Isles could neither refuse to co-operate, nor insist on being in command over one of lesser rank. As King's nephew, and an earl, Randolph's position would be safeguarded, and offence by Angus Og be made difficult.

It was apparent that the monarch had indeed been thinking, and to considerable effect.

Thereafter, Bruce went on to deal with matters tactical and organisational, in businesslike fashion, so that the atmosphere lost much of its tension and drama. Christina MacRuarie looked cynical — but then she often did.

The two expeditions would part company next day.

During the night, Edward Bruce took the opportunity to slip back across the Solway sands, at low tide and in darkness. He came on from Dumfries to rouse his brother, full of news, question, advice and demands.

The King, who did not relish Edward's headstrong presence in either expedition, informed him that he was taking most of his brother's men to Tynedale; but that he wanted him to go north, forthwith, and set up the inevitably prolonged sieges of Stirling Castle and Dundee. Edward was not enthusiastic, pointing out the wearisome and static nature of the tasks — to have pointed out to him in return that means might be found, as at Perth, to expedite that procedure. The other was, understandably, a little hipped over Perth's fall — as he was about the Dumfries terms and surrender, after he had done all the work. He could hardly refuse the remit — but he took the opportunity to strike a blow for a concern of his own. Without actually framing it as a bargain, he indicated that he would tackle the task more enthusiastically if Robert would agree, as had been suggested on a number of occasions, to have him officially adopted as heir to the throne.

The King was careful, as in the past, not to commit himself. He would consider it — but his daughter's interests must not be overlooked, even though she was a captive in England . . .

Edward's vigorous exposition on the follies of having a reigning queen on the throne of battling Scotland — especially a young and absentee one — kept the King from his sleep for considerably longer.

* * *

So, while a somewhat disgruntled Earl of Carrick headed north, and a not entirely contented Lord of the Isles took the new Earl of Moray and a great fleet south-west to the Isle of Man, the King of Scots personally led a light cavalry force of some 1,500 south-east into England, by the same route as before. And this time he pulled no punches. Ignoring the Vale of Irthing, which had not yet recovered from the assault of two years earlier, he made straight down Tyne, spreading fire and destruction. Hexham was of course his especial target; and after cutting down the still hanging bodies of his commissioners, he destroyed the town entirely — save for the Priory itself, which he left undamaged, although he appropriated all its silver and treasure that he could find. It seemed that Prior Thomas de Fenwick had been replaced by a younger man, one Robert de Whelpington, with instructions from Archbishop Greenfield of York to have no more truck with the Scots.

Bruce decided that the Archbishop required instruction also.

Setting up his base at Corbridge, downstream from Hexham, he subjected the South Tyne area to a systematic devastation such as even Wallace's 1297 invasion had not equalled. Then, with no major opposition materialising, he drove on south-wards, not so much burning and harrying now as making demonstration and demanding tribute, payment for relief, and at high rates — and getting it. On to the very gates of Newcastle they pressed. But finding that strongly walled city too tough a nut to crack quickly, they by-passed it, assailing the Teame valley instead, with rich reward. Then on to Durham itself.

They were now nearly a hundred miles deep into England, and Bruce was growing a little anxious. His scouts gave him no intimation of any large enemy force being mustered against them; but if any were being raised in the west, he could be all too easily cut off from home. He decided that Durham — or at least, Hartlepool, where he had family lands whose revenues had long been denied him — was as far as he dared go on this occasion; York must wait. And, woefully, his wife Elizabeth, seventy miles farther than York, must wait also.

Bishop Kellew of Durham, successor to the late and unlamented Beck, was away at a parliament in the south, and his great castle on its rock safe from all but prolonged siege. But the rich city itself was vulnerable; and after some part of it was reduced to ashes, its chief citizens were urgent to persuade Bruce to accept an immediate 2,000 merks, with promises of a total of £5,000, and hostages to ensure payment. With the humiliating rider that they must agree to provide free ingress and egress through the County Palatine whenever the King of Scots chose to invade England, Bruce accepted their terms for one year's protection. The fact that it was the Prince-Bishop's land, and largely his money also, was the best of it.

The King turned for home not dissatisfied, the Scots Treasury in a better state, by a total of nearly £40,000, than it had been for many a year, the county authorities of Northumberland, Cumberland and Westmorland each having agreed to pay £2,000 over and above their constituent places, for a year's peace.

The Scots reached the Border area without interception; but Bruce's luck changed nevertheless, and the last stages of that ride were something of a personal nightmare. Sickness struck him, of the same variety that he had suffered at Inverurie six years before, brought on no doubt by the same causes — lack of rest and proper feeding, plus the hard and insanitary conditions of continuous campaigning. Once again fever, vomiting, skin-rash and intolerable itch was his lot, with ever-increasing weakness. But now he had to continue to ride.

Possibly his sickness was basically responsible for the second misfortune. His advance party was attacked and badly cut up by a company out from the Carlisle garrison, in the Haltwhistle area; and just because the King was only too well aware of the hindrance he had become to his people, he agreed to fierce demands for retaliation on the fortress of Carlisle itself, to which he probably never would have listened in less fevered state. In the event, the typical secret night attack was repulsed with serious losses, a barking dog alarming the guards, and the main garrison rallying swiftly. It was a sobered and reduced company which recrossed the Border line at length, with their semi-delirious monarch demanding to be taken to Jamie Douglas's camp at the siege of Roxburgh Castle.

Bruce was not aware of his arrival at Roxburgh, where Teviot joined Tweed; nor of the loving care he received *en route* or at Douglas's hands. And only dimly aware of the hot summer weeks that followed, while he lay helpless, and of the succession of his friends who came sorrowfully from far and near to visit him. At some stage he realised that Christina MacRuarie was back, nursing him, but did not know that it was for Elizabeth de Burgh that he constantly moaned and cried — with whom sometimes he believed that he gripped in his arms — thereby twisting a sharp knife in the Highlandwoman's heart.

309

Strangely enough, it was his brother again who really set him on the road to recovery, a recovery of the spirit primarily, rather than of the body. For in August Edward came in triumph to Roxburgh, thinking to cheer the King into health by the tale of his successes. Dundee had fallen at last, he announced. And Stirling would be theirs within the year.

Robert, on his sick-bed, required a little while to take this in, and Edward expiated on his tactics at Dundee and what he had done to the English and the traitors therein. But it was not on this that his brother's mind fixed.

"Stirling . . .?" he said thinly. "You said . . . Stirling will be ours? Within a year. How can you be so sure?"

"Because I have come to terms with the captain, Sir Philip Moubray. If it is not relieved within the year, he yields Stirling to me. Moubray — he who struck you down at Methven fight . . ."

"You gave him a year! To be relieved? And . . . and raised the siege? You did that?"

"Yes. So we win Stirling cheaply. I have his written word . . ."

"Cheap!" However weak the King's voice, it was intense enough. "You are a fool, Edward! A bigger fool than even I judged!"

"But . . . do you not understand? We are spared a long and wasteful siege. Such as you are ever against. Who will relieve Moubray? My men are freed — and are now investing Linlithgow. Then it will be Edinburgh's turn . . ."

"Edward — what did our sire endow you with, for wits?" his brother demanded. "You have given your plighted word? That Moubray has a year unassailed?"

"To be sure. Why not? Do you hate Moubray so much? Because he unhorsed you once! I say you should have hated MacDouall more, who slew our brothers! Yet he you gave honourable terms to . . ."

"God's mercy — listen to me, Edward! You have ensured the invasion of our country. On a scale we have not seen since Falkirk. Stirling is the key to Scotland, as all do know. The English cannot, I say, ignore this. Cannot fail to come to the relief of Stirling. Once that is yielded, they have lost this long war. Moubray knows that, if you do not. And now you have committed my honour, with your own. Given Edward of Carnarvon a year . . ."

"You have been giving English towns a year's truce. For money!"

The King, whose strength was ebbing, ignored that. "King Edward is now released from his foolish passion for his catamite, Gaveston. The English are no longer divided over that, for and against the King. His lords are spurring him to action against us, after all his folly and sloth. He is a weakling, but he has hard men round him. Men who will now control him. This of Stirling will give them what they need — a challenge. A challenge with a set time. To relieve Moubray and the key to Scotland. Edward will seek to redeem his name and fame. I see it all. All over England trumpets will blow . . ."

Robert Bruce's voice died away.

Chapter Twenty

Robert Bruce was right. All England saw that year's bargain at Stirling as a challenge and a rallying-cry, not to be ignored. Strangely, Bruce's own raids over the Border, with all their attendant blackmail, seemed to have little effect on opinion in the far south; but the Stirling ultimatum was different. England's name, fame and honour were at stake. That winter of 1313–14, plans were laid for the greatest invasion of Scotland ever mounted. Not only was Stirling to be relieved, and dramatically, but the whole wretched country was to be ground into the dust, once and for all. By spring the trumpets were sounding indeed, for muster from one end of England to the other. King Edward set his invasion for Easter.

Bishop Lamberton arrived back in Scotland, finally, for good or ill, to celebrate that Eastertide in his own land, parole broken — since no one seemed interested in it any longer, anyway. He brought word that the invasion had been postponed until late May, when there would be more grass to feed the hundreds of thousands of horses involved — always a major problem.

So, by late May, the Bruce, almost himself again, though thin, had reluctantly taken up his position just south of Stirling. A head-on confrontation with the embattled might of England was still the last thing that he desired; but now there was no alternative, unless he was prepared to abandon all but the Highlands to the enemy. The waist of Scotland had to be held.

The English would, of course, seek to relieve the castle. But that was not the vital matter. It was the crossing of the Forth at the narrow slip of firm land between the vast morasses of the Flanders Moss and the widening firth, that mattered — Stirling Bridge, as ever the key.

The enemy must approach that key crossing east-about or west-about; round Stirling Rock, castle and town, by the flat links of the Carse, boggy and broken by burns, runnels, ditches; or west by the scattered woodlands and hillocks of the former royal hunting park, really only an extension of the great forest of the Tor Wood. One, or both, of these. There was no alternative.

So, as his forces assembled from all over the land, Bruce applied his wits to the task of turning this entire approach area into a maze of traps. It was not difficult in the low-lying Carse, for the flats were already waterlogged and pitted with holes. It was the causeways and banks and dykes through it on which they had to concentrate, and, as mud-slaistered as his men, the King spent long May days cutting, digging, undermining and covering over, so that to the untutored eye the place appeared as before — but was not.

The inland higher ground was a much more difficult proposition. The scattered woodland would admittedly tend to break up enemy heavy cavalry formations; but the whole area was too widespread and open for defensive works. Only at one point was there any opportunity to improve on nature. All this upland of knowes and hollows was drained by small burns south-eastwards into a major stream, the Bannock Burn, which cut a deepish ravine for itself down to the windings of the Carse flats. The road from the south crossed this stream, just above the edge of the low ground, and there was no other convenient crossing near by. The ground on either side of this crossing was open, so there was no opportunity for ambush; anyway, a huge army cannot be ambushed. But some distance beyond the crossing, the road forked, one prong following the flats, the direct route to the town and Stirling Bridge; the other striking off to the left, and upwards, across King Alexander's New Park, round the west side of the Rock and so along the south lip of the Flanders Moss. If the English decided on a west-about approach, they were bound to take this road. And before it actually climbed to enter the wooded area, there was a wide grassy level entry — indeed, it was known as The Entry, especially constructed for deer-driving. The Entry was flat and nearly half a mile wide to the south, but narrowing-in like a funnel to a mere fifty or so yards on either side of the road.

Here Bruce got to work, using the same ideas that he had developed at the Battle of Loudoun Hill — and hoped that it would not again be Pembroke who led the English. Deep lateral trenches were dug at irregular intervals across that triangle of green, with stakes in their foot, and all carefully covered with woven brushwood and then grassy turfs brought from areas out of sight. The wooded flanks were honeycombed with individual pits, and the glades sown with spiked iron caltrops. It was all done on a vast scale, ten times that of Loudoun Hill, with thousands of men working, Bruce and some of his lords amongst the others, like labourers;

even bishops and abbots might be seen leading trains of pack-horses laden with turf and brush. All men, great and small, knew that Scotland's continued existence was in the balance.

And still the English did not come. Large numbers had assembled at Wark, on the south side of Tweed, spies informed — but the main armies delayed. To some extent, Bruce was grateful for more time — Angus Og, after capturing Man, had returned to his Hebrides, and dispersed his host. Summoned again urgently, he had not yet put in an appearance. It was possible that he might be sulking. But in another respect, this delay was a problem, for the camouflage over his pits and trenches tended to dry up a day or two after it was cut, and constant replacement was necessary. Bruce even had squads of men watering the turfs, like monks in a garden.

Then, in mid-June, word reached the King that the invasion had indeed started. The English had crossed Tweed with an incalculable host, its baggage-train alone extending for twenty miles. King Edward was leading in person, with the High Constable, the Earl of Hereford, and the Earl of Gloucester as deputies. Rumour had it that there were no fewer than ninety-three other English barons and lords present, with their levies, not to mention great contingents from Wales, France, Brittany, Guienne and the Low Countries. There were said to be twenty-three Anglo-Irish chiefs under the Earl of Ulster, Bruce's own father-in-law. Total numbers were impossible to ascertain, accounts varying from 70,000 to 200,000. Not that such figures were really significant. None knew better than Bruce that the true worth of any army depended not on sheer size — since this could only add to the problems of commissariat and mobility — but on its spirit, leadership and composition. It was that composition he demanded of his informants now; above all, what were the numbers of heavy armoured cavalry, and of longbowmen — the two vital arms in which Scotland was weakest.

Reports were now flowing in to the Scottish camp below the frowning battlements of Stirling, in a steady stream. The English were advancing, not by Berwick and the coast, but up Tweeddale and Lauderdale. They comprised ten distinct divisions, with Hereford's and Gloucester's in the van. Cavalry might number 40,000 or 50,000, but the heavy armoured chivalry, the knightly host, would be perhaps a tenth of that. Archers could be put at 7,000. Infantry was without number.

These figures, although still vague, were daunting. In a set battle, as this must be, the heavy chivalry were all-important — that is, knights and their like in full armour, mounted on destriers also fully armoured. Since the men's full armour weighed up to 100 pounds, and the beasts' five times that, only the most powerful horses could carry it for any length of time. Inevitably these were slow — but they were almost impervious to any assault save of their own kind. And of such Bruce would be hard put to it to raise 100; Scotland just did not breed such horses. Of light horse, moss-troopers and the like — hobelars, the English called them — he had perhaps 4,000; but against armoured chivalry these were of little avail, however splendid at mobile warfare. As to archers, he did not have 500, and no longbowmen.

And still no sign of Angus Og and the Islesmen — though it was known that they were on their way.

Bruce drew up his army in four main divisions, facing east so as to cover both possible approaches. The van, of picked infantry, with their long pikes for forming schiltroms, he put under his nephew Moray, as a sufficiently sober and steady man not to lose his head in the face of overwhelming odds. Edward, of course, wanted this place of honour; but his brother just did not dare risk it, with all at stake. Edward's brilliance was as a dashing commander of light cavalry, not the spearhead of a static and defensive host. He gave him instead half of the light horse, to hold the right flank, based on the line of the Bannock Burn. The other half was for Douglas, on the left — although nominally commanded by the High Steward; old James Stewart had recently died, and young Walter was now the Steward, a notable youth but inexperienced. Bruce himself commanded the main body, not exactly in the rear but somewhat back on the higher ground, where he could survey all, and especially the approaches to The Entry. Randolph's van was based on St. Ninian's Kirk, a strategic site above the Carse route.

It was Saturday, the Eve of the Vigil of St. John the Baptist, the 22nd of June — midsummer. Spies declared the English van to be at Falkirk, only ten miles away — though its rearguard and baggage was still rumbling through Edinburgh twenty-five miles to the south-east.

There was little sleep that night, and at four a.m. of a misty dawn, trumpets in the Scots host called men to Mass. There had to be, of course, many services — but there was an ample sufficiency of clergy, armed and armoured, to provide them. William Lamberton himself celebrated for the King's company. He sternly prescribed only bread and water for the day's substinence, as the Vigil required — poor fare as it was on which to fight a vital battle but he knew his fellow-countrymen, and the streak of fanaticism in them.

Bruce was still concerned to have detailed news of his enemy's numbers and quality, assessed not just by spies but by experienced commanders. He sent out a swift-riding vadette under Douglas and Keith the Marischal, to gain him the information he needed, risky as this was.

Then, as they stood to arms, the King reviewed his whole force, riding round the divisions, alone, on a small and wiry grey garron. He was clad in light chain-mail, under a gorgeous heraldic surcoat of the red Lion Rampant on gold, and on his helmet was a leathern crest of a demi-lion, ringed by a high crown. His review took a long time, with so many to exchange a word with — for surely never had a king and commander known personally so many of his host, veteran warriors with whom he had fought almost continuously for seventeen long years. Always concerned with the personal touch, today, which might well be the last for him as for them, he desired his identification with all to be complete. Besides, this uneasy waiting period had to be got over.

As he went his rounds, however, Bruce looked all too often back over his shoulder, westwards. Had he misjudged one man, in all these — Angus Og MacDonald?

Then back through the secret glades of the Tor Wood came Douglas and Keith, grave-faced. They had risked much, got very close to the enemy, and spoken with many scouts who dogged the English columns. And what they had seen and heard obviously had affected them direly.

"The van is not far off, Sire," Douglas reported, panting. "Indeed, it should be in sight at any time. The main host covers all the plain between the Sauchie Ford and Falkirk. And far beyond. I have never seen the like. As far as eye can see . . ."

"Sir James," the King interrupted him harshly. "Of course you have never seen the like! I did not send you out to tell me that. Such stories we have been listening to for days. I want facts. Firm details. Have you brought me none?"

Flushing, the younger man swallowed. "Yes, Sire. The van is of medium cavalry, under Gloucester and Hereford — about 6,000. It is said that there is bad blood between these, for though Hereford is High Constable of England, their King has appointed his nephew Gloucester, although but twenty-four, to be Constable for this battle. They have 500 mounted Welsh archers . . ."

"Pembroke? He does not ride with the van?"

"No — not Pembroke. But Clifford does . . ."

"Ha — Clifford! Clifford came too late for Loudoun Hill!"

"Pembroke, under King Edward, commands the main chivalry, Your Grace," Keith put in. "Three or four thousand strong, of barded destriers, a terrible sight."

"Only if they have ground they may fight on, sir!" Bruce snapped. "An armoured knight on a destrier, in a bog or a pit, is no terrible sight!"

His informants said nothing.

"It is my aim to make this an infantry, not a cavalry battle, God willing," the King went on. "Where is the English infantry?"

"Well back, Sire, I fear . . . the enemy will it otherwise. They will have it a cavalry battle."

"So much the better — so long as *I* choose the ground! It is all-important, therefore, that this day be fought where I want it. You understand? This day — and all days to come — depends on it. And, for the sweet Christ's sake — lift your visages! Smile, my friends! Men are watching you. Would you lose all, before we begin? I am fighting this battle with the land, and men's spirits. Have you naught of cheer for me to tell them?"

James Douglas blinked. "They are tired. The English are tired at least. Yesterday they rode over twenty miles. They have hurried. Men and horses are exhausted, they do say — in this hot dry weather. They can have slept little last night — and you burned all Falkirk's food and forage . . ."

"Aye — so be it. Order the trumpets to blow. I will address my folk."

"Angus, Sire? The Lord of the Isles? He has not come . . .?"

"No."

Edward Bruce had come up. "Did you really expect him, Douglas? I did not! The Islesman has ever fought for his own hand. And when it suited him. Now, at the pinch, why should he come?"

"He is on his way. That we know, my lord . . ."

"On his way! But will he arrive? In time? I think not. If we win — then, yes, he was on his way! And if we lose, he remains unscathed. And returns to his Isles faster than he came! That, I swear, is the MacDonald."

"And you, I swear, are wrong, my lord of Carrick!" Bruce exclaimed. "And even were you right — say nothing of it now, I charge you. This day depends on faith. Faith in God, in me, and in each other. Let no word or look or act destroy that faith."

When the trumpets had brought together a great part of the host, from its various positions, Bruce rode out alone on his grey pony, to westwards of them, so that his voice would carry from the slightly higher ground and on the westerly breeze.

"My friends," he cried, arm raised, when quiet was gained. "Today we put all to the test. Today Scotland stands or falls. And

316

not only Scotland, but right, freedom and faith. If we fail today, these fall, with Scotland. Let none mistake. Today is fate hammered out on the anvil, hammered into shape."

There was a deathly silence at these grave words.

He went on. "But mark you, today we are the *hammer*, not the iron! And the land, our land, is the anvil. The iron is the arrogant invading English host, which once more desecrates our land. But this time, friends, is the last. This time, we shall hammer and bend and mould that great unwieldy host until it is fit — yes, and glad — only to be tossed into yonder pools and pows of the Carse, to cool its heat and hurt! This, God willing, we shall do. For it is a host as tired as it is great. Empty of belly, for it has outmarched its baggage train. At enmity within itself, out of envy and suspicion. And ill-led by a King whom men despise, and a Constable who has never fought a battle."

That aroused suitable spirited reaction, however exaggerated.

"We are otherwise. Few in numbers, yes — but united. We are rested, and if we fast, do so of our choice. Best of all, we know each other, have fought together over these long years. We are fighting men all. We know every inch of the ground. And our all is at stake. We win, or die."

Men cheered now, if a little grimly.

"I say, my friends, we win or die. The issue is simple as that. Therefore, I would have to command this day only those prepared to make the choice — to win, or die. Any who, losing would still live, I give fullest leave now to go. While there is yet time. I say this in good faith, and mocking none, deceiving none. Some may not be prepared to die, today, and for this cause. To all such, I say — go now. Any who have no heart in the business or qualms of spirit, it is best should leave us. Even should it be half our numbers. It is better for the rest . . ."

The King got no further. The snarling growl that rose from the packed ranks was angry, menacing, almost ferocious. If there was any movement, it was an edging forward.

Bruce was satisfied. He raised his hand again for quiet.

As he waited for it, and before he could speak, another sound than growling men reached all their ears. Thin, high, on the westerly breeze, came the wail of bagpipes at a distance.

Every head turned, to stare, the King's included — and, being higher than the rest, Bruce was able to see, curving round the base of the great Rock, north-westwards, the glitter of arms in the sun, and the waving of many banners.

"Thank God!" he breathed. "Thank God!" He raised his voice, to shout. "The Isles, my friends — the Isles! They come! They

317

come! Angus of the Isles comes — in time. Constant was my faith in him — and justified!"

In the uproar that followed, Douglas it was who spurred out to the King's side, to grab his arm and point in exactly the opposite direction. There, eastwards, sunlight glittered on more arms and banners, more, vastly more. Rounding the shoulder of the land behind the township of Auchterbannock, where the road, the ancient Roman Road of Antonine, drove its causewayed course above the marshlands of Forth, came the English van. Calling for trumpets, Bruce commanded the swift dispersal to positions.

There was now no more waiting and talk. Deputing Campbell to welcome Angus Og, and to attach his force meantime to the main rearward, the King himself took the 300 or so light cavalry allotted to the main body, Carrick and Annandale mosstroopers, and rode with them at fullest speed south-westwards and into the cover of the scattered tree-dotted flanks of the Tor Wood. Hidden therein he swung eastwards, down through the twisting hollows of the broom-grown knowes, until they came out into the open level ground, the little grassy plain between the Bannock Burn and the mouth of The Entry to the New Park, with the road running through it. With the enemy not yet in sight from here, he and his men dismounted and seemed to take their ease in the sun. They were bait, royal bait, for the trap.

They had not long to wait. From here they could see the houses of the Milton of Bannock, where the road crossed the Bannock Burn; and here, presently, the English van began to appear, advancing cautiously, only two miles from Stirling and with some at least of the Scots army in view.

Bruce waited, himself hidden, fretting in the face of that daunting threat, until a considerable portion of the enemy cavalry was across the burn, and not only in full view but less than half a mile away. Then he ran out from cover towards his own scattered men, Irvine bearing a small version of the Lion Rampant banner behind him. Waving and shouting, as though in some panic, he got his 300 mounted, but slowly, awkwardly, and into some sort of order, seemingly just aware of the English approach. About one-third of the party he then sent streaming off, north-westwards into The Entry, along a line that would seem haphazard but was in fact carefully avoiding the hidden transverse trenches and lateral pits. The others he kept milling around, as though uncertain or waiting for stragglers.

To some degree the stratagem worked — but only partially. The apparently panic-stricken and retreating Scots did entice the English, but only a small portion of the van. One or two squadrons of cavalry, numbering about 400 riders, detached themselves from the mass and came spurring forward at speed.

Bruce cursed. This was of no use to him; no use in springing his elaborate trap for a few hundred, and so reveal it for all the rest. Swiftly he had to re-assess his position.

The lame-duck procedure would not serve now. But if they were instead to stand and fight, or seem to, the main van might be coaxed to come to the rescue of its spearhead. Unfortunately he had sent fully 100 of his men away in obvious flight already, which left him with only about half the numbers that were descending upon them. If he could get his detached hundred back . . .

Bruce sent a single rider after them, and then waved his 200 into two squadrons, to advance towards the now charging enemy at a trot, leaving a gap in the centre. Two-to-one was rather better odds than the day would average, after all.

"That banner?" he jerked, to Irvine, as he rode out, a little in front of the rest, into the gap. "That is the cotised bend between six lions, white on blue, of Bohun, is it not? Hereford. The High Constable. But . . . he would never lead so small a band."

"There are three mullets in chief, Sire. A second son, perhaps. But, Your Grace — this is folly! To hazard yourself thus. To give battle. On . . . on a garron! Unarmed! If you were to fall, now, all is lost before it is begun . . .!"

"Never fear, Willie! This is scarce giving battle. We but coax and draw and cozen. And this garron can outrun the heavier English beasts. And I am not unarmed." He drew out a light battle-axe from its socket at his saddle. "Hereford has no son. That must be his nephew, Sir Henry de Bohun. See — get back to the others. Tell them to wheel and sidestep. A mêlée. No true battle, but a mêlée. Go — quickly."

The enemy were less than 300 yards away now, their knightly leader and his esquire with the banner somewhat in front — a young man by his manner of riding. Pray that he was inexperienced.

Bruce was still moving forward, at a slow trot, vigilant, calculating. This must be timed to a nicety . . .

Then, suddenly, unexpectedly, the entire situation changed. That young knight had sharp eyes, it seemed, quick wits, and a lofty ambition. Even at 200 yards he must have spotted the gold crown that circled the King's basinet — the sun would be gleaming on it. Clearly his shouts rang out.

"The Bruce! It is the Bruce! Himself!" Then he was turning in his saddle, waving back his ranks. "He is mine! Mine! Back! Back, I say!" And couching his long lance, he stooped low, digging in his golden spurs. "A Bohun! A Bohun!" he yelled, as he thundered forward, alone.

Bruce caught his breath, taken by surprise. Here was a fix! Folly indeed. For both of them. To dodge and wheel and bolt now, before this open challenge to single combat, was inconceivable for the King of Scots. Yet he was undermounted and under-armed, without lance or even sword — these left with his heavy charger up on the hill. He had only this light battle-axe and a dirk. Yet he had no choice but to stand — or be for ever shamed. Irvine had been right. If he fell now, all was lost. This — this was worthy of his brother Edward!

There were only moments for racing thoughts. Grimly the King reminded himself that he was the veteran, the man of experience, his nerve tried in a hundred frays. He had other advantages — a more nimble horse, and a notable reputation with the battle-axe.

He altered nothing, therefore, as the other hurtled down on him. He did not draw aside, crouch, or even change his mount's quiet trot. Above all, he did not pull up — for a horse can much more swiftly answer the rein and knee when already in movement, than when halted.

It might so well have been a tournament, under the afternoon sun — save that one jouster had no lance. Now only a few yards separated them, and eye looked into hot eye. Bruce made his only disposition. Suddenly he tossed the battle-axe from his right hand to his left.

The Bohun saw it, and in the split seconds left to him, adjusted accordingly. It could only mean that his opponent was going to pull to his right, to the left of himself, and so any blow would have to be left-handed. He therefore swung his lance just a few degrees to his own left.

With only feet to spare, Bruce jerked and kicked his garron to the left, not the right, directly across the front of the galloping charger, causing it to veer and peck. In almost the same movement he flung his axe back into his right hand.

Only by bare inches was a collision avoided. But the lance-tip, swinging round wildly at the last moment to the other side, did not come within a foot of Bruce's shoulder. And as the other plunged past, bent low over his couched lance, the King rose higher in his stirrups, reaching up, and brought down that battle-axe right on the crown of the Bohun's crested helm, with all the violent strength of a mighty spring released.

With the deep crunching of shorn steel and bone both, the gleaming blade drove down and down, splitting the head open, in spouting blood, to the very breastbone and gorget, where it was jerked to such an abrupt stop that the wooden shaft snapped off in its wielder's hand. Charger and reeling, ghastly rider careered on until Bohun fell with a resounding crash.

The victor, his garron still trotting forward, was left with a foot or so of splintered timber and a wrist and arm numb with the shock. He had scarcely realised the power of that right arm, recent sickness or none.

The enemy line was still halted, under Bohun's esquire, so swiftly left leaderless. There were shouts from behind Bruce as his 200, ignoring previous commands, surged forward for the King.

The uncertainty, now, of Bohun's line, still 250 yards away, and stationary, was very evident, hesitating whether to resume the spoiled charge, stand still, or retire. Their doubts could only have been advanced by activity behind as well as in front. Trumpets sounded from the main English van, and some part of it at least began to move forward. At the same time, renewed shouting from still farther in front heralded the return to the fray of the 100 lame ducks. Bohun's esquire did what any sensible man would have done — nothing. He waited.

Bruce again was faced with decision. It would be suicide to confront the entire English van, with his 300. But by turning back, he still might be able to lead the enemy into his pits . . .

Then there was a new development, intimated by new trumpet-blowing from the right flank, from the Tor Wood. Down through the glades came Edward Bruce, to the rescue of his brother, with some 500 horse. The King almost wept. Everything was forcing him into battle, the wrong battle. Yet he could scarcely blame Edward.

It was with relief, therefore, that he perceived that only a small proportion of the English van was in fact advancing to the aid of the Bohun company — even though they did so under the ken-speckle banner of Gloucester himself. Hereford, the veteran, was holding the main host back. Those trenches and pits were still to be unused.

With Edward now charging down on the right, there could be no real choice for the King. He had to go forward, into the attack — and hope that it could indeed be a limited engagement. All would depend on Hereford.

Caught up by his own 300 now, Bruce rode straight for Bohun's waiting line, useless axe-shaft in hand. With a crash they met, and, since the English were in only two ranks, plunged through, on impetus rather than fighting, and little of casualties on either side. There was Gloucester, with perhaps another 500, not far ahead.

That Earl was a young man, barely twenty-four, and though

gallant, unused to battle. Seeing the King of Scots unhalted in his advance directly in front, and a new and large force charging down on his left flank, he did not panic, but sought to change his dispositions — not easy in a headlong cavalry attack. While retaining half his men to confront the King, he sought to swing the other half round to face Edward Bruce's assault. It was not entirely successful as a manoeuvre — and his whole force lost vital speed.

In the event, the result was complete chaos, on both sides, with mounted men crashing into each other, milling, falling, and no coherence or control anywhere, the sort of battle commanders suffer in nightmares. Gloucester himself was one of the first to be unhorsed. But any advantage was with the Scots, since they retained the impetus. In a whirling impenetrable mêlée, the clash moved south-eastwards. The English were not in fact defeated — but it looked as though they were.

In the confusion, two trends in the leaders' thinking had their inevitable effect on the struggle. Bruce did not want to get drawn within striking distance of Hereford's main van; and Gloucester desired to get back to that same van. As a consequence, both sides tended, almost imperceptibly, to draw back. Only Edward Bruce would have reversed the process — but his brother reached his side, and made his wishes known in no uncertain tones. He in fact ordered Edward's trumpeter to sound the retiral.

Whether Gloucester, shaken and remounted on a riderless beast, realised this is not to be known. But he was only too glad to be able to lead his own people in detaching themselves from the disorderly embroilment. In groups and batches and handfuls the English disengaged and streamed back towards their main body.

The Bruces found themselves masters of the field, such as it was. Edward would have pursued farther but the King was adamant.

"Back, Edward," he cried. "Back to your own position on the hill. As do I. God is good — but if Hereford attacks now . . .! Quickly, or we may have won a bicker and lost a battle!"

So the two Scots companies separated, and turned to ride back whence they had come, leaving the shambles behind. Sir Henry de Bohun was not alone, after all, on the trampled grass.

Avoiding the unused trenches, pits and caltrops, Bruce headed for the high ground. Hay, Campbell and Boyd, from the main rearward, came riding to meet the King's party, in highly doubtful frame of mind, not knowing whether to cheer or weep, to praise or rail. The grizzled Boyd was most certain, and outspoken.

"Sire," he accused, "you hazarded all! It was ill done. If you had fallen there, in that fool's ploy, Scotland would have gone down. Yon was a laddie's victory — not a king's."

"I know it, Robert my friend," Bruce admitted. "But my hand was something forced. You must bear with me. See — I have spoiled a good axe! Can anyone find me another?"

"Who was the Englishman, Sire?" Hay asked. "In the first fray. We saw it all, but could not tell the arms."

"Henry Bohun, I think — nephew to Hereford. Would you have had me run from him, in single combat? Before two armies?"

There was no answer to that, of course — save for the roaring cheer of the Scots massed ranks as their King rode up. That first blood of the battle may have been folly, bad generalship — but there was no doubt as to what it did for the Scots morale.

* * *

"Those are Clifford's colours," the King declared. "I know them all too well! Where is he going?"

"He takes the Carse road," Gibbie said. "Hereford will have sent him forward, as scout, to see if they may win round by the north and east, to Stirling Bridge. By the flats . . ."

"That is no scouting party. There are 700 or 800 there. And they have left the Carse road. They are heading farther out, in the marshes. Picking their way. Medium cavalry again."

"They must have a guide," Campbell suggested. "From Bannock, belike. Who knows the marshes."

"A guide, yes. But more than that, I swear. One who knows more than the marshes. Our traps and defences! Someone from Stirling Castle, perhaps. Who has watched us cutting and digging the Carse causeways. From the castle they could see all that we did. Someone may have won out, and reached Hereford. And now leads Clifford northwards through the outer marshes, by divers ways."

The King was back, with his rearward leaders, on the vantage knoll where he had spent the first part of the day, the rest of the Scots host returned to their allotted positions. The great English van was still stationary, cautious, around the Milton of Bannock, holding the burn-crossing. Obviously Hereford was awaiting the arrival of the main invading army under King Edward and Pembroke, which must have been far behind. But meantime he had despatched this powerful cavalry force under Clifford, to probe a way north-abouts to Stirling Bridge.

Angus Og, weary and yawning — for he had marched all yesterday, all night, and most of this day, after having had to fight a sea-battle with John of Lorn and the English fleet at the mouth of Clyde — pointed.

"These Carse marshes — who knows them well? Can the English

win round to Stirling, by the shore? The tidelands? If so, we must retire, behind the Rock. By the west. Or be cut off."

"Myself I know them well enough," Bruce answered. "Clifford can go another mile or so, twisting and turning. Then he will reach the Pelstream Burn, flowing into the Bannock. It is wide, with soft mud banks. Tidal there, a mile inland. They cannot cross that. They must turn inland also. There is no ford or crossing place until they reach the road again. That bridge we have demolished. But there is a ford there. And they will have avoided all our traps."

"We cannot halt them, then?"

"We must — God aiding! That is why Moray is posted at St. Ninian's Kirk, with our van. He is just above that reach of the Carse. Can see it all from there. But ... I never thought to see cavalry take the soft road through the marshes. Foot, perhaps — not horse. So Moray has only foot . . ."

"Then send these, your own cavalry, to aid him."

"I dare not, Angus. Not yet. This may be but a ruse, to draw off our cavalry. That will never be the main battle, in those swamps and pows. So long as Hereford and Gloucester stand there, with the main van, I dare not detach my cavalry. Any of it. There are still 5,000 enemy cavalry waiting below us, in their van. My nephew must make do with his foot. Pray he uses them well . . ."

"Sire!" Hay exclaimed, gulping. "Look there! He comes — my lord of Moray! Himself." And he pointed north-eastwards.

"Christ God in Heaven!" the King swore. "Has he taken leave of his wits, as well as his men?" Cursing, he left them, spurring.

"Sire — I have word for you," Randolph called, as they neared. "Ill word. We could be in trouble. I fear the English will know of the Carse traps . . ."

"Damnation, man!" his uncle cried. "The more reason you be not here! What madness is this . . .?"

"I had to see you. We must change our plans. I could not send another. One of the Carse fowlers came to me. He saw three men slipping through the marshlands, southwards. After midday. Secretly. One he swears was Sir Philip Moubray himself. From the castle. If it is he, he will know all. Our dispositions. Traps."

Bruce actually grabbed his nephew's arm. "Quiet, man! And look! See you there!"

Moray had cut across through the hillocks from St. Ninians, a mile away. For the first time, staring, he saw Clifford's force out on the low ground. "Merciful saints!" he groaned. "Already! And Cavalry . . .!"

"Aye, cavalry. And you are here! Get back, man. Quickly!"

"But — here is what I came to say, Sire. This makes it more than

324

ever vital. We must change plans. If we cannot hold the Carse road, you can be cut off. Your main host. We must retire on Stirling Bridge . . ."

"There is neither time nor the men to change our plans now, sir. Retire from our strong position, in face of the enemy ready to move, and we are lost. Better that we *be* cut off, I say — since if lose we die here. But, by the Rude — we have not lost the Carse road yet! Get you back, my lord of Moray, to your post. A rose has fallen from your chaplet, today! But you may pick it up again, yet! You have time, still. Get you down, with your foot, into those marshes, and halt me Clifford. At all costs. He must not cross the Pelstream ford. A schiltrom, this side of it . . ."

Without waiting for the rest, or another word, Moray went.

Bruce sent a runner to Douglas, on the left flank, to be ready to go to the assistance of Moray. But only if need be, and with only half his cavalry. Leave the Steward with the rest, in case the English main attack developed meantime.

Anxiously the King and his colleagues returned to the vantage-point, to watch.

Presently they saw Clifford's cavalry reach the south bank of the Pelstream Burn near its junction with the Bannock, and then turn westwards, inland, following it. No cavalry — nor foot either — could cross that mud-lined, mud-bottomed, tidal stream. If Moubray was leading them, he must have told them so.

The Pelstream meandered across the flats in serpentine coils, and Clifford's hundreds made slow work of following its sodden, sedge-lined banks. But even so, not slow enough for Robert Bruce, grudging them every step. He groaned at the thought of all their barriers and ditches avoided.

They could see the tip of St. Ninian's Kirk's tower from here, but Moray's force was not in view. Time — it was always timing that counted. Could they be in time? And would Hereford wait?

The first hint of action the watchers gained was from the enemy. Clifford had halted, facing almost due west now. Then his long straggling column began to fan out and form into some sort of line abreast over the marshy ground, no longer following the burn's edge. It was clear that they had seen something the King's group could not see.

"Moray must be down!" Bruce exclaimed. "The English prepare to attack."

Then the Scots began to appear, from the dead ground at the foot of St. Ninian's hill, just where the Pelstream Burn passed out of view, banners brave amongst them, but looking a rabble nevertheless. They were this side of the burn.

"What chance have they?" Hay demanded. 'Foot against cavalry. They must be ridden down . . ."

"They have a chance. If Moray holds them tight. Remember Wallace at Falkirk. The schiltroms held. The English cannot charge strongly in bog . . ."

This last was very obvious, even from more than a mile off. Distant trumpets shrilled, and in some sort of extended order, Clifford's cavalry began to advance again. But it was no charge, and no true line could be kept.

The Scots could be seen to be forming, now, into a single great square, based on the Pelstream ford. So their backs were secure, at least; only three sides might be attacked. The bristle of their long spears, thrust out like a hedgehog's spikes, could not be seen from this distance — but they could be visualised. Moray's and Hugh Ross's standards flew above the eight-packed ranks.

It was a strange battle to watch, so remote, so slow-motion. Like the cumbrous waves of a heavy tide, the cavalry lapped and swirled and seethed around the rock of the packed spearmen, unable to gain sufficient space or hard ground for the charging impetus they required, while the Scots had to adopt a purely defensive role. Moray was the right man for that, however. If anyone could hold those dense ranks tight, disciplined, unyielding either to panic or the temptation to rush out and break position, he could.

Bruce's glance often turned in the other direction, south-east instead of north-east. The main English van remained stationary, neither sending further reinforcement for Clifford nor itself moving out along the road towards the high-ground Scots positions. Either there was division in policy amongst the commanders, or the orders to await the arrival of the King and Pembroke, with the heavy chivalry, were paramount.

How long the struggle at the Pelstream Burn lasted, none could have told — but it seemed endless. Had Clifford had archers, all would have been otherwise of course; but lacking them, it was almost stalemate. At ône stage, admittedly, it seemed as though the English were achieving a break-in, the schiltrom sagging in front until, at least from a distance, it appeared nearly divided. The watchers fretted helplessly — and then perceived a division of cavalry spurring over the higher ground, this side of St. Ninians, Douglas's well-known banner at their head. But Douglas halted there, on the lip of the descent, and waited, inactive but yet a threat. He could see the position better, and presumably decided that Moray did not actually require his intervention. He was obeying Bruce's commands to the letter.

Presently it was apparent that the English advantage was indeed not sustained, and the schiltrom restored to its proper shape. And gradually a new element in the battle became evident; a great bank of fallen horseflesh, dead and dying, was building up in front of the ranks of spearmen, helping to protect the Scots. No doubt there were fallen men amongst the beasts, but inevitably it was the horses that took the brunt of the punishment from that savage frieze of pikes, rather than their mail-clad riders.

This grim barrier of their own slain obviously became an increasing obstacle to the enemy. Still they continued to attack, but noticeably the pace flagged, intervals lengthened.

"Clifford is held!" the King declared, at length. "He cannot break Moray, and cannot cross the burn. He must turn back. Praise God — that fight is ours also!"

Soon it was apparent that Clifford perceived the fact as clearly as Bruce. A trumpet sounded the recall, out there on the flats, and the English cavalry, having lost perhaps a third of their number, drew off. Reforming, they turned heavily to ride back whence they had come. The sound of throaty cheering came echoing across the Carse — and everywhere re-echoed along the Scots positions.

"Whatever the result of the greater battle, there we have seen something men will wonder at for long," Bruce told his companions. "I have not heard, in all the story of war, where infantry have defeated a greater force of mailed cavalry in the open field. If Moray does naught else, he has had his hour, I say!"

"But by your contriving and devising, Sire," Hay pointed out.

The King shook his head. "Moray's glory is not thereby lessened."

Some time later, with the sun already sinking behind the Highland Line to the north-west, Moray, with Hugh Ross, was summoned to the monarch's presence, to receive a very different welcome from the last.

"Your chaplet is secure again, my lord," Bruce said, holding out his hand. "Would that I might add to it. But I am in no position to do so, this day — since my own wears none so well, as you will hear! But I thank you, and yours, in the name of all. Had you failed, and Clifford won behind us to Stirling and the bridge, we could I think, have but prayed that we might die bravely tomorrow, all of us. We may so have to do, for the main battle is still to be fought. But our rear is secure and our spirit high — thanks to you."

"I but obeyed Your Grace's orders," his nephew said, flushing. "For the rest, I have not even blooded my sword! Sir Hugh also. All was done by my stout spearmen."

"Very well so. It is as it should be. You have proved better commanders than I, today. We shall see if I can do better tomorrow!"

"Tomorrow, Sire?" James Douglas had come up, to add his tribute to Randolph, whom he had so chivalrously refrained from aiding lest any of his glory be diluted. "There are still two hours of daylight. And a midsummer night . . ."

"See there, Jamie," Bruce said, pointing. "King Edward has come, at last, with his main force. There will be no attack tonight, I swear. The English have much talking to do! Having waited so long, Hereford will not attack now that the King is here. And Edward will be in no state, after long marching, to throw in his army just arrived. At this hour. We have tonight."

The Scots stood to their arms for another hour and more, nevertheless, as ever more of the vast array of power and might came into view. It was a tremendous, a terrifying sight — although scarcely so for Bruce himself, whose commander's eye was inevitably taken up with the problems and logistics of it all. That enormous mass of men and beasts crowding in over the Bannock Burn, and stretching far out of sight beyond — where were they to be put? That night? The terrain just would not hold them.

Presently the King burst out with a mighty and wondering oath. The English van, so long stationary, had started to move again — but not now in battle array, or towards the foe. They were moving down into the Carse, slowly, in troops and squadrons and columns, picking their way amongst the pools and pows, the runnels and ditches, spreading out over the wide marshlands. On and on they went, and on and on others came after them, to appropriate any and every island and patch of firm ground, to settle and camp for the night. Down into that great triangle of waterlogged plain, rimmed by the Bannock Burn, the River Forth and the escarpment of St. Ninians, went the flower of England's chivalry and score after score of thousands of her manhood, in an unending stream.

Almost speechless, Robert Bruce shook his head. "Dear God," he muttered, "I would not . . . I would not have believed it. The folly of it!"

"They have little choice," Douglas said. "And is it so ill a choice? It will be uncomfortable, yes. But there is water for all their horse, at least. And the men, though scattered, are safe there from any night assault from us. Their flanks protected by the burn and the Forth . . ."

Bruce stared at him with a strange look in his narrowed eyes. "You think so? Pray God, then, that they stay there! Pray God, I say! And now — call me a council. We shall eat while we have it. Every commander here to this knoll . . ."

CHAPTER TWENTY-ONE

THERE was little of darkness that June night, and little sleep in it for Robert Bruce at least. Despite the pleas of his friends that he should rest, much of it he passed in restless pacing, anxious eyes ever turned eastwards, down to where the myriad fires of the English host pinpointed the dusk and made the floor of the Carse like the reflection of a star-strewn sky.

The King was, for that stark period, a prey to doubts and dreads. He was that, indeed, a deal more often than even his closest colleagues knew, and always had been. In a few hours he might well be dead, along with so many others. But it was not that thought which unmanned him, but the fear that what he had fought for so terribly for seventeen long years might well be thrown away in one brief day. All along, he had had that dread, and so had resolutely refused to hazard his all in any great fixed battle. That evening, during the council-of-war, he could have been persuaded, even yet, to give up all and withdraw, under cover of night, far to the west, to Lennox perhaps, as that Earl had suggested, and the skirts of the Highland hills, where no English army could follow, so that at least total disaster was avoided. He had been tired, of course, as he was tired now — yet could not rest.

Oddly, almost as strong a fear in his mind was of a reverse sort. Fear that the English would perceive how dangerous was their present position, and move out of it, to the attack, before he could take advantage of their mistake. Attack — there was the crux of the matter. The enemy position in that marshland was fair enough as a resting place, if inconveniently waterlogged. At least it could not be outflanked. It was only a trap if the host had to fight therein, an armoured and horsed host. It was no place for fighting, and undoubtedly the English had only gone there to bivouac. But if they could be brought to battle there . . .! Which meant attack, early attack. By the Scots. But only if the Scots left their strong defensive positions, with their clear line of retreat westwards. Only thus could the potentialities of the carseland be exploited. Was this folly upon folly?

So Bruce paced the dew-drenched turf of his green knoll, and fought in his mind and spirit and will his own Battle of Bannockburn that night. Yet, at the back of it all, he knew what he was going to do, and his greatest fear was that the enemy would be aroused and on the move, out of the trap, before he could spring it.

When he could restrain himself no longer, soon after three o'clock of the Monday morning, the King had all others roused from their rest — but quietly and not by any blowing of bugles. Then, in the dove-grey, pre-sunrise light, Maurice, Abbot of Inchaffray, celebrated High Mass before the coughing, yawning shadowy host, and, aided by the other clergy, great and small, went round the serried ranks with the Sacrament.

As, thereafter, they all partook of a more material but still austere refreshment, Bruce addressed them sternly, but confidently, swallowing his own fears, telling them what he, and Scotland, expected of them this day, the birthday of John the Baptist, and of how it was to be achieved — with the help of the said saint, also Saint Andrew of Scotland and the martyr Saint Thomas. And not least, their own abiding belief in freedom. Where he led them today there could be no turning back, for him or for any. Holy Church had blessed them. And the Chancellor, the Abbot Bernard, would carry the sacred Brecbennoch of Saint Columba before them in the fray. As would the Dewar of the Main carry Saint Fillan's arm-bone. For himself, he here and now proclaimed full pardon for all and every offence committed against the Crown to all who fought that day, and relief from every tax or duty of any who fell in the battle. Let the victories of the day before hearten them — but also let them remember that today the veterans Pembroke and Ulster were with King Edward, and they must look for firmer command. Therefore, the Scots would strike first — and God be with them, and surprise likewise!

With a minimum of noise, no shouting or trumpeting, the Scots army then marshalled itself into its four great divisions under the same commanders as before — only this time, all the cavalry was put under the command of Sir Robert Keith the Marischal, to take the extreme left wing, nearest Stirling; and the non-fighting clergy, with the porters, grooms and other non-combatants, sent, with the baggage and pack-horses, to a green ridge north of St. Ninians, where they might watch and wait.

With the sunrise just beginning to stain the eastern sky in their faces, the silent advance commenced.

They gradually moved into line abreast, Edward Bruce's division this time in the place of honour on the extreme right, and very slightly ahead; then Moray; the Douglas and Walter the Steward; then the King with the largest number, including the Islesmen under Angus Og. Keith and the cavalry, farther left still, held back meantime. Bruce, only chain-mail again under his vivid surcoat, marched with the rest, Irvine leading his grey pony. Where he was going was no place for chargers — as he hoped he might have opportunity to prove to Edward of Carnarvon.

At every pace of the misty, mile-long, downhill march, the King listened with ears stretched for the sound he dreaded — English bugles blowing — and heard none.

At length, on the very lip of the Carse, the light growing and the night mists dispersing, the English outposts became aware of the untimely and outrageous Scots advance, and everywhere trumpets began to shrill.

"I swear King Edward must have had a better night than I!" Bruce commented to Angus Og, feeling better already with the prospect of action at last. "Now, let us give him a busy day!"

When Bruce had told his own trumpeter to make the first, short flourish of the day, he stepped forward, with Abbot Bernard and the Brecbennoch reliquary, a little in front, and sank to his knees. And behind him, while fiercest excitement and bustle, not to say panic, seethed in the roused and far-scattered English camp, the Scots ranks knelt in their thousands, and a ragged but heartfelt rendering of the Lord's Prayer rose amongst the shouting larks above the Carse of Stirling.

"Your prince is become much concerned with God, these days. For an excommunicate!" the Lord of the Isles murmured, to Lennox, as the droning prayer ascended. "Is it for his own soul? Or to encourage the faint-hearted? Or perhaps to please the flock of priests it is our misfortune to have with us?" The new Pope Clement had, unfortunately, been persuaded to renew the excommunication.

"I think that anathema weighs on his mind," the Earl said. "As does his recurring sickness. But — he will fight none the less well for it. As must we, to survive this day."

" 'Fore God — let us but commence it, Malcolm man!"

Rising from his knees, Robert Bruce slowly drew his great two-handed sword, and raised it high above his head. Then, swiftly, dramatically, he brought it down — but with explosive effort and every ounce of the strength of his powerful wrists, arrested the descent of its five-foot length so that it held sure, steady, pointing directly at the enemy's centre. No words were needed now. With a roar that drowned all the trumpet-calls, their own and the enemy's, the long Scots line surged forward.

The tactical situation was simple, astonishingly so considering the large numbers of men involved. The huge English army was penned in an enormous trap of level, pool-pitted and ditch-crossed swamp, with islands of firm ground, hemmed in on three sides by

331

the Bannock Burn, the River Forth and the Pelstream Burn. The fourth side, to the west, where the ground lifted to the New Park escarpment, was now barred by the half-mile-long line of advancing Scots.

It was no charge, of course, even of infantry — the ground precluded that. Cut up with runnels and stanks and sumps draining into larger canals and ditches, it was terrain to be hopped and picked and sidled over, even by nimble men. For cavalry it was practically impassable, save by circuitous routes.

The English, of course, were not idle while this wholly unexpected attack on so broad a front was being mounted. Swiftly they were rallying, forming up into their troops, squadrons and companies. Already there was a distinct drift of mounted men southwards towards the entrance point to the carseland of the night before. Then the drift turned to something more definite as the cavalry of the English extreme left, bivouacked nearest to the Milton of Bannock, achieved some sort of formation and began to hasten to gain and hold that vital bridgehead. First to enter, the night before, it was Gloucester's section of the van. Yesterday's misfortunes had not quenched the young Earl's eagerness. His great banner well to the fore, his trumpets braying, he was going to be first into action again.

But another and equally impatiently active earl was intent on gaining the same bridgehead — Edward, Earl of Carrick. For this very reason Bruce had given his brother the extreme right today. Leaping, bounding, even using their long pike-shafts as vaulting-poles across the pows and ditches, the Scots foot raced for the bridge.

Gloucester's cavalry was grievously hampered by the terrain, though it was better here than elsewhere, as the English had pulled off the doors and roof-timbers of every building in the Milton and around to form little gangways and bridges across the ditches. But even so the horsemen had to twist, go slowly and most often in many single files. As a result, though a few reached the bridge first, they were isolated, and went down before the charge of the thrusting pikemen. By the time that Gloucester himself reached the scene, Edward Bruce had roughly formed his men into two schiltroms, side by side, at the bridge. There was no room, firm ground, for the English to pause and marshal their horsed ranks. Oncoming riders pushed earlier arrivals forward. Undoubtedly Gloucester would have formed up for a less piecemeal attack if he could; but like Clifford the day before the lack of firm ground gave no opportunity. He and his men plunged at and circled the schiltroms disjointedly.

Gallantly impetuous yet, and an example to his men, the Earl plunged into the narrow gap between the schiltroms, hoping no doubt further to divide them. None of his people followed him therein, not even his standard-bearer. With a wild yell the pikemen of the inner sides of both formations broke and surged towards each other, spears and dirks jabbing. Gloucester's horse went down, and its rider disappeared under the press.

Edward Bruce yelled also, not to kill, to save the Earl as prisoner, for his great ransom; but it was too late. Gilbert de Clare, nephew of King Edward and kinsman of the Bruces also, was dead, in the first minutes of the battle.

Unhappily his scattered cavalry drew back into the marsh's safety.

All of this was not, of course, evident to the rest of the advancing Scots line; but that their right had had the best of it was clear, and greatly enheartened many. Bruce himself, though cheered, was otherwise preoccupied. As well as having to pick an awkward way for himself, like the others, across the shocking terrain that he had chosen to fight on, his primary concern at this stage was the menace of the English bowmen. Properly handled they could yet end everything. The enemy might in heavy cavalry he believed he had neutralised, by fighting here; but the archers . . .?

Bowmen, to be of real advantage in any battle, had to be massed, preferably on a flank and if possible on ground somewhat higher than the rest, where they could see, and enfilade the enemy without endangering their own ranks. The previous night Bruce had recognised all too clearly where, in this situation, the archers should be placed. Indeed, there was little choice. Well to the north-west of the English position, on their extreme right not far from where Moray had fought Clifford at the Pelstream ford, was an isolated hogback of slightly rising ground amongst the marsh. Here the bowmen could stand secure and do maximum damage. But, in fact, no archers stood there this morning; instead heavy cavalry occupied this key position, excellent for weighty horses admittedly, but quite useless tactically in that they could not move from it without plunging into soft bog again. There the pride of England's chivalry was safe, but unserviceable. It had been the first magnet for Bruce's glance, when the mists cleared. Surely if Edward Plantagenet had not the wits to see it, Pembroke or Ulster should have done.

Now, amongst all that wild upheaval in the Carse, one double movement at least was clear, definite. The heavy chivalry at last was being moved south, out of the precious island, and from behind, nearer the Forth where the enormous numbers of English infantry had been allotted the softest ground of all, the archers were being marched out north-westwards. Somebody had recovered his wits.

Bruce himself, leading the left and most northerly of the Scots divisions, was most nearly opposite this danger point. But there was much of grievously waterlogged ground between. That was why he had given Keith the cavalry, and sent them still farther to the north. They could sweep down from the escarpment, cross the Pel-stream ford, and reach the edge of that raised island via that burn's south bank — the way Clifford had come.

Bruce shouted to his trumpeter to sound the special call that would set Keith moving. It would be a race between light cavalry with a difficult mile to cover, and bowmen on foot, ploughing their way not only through marsh but through the confusion of their own moving and marshalling cavalry, with half that distance to go.

The King could do nothing more about that meantime. Because of the lie of the land, he had the widest stretch of carse to cover before making contact with the enemy. He could only continue his slow advance.

Moray, away to the right and nearest Edward Bruce, had already made contact, and, formed up into two schiltroms also, was creeping forward behind his frieze of long pikes. Douglas in similar formation would soon be doing the same. This was the chosen strategy and pattern of attack. In close hedgehog formation the Scots line was to move slowly but inexorably forward, whatever the state of the ground, pivoting on Edward Bruce at the Milton bridge, eventually one long line of no fewer than nine mobile schiltroms — for the King's own was to form into three — pushing back and compressing the enemy into the Forth. Such was the crazily ambitious design.

The English, admittedly, were in an appalling situation tactically as well as strategically. In essence they were a cavalry army, and their cavalry was all to the front. But to bring it to bear successfully on the advancing Scots, its commanders required space for marshalling and manoeuvre and firm ground to gain any impetus. Here and there, of course, there were better stretches, patches of solid footing, drained re-entrants. And here the knightly chivalry did well — although nothing like a real charge could be mounted. But though half a mile of front might sound a lot, in any modest battle, for the vast English numbers it was wickedly narrow. The enormous majority even of their cavalry could not be brought to bear on the Scots. As for the infantry, hidden behind all this, it might as well not have been there. Not at first, at any rate. Its time might come.

Bruce, with only 200 yards or so between him and the first of the milling enemy, paused to form into three schiltroms under Angus Og, Gilbert Hay and Neil Campbell. He remained with Angus in the centre. But while this went on, standing in mud up to the knees, his glance was ever turning northwards. Keith's horse were streaming across the Pelstream Burn with a bare 600 yards to go. The first of the bowmen had reached their stance, but only in twos and threes. They would all know the result of that race in a few minutes. And, if Keith lost it, his liege lord and many another might well be dead men in as brief minutes thereafter, skewered by the dreaded English cloth-yard shafts.

They moved on, stumbling, floundering, wading, cursing, in the mire, all the knights' fine surcoats and emblazoned shields now mud-covered, anonymous. The great Lion Rampant Standard of Scotland itself was blackened with slime, borne by Sir Nicol Scrymgeour, son of Wallace's faithful Alexander, whom Bruce had knighted only that morning, along with young Irvine and not a few others. On their right Douglas and the Steward's schiltroms were already engaged, but still moving forward by fits and starts, a sorry-looking crew of mud-plastered bog-trotters, but a-bristle with forward-pointed, jabbing pikes that no horsemen had yet penetrated.

Then the King's division were into the fray. Bruce had sheathed his great sword in exchange for a battle-axe, much handier in close fighting. Not that he had opportunity to wield it. The front ranks had to be pike-bearers, with their long spears outthrust. So long as they remained upright, those behind could only contribute moral and vocal support. Even the last was difficult for lurching, ploutering, bemired men needing all their breath.

Some of the English knights and chivalry, infuriated at the use-lessness of their horses in this swamp, had dismounted and were fighting on foot, using their lances as spears. These presented the most serious threat. But the majority of the quality, the lordly ones, were so encumbered with heavy plate armour, weighing up to a hundredweight, that they could scarcely walk on firm ground, much less fight in a bog. Most therefore remained in the saddle — at least until their frightened and mud-fettered chargers were speared under them, and they crashed helplessly.

It was not a battle, in truth — only a vast, horrible and unimaginable chaos of mud and blood and screaming frustration. On both sides, but inevitably much the more so with the English, horse-and-armour-encumbered and lacking any true formation or plan of action. If battle it was, it was men against clutching, engulfing bog, the land of Scotland given its own chance to fight.

In all the excitement and confusion, it was some time before Bruce realised that they were not being showered with arrows. He could not pause in this undignified plunging amidst other jostling bodies, but he did make darting glances to the left. And there, on the higher ground, he could see Keith's banner flying bravely, and horsemen hacking and swiping at fleeing archers in every direction. The King's sigh of relief was only metaphorical, but very genuine.

He knew now that this battle could indeed be won.

But that, of course, was only a future possibility, however heartening. Meantime there was only bog to cover and English to kill, by the thousand, the ten thousand. That June Monday of 1314, hell had come to the Carse of Stirling, hell for all men, almost as much for the Scots as for their foes.

In fact, it was the Scots who grew exhausted first, since on them fell the greatest and most sustained exertions. And there were so many English to confront, to beat down, to drive before them, but still to cope with. Endless hosts and legions of men, penned in and therefore unable to escape, to be fought. There was no limit to it, no relief for flesh and blood on that terrible plain, hour after bloody hour.

At some stage Bruce realised, from his own state, that the said flesh and blood could not indeed stand much more. His men were dropping now, not so much from wounds as from exhaustion, stumbling into runnels and pools and just not rising again. The nine schiltroms now represented a barely recognisable line; in fact few were recognisable as even schiltroms any more. It was long since there had been any shouting and slogan-crying; only the involuntary screaming of agonised men and injured horses. And not half, perhaps not a third of the English host was accounted for. The vast mass of it was still there before them, ever more tightly compressed in its dreadful trap. Dying, yes — but dying so very slowly, selling its life so very dearly. This could not go on.

Yet — and here was the deepest hell of it — there could be no let-up. The Scots could not, dare not, stop and go back, content with their partial victory. Still outnumbered fantastically, if they turned now, with all that quaking bog to cover again, they could and would be overwhelmed in disaster. There were still scores of thousands of the enemy who had not yet had opportunity to strike a blow, had barely moved, were fresh, unblooded. Give the demoralised cavalry a chance to get out of the way, and the untouched infantry behind could swarm forward to ultimate victory.

Bruce racked his tired, benumbed brain for what was to be done. He was still the commander, the only man in all this tortured plain who could still influence other men, by his decision, to any effective action — since the English leadership seemed to be completely at a discount. He had long since given up looking for King Edward, or Pembroke, or Ulster his own father-in-law. He was just one man struggling painfully on, in all-enveloping mud, amongst other weary men. What could he do?

If he halted the entire forward movement, however sluggish now, by trumpet call? What then? Exhausted men would sink, practically into torpor. He would never get them started again. The English would be given time to rally. At the very least, they would see opportunity to cut their way through, to escape. And on firm land again, those untouched thousands would recover.

What else? For once, Robert Bruce's mind, so fertile for stratagem, produced no alternative to this treadmill of horror.

Then, strangely, the matter was taken out of his drooping hands. Distant trumpets and thin high cheering, from far behind, turned some heavy heads, the King's included. There, coming rushing down the escarpment from the New Park, was a new host, horse and foot, banners flying. From nearly a mile away it could not be seen that its leader was a gaunt stooping bishop, William Lamberton, on a palfrey; that its cavalry were priests and grooms on packhorses; that its infantry were porters and cooks and old men, even women, with staves and meat-choppers and carving-knives; its banners blankets and plaids tied to tent-poles. On it came, out of hiding amongst the knowes, a new and vociferous host, with no hint of exhaustion about it.

In that moment the Battle of Bannockburn was finally won. Appalled, the English commanders saw their enemy reinforced, and accepted it as the last straw. King Edward had esteemed the battle lost long before. He was no coward, however poor a monarch, and had been agitating, not how to save himself but how to extricate any large number of his people from this trap. But now even the veterans Pembroke and Ulster urged immediate flight — and when the King would have turned his horse instinctively southwards, towards their entry to that place of disaster, Pembroke it was who grabbed the royal arm and practically pulled his monarch off his massive destrier. Unseating squires and heralds from lighter, faster horses, the two Earls got the King mounted again, and were off with him, northwards. They had learned from Clifford of the north-about route to Stirling by the Pelstream ford, and rightly guessed that it was unlikely to be guarded now. A score or so of determined, cruelly-spurring men, they left that stricken field while yet most men stared unbelieving at the baggage-train army.

Quickly, of course, the English command's flight was perceived, and swiftly men reacted. The Scots, suddenly reinvigorated, yelled their triumph and surged forward. The English decided that it was every man for himself, and acted accordingly.

Abruptly, then, the battle was over, although the fighting was not. That was to go on for hours yet, as men tried to hack or race or swim their way to freedom, and died in the process, thousands upon thousands of men, so that the very River Forth was choked with bodies. Not all died, of course, but a great many did, singly, in groups and in large companies that stood and sold their lives dearly — for there was a mighty backlog of old scores to pay off, and ordinary soldiers and men-at-arms were not worth taking prisoner. Lords and knights and gentry, of course, were different; their ransoms would set up many for life.

It was not much past noon, in fact, when King Edward fled the field; but King Robert was still there when the sun was sinking, still seeking to command, to control, to bring order if not mercy out of utter shambles and chaos. He had, indeed, exerted some major control from the beginning, detaching Douglas and sending him and Keith, with some part of the cavalry, in hot pursuit of King Edward and his fleeing nobility, round Stirling Rock. Then he set up some sort of headquarters on the green mound from which the archers had been dislodged, and from there endeavoured to bring order out of bedlam, fatigued as he was. And there, presently, William Lamberton came to him, and they gripped hands in silent, eloquent thankfulness, hearts too full for words, tears in their eyes for all to see, neither ashamed.

They were there still, as the sun sank, the Bishop superintending the treatment of wounded, Bruce, swaying on his feet, directing, directing, with all his commanders out supervising the clearance of that desperate field, halting massacres, shepherding prisoners, receiving belated surrenders, collecting and separating the dead, garnering and protecting booty — all this, when a party approached under Gilbert Hay. He brought a number of bodies borne on shields and hurdles, and beside one of these limped a tall, smooth-faced man in middle years whose magnificence was only partly hidden by the universal mud and dried slime.

"Here is one, Sire, who claims you owe him much," Hay said. "It may be that he speaks false — for also he claims to be Earl of Gloucester. Whereas here is the true Gloucester!" And he gestured to one of the corpses.

"Robert Bruce knows who I am," the prisoner declared, with dignity. "And if I know *him*, he will not forget."

"Aye — Monthermer! My lord — it is a long time. Twelve years, no less," Bruce said, and held out his hand. "I have not forgot.

338

Here are changed days — but had it not been for you, I would not have lived, I believe, to fight this day. My lord High Constable — this is the Earl Ralph de Monthermer, who held the earldom of Gloucester during his stepson's minority. He once served me more than well."

This was, indeed, the man who had sent Bruce the spurs and the shilling, that night in London in 1302, as hint to flee, when the Comyn had betrayed him to King Edward and he was to be arrested the next morning; the man who was Edward Longshanks' son-in-law, having married Edward's daughter, after her widowing from the de Clare Earl of Gloucester, Bruce's cousin, and so had been given the earldom until the child heir should reach man's estate. And that child heir it was who now lay, pierced by a score of Scots pikes, there beside his stepfather.

Bruce went to look down at the dead, once-handsome young man, his second cousin whom he had never met in the flesh, and shook his head. "Gilbert," he said, sighing. "Gilbert de Clare. At least you died nobly."

"Aye. He leaves this sorry field in better state than do most of us!" the older man said. "God knows, I could wish myself in Gilbert's place. Here, for the rest of us, was shame on shame."

"The fortunes of war, friend. Do not blame yourself. At least you did not run! With your brother-in-law!"

"I was not with him, the King, at the end. I took command of Gilbert's men, when he fell. But ... Edward, the King — he is a fool! And has shamed us all this day. Yet, he could not stay to be captured, Robert. The King. You must see it. His ransom — his ransom would have bought all Scotland's freedom!"

Strangely, levelly, the tired Bruce looked at Monthermer, and then nodded. "Scotland's freedom is bought, I think!" he said softly. "Not by a king's ransom, but by the courage and blood and sacrifice of her people. Remember it!" Then he smiled, however slightly. "But you, Ralph — you are now my guest. You shall be treated as such. No ransom is required of you. I pay my debts — all of them! My lord Constable — have the Earl Ralph conducted to the Abbey of Cambuskenneth, to the Abbot's good keeping. And bestow the body of Earl Gilbert, my cousin, in his chapel. I will come there anon ..."

But Hay had another body to show his monarch, covered by a cloak. Wordlessly twitching back the cloth, he revealed the dead but still arrogant face of Robert, Lord Clifford.

"Clifford!" Bruce cried, chokingly. "Robert Clifford, 'fore God!" And then more quietly, "Aye — before God, at last! May He ... have mercy ... on his soul! May he ... rest in peace."

339

The King had made many merciful pronouncements of late. But this was as hard a sentence to say as any he had ever enunciated.

He turned blindly away, as William Lamberton gripped his arm.

Chapter Twenty-two

In the refectory of the Abbey of Cambuskenneth, almost islanded in a great bend of the Forth only a mile or so north of the battlefield, Robert Bruce played a new role, armour, weapons and the panoply of war for once cast aside. He sat at a table, with the Abbot Bernard, his Chancellor, and other clerks who yesterday had been soldiers, and was flanked by other tables manned by monks and priests, even of high degree — any who could write and figure on paper. And all around them men came and went, bringing, stacking, piling high, arranging, documenting the greatest treasure Scotland had ever seen. When the King of England went to war, it seemed, he did so in style — and in his haste to be gone, he had left his style behind. Cambuskenneth had become a counting-house.

Gold and silver vessels and plate, personal jewellery, gem-studded ceremonial weapons, crosses, orders and the like, gold-worked clothing, saddle-cloths, standards and banners, rich harness, was the last of it — even though there were over 200 pairs of knights' golden spurs alone. It was the armour, helmets and shields, much of it gold- and silver-enriched, captured or cast away by fleeing men, that half-filled the hall. King Edward's own shield, even his royal seal, lay on the table at Bruce's elbow.

The King yawned nevertheless. He was not much of an account-ant — although none recognised better what this wealth meant to bankrupt, war-ravaged, all but starving Scotland. He had in fact slept no more that night than the nights before — though on this occasion he had been conducting a knight's vigil, in the Abbey chapel, over the body of Gilbert de Clare, of Gloucester, his cousin, a vigil and personal thanksgiving combined. Few, indeed, had slept much anywhere in Scotland that night, save for the drunken — the bells had seen to that. Every bell in the land had been ringing since nightfall — and not all were so mellow and harmonious as the great carillon of Cambuskenneth which even yet kept the warm noontide air throbbing around them. The jangle from nearby Stirling's host of belfries across the river was head-splitting, nerve-shattering, and dearly the King would have liked to command its cessation — but did not.

"I calculate the treasure already listed now at worth no less than £200,000, Sire," Bernard de Linton mentioned, pen pausing for a moment.

"Aye. No doubt," the King conceded. "Very good. A great sum. But — this is not a cattle-mart! Do you have me here to price and sum . . .?" He yawned cavernously.

"Your Grace," the Abbot said severely. "Here is new life for your kingdom. Yesterday we shed sweat and blood. Here is life's blood of a different sort. But a sort that the realm must have."

"I know it, friend. Know also that to you, as Chancellor, this is all-important. But for myself, I am more concerned to hear the figures of our losses yesterday, which still you do not find for me."

"It takes time, Sire. Until the Lord Edward comes back. And Sir James, with the Marischal. And Sir Neil, and the others, pursuing the enemy. We cannot know for sure. Even bodies counted are no sure token. For who can tell a Scots corpse from an English, sunk in mire? Stripped. Drowned in Forth. But — comfort Your Grace — we believe that our losses are small, as against those of the English. In dead. Even in wounded. Of these, they say there are more men injured by their own splintered pike-staffs than by enemy steel. Of knights we do know numbers. But three are dead. Sir William, younger son of the Earl of Ross. Sir William de Vipont. And Sir William Airth. Only these, though more are wounded. Against already counted thirty-five English barons and nobles, over 200 knights and 700 esquires and gentry. Dead. So great a victory is scarce believable . . ."

There was an interruption. A small party of Islesmen came into the hall, pushing before them a white-haired elderly man dressed only in blood-stained silken shirt and breeches, his fine features lined with pain and fatigue. Yet this man, though roughly handled, still clutched a sword to him, determinedly though not aggressively. After a word with the guard at the door, the little pary was permitted to approach the King.

"Lord," their spokesman said, in the soft Gaelic, "this man we have but now found. In a bush. He says that he will yield his sword to none but you. He said we could kill him before he gave it up. Almost we did . . ."

"Enough of this heathen gibberish!" the old man interrupted strongly, for so frail-seeming a captive. "I am Marmaduke Tweng. Will Your Majesty accept my sword?"

"Ha! Sir Marmaduke!" Bruce actually rose to his feet. "I greet you, sir. Yours is a name all men would honour. You are hurt?"

"Honour . . .?" the other demanded. "Is there honour for any Englishman hereafter? Our honour is fled! Better that it was trampled in yonder mire!"

"Not so, sir. Honourable men do not lose their honour so easily. Because others forget theirs. Yours is safe, I say. It came intact from Stirling once before!"

Sir Marmaduke Tweng was, in fact, one of the very few notable Englishmen who had come out of Wallace's campaigns, especially the Battle of Stirling Bridge, seventeen years before, with name unsullied — even though he had held Stirling Castle against the Scots for long years thereafter. Wallace had said that if there were but a few more Twengs in England, Scotland would never win her freedom.

"Aye — this foul corner of Scots mire has been the curse on me! I say, the curse of me." He had to shout, above the clamour of the bells. "King Robert — will you accept my sword?"

"That I will not, Sir Marmaduke! Keep your sword. No man wears one more worthily. You are no prisoner. So you pay no ransom." Bruce turned to the Chancellor. "Give these MacDonalds something for their trouble. A gold spur perhaps. And let them go. You, Sir Marmaduke, may not have lost your honour or your sword — but you have lost much, I see. Blood, it seems — and armour, helmet, mount, shield, seal? See you — take what you will from here." He waved a hand at all the stacked booty. "And choose you a horse. Moreover, show yourself to my physicians. You are my honoured guest until you leave this Scotland."

The older man's voice quavered now, and was barely to be heard above the bells. "You are kind. Noble. There speaks a king indeed!" He coughed, to hide his emotion. "Would . . . would we had such a king, in England. May I . . . kiss your Majesty's hand?" He raised his white head. "One matter more, Sire — of your patience. I have a friend. Sir Edmund de Mauley. Lord Seneschal of England. Do you know . . .?"

"I fear he lies in the chapel crypt, here, sir. With . . . others. He at least did not flee."

"And . . . and my cousin? Sir William, Lord of Higham? The Lord Marshal of Ireland?"

"He also, Sir Marmaduke. Their honour is safe."

"For that I thank God . . ."

A disturbance turned all eyes. A gorgeously-clad figure in splendid surcoat and gold-inlaid armour was being carried in on a cothouse door, a great eight-pointed cross picked out in rubies on his breast, one who had escaped the mud — but not the blood. Gilbert Hay escorted the body in.

"Sire — I know not who this is. None know. They found him beneath a heap of slain. But the cross, of St. John. Of Rhodes. A stranger knight. But important, I think . . ."

"Important, yes." That was Tweng, strongly. "*I* know who that is. He was with the King. But turned back when the King fled. Saying it was not his custom to flee. *He* would not run. Not he who is named the third greatest knight in Christendom!"

"Dear God!" Bruce exclaimed. "You mean . . .?"

"Aye, you should know — since you yourself are called the second such, Sir Robert! The first is the Emperor Henry of Luxemburg. And this, Sir Giles d'Argentin, was the third. God rest his noble soul!"

"Amen!" the King said. "D'Argentin! The Crusader. Name me not in the same breath with this man, sir. A man whose harness I am scarcely worthy to unloose! One day, I had hoped — do hope — myself to carry my sword against the Infidel. He, d'Argentin, would have been my choice as leader. Sweet Christ — what a loss is here! Had I but known his presence . . ."

"What could you have done, Sire . . .?"

Hay's words were drowned in the clatter of hooves and clank of armour outside. A new and larger party came stamping into the refectory, to bow, the Earl of Moray leading.

Bruce sighed, and shook his head. "Well, nephew?" he said, but scarcely welcomingly.

"Stirling Castle has surrendered, Sire," Randolph declared. "Your standard now flies over it, at last. Here is Sir Philip Moubray, the governor."

"Ha — Moubray!" Bruce stared at the narrow-faced, prematurely grey, youngish man, one of his principal enemies. "Moubray, who has cost me dear indeed. He gives me back my principal fortress? And himself! What shall I do with him, nephew?"

"Hang him, Sire!" Hay asserted, briefly.

"I asked my lord of Moray, Gibbie. Let him answer, for he is his prisoner, it seems."

"Your Grace," Randolph said slowly. "I would urge you to do with him as you did with me."

"You would? He is a traitor, my lord."

"As was I."

"You were my own kin."

"You seek my mercy on him, then?"

"I do. Two nights ago you praised my stand. At the Pelstream. Offered me reward. Now I ask it. This man's life. He was my friend once. He is a valiant knight. He would not have cost you so dear were he not. You have need of such still, I think."

343

"M'mmm. Sir Philip — how say you? It was on Methven field last we met, was it not?"

"Yes, Sire." The prisoner came forward, and fell on his knees. "I struck you from your horse. Sought to capture you. I have never failed to be your foe."

"Why?"

"I believed your cause wrong. And Comyn's right."

"And now?"

"I do not beg for my life, Sire. But if you choose to grant it, I will serve you faithfully until its end."

Bruce took a turn away, and looked down at the dead face of Sir Giles d'Argentin. "So be it, Sir Philip," he said. "Too many brave men have died, to no advantage. Live, then — and serve me as well as you served my enemies." And he gave him his hand to kiss.

When the King sat down again, the Abbot Bernard spoke as low-voiced as was practical, in the bells' clamour. "You are over-generous, Sire," he complained. "Needlessly so. Mercy is good. But . . . Sir Marmaduke Tweng is a rich man. He could well have paid a great ransom. And this Sir Philip Moubray has great lands. In Lothian. They should be forfeit. Your Treasury needs all such, with a whole realm to build anew."

"It will take more than siller to build it anew, Master Bernard! All this accounting and inventory is turning you huckster. Let us not become merchants, in this our deliverance. Forbye, we have plenty. Plenty for ransom, have we not? What did you say? Thirty-five lords and barons? 200 knights . . .?"

"No, no, Sire — that was the numbers slain. Captured, and for ransom, there are but twenty-two lords. Though some 500 of knightly rank."

"Mercy on us — and you grudge me Sir Marmaduke!"

"Yesterday Your Grace freed the Earl Ralph. He would have brought a mighty ransom. I but remind you not to be too kind in your triumph, too gentle . . ."

"Gentle! Save us — do you really esteem me so gentle, man? My brother Edward once named me that, I mind. But you are a wiser man, I thought! I am nothing gentle. I but choose my victims! Some, I swear, will not find me kind, nor gentle, hereafter."

The next visitors to Cambuskenneth Abbey proved the King's words, despite all their nobility. For this was a noble band indeed, brought in by Edward Bruce and Robert Boyd, weary with long riding, all of them, but proud still.

"These I have brought from Bothwell Castle, in Lanarkshire," Edward announced, without ceremony. "Fleeing, they took refuge there. But that place's governor, one Gilbertson, decided to turn his

344

coat. He delivered them all into my hands, in return for his own life." He paused, grinning. "Henry de Bohun, Earl of Hereford, Lord High Constable of England. Robert de Umfraville, Earl of Angus. Sir Ingram de Umfraville, former Guardian of this realm. Maurice, Lord Berkeley. John, Lord Segrave. Hugh, Lord Despenser. John, Lord Ferrers. John, Lord Rich. Edmund, Lord Abergavenny. Sir Anthony de Lucy. Aye — and a troop of lesser men outside."

"So-o-o! Here is the cream in the pitcher!" This time Bruce did not rise to his feet. "Save for the illustrious dead, here is England's pride and glory! With . . . some leavening of my own! I thank you, my lord of Carrick. And Sir Robert Boyd. You have done notably well. You have not heard how James Douglas fares? Chasing the Plantagenet? And Pembroke? And my good-sire?"

"Pembroke left them behind Stirling," Edward reported. "There he halted, they say, to rally his own fleeing Welsh marchmen and archers. He has over 1,000 of them. He is marching them to Carlisle. In good order. Too many for me to hunt, with my sixty horse. Besides, I had another game!"

"Aye. Aymer de Valence plays the man, at last! But — the King? Ulster?"

"Douglas will never catch them. They have better horses and near an hour's start. We heard that they had not drawn rein by Linlithgow! And they were still passing their own baggage-train heading north! They will be in Berwick, by this."

"A pity. I would have welcomed a word with my good-sire. About his daughter!" Bruce looked for the first time directly at the galaxy of stiff-necked if wary-eyed English lords — for the Umfraville brothers, though they held the Scots earldom of Angus, through marriage, were English in all else. "My lords," he said, "I have been accused this day of being over-kind, over-gentle. Insufficiently a huckster, a merchant! You are all King Edward's men — the old Edward. He trained you, as he sought to train me. You know how he would have acted, had he sat here today!"

There was absolute silence. All knew only too well what their master, Edward the Hammer of the Scots, would have done.

"He slew my brothers, as prisoners — three of them. Hanged, drawn and quartered. And my good-brother, Seton. And innumerable of my friends. Wallace he butchered unspeakably. *Your* King hanged his prisoners, my lords — and the earls he hanged highest of all! Tell me why should not I do the same with you?"

"*We* are not rebels, sir," Hereford said, coldly.

"Ha! Not rebels, no. You still say *we* were?" And when none answered that, Bruce went on tensely. "I would you *had* been

345

rebels. I would have honoured you more. One rebel I have freely pardoned. Moubray! You are not rebels — you are cowards! Dastards! Your late liege lord Edward Longshanks would not have lifted a single finger to save you, this day. You know it. He would have forsworn you all. He, from being a noble knight, grew to become a savage, a brute-beast! But he was never a coward. Never would he have fled a field leaving scores of thousands who still could fight. As did his son. And as did you, my lords!"

"I pray you — spare us your strictures, sir," the Lord Berkeley requested with heavy patience. "We are your prisoners, and there's an end to it. Do your worst — but no preaching. From a brigand, a rebel! Of a mercy!"

Bruce motioned to his brother, and the other Scots, for patience. "You are courageous with your tongue, at least! Or is it mere proud English insolence? You are my prisoners, yes. And a brigand would hang you, out of hand. Would he not?"

"I think not. A brigand, impoverished and beggarly, would sell us! As you will do. For as high a price as he could gain! Never fear, Robert Bruce — we will pay our ransoms!"

Fists tight clenched, the King looked at the row of cold, arrogant, all but bored-seeming faces. Urgently he sought to control his temper. "Sir Marmaduke Tweng — who stayed to fight — named me the second knight in Christendom. You name me rebel and brigand. Which is it to be, my lords? How do you elect to be treated? By the knight? Or by the brigand? Choose now, and make no complaint hereafter."

"What matters it? The leopard does not change its spots."

"Nor the jackal become lion because it dons a king's robe!" That was Ferrers.

"Sire — you have won a battle. You will not stain it with dishonour?" That was Ingram de Umfraville, the former Guardian, who, with his brother, was in somewhat different case from the others, being, in theory at least, Scots citizens — and therefore *ipso facto* themselves rebels.

"So be it," Bruce said. "I shall disappoint none of you, my lords. You shall all go into the deepest pits of Stirling Castle. Each alone. You shall not hang — not yet! Bread and water shall be your diet — lest you grow contented with your chains. And there you will lie until your ransoms are paid. A brigand, I will sell you for a high price, as you say!"

"And your price, sir? What is it?" That was Hereford, the Constable. "We are not paupers. We will pay your price, in gold or silver, never fear. How much?"

"Gold and silver? Aye, that too. But I will have more than gold

346

and silver, my lords." Bruce leaned forward, speaking slowly, carefully. "I will have what is mine restored to me, first. And you have much that is mine, in your England. My wife. My daughter. My sisters. The Countess of Buchan. My friends a-many. Held prisoner for long years. Shut away. In cells and cages. Grown old in your foul prisons. I have waited long for this. You cannot give me back my dead brothers. But every one of these shall be returned forthwith. My Queen first of all. Before any one of you see the light of another day from your deep pits. The surest messengers and fleetest horses are yours, to send for them, this very day. And if they do not come, within six weeks — no, a month — then you die. All of you. Die as my brothers died, as Wallace died, hanged, disembowelled and your entrails burned before your eyes! You understand . . ."

Without waiting, without daring to wait for an answer, the King of Scots rose, his heavy chair thrust back to fall with a crash, and turning, strode from the refectory without a backward glance, lest any should see the tears that streamed from his eyes.

Outside in the Abbey garden, as the bells clanged their joyful paeans across the marshes, Robert Bruce stared away and away southwards, blinking.

"Elizabeth!" he whispered. "Elizabeth, my heart . . .!"

Author's Note

BANNOCKBURN was one of the great battles of history. But it was not the end, either of Robert Bruce's epic task, or of the English determination to subdue and control Scotland. It was not even the beginning of the end; the end of the beginning, rather. Long years of struggle lay ahead, for King as well as people — for his was indeed a life's work. But it would be true to say that after Bannockburn nothing was ever quite the same again. It had proved that even the mightiest English army could be beaten in open battle; and that the Scots, if properly led, and united, had a genius for war — something that the world was to learn century by century thereafter.

But some of the very qualities which went to make up that genius, themselves ensured their ruler's trial and heartbreak — the Scots' intense individualism, fierce stubbornness, prickly pride, and suspicion of each other's motives. These, with the recurrent thread of treachery woven so indelibly into the tapestry of Scotland's colourful story, even more surely than the English threat, made certain that Bruce's greatest challenge remained yet to come.

Aged forty, with no male heir other than a brother whom he knew could no more rule Scotland than fly through the air, with a wife whom he had not seen for eight years, and a daughter he scarcely knew, the second greatest knight in Christendom — now moved up, indeed, to first place — faced the future with a disillusioned eye, the seeds of grim fate in his body, but a brave heart, none braver. THE PRICE OF THE KING'S PEACE will complete this trilogy of Robert the Bruce.

N.T.

ROBERT THE BRUCE TRILOGY:

Book 1: The steps to the Empty Throne

The Heroic story of Robert the Bruce and the Turbulent Struggle for an independent Scotland

The year is 1296 and Edward Plantagenet – King of England, is determined to hammer the rebellious Scottish into submission. Bruce, despite internal clashes with that headstrong figure, William Wallace, and his fierce love for his antagonist's god-daughter, gives himself the task of uniting the Scottish against the invaders from the South.

And so begins this deadly game for national survival with battle-scarred Scotland as the prize.

"Very readable ... the author weaves his way authoritatively through the highways and byways of this bloodthirsty period and paints some life-like portraits of top people of the time" – *Daily Telegraph*

"Mr Tranter writes with knowledge and feeling" – *The Scotsman*

Book 3: The Price of the King's Peace

Bannockburn was far from the end for Robert Bruce and Scotland; not even the beginning of the end – only the end of the beginning. There remained fourteen years of struggle, savagery, heroism and treachery before the English could be brought to sit at a peace-table with their proclaimed rebels, and so to acknowledge Bruce as a sovereign king.

In these years of stress and fulfilment, Bruce's character burgeoned to its splendid flowering. The hero-king, moulded by sorrow, remorse and a grievous sickness, equally with triumph, became the foremost prince of Christendom – despite continuing Papal excommunication. That the fighting now was done mainly deep in England, over the sea in Ireland, and in the hearts of men – his own not the least – was none the less taxing for a sick man with the seeds of grim fate in his body, and the sin of murder on his conscience. But Elizabeth de Burgh was at his side again, after the long years of imprisonment, and a great love sustained them both.

Freedom, then, with love – here is the theme and trumpet-call of this, the final volume of Nigel Tranter's trilogy about Robert the Bruce.

The Wallace

Scotland at the end of the thirteenth century was a blood-torn country under the harsh domination of a tyrant usurper, the hated Plantagenet, Edward Londshanks. During the appalling violence of those unsettled days one man rose as leader of the Scots. That man was William Wallace. Motivated first by revenge for his father's slaughter, Wallace then vowed to cleanse his country of the English and set the rightful King, Robert the Bruce, upon the Scottish throne.

Chain of Destiny

His father had been murdered at Bannockburn, and now James Stewart, aged fifteen, was the new King of Scots. His reign was to be dramatic and colourful, and to end in tragedy, but during those eventful years James became the finest and best-loved king in Scotland's history. Vigorous, headstrong, romantic, he inspired deep loyalty from men – and passionate love from women. And so great was his people's affection that the flower of a whole nation finally laid down its life for him – at the tragic Field of Flodden ...

GREAT HISTORICAL NOVELS
BY NIGEL TRANTER

Robert the Bruce:

All these books are available at your local bookshop or newsagent, or can be ordered direct from the publisher. Just tick the titles you want and fill in the form below.
Prices and availability subject to change without notice.

CORONET BOOKS, P.O. Box 11, Falmouth, Cornwall.
Please send cheque or postal order, and allow the following for postage and packing:
U.K. – One book 19p plus 9p per copy for each additional book ordered, up to a maximum of 73p
B.F.P.O. and EIRE – 19p for the first book plus 9p per copy for the next 6 books, thereafter 3p per book.
OTHER OVERSEAS CUSTOMERS – 20p for the first book and 10p per copy for each additional book.

Name ....

Address ....

....